DIE
FOR ME

DIE
FOR ME

KAREN ROSE

headline

First published in Great Britain in 2007
by HEADLINE PUBLISHING GROUP

1

Cataloguing in Publication Data is available from the British Library

Hardback ISBN 978 0 7553 3704 0
Trade paperback ISBN 978 0 7553 3705 7

Typeset in Palatino by Avon DataSet Ltd,
Bidford-on-Avon, Warwickshire

Printed and bound in Great Britain by
Clays Ltd, St Ives plc

HEADLINE PUBLISHING GROUP
An Hachette Livre UK Company
338 Euston Road
London NW1 3BH

www.headline.co.uk
www.hodderheadline.com

Dedicated to the memory of
Dr Zoltan J. Kosztolnyik,
Professor Emeritus of Medieval History,
Texas A&M University.

Although I never had the privilege of knowing him
personally, I have had the honor, privilege, and
pleasure of knowing the daughter he raised.

And as always, to my precious husband Martin.
You touch the lives of your students every day,
bringing history to life with the same unique
combination of passion, intelligence, and acerbic
wit that made me fall in love with you
twenty-five years ago.

Whether you're dressing up like Cleopatra,
illustrating the Declaration of Independence
using the rock music videos of '80s hair bands,
or explaining the Monroe Doctrine through the
'Badger-Badger-Mushroom' Dance,
you have assured that no student that passes
through your class will ever forget you.

You inspire me. I love you.

Acknowledgments

So many people contributed to my knowledge base as I wrote this book. To all of you – my sincerest thanks!

Danny Agan for answering all my detective questions and especially for helping my hero locate things underground.

Tim Bechtel of Environscan, Inc. for background and technical details on ground penetrating radar.

Niki Ciccotelli for her description of growing up in Philadelphia that was so real that I felt as if I were physically there myself.

Monty Clark of the Art Institute of Florida in Ft. Lauderdale, for the invaluable and very cool information on video game design and designers.

Marc Conterato for all things medical and Kay Conterato for clipping all those extremely useful newspaper articles on insurance and hackers.

Diana Fox for a great title.

Carleton Hafer for answering all my computer questions in a way I could clearly understand.

Linda Hafer for the wonderful introduction to opera and for opening a world of music I never thought I would like but that I do!

Elaine Kriegh for her vivid descriptions of medieval tomb monuments.

Sonie Lasker, my *sempai*, for demonstrating weapon technique and teaching me how personally rewarding martial arts can be. *Domo arigato.*

Deana Seydel Rivera for showing me Philadephia – and three days before her wedding, no less.

Loretta Rogers for her motorcycle expertise. How I wish I had the courage to fly on two wheels!

Sally Schoeneweiss and Mary Pitkin for keeping my Web site organized, functional and beautiful.

My language advisors: Mary C Turner and Anne Crowder – *Merci beaucoup*, Bob Busch and Barbara Mulrine – *Spasiba*, Kris Alice Hohls – *Danke*, Sarah Hafer – *Domo arigato*.

Friends who answered my catch-all questions here and there – Shari Anton, Terri Bolyard, Kathy Caskie, Sherrilyn Kenyon, and Kelley St. John.

My editor, Karen Kosztolnyik, and my agent, Robin Rue, who make this so much *fun*.

As always, all mistakes are my own.

Prologue

Philadelphia, Saturday, January 6

The first thing that hit Warren Keyes was the smell. Ammonia, disinfectant . . . and something else. What else? *Open your eyes, Keyes.* He could hear his own voice echo inside his head and he struggled to lift his eyelids. Heavy. They were so heavy, but he fought until they stayed open. It was dark. No. There was a little light. Warren blinked once, then again with more force until a flickering light came into focus.

It was a torch, mounted on the wall. His heart started thudding hard in his chest. The wall was rock. *I'm in a cave.* His heart began to race. *What the hell is this?* He lunged forward and white-hot pain speared down his arms to his back. Gasping, he fell back against something flat and hard.

He was tied. *Oh God.* His hands and feet were tied. And he was naked. *Trapped.* Fear rose from his belly, clawing his insides. He twisted like a wild animal, then fell back again, panting, tasting the disinfectant as he sucked in air. Disinfectant and . . .

His breath hitched as he recognized the odor under the disinfectant. Something dead. Rotting. *Something died here.* He closed his eyes, willing himself not to panic. *This isn't happening. This is just a dream, a nightmare. In a minute I'll wake up.*

But he wasn't dreaming. This, whatever it was, was real. He was stretched out on a board on a slight incline, his wrists tied together and his arms pulled up and behind his head. *Why?* He

1

tried to think, to remember. There was something . . . a picture in his mind, just beyond his reach. He strained for the memory and realized his head ached – he winced as the pain sent little black spots dancing across his eyes. God, it was like a really bad hangover. But he hadn't been drinking. Had he?

Coffee. He remembered drinking coffee, his hands closing around the cup to get warm. He'd been cold. He'd been outside. *Running.* Why was he running? He rotated his wrists, feeling his raw skin burn, reaching until the tips of his fingers touched rope.

'So you're finally awake.'

The voice came from behind him and he craned his neck, trying to see. Then he remembered and the pressure on his chest lessened a fraction. It was a movie. *I'm an actor and we were making a movie.* A history documentary. He'd been running with . . . with what? He grimaced, focusing. *A sword, that's it.* He'd been in medieval costume, a knight with a helmet and shield . . . even chain mail, for God's sake. The entire scene came back now. He'd changed his clothes, even his underwear, for some scratchy, shapeless burlap that irritated his crotch. He'd had a sword, and he'd carried it as he ran through the woods outside Munch's studio, yelling at the top of his lungs. He'd felt like a damn idiot, but he'd done it all because it was in the damn script.

But this – he jerked at the ropes again with no success – *this was* not *in the script.*

'Munch.' Warren's voice was thick, grating on his dry throat. 'What the hell is this?'

Ed Munch appeared to his left. 'I didn't think you'd ever wake up.'

Warren blinked as the dim light from the torch flickered across the man's face. His heart skipped a beat. Munch had changed. Before he'd been old, shoulders stooped. White hair and a trim mustache. Warren swallowed, his breath shallow. Now Munch stood straight. His mustache was gone. So was his hair, his head shaved shiny bald.

Munch wasn't old. Dread coiled in his gut, seething and roiling. The deal was five hundred for the documentary. Cash if he came that day. Warren had been suspicious – it was a lot of money for a history documentary they'd show on PBS if he was lucky. But he'd agreed. One odd old man was no threat.

But Munch wasn't old. Bile rose, choking him. *What have I done?* Close on the heels of that question came the next, more terrifying. *What will he do to me?*

'Who are you?' Warren croaked out and Munch held a bottle of water to his lips. Warren pulled away, but Munch grabbed his chin with surprising strength. His dark eyes narrowed and fear made Warren freeze.

'It's just water this time,' Munch ground out. 'Drink it.'

Warren spat the mouthful of water back in the man's face and held himself rigid when Munch raised his fist. But the fist lowered and Munch shrugged.

'You'll drink eventually. I need your throat moist.'

Warren licked his lips. 'Why?'

Munch disappeared behind him again and Warren could hear something rolling. A video camera, Warren saw when Munch rolled it past him, stopping about five feet away. The camera was pointing straight at his face. 'Why?' Warren repeated, louder.

Munch peered through the lens and stepped back. 'Because I need you to scream.' He lifted a brow, his expression surreally bland. 'They all screamed. So will you.'

Horror bubbled up and Warren fought it back. *Stay calm. Treat him nice and maybe you can talk your way out of this*. He made his lips curve. 'Look, Munch, let me go and we'll call it even. You can keep the sword fight scenes I did already at no charge.'

Munch just looked at him, his expression still bland. 'I never planned to pay you anyway.' He disappeared again and reappeared, pushing another video camera.

Warren remembered the coffee, remembered Munch's insistence that he drink it. *Just water this time*. Rage geysered inside him, momentarily eclipsing the fear. 'You drugged me,'

3

he hissed, and he filled his lungs with air. *'Somebody help me!'* he yelled as loud as he could, but the hoarse sound from his throat was pathetically useless.

Munch said nothing, just set up a third camera on a boom so that it pointed down. Every movement was methodical, precise. Unhurried. Unconcerned. Unafraid.

And then Warren knew no one could hear him. The hot rage drained away, leaving only fear, cold and absolute. Warren's voice shook. There had to be something . . . some way out. Something he could say. Do. Offer. Beg. He'd beg. 'Please, Munch, I'll do anything . . .' His words trailed away as Munch's words replayed in his mind.

They all screamed. Ed Munch. Warren's chest constricted, despair making it difficult to breathe. 'Munch isn't your real name. Edvard Munch, the artist.' The painting of a ghoulish figure clutching its face in agony flashed into his mind. *'The Scream.'*

'Actually, it's pronounced "Moonk", not "Munch", but nobody ever gets it right. Nobody gets the details right,' he added in a disgusted voice.

Details. The man had been all about details earlier, frowning when Warren argued against the scratchy underwear. The sword had been real, too. *I should have used it on the bastard when I had the chance.* 'Authenticity,' Warren murmured, repeating what he'd thought had been the ramblings of a crazy old man.

Munch nodded. 'Now you understand.'

'What will you do?' His own voice was eerily calm.

One corner of Munch's mouth lifted. 'You'll see soon enough.'

Warren dragged in each breath. 'Please. *Please*, I'll do anything. Just let me go.'

Munch said nothing. He pushed a cart with a television just beyond the camera at his feet, then checked the focus of each camera with calm precision.

'You won't get away with this,' Warren said desperately, once again pulling at the ropes, struggling until his wrists burned and his arms strained in their sockets. The ropes were thick, the knots unyielding. He would not break free.

'That's what all the others said. But I have, and I will continue to do so.'

Others. There had been others. The smell of death was all around, mocking him. Others had died here. He would die here, too. From somewhere deep inside him, courage rallied. He lifted his chin. 'My friends will come looking for me. I told my fiancée I was meeting you.'

Finished with the cameras, Munch turned. His eyes held a contempt that said he knew it was a last, desperate bluff. 'No, you didn't. You told your fiancée you were meeting a friend to help him read lines. You told me so when we met this afternoon. You said this money would pay for a surprise for her birthday. You wanted it to stay a secret. That and your tattoo were the reasons I chose you.' He lifted one shoulder. 'Plus, you fit the suit. Not everyone can wear chain mail correctly. So no one will be looking for you. And if they do, they'll never find you. Accept it – you belong to me.'

Everything inside him went deathly still. It was true. He had told Munch the money was for a surprise for Sherry. Nobody knew where he was. Nobody would save him. He thought of Sherry, of his mom and dad, of everyone he cared about. They'd wonder where he was. A sob rose in his throat. 'You bastard,' he whispered. 'I hate you.'

One side of Munch's mouth quirked, but his eyes lit up with an amusement that was more terrifying than his smile. 'The others said that, too.' He shoved the water bottle at Warren's mouth again, pinching his nose until he gasped for air. Wildly Warren fought, but Munch forced the water down. 'Now, Mr Keyes, we begin. Don't forget to scream.'

Chapter One

Detective Vito Ciccotelli got out of his truck, his skin still vibrating. The beat-up old dirt road that led to the crime scene had only served to further rile his already churning stomach. He sucked in a breath and immediately regretted it. After fourteen years on the force, the odor of death still came as a putrid and unwelcome surprise.

'That shot my shocks to holy hell.' Nick Lawrence grimaced, slamming the door of his sensible sedan. 'Shit.' His Carolina drawl drew the curse out to four full syllables.

Two uniforms stood staring down into a hole halfway across the snow-covered field. Handkerchiefs covered their faces. A woman was crouched down in the hole, the top of her head barely visible. 'I guess CSU's already uncovered the body,' Vito said dryly.

'Y'think?' Nick bent down and shoved the cuffs of his pants into the cowboy boots he kept polished to a spit shine. 'Well, Chick, let's get this show on the road.'

'In a minute.' Vito reached behind his seat for his snow boots, then flinched when a thorn jabbed deep into his thumb. 'Dammit.' For a few seconds he sucked on the tiny wound, then with care moved the bouquet of roses out of the way to get to his boots. From the corner of his eye he could see Nick sober. But his partner said nothing.

'It's been two years. Today,' Vito added bitterly. 'How time flies.'

Nick's voice was quiet. 'It's supposed to heal, too.'

And Nick was right. Two years had dulled the edge of Vito's grief. But guilt . . . that was a different matter entirely. 'I'm going out to the cemetery this afternoon.'

'You want me to go with you?'

'Thanks, but no.' Vito shoved his feet into his boots. 'Let's go see what they found.'

Six years as a homicide detective had taught Vito that there were no simple murders, just varying degrees of hard ones. As soon as he stopped at the edge of the grave the crime scene unit had just unearthed in the snow-covered field, he knew this would be one of the harder ones.

Neither Vito nor Nick said a word as they studied the victim, who might have remained hidden forever were it not for an elderly man and his metal detector. The roses, the cemetery, and everything else was pushed aside as Vito focused on the body in the hole. He dragged his gaze from her hands to what was left of her face.

Their Jane Doe had been small, five-two or five-three, and appeared to have been young. Short, dark hair framed a face too decomposed to be easily identifiable and Vito wondered how long she'd been here. He wondered if anyone had missed her. If anyone still waited for her to come home.

He felt the familiar surge of pity and sadness and pushed it to the edge of his mind along with all the other things he wanted to forget. For now he'd focus on the body, the evidence. Later, he and Nick would consider the woman – who she'd been and who she'd known. They'd do so as a means to catch the sick sonofabitch who'd left her nude body to rot in an unmarked grave in an open field, who'd violated her even after death. Pity shifted to outrage as Vito's gaze returned to the victim's hands.

'He posed her,' Nick murmured beside him and in the soft words Vito heard the same outrage he felt. 'He fucking posed her.'

Indeed he had. Her hands were pressed together between

8

her breasts, her fingertips pointing to her chin. 'Permanently folded in prayer,' Vito said grimly.

'Religious murderer?' Nick mused.

'God, I hope not.' A buzz of apprehension tickled his spine. 'Religious murderers tend not to stop with just one. There could be more.'

'Maybe.' Nick crouched down to peer into the grave which was about three feet deep. 'How did he permanently pose her hands, Jen?'

CSU Sergeant Jen McFain looked up, her eyes covered with goggles, her nose and mouth by a mask. 'Wire,' she said. 'Looks like steel, but very fine. It's wound around her fingers. You'll be able to see it better once the ME cleans her up.'

Vito frowned. 'Doesn't seem like wire that thin would be enough to trip the sensor on a metal detector, especially under a couple feet of dirt.'

'You're right, the wire wouldn't have set it off. For that we can thank the rods your perp ran under the victim's arms.' Jen traced one gloved finger along the underside of her own arm, down to her wrist. 'They're thin and bendable, but have enough mass to set off a metal detector. It's how he kept her arms fixed in position.'

Vito shook his head. 'Why?' he asked and Jen shrugged.

'Maybe we'll get more from the body. I haven't gotten much from the hole so far. Except . . .' She nimbly climbed from the grave. 'The old man uncovered one of her arms using his garden spade. Now, he's in pretty good shape, but even I couldn't have dug that deep with a garden spade this time of year.'

Nick looked into the grave. 'The ground must not have been frozen.'

Jen nodded. 'Exactly. When he found the arm he stopped digging and called 911. When we got here, we started moving dirt to see what we had. The fill was easy to move until we got to the grave wall, then it was hard as a rock. Look at the corners. They look like they were cut using a T square. They're frozen solid.'

Vito felt a sick tug at his gut. 'He dug the grave before the ground froze. He planned this pretty far in advance.'

Nick was frowning. 'And nobody noticed a gaping hole?'

'Perp might've covered it with something,' Jen said. 'Also, I don't think the fill dirt came from this field. I'll run the tests to tell you for sure. That's all I got for now. I can't do anything more until the ME gets here.'

'Thanks, Jen,' Vito said. 'Let's talk to the property owner,' he said to Nick.

Harlan Winchester was about seventy, but his eyes were clear and sharp. He'd been waiting in the back seat of the police cruiser and got out when he saw them coming. 'I suppose I'll have to tell you detectives the same thing I told the officers.'

Vito put a little sympathy into his nod. 'I'm afraid so. I'm Detective Ciccotelli and this is my partner, Detective Lawrence. Can you take us through what happened?'

'Hell, I didn't even want that damn metal detector. It was a present from my wife. She's worried I don't get enough exercise since I retired.'

'So you got out this morning and walked?' Vito prompted and Winchester scowled.

' "Harlan P. Winchester," ' he mimicked in a high, nasal voice, ' "you've been in that good-for-nothin' chair for the last ten years. Get your moldy butt up and walk." So I did, 'cause I couldn't stand to listen to her nag me anymore. I thought I might find something interesting to make Ginny shut up. But . . . I never dreamed I'd find a *person*.'

'Was the body the first object your detector picked up?' Nick asked.

'Yeah.' His mouth set grimly. 'I took out my garden spade. It was then I thought about how hard the ground would be. I didn't think I'd be able to break the surface, much less dig deep. I almost put my spade away before I started, but I'd only been gone fifteen minutes and Ginny would have nagged me some more. So I started digging.' He closed his eyes, swallowed hard,

10

his bravado gone like so much mist. 'My spade . . . it hit her arm. So I stopped digging and called 911.'

'Can you tell us a little more about this land?' Vito asked. 'Who has access to it?'

'Anybody with an ATV or four-wheel drive, I guess. You can't see this field from the highway and the little drive that connects to the main road isn't even paved.'

Vito nodded, grateful he'd driven his truck, leaving his Mustang parked safely in his garage alongside his bike. 'It's definitely a rugged road. How do you get back here?'

'Today I walked.' He pointed to the tree line where a single set of footprints emerged. 'But this was the first time I've been back here. We only moved in a month ago. This land was my aunt's,' he explained. 'She died and left it to me.'

'So, did your aunt come out to this field often?'

'I wouldn't think so. She was a recluse, never left the house. That's all I know.'

'Sir, you've been a big help,' Vito said. 'Thank you.'

Winchester's shoulders sagged. 'Then I can go home?'

'Sure. The officers will drive you home.'

Winchester got in the cruiser and it headed out, passing a gray Volvo on its way in. The Volvo parked behind Nick's sedan and a trim woman in her midfifties got out and started across the field. ME Katherine Bauer was here. It was time to face Jane Doe.

Vito started toward the grave, but Nick didn't move. He was looking at Winchester's metal detector sitting inside the CSU van. 'We should check the rest of the field, Chick.'

'You think there are more.'

'I think we can't leave until we know there aren't.'

Another shiver of apprehension raced down Vito's back. In his heart he already knew what they would find. 'You're right. Let's see what else is out there.'

Sunday, January 14, 10:30 A.M.

'Everybody's eyes closed?' Sophie Johannsen frowned at her graduate students in the darkness. 'Bruce, you're peeking,' she said.

'I'm not peeking,' he grumbled. 'Besides, it's too dark to see anything anyway.'

'Hurry *up*,' Marta said impatiently. 'Turn on the lights.'

Sophie flicked on the lights, savoring the moment. 'I give you . . . the Great Hall.'

For a moment no one said a word. Then Spandan let out a low whistle that echoed off the ceiling, twenty feet above their heads.

Bruce's face broke into a grin. 'You did it. You finally finished it.'

Marta's jaw squared. 'It's nice.'

Sophie blinked at the younger woman's terse tone, but before she could say a word she heard the soft whir of John's wheelchair as he passed her to stare up at the far wall. 'You did all this yourself,' he murmured, looking around in his quiet way. 'Awesome.'

Sophie shook her head. 'Not nearly by myself. You all helped, cleaning swords and armor and helping me plan the sword display. This was definitely a group effort.'

Last fall, all fifteen members of her Weapons and Warfare graduate seminar had been enthusiastic volunteers at the Albright Museum of History, where Sophie spent her days. Now she was down to these faithful four. They'd come every Sunday for months, giving their time. They earned class credit, but more valuable was the opportunity to touch the medieval treasures their classmates could only view through glass.

Sophie understood their fascination. She also knew that holding a fifteenth-century sword in a sterile museum was but a shadow of the thrill of unearthing that sword herself, of brushing away the dirt, exposing a treasure no eyes had seen in five hundred years. Six months ago as a field archeologist in southern France, she'd lived for that rush, waking every morning wondering what buried treasure she'd find at the dig that day. Now, as the Albright Museum's head curator, she could only touch the treasures unearthed by others. Touching them, caring for them would have to be enough for now.

And as hard as it had been to walk away from the French dig of her dreams, every time she sat at her grandmother's side as she lay in a nursing-home bed, Sophie knew she'd made the right choice.

Moments like this, seeing the pride on the faces of her students, made her choice easier to bear, too. With pride of her own, Sophie admired what they'd accomplished. Large enough to easily accommodate groups of thirty or more, the new Great Hall was a spectacular sight. Against the far wall, three suits of armor stood at attention under a display of one hundred swords, arranged in a woven lattice pattern. War banners hung on the left wall, and on the right wall she'd mounted the Houarneau tapestry, one of the jewels of the collection amassed by Theodore Albright I during his brilliant archeological career.

Standing in front of the tapestry, Sophie took a moment to enjoy looking at it. The twelfth-century Houarneau tapestry, like all the other treasures in the Albright collection, never failed to steal her breath away. 'Wow,' she murmured.

' "Wow?" ' Bruce shook his head with a smile. 'Dr J, you should be able to think of a better word than that, in any one of a dozen languages.'

'Only ten,' she corrected and watched him roll his eyes. For Sophie, the study of language had always been a practical pleasure. Fluency in ancient languages enabled her research, but more, she loved the fluid rhythm and nuance of words themselves. She'd had few opportunities to use her skill since coming home and she missed it.

So, still admiring the tapestry, she indulged herself. '*C'est incroyable.*' The French flowed through her mind like a welcome melody, which was no surprise. Excepting a few short visits back to Philly, Sophie had made France her home for the last

13

fifteen years. Other languages required more conscious effort, but still her mind skimmed easily. Greek, German, Russian . . . she picked the words like flowers from a field. *'Katapliktikos. Hat was. O moy bog.'*

Marta raised a brow. 'And all that translated, means?'

Sophie's lips curved. 'Essentially . . . wow.' She took another satisfied look around. 'It's been a huge hit with tour groups.' Her smile dimmed. Just thinking about the tours, or more specifically the tour *guides*, was enough to suck the joy right out of her day.

John turned his chair so he could stare up at the swords. 'You did this so fast.'

She set the unpleasant tours aside in her mind. 'The trick was Bruce's computer-generated mockup. It showed where to place the supports, and once that was done mounting the swords was easy. It looks as authentic as any display I've ever seen in any castle anywhere.' She aimed a smile of appreciation toward Bruce. 'Thank you.'

Bruce beamed. 'And the paneling? I thought you were going with painted walls.'

Once again her smile dimmed. 'I was overruled on that. Ted Albright insisted that the wood would make the place look more like a true hall and not a museum.'

'He was right,' Marta said, her lips pursed tightly. 'It looks better.'

'Yeah, well maybe it does, but he also cleaned out my operating budget for this year,' Sophie said, annoyed. 'I had a list of new acquisitions that I now can't afford. We couldn't even afford to have the damn paneling installed.' She looked at her abused hands, nicked and scraped. 'While you all were back home sleeping until noon and pigging out on turkey leftovers, I was here with Ted Albright every day, putting up all this paneling. God, what a nightmare. Do you know how high these walls are?'

The whole paneling debacle had been the source of yet another argument with Ted 'the Third' Albright. Ted was the only grandson of the great archeologist, which unfortunately made him the sole owner of the Albright collection. He was also the owner of the museum, which unfortunately made him Sophie's boss. She rued the day she'd ever heard of Ted Albright and his Barnum and Bailey approach to running a museum, but until a position opened up in one of the other museums, this job was it.

Marta turned to look at her, her eyes cold and . . . disappointed. 'Spending two weeks alone with Ted Albright doesn't sound like a hardship. He's an attractive man,' she added, her tone acidic. 'I'm surprised you managed to get any work done at all.'

Uncomfortable silence filled the room as Sophie stood, shocked and staring at the woman she'd mentored for four months. *This can't be happening again.* But it was.

The men exchanged looks of wary confusion, but Sophie knew exactly what Marta was saying, exactly what she'd heard. The disappointment she'd seen in Marta's eyes now made sense. Rage and denial screamed through Sophie's mind, but she decided to address the current insinuation and leave the past covered, for now.

'Ted's married, Marta. And just so you can set the record straight, we weren't alone. Ted's wife, son, and daughter were working with us the whole time.'

Maintaining her icy stare, Marta said nothing. Awkwardly Bruce blew out a breath. 'So,' he said. 'Last semester we revamped the Great Hall. What's next, Dr J?'

Ignoring the churning of her stomach, Sophie led the group to the exhibition area beyond the Great Hall. 'The next project is redoing the weapons exhibit.'

'*Yes.*' Spandan socked the air. 'Finally. This is what I've been waiting for.'

'Then your wait is over.' Sophie stopped at the glass display cabinet that held a half-dozen very rare medieval swords. The Houarneau tapestry was exquisite, but these weapons were her favorite items of the entire Albright collection.

'I always wonder who owned them,' Bruce said softly. 'Who fought with them.'

John brought his chair closer. 'And how many died at their tip,' he murmured. He looked up, his eyes hidden behind the hair that was always in his face. 'Sorry.'

'It's okay,' Sophie said. 'I've often wondered the same thing.' Her mouth quirked up at a sudden memory. 'My very first day as curator, a kid tried to pull the fifteenth-C Bastardsword off the wall and play Braveheart. Nearly gave me heart failure.'

'They weren't behind glass?' Bruce gasped, appalled. Both Spandan and John wore similar looks of horror.

Marta hung back, arms crossed and jaw cocked to one side. She said nothing.

Sophie decided to deal with her privately. 'No, Ted believes that putting glass between artifacts and museum patrons degrades the "entertainment experience."' It had been their first argument. 'He agreed to put these behind glass if we displayed some of the less valuable swords out in the Great Hall.' Sophie sighed. 'And if we displayed these rare swords in an 'entertaining' way. This display case was a temporary compromise until I could get the Great Hall finished. So this is the next project.'

'What exactly does "entertaining" mean?' Spandan asked.

Sophie frowned. 'Think mannequins and costumes,' she said darkly. Costumes were Ted's passion, and when he'd only wanted to dress up mannequins, she could go with the flow. But two weeks ago he'd unveiled his newest scheme, adding another role to Sophie's job description. To kick off the new Great Hall, they'd give tours . . . in period garb. Specifically, Sophie and Ted's nineteen-year-old son, Theo, would lead the tours and nothing Sophie could say would change Ted's mind. Finally she'd outright refused – and in a rare fit of serious temper Ted Albright had threatened to fire her.

Sophie had very nearly quit – until she'd gotten home that night and looked through the mail. The nursing home was raising the cost of Anna's room. So Sophie swallowed her pride, donned the damn costume and did Ted's damn tours during the day. In the evenings she'd redoubled her search for another job.

'Did the boy damage the sword?' John asked.

'Thankfully, no. When you handle them, be sure you wear your gloves.'

Bruce waved his white gloves like a truce flag. 'We always do,' he said cheerfully.

'And I appreciate it.' He was trying to lighten her mood and Sophie appreciated that as well. 'Your assignment is the following – each of you will prepare an exhibit proposal, including the space requirements and cost of materials you'll need to build it. It's due in three weeks. Keep it simple. I don't have the budget for anything grand.'

She left the three men to work and walked to where Marta stood motionless and stony-faced. 'So now what?' Sophie asked.

A petite woman, Marta craned her neck to meet Sophie's eyes. 'Excuse me?'

'Marta, you obviously heard something. You've also obviously chosen not only to believe it but to publicly challenge me on it. Your choices as I see them are to either apologize to me for your disrespect and we go on, or continue this attitude.'

Marta frowned. 'And if I continue?'

'Then there's the door. This is a volunteer experience, on both our parts.' Sophie's expression softened. 'Look, you're a nice kid and an asset to this museum. I'd miss you if you were gone. I'd really rather you chose door number one.'

Marta swallowed hard. 'I was visiting a friend. A grad student at Shelton College.'

Shelton. The memory of the few months she'd been enrolled at Shelton College still made Sophie physically ill, more than ten years later. 'It was just a matter of time.'

Marta's chin trembled. 'I was bragging on you to my friend, how you were such a great role model, my mentor, that you're a woman who made a name for herself in the field using her brain. My friend laughed and said you'd used other parts of your body to get ahead. She said you slept with Dr Brewster so you could get on his dig team at Avignon, that that's how you got your start. Then when you went back to France, you slept with Dr Moraux. That's why you moved up so fast, why you got your own dig team when you were so young. I told her it wasn't true, that you wouldn't do that. Did you?'

Sophie knew she would be well within her rights to tell Marta that this was none of her business. But Marta was obviously disillusioned. And hurt. So Sophie reopened a wound that had never really healed. 'Did I sleep with Brewster? Yes.' And she still felt the shame of it. 'Did I do it to get on his dig team? No.'

'Then why did you?' Marta whispered. 'He's married.'

'I know that now. I didn't then. I was young. He was older and . . . he deceived me. I made a stupid mistake, Marta, one I'm still paying for. I can tell you I got to where I am without Dr Alan Brewster.' His very name still left a vile taste on her tongue, but she watched Marta's expression change as she accepted that her mentor was human, too.

'But I *never* slept with Etienne Moraux,' she went on fiercely. 'And I got to where I was by working my ass off. I published more papers than anyone else and did all the grunt work to prove myself. Which is how you should do it, too. And Marta, no more comments about Ted. However we disagree over this museum, Ted's devoted to his wife. Darla Albright is one of the nicest people I've ever met. Rumors like that can destroy a marriage. Are we clear?'

Marta nodded, relief in her face and respect back in her eyes. 'Yes.' She tilted her head thoughtfully. 'You could have just thrown me out.'

'I could have, but I have a feeling I'm going to need you, especially for this new exhibit.' Sophie looked down at her own ratty jeans. 'I have no fashion sense, twenty-first or fifteenth century. You'll have to dress Ted's damn mannequins.'

Marta laughed softly. 'That I can do. Thanks, Dr J. For

keeping me. And for telling me when you didn't have to. Next time I see my friend I'll tell her my original opinion stands.' Her lips turned up charmingly. 'I still want to be you when I grow up.'

Embarrassed, Sophie shook her head. 'Trust me, you don't. Now get to work.'

Sunday, January 14, 12:25 P.M.

Vito had placed a red flag in the snow every place Nick picked up a metal object. Now Nick and Vito stood with Jen, staring in dismay at five red flags.

'Any or all of those could be more Jane Does,' Jen said quietly. 'We have to know.'

Nick sighed. 'We're going to have to search this whole field.'

'That's a lot of manpower,' Vito grumbled. 'Does CSU have the resources?'

'No, I'd have to request support. But I don't want to go up the ladder with that kind of request until I'm damn sure these flags don't mark arrowheads or buried Coke cans.'

'We could just start digging at one of the flags,' Nick said. 'See what we turn up.'

'We could.' Jen frowned. 'But I want to know what's under our feet before we do. I don't want to lose evidence because we moved too fast or the wrong way.'

'Cadaver dogs?' Vito suggested.

'Maybe, but what I'd really like to have is a scan of the property. I saw it on the History Channel. These archeologists used ground-penetrating radar to locate the ruins of an ancient wall. It was very cool.' Jen sighed. 'But I'd never get the funds to pay a contractor. Let's bring in the dogs and get it done.'

Nick held up a wagging finger. 'Not so fast. The show was about archeologists, right? Well, if we had an archeologist, he might be able to do that . . . radar thing.'

Jen's eyes sharpened. 'Do you know an archeologist?'

'No,' Nick said, 'but the city's chock full of universities. Somebody must know one.'

'They'd have to work for cheap,' Vito said. 'And they'd have to be somebody we could trust.' Vito thought about the body, the way the hands were posed. 'The press would have a field day with this if it leaked.'

'And our asses would be deep fried,' Nick muttered.

'Who do you need to trust?'

Vito turned to find the ME standing behind him. 'Hi, Katherine. Are you done?'

Katherine Bauer nodded wearily, peeling off her gloves. 'The body's in the bus.'

'Cause?' Nick asked.

'Nothing yet. I'm thinking she's been dead two or three weeks at least. I can't give you anything more until I get some tissue samples under my microscope. So,' she tilted her head sideways. 'Who do you need to be able to trust?'

'I want to get a scan of the property,' Jen said. 'I was going to see if anyone knows any of the professors in the archeology departments in the local universities.'

'I do,' Katherine said, and the three of them stared at her.

Jen's eyes widened. 'You do? A real *live* archeologist?'

'A dead one won't do us much good,' Nick said dryly and Jen's cheeks turned red.

Katherine chuckled. 'Yes, I know a real live archeologist. She's home on . . . a sabbatical of sorts. She's considered an expert in her field. I know she'd help.'

'And she's discreet?' Nick insisted and Katherine patted his arm maternally.

'Very discreet. I've known her for more than twenty-five years. I can call her now if you want.' She waited, her gray brows lifted.

'At least we'll know,' Nick said. 'I vote yes.'

Vito nodded. 'Let's call her.'

Sunday, January 14, 12:30 P.M.

'God, it's incredible.' Spandan held the Bastardsword in his gloved hands with all the care and respect due a treasure that had survived five hundred years. 'I bet you wanted to kill that kid for trying to rip this off the wall.'

Sophie looked down at the two-handed longsword she'd taken from the case. The students were taking a 'creativity break' to better help them 'envision the assignment'. Sophie knew they really just wanted to touch the swords and she couldn't blame them. There was a fundamental power in holding a weapon this old. And this lethal.

'I was more angry at his mother who was too busy talking on her cell phone to watch her kid.' She chuckled. 'Luckily my brain hadn't fully settled back into English, so when I cussed her out, it was in French. But, uh, some things transcend language.'

'So what did she do?' Marta asked.

'Went crying to Ted. He gave her a refund, then came after me. "You can't frighten the guests, Sophie," ' she mimicked. 'I still remember the look on that woman's face when I dragged her little brat over to her. She wasn't much bigger than the kid. Nearly broke her neck looking up at me. It was one of the few times being tall was an asset.'

'You need better security in this place,' John commented, his eyes focused on the Viking Age sword he held. 'It's a wonder nobody's walked off with any artifacts.'

Sophie frowned. 'We have an alarm system, but you're right. Before, hardly anyone knew we were here, but now, with all these tours, we definitely need a guard.' The salary for a guard had been in her operating budget for the coming year. But nooo . . . Ted wanted *paneling*. It was enough to make her twitch. 'I know of at least two Italian reliquaries that are no longer on their shelf. I keep checking for them on eBay.'

'Makes you wish for medieval justice,' Spandan grumbled.

'What would have been the penalty for theft?' John asked, slanting a look up at her.

Sophie carefully settled the longsword back in the display case. 'Depends on what point in the Middle Ages – early, high, or late – and on what was stolen, if it was stolen by force or by stealth, and who the victim was and who the thief was. Felony thieves might be hanged, but most small thefts were settled by recompense.'

'I thought they cut off a hand or gouged out an eye,' Bruce said.

'Not commonly,' Sophie told him, her lips quirking at his obvious disappointment. 'It didn't make sense for the lord to disfigure the people who were working his land. Without a hand or a foot they couldn't make him as much money.'

'No exceptions?' Bruce asked and Sophie shot him an amused look.

'Bloodthirsty today, aren't we? Hmm. Exceptions.' She considered it. 'Outside Europe, there were cultures that certainly still practiced eye-for-an-eye justice. Thieves lost one hand and the opposite foot. In European culture, go back to the tenth century and you'll find amputation of 'the hand with which he did it' as a punishment in the Anglo-Saxon Dooms. But the culprit had to be caught stealing from a church.'

'Your reliquaries would have been in a church back then,' Spandan pointed out.

Sophie had to chuckle. 'Yes, they would have been, so it's a damn good thing they were stolen from here and now, not there and then. Now your 'creativity break' is over. Put the swords away and get back to work.'

Sighing heavily they did as she asked, first Spandan, then Bruce and Marta. Until only John remained. In almost an offertory way, he lifted the sword with both hands and with both hands Sophie took it. Fondly she studied the stylized pommel. 'I found one like this once, at a dig in Denmark. Not this nice, and not all in one piece. The blade had corroded completely through, right in the middle. But what a feeling it was, uncovering it for the first time. Like it had been sleeping for all those years and woke up, just for me.' She glanced down at him with an embarrassed laugh. 'That sounds crazy, I know.'

His smile was solemn. 'No, not crazy. You must miss it, being in the field.'

Sophie arranged the contents of the case and locked it. 'Some days more than others. Today I miss it a great deal.' Tomorrow, when she was leading a tour in *period garb*, she'd miss it a great deal more. 'Let's go—'

Her cell phone rang, surprising her. Even Ted gave her one day of rest. 'Hello?'

'Sophie, it's Katherine. Are you alone?'

Sophie straightened at the urgency in Katherine's voice. 'No. Should I be?'

'Yes. I need to talk to you. It's important.'

'Hold on. John, I need to take this. Can I meet you and the others in the hall in a few?' He nodded and turned his chair toward the Great Hall and the other students. When he was gone, she shut the door. 'Go ahead, Katherine. What's wrong?'

'I need your help.'

Katherine's daughter Trisha had been Sophie's best friend since kindergarten and Katherine had become the mother Sophie had never had. 'Name it.'

'We need to excavate a field and we need to know where to dig.'

Sophie's mind instantly put 'medical examiner' and 'excavation' together, conjuring a picture of a mass grave. She'd excavated dozens of gravesites over the years and knew exactly what needed to be done. She found her pulse increasing at the thought of doing real fieldwork again. 'Where and when do you need me?'

'In a field about a half hour north of town, an hour ago.'

'Katherine, it'll take me at least two hours to get my equipment up there.'

'Two hours? Why?' In the background Sophie heard several disgruntled voices.

'Because I'm at the museum and I have my bike. I can't tie all that equipment to the seat. I have to go home first and get

Gran's car. Plus, I was going to sit with her this afternoon. I need to stop by the nursing home and check on her at least.'

'I'll check on Anna myself. You go to the college and get the equipment. One of the detectives will meet you there and transport you and the equipment to the site.'

'Have him meet me in front of the humanities building at Whitman College. It's the one with the funky ape sculpture in front. I'll be out front by 1:30.'

There was more murmuring, more intense. '*Okay*,' Katherine said, exasperated. 'Detective Ciccotelli wants to be sure you understand this is to be kept in the utmost confidence. You must exercise extreme discretion and say nothing to anyone.'

'Understood.' She returned to the Great Hall. 'Guys, I need to go now.'

The students immediately began to gather their work. 'Is your grandmother okay, Dr J?' Bruce asked, his forehead creasing in concern.

Sophie hesitated. 'She will be.' Not the whole truth and hopefully for Anna, not a lie. 'For now, you get a few free hours this afternoon. Don't have too much fun.'

When they were gone, she locked up, set the alarm, and headed toward Whitman College as fast as she legally dared, her heart beating rapidly in her chest. For months she'd been missing the field. It looked like she was finally about to find one.

Chapter Two

Sunday, January 14, 2:00 P.M.

He sat back in his chair and nodded at his computer screen, his lips curving in a satisfied smile. It was good. Very, very good. *If I do say so myself*. Which he did.

He raised his eyes to the still photos he'd taken from the video of Warren Keyes. He'd chosen his quarry well – height, weight, musculature. The young man's tattoo had been Fate sealing the deal. Warren was meant to be his victim. He'd suffered brilliantly. The camera had captured the exquisite agony on his face. But his screams . . .

He clicked on an audio file and a chilling scream blasted from the speakers with crystal clarity, sending a shiver of pleasure racing down his back. Warren's screams had been perfect. Perfect pitch, perfect intensity. Perfect inspiration.

His eyes moved to the canvases he'd hung next to the stills. This series of paintings might be his best work yet. He'd titled the series *Warren Dies*. It was done in oil, of course. He'd found oil the best medium for capturing the intensity of expression, the victim's mouth stretching open on one of those perfect screams of excruciating pain.

And the eyes. He'd learned there were stages to death by torture. All were most clearly seen through the victim's eyes. The first stage was fear, followed by defiance, then despair as the victim realized there was truly no escape. The fourth stage, hope, depended entirely on the victim's tolerance for pain. If the victim persisted through the first wave, he might give them respite, just long enough to allow hope to surface. Warren Keyes had had a remarkable tolerance for pain.

Then, when all hope was gone, there was the fifth stage – the plea, the pitiful appeal for death, for release. Toward the end, there was stage six, the final surge of defiance, a primitive fight for survival that predated modern man.

But the seventh stage was the best and most elusive – the instant of death itself. The burst . . . the flash of energy as the corporeal yielded its essence. It was a moment so brief that even the camera lens was incapable of complete capture, so fleeting that the human eye would miss it if one weren't expressly watching. He had been watching.

And he'd been rewarded. His eyes lingered on the seventh painting. Although last in the series, he'd painted it first, rushing to his easel while Warren's released energy still vibrated along every nerve and Warren's final, perfect scream still rang in his ears.

He saw *it* there, in Warren's eyes. That indefinable *something* he alone had found in the instant of death. He'd first achieved it with *Claire Dies* more than a year ago. Had it really been that long? Time did fly when you were having fun. And he was finally having fun. He'd been chasing that indefinable *something* his entire life. He'd found it now.

Genius. That's what Jager Van Zandt called it. He'd first gained the entertainment mogul's attention with *Claire*, and although he personally considered his *Zachary* and *Jared* series to be superior, *Claire* remained VZ's favorite.

Of course, Van Zandt had never seen his paintings, only his computer animations in which he'd transformed Claire into 'Clothilde,' a World War II Vichy French whore strangled to death by a soldier who'd been betrayed by her treachery. A crowd pleaser wherever the clip was shown, Clothilde had become the star of *Behind Enemy Lines*, Van Zandt's latest 'entertainment venture.'

Most people called them video games. Van Zandt liked to think he was building an entertainment empire. Before *Behind*

Enemy Lines, VZ's empire existed only in the man's dreams. But VZ's dreams had come true – *Behind Enemy Lines* had flown off the shelves – a runaway success thanks to Clothilde and the rest of his animations. *My art.*

Van Zandt understood that as well and had chosen Clothilde, caught in her moment of death, to adorn the *Behind Enemy Lines* box. It always gave him a rush to see it, to know that the hands gripping 'Clothilde's' throat were his own.

VZ clearly recognized his genius, but he wasn't sure the man could handle the reality of his art. So he'd go on letting VZ believe what he wanted to – that Clothilde was a fictional character and that his own name was Frasier Lewis. In the end both he and Van Zandt would get what they wanted. VZ would get a best-selling 'entertainment venture' and make his millions. *And millions will see my art.*

Which was the ultimate goal. He had a gift. VZ's video game was merely the most efficient way to showcase that gift to the most people in the shortest time. Once he was established he wouldn't need the animations. His paintings would be in demand on their own. But for now, he needed Van Zandt and Van Zandt needed him.

VZ was going to be very pleased with his latest work. He clicked his mouse and once again watched his animation of Warren Keyes. It was perfect. Every muscle and sinew rippled as the man struggled against his bonds, arching and writhing in pain as his bones were slowly pulled from their sockets. The blood looked good, too. Not too red. Very authentic. Careful study of the video had enabled him to duplicate every aspect of Warren's body, down to the simplest twitch.

He'd done an especially skillful job with Warren's face, capturing the fear and the defiance as Warren resisted the demands of his captor. *Which would be me.* The Inquisitor. He'd depicted himself as the old man who'd lured Warren to his dungeon.

Speaking of such, now that *Warren Dies* was complete it was time to lure his next victim. He opened UCanModel, the delightful little website with which he'd had such success in locating the perfect faces for his work. For a modest fee, actors and models could post their portfolios on UCanModel so that any Hollywood director had only to click on their picture to launch them to instant stardom.

Actors and models made the perfect subjects. They had beauty, the ability to emote, and their faces translated well to film and canvas. They also were so eager for fame and so poor that they'd take just about any job. Luring them with a part in a documentary had worked every time and allowed him to purport himself as the nonthreatening old history professor named Ed Munch. He was getting tired of being Edvard Munch, though. Maybe he'd be Hieronymus Bosch next time. Now, *there* was artistic genius.

He perused the lineup his current search had produced. He'd identified fifteen prospects, but he'd already eliminated all but five. The others weren't nearly poor enough to be easily hooked. Of the five, only three were truly destitute. His financial checks had shown them all to be in or on the verge of bankruptcy.

He'd shadowed these three prospects for a week and found only one to be solitary and secretive enough not to be missed afterward. That was an important component. His victims must not have anyone to look for them. They were runaways like pretty Brittany with her folded hands. Or, like Warren and Billy before him, they had to be so secretive that no one would know they'd been contacted.

Of all the current candidates, Gregory Sanders was the perfect choice. Rejected and cast out by his family, Sanders was alone. This he'd found the night before when he'd followed Sanders to his favorite bar. Disguised as an out-of-town businessman, he'd bought Sanders a few drinks and waited until the man blubbered his sad tale. Sanders had no one. So he was perfect.

Clicking Gregory's contact button, he zipped off his standard e-mail, confident in the steps he'd taken to mask his own identity, both physical and electronic. By tomorrow, Greg would accept his offer. By Tuesday, he'd have a new victim. And a new scream.

He pushed away from his desk and stiffly came to his feet, rubbing his right thigh. Damn these Philly winters. The pain was bad today. Apart from the sheer thrill, his art accomplished another important benefit – while he painted, he could forget about the phantom pains for which there was no treatment. No cure. No goddamn relief.

He'd reached the door of his studio when he remembered. *Tuesday*. The old man's bills were due on Tuesday. Paying them was a necessity. As long as the mortgage and utilities were paid on time, no one would wonder where the old man and his wife had gone. No one would look for them, which was the way he wanted it. He walked back to his computer. He'd be busy with his new victim on Tuesday, so he'd pay the bills now.

Dutton, Georgia, Sunday, January 14, 2:15 P.M.

'I appreciate you coming so quick, Daniel.' Sheriff Frank Loomis threw a glance over his shoulder before turning to unlock the front door. 'I wasn't sure you would.'

Daniel Vartanian knew the observation was fair. 'He's still my father, Frank.'

'Uh-huh.' Frank frowned when the lock didn't budge. 'I was sure that was the one. I've had this key since the last time your folks took a long vacation.'

Daniel watched Frank try five different keys, the feeling of apprehension in his gut swelling to dark dread. 'I've got a key.'

Frank stepped back with a glare. 'Then why the hell didn't you say so, boy?'

Daniel lifted a brow. 'Wouldn't want to go steppin' on toes,' he said sarcastically. ' "Jurisdictions bein' what they are." ' The words had been Frank's own, uttered just last night when he'd called to say Daniel's parents might be missing.

'Pull that GBI stick outta your ass, *Special Agent* Var-tanian, or I will, and then I'll whip you with it.' The threat was not an idle one. Frank had tanned Daniel's hide more than once for one prank or another. But it was because Frank cared, which was more than he could say for his father. Judge Arthur Vartanian had been too busy to care.

'Don't knock those GBI sticks,' Daniel said mildly, though his heart had begun to pound. 'They're the latest technology, like all our toys. Even you might be impressed.'

'Damn bureaucrats,' Frank muttered. 'Offer "technology" and "expertise", but only if they run the show. Give 'em an inch and pretty soon they've descended like locusts.'

That, too, was a fair observation, although Daniel doubted his superiors at the Georgia Bureau of Investigation would see it as such. He'd found the key, but now had to focus on steadying his trembling hand. 'I'm one of those locusts, Frank,' he said.

Frank huffed, irritated. 'Dammit, Daniel, you know what I meant. Art and Carol are your parents. I called you, not the GBI. I don't want my county overrun by bureaucrats.'

Daniel's key didn't fit the lock either. But it had been a long time, so that in and of itself was not a cause for alarm. 'When was the last time you saw them?'

'November. About two weeks before Thanksgivin'. Your mama was headed in to Angie's and your daddy was down at the courthouse.'

'Then it was a Wednesday,' Daniel said and Frank nodded. Angie's was the town's beauty shop where his mother had kept a standing Wednesday appointment since before he was born. 'But why was Dad at the courthouse?'

'Retirement was hard on your father. He missed the work. The people.'

Arthur Vartanian missed the power of being the circuit court judge in a little Georgia town, Daniel thought, but kept it to himself. 'You said my mother's doctor called you.'

'Yes. That's when I realized how long it had been since I'd

seen either of them.' Frank sighed. 'I'm sorry, son. I assumed she'd at least told you and Susannah.'

That his mother had kept such a thing from her own children had been hard to accept. Breast cancer. She'd had surgery and chemo and had never said a word.

'Yeah, well, things haven't been so good between any of us for a while.'

'Your mama missed several appointments, so the nurse got worried and called me. I checked around and found your mother told Angie she and your father were going to visit your grandma in Memphis the day she canceled her December hair appointments.'

'But they didn't go to Memphis.'

'No. Your grandma said that your mother told her that they were spending the holidays with your sister, but when I called Susannah she said she hadn't heard from your parents in more than a year. That's when I called you.'

'That's just too many lies, Frank,' Daniel said. 'We're going in.' He shattered the small windowpane to the side of the door with his elbow, reached in and unlocked the door. The house was quiet as a tomb and smelled musty.

Stepping over the threshold was like stepping back in time. In his mind Daniel saw his father standing at the foot of the stairs, his knuckles battered and bloody. Mama stood at his father's side, tears running down her face. Susannah stood alone, a desperate plea on her face for him to abandon the confrontation that she didn't understand. It would be easier on Susannah if she never knew, so he'd never told her.

He'd walked away, planning never to return. The best-laid plans . . . 'You take the upstairs, Frank. I'll take this level and the basement.'

Daniel's first look confirmed his parents had gone on a trip. The water was off and every appliance unplugged. His mother had a fear of fire by toaster oven, he recalled.

He cleared the first floor and, heart pounding, descended into the basement, visions of bodies he'd found throughout his years as a cop bombarding his mind. But there was no smell of death and the basement was as orderly as it had always been. He climbed the stairs to find Frank waiting in the hall by the front door.

'They took lots of clothes,' Frank said. 'Their suitcases are gone.'

'This doesn't make a lick of sense.' Daniel walked into each room again, pausing in his father's office. 'He was a judge for twenty years, Frank. He made enemies.'

'I considered that. I asked Wanda to pull records of his old cases.'

Surprised and comforted, Daniel gave Frank a weary smile. 'Thanks.'

Frank shrugged. 'Wanda will be thankful for the overtime. Come on, Daniel. Let's go back to town, get something to eat and figure out what to do next.'

'In a minute. Let me check his desk.' He pulled on the drawer, surprised when it slid right open. Staring up at him was a brochure for the Grand Canyon and his throat tightened. His mother had always wanted to see the Grand Canyon, but his father was always too busy and they never went. It looked like he'd finally made the time to go.

Suddenly the reality of his mother's cancer hit him square in the face, becoming more than a secret she'd withheld. *My mother's going to die.* He cleared his throat harshly. 'Look, Frank.' He moved the brochures to the blotter, fanning them out.

'Grand Canyon, Lake Tahoe, Mount Rushmore.' Frank sighed. 'I guess your daddy finally took her on that trip he'd been promising all these years.'

'But why not just say that's where they were going? Why all the lies?'

Frank squeezed his shoulder. 'I guess your mama doesn't want anyone to know she's sick. For Carol, it's a pride thing. Let her have her dignity. Let's go get supper.'

His heart heavy, Daniel started to rise but a noise stopped him. 'What was that?'

'What?' Frank asked. 'I didn't hear anything.'

Daniel listened and heard it again. A high whirring sound. 'His computer is running.'

'That's impossible. It's turned off.'

The monitor was dark. But Daniel laid his hand on the computer and his breath caught. 'It's warm and it's running. Somebody is using this computer, right now.' He hit the button on the monitor and together they watched an online banking screen appear. The cursor moved with ghostly precision, untouched by either of them.

'Shit, it's like watching a Ouija board,' Frank murmured.

'It's Dad's online bill pay system. Someone just paid Dad's mortgage.'

'Your daddy?' Frank asked, confusion obvious in his voice.

'I don't know.' Daniel's jaw hardened. 'But you can be damn sure I'll find out.'

Philadelphia, Sunday, January 14, 2:15 P.M.

Vito stared at the 'funky ape sculpture' with increasing annoyance. He'd been waiting for more than half an hour but there was no sign of Katherine's friend. He was frustrated and cold, having rolled down his window for fresh air. The smell of Jane Doe was in his hair and his sinuses and he couldn't stand himself.

He'd called Katherine a half dozen times with no success. He couldn't have missed her. He'd been early and the only person he'd seen was a college girl sitting on a bench at the bus stop about fifteen feet behind his truck.

The girl looked about twenty and had long, long blond hair that had to touch her butt when she stood up. A red bandana covered the top of her head and two thin braids hung from her temples, but the rest of her hair fell loose, covering her like a cape. Enormous gold hoops swung from her ears and her face was half-covered by the round frames of her purple sunglasses.

And to top it all off, she wore an old army surplus camouflage jacket that looked about four sizes too big.

College kids, he thought, shaking his head. She looked up the street, then down before drawing her knees up under her coat, propping her thick-soled army boots on the bench. She must be freezing. God knew he was and he had the truck's heater going.

Finally his cell rang. 'Dammit, Katherine, where have you been?'

'In the morgue, getting your Jane Doe settled for the night. What do you need?'

'Your friend's cell number.' He looked up at the knock on the passenger window. It was the college girl. 'Hold on, Katherine.' He rolled the far window down. 'Yes?'

The girl's full lips were quivering. 'Um . . . I'm waiting for someone and I think it might be you.'

She was even prettier up close, and asking for trouble approaching men like that. 'Hell of a pickup line, but I'm not interested. Go practice on somebody your own age.'

'Wait!' she shouted, but he rolled the window back up.

'Who was that?' Katherine asked, amusement in her voice.

Vito was not amused. 'College kid trying for an older guy. Your friend isn't here.'

'If she said she'd be there, she's there, Vito. Sophie's very reliable.'

'And I'm telling you – Goddammit.' It was the girl again, at his window now. 'Look here,' he said to the girl, 'I said I'm not interested. That means go away.' He started to raise the window, but she slammed her palms on the edge of the glass, curling her fingers into claws as she fought the window's ascent. The gloves she wore were thin knit and every finger was a different color of the rainbow, clashing with the camouflage.

Vito was reaching for his badge when the girl took off her sunglasses. She rolled eyes that were bright green. 'Do you know Katherine?' she demanded and it was then he realized she was no girl. She was at least thirty, maybe a few years older.

He gritted his teeth. 'Katherine,' he said slowly. 'What does your friend look like?'

'Like the woman standing at your window,' Katherine said, chuckling. 'Long hair, blond, thirtyish. Eclectic fashion sense. Sorry, Vito.'

He bit back his smartass retort. 'I was looking for someone your age. You said you'd known her for twenty-five years.'

'Twenty-eight, actually. Since I was in kindergarten,' the woman said brusquely and stuck out her multicolored hand. 'Sophie Johannsen. Hello, Katherine,' she called into the phone. 'You should have given us cell phone numbers,' she added in a tone that was singsong on top, but underneath was taut with impatience.

Katherine sighed. 'I'm sorry. I've got to go, Vito. I have company coming for dinner and I still have to check on Sophie's grandmother on my way home.'

Vito closed his phone and met the woman's narrowed green eyes, feeling like a total and complete idiot. 'I'm sorry. I thought you were twenty.'

One side of her full mouth lifted in a wry smile and he was struck with the certainty that he'd been wrong yet again. She wasn't simply pretty up close. She was absolutely beautiful. Vito found his fingers itching to touch her lips. *A woman could do amazing things with that mouth.* Abruptly he clenched his jaw, both annoyed and shocked at the vividness of the images stampeding through his mind. *Rein it in, Chick. Now.*

'I guess I'm flattered. It's been a long time since somebody mistook me for a college coed.' She pointed an electric blue finger at the building. 'The equipment we need is just inside. There's too much for one trip and I didn't want to leave it on the curb while I went back for the rest of it. It's pretty expensive. Can you give me a hand?'

Controlling his thoughts with considerable difficulty, he followed her to the building. 'We appreciate your help, Dr Johannsen,' he said as she unlocked the door.

'It's my pleasure. Katherine's been there for me more times than I can count. And please, call me Sophie. Nobody calls me Dr Johannsen. Even my students call me Dr J – but I think that's more of a basketball reference, because I'm tall.'

She offered the last line with a self-deprecating smile and Vito couldn't take his eyes off her face. Devoid of a speck of makeup, she had a natural, wholesome glow despite the hippie earrings and army surplus clothes and rainbow fingers. He was hit with a rush of yearning so keen it nearly stole his breath. Before . . . that had been lust. This was something different. He searched for a word, but only one came to mind. *Home.* Looking at her face was like coming home.

Her cheeks grew pink and Vito realized he'd been staring. For three beats of his heart she stared back, then abruptly turned to tug hard on the heavy door, taking a stumbling step back against him when it flew open. His hands gripped her shoulders to hold her upright, bringing her against him. *Let her go.* But his hands did not obey. Instead they held on and for one moment she seemed to relax, resting against him.

Then she leaped forward as if stung, lunging to catch the door before it closed again, breaking the contact and ending the moment.

He'd held her for only a few seconds, but it was like touching a live wire, and he took a step back, physically and mentally. Shaken and not liking it, he drew a breath. *It's just because it's today*, he told himself. *Get a grip, Chick, before you make a fool of yourself.* But he blinked in surprise as the next words tumbled from his mouth.

'Call me Vito.' He usually preferred being called 'Detective' when he was working. It kept things nice and separate. But it was too late now.

'Okay.' The single word came out on an exhale, as if she'd been holding her breath. 'Here are the things we need to take.'

Four suitcases sat by the door and Vito picked up the two largest. She got the other two and pulled the door closed. 'I'll need to get these back to the university tonight,' she said briskly. 'One of the professors has the GPR signed out for a field trip tomorrow.'

It seemed she'd shrugged the moment away and Vito decided to do the same, but his eyes had a mind of their own. He couldn't stop looking at her face, searching her profile as they walked to his truck. Her lips were still quivering from the cold and he felt a pang of guilt. 'Why didn't you just come up to me earlier?' he asked.

'You said to be discreet,' she said, looking straight ahead. 'I wasn't sure you were Katherine's cop and you weren't in a police car. I kept thinking that if you weren't the right one, you might not appreciate me blabbing your name. Katherine didn't tell me what you looked like and she didn't give me the secret handshake. So I waited.'

While she froze, he thought, remembering the way she'd drawn her body up under the coat for warmth. He put the two large suitcases in the bed of his truck and secured them. When he reached for the smaller cases she held, she shook her head. 'These are delicate. Given a choice, I'd ride in the bed and buckle these in my seat.'

'I think I can find room for you both.' He stowed the cases in the back floorboard, then opened her door. 'After you . . .' His mind derailed when she moved past him. She smelled like the roses he'd thrown behind his seat in the truck, fragrant and sweet.

He stood motionless, just breathing in her scent. She looked nothing like his Andrea, who'd been dark and petite. Sophie Johannsen was an Amazon, tall, blond, and . . . alive. *She's alive, Chick. And today, that's just enough to get you into trouble.* By tomorrow, he'd be blessedly numb once more.

'Sophie,' she said warily. 'I'm Sophie.'

'I'm sorry.' *Focus, Chick.* One unidentified body, perhaps more. That was what should be occupying his thoughts, not Sophie Johannsen's perfume. He gestured to the front seat, determined to pull their interaction back to the professional level. 'Please.'

'Thanks.' She climbed in and he heard the clinking of metal coming from her coat.

'What do you have in your pockets?'

'Oh, all kinds of things. This is my field jacket.' From one of the pockets she pulled a handful of garden stakes. 'Markers for what we find.'

I sure as hell hope you brought enough, he thought, remembering the red flags Nick would be removing before they got back. They wanted a clean investigation with no prejudicing the expert before she started her scan. 'Let's go.'

Once they were under way, Sophie held her frozen fingers up to the truck's heater. Without a word, Vito leaned forward and twisted a knob, turning the temperature up.

When her fingers were warm again, she settled into the seat and studied Vito Ciccotelli. His appearance had come as a surprise. With a name like Vito, she'd expected him to be a brawny thug with a face that had gone too many rounds with the champ. She could not have been more mistaken. Which was why she'd stared. She'd been taken off guard. *You go right on thinking that*.

He was at least six-two. She'd had to look up to meet his eyes, and at five-eleven herself, that didn't happen very often. His shoulders were broad in his leather jacket, but there was a lean toughness to him that spoke more of a large cat than a scrappy bulldog. He had the kind of rugged, chiseled face that one saw in fashion magazines. Not that she read fashion magazines herself, of course. That was Aunt Freya's vice.

Sophie imagined most women would consider Vito Ciccotelli swooningly handsome and fall helplessly at his feet. That was probably why he'd been so quick to rebuff her earlier – women probably hit on him all the time. It was a good thing she wasn't most women, she thought dryly. Falling helplessly at his feet was the last thing on her mind.

Although that's very nearly what she'd done. How embarrassing. But for that one moment when he'd held her against him she'd felt comfort and the solidity of welcome. As if she could lay her head back against his shoulder and rest. *Don't be ridiculous, Sophie.* Men that looked like Vito were too accustomed to getting exactly what they wanted with the bat of an eyelash. But somehow that assessment felt unfair. As if it mattered. He'd come for her GPR. Nothing more. *So focus on what you're here for.* A chance to work again. To do something important. Still, her eyes were drawn to his face.

He was wearing sunglasses, but she could just see the corner of his eye where the darkness of his skin was broken by tiny white lines, as if he was quick to smile. He wasn't smiling now. At this moment, his expression was sober and brooding which made her feel a little guilty for feeling so excited and energized.

For the first time in months she'd be doing something that got her back into the field. That was what had her heart pumping and goosebumps pebbling her skin. The thrill of the hunt, of finding secrets hidden below the surface of the earth, not the memory of his hands gripping her shoulders. *He was just keeping you from falling on your ass.* It had been way too long since she'd been touched by a man, for any reason. She frowned and focused. 'So Vito, tell me about this gravesite.'

'Who said anything about graves?' he asked, his tone casual.

She fought the urge to roll her eyes. 'I'm not stupid. An ME and a cop are looking for something under the ground. So how many graves are we talking about?'

He shrugged. 'Maybe none.'

'But you've found at least one.'

'What makes you say that?'

She wrinkled her nose. '*L'odeur de la mort.* It's quite noticeable.'

'You speak French? I took it in high school, but I only learned the swear words.'

Now she did roll her eyes, her temper flaring. 'I'm fluent in ten languages, three of them deader than the body you just came from,' she snapped, then instantly wished her words back as he flinched, a muscle twitching in his clenched jaw.

'The body I just came from was somebody's daughter or wife,' he said quietly.

Her face heated, her annoyance becoming embarrassment and shame. *Shoved your foot in your mouth, army boot and all.* 'I'm sorry,' she said, just as quietly. 'I didn't mean to be disrespectful. The bodies I come across have been dead several hundred years. But it's not an excuse. I got a little . . . jazzed at the prospect of doing something interesting. I let myself get carried away. I apologize. It was insensitive of me.'

He kept his gaze fixed ahead. 'It's all right.'

No, it wasn't, but she didn't know what to say to make it right. She pulled off her gloves and began to braid her hair that still hung loose so it would be out of her way when she got to where the detective was taking her. She was almost done when he spoke, startling her.

'So,' he said. 'You speak French? I took it in high school, but . . .'

His mouth turned up in a rueful smile and she smiled back. He'd thrown her a do-over. This time she would keep her feet out of her mouth. 'But you only learned the swear words. Yes, I speak French and several other languages. It comes in handy translating old texts and conversing with the locals when I'm working.' She went back to braiding her hair. 'I'll teach you a few swear words in other languages if you want.'

His lips twitched. 'It's a deal. Katherine said you were on sabbatical.'

'Of sorts.' She secured the braid into a tight ball at her nape. 'My grandmother had a stroke, so I came back to Philly to help my aunt take care of her.'

'Is she recovering?'

'Some days we think so. Other days . . .' She sighed. 'Other days it's not so good.'

'I'm sorry.' He sounded very sincere.

'Thank you.'

'And where did you come back from?'

40

'Southern France. We were excavating a thirteenth-century castle.'

He looked impressed. 'Like, with a dungeon?'

She chuckled. 'At one time, most likely. Now we'll be lucky to find the outer walls and the foundation of the keep. *They'll* be lucky,' she corrected. 'Listen, Vito . . . I'm sorry I was out of line, but it really would help me to know a little more about what you need me to do before I begin.'

He shrugged. 'There's really not much to tell. We found one body.'

Back to square one. 'But you think there are more.'

'Maybe.'

Keeping her feet well away from her mouth, she injected a note of lightness into her voice. 'If I uncover something, I'll know your secrets. I hope this isn't one of those "now I'll have to kill you" things. That would ruin my day.'

The corners of his mouth quirked. 'Killing you would be illegal, Dr Johannsen.'

They were back to formalities. Too bad. She was still calling him Vito. 'Well then, Vito, unless you plan to erase my memory, you'll have to trust that I won't blab. You don't have one of those memory-zapping guns like they used in *Men in Black*, do you?'

His lips twitched again. 'I left it in my other suit.'

'Forewarned is forearmed, they say. Which suit is it? I promise I won't tell.'

Abruptly he grinned, exposing a deep dimple in his right cheek. *Oh, my*, she thought. *Oh my, oh my*. A smile turned Vito Ciccotelli from merely magazine-handsome to movie-star-gorgeous. Aunt Freya's heart would be going pitter-pat. *Just like yours is right now*. Then he spoke.

'That information is classified,' he said and Sophie stiffened.

'So much for establishing rapport.'

His grin faded. 'Dr Johannsen, it's not that I don't trust you. You wouldn't be here if I didn't. Katherine vouches for you and that was enough for me.'

'Then—'

He shook his head. 'I don't want to give you any information that could bias your findings. Go in with a clean slate and tell us what you see. That's all we want.'

She considered. 'I suppose that makes sense.'

'Thank God,' he muttered and she chuckled.

'Can you at least tell me how big this area is?'

'One, two acres tops.'

She winced. 'Oh. That'll take a while.'

His black brows went up. 'How long is a while?'

'Four, five hours. Maybe more. Whitman's ground-penetrating radar is a small unit. We use it for teaching purposes. The biggest plot we ever scan with students is maybe ten meters square. Sorry,' she added when he scowled. 'If you need an area that big scanned I can recommend some geophysical survey companies that are really good. They'll have bigger units they can drag with a tractor.'

'With big price tags,' he said. 'We can't afford to hire a contractor. Our department budgets have been cut so much . . . We simply don't have the funds.' He threw her a cautious glance. 'Can you give us four or five hours?'

She checked her watch. Her stomach had already started to rumble. 'Can your department budget spring for pizza? I didn't have lunch.'

'That we can do.'

Chapter Three

Philadelphia, Sunday, January 14, 2:30 P.M.

Vito stopped the truck behind the CSU van. 'This is the place.'

'I kind of figured that out for myself,' she murmured. 'The yellow police tape and CSU van were my first clues.' Before he could say another word she opened her door and hopped out, flinched, then swallowed hard.

'It's strong,' he said sympathetically. '*Eau de* . . . what did you call it?'

'*L'odeur de la mort,*' she said quietly. 'Is the body still here?'

'No. But removing the body doesn't always remove all the odor right away. I can get you a mask, but I don't think it really helps.'

She shook her head and the big hoops at her ears swayed. 'I was just surprised. I'll be fine.' Her jaw set determinedly, she grabbed the two smaller cases. 'I'm ready.'

She said it with a hard little nod, more as if to convince herself than anyone else.

Nick climbed from the CSU van and Vito had the satisfaction of seeing his partner's face go blank. Jen McFain's reaction was much the same. Of course they weren't getting the full effect as Johannsen had braided the hair that hung an inch past her butt.

'Jen, Nick, this is Dr Johannsen.'

Jen hurried forward with a smile, craning her neck to see Johannsen's face. The difference in the women's heights was almost comical. 'I'm Jennifer McFain, CSU. Thank you so much for coming out to help us on such short notice, Dr Johannsen.'

'You're welcome. And please call me Sophie,' she said.

'Then I'm Jen.' Jen eyed the small suitcases. 'I've always wanted to play with one of these. If you don't mind, could you take off the earrings?'

Johannsen immediately dropped her earrings into one of the pockets of her jacket. 'Sorry. I forgot I had them on.' She glanced over Jen's shoulder at Nick. 'You are?'

'Nick Lawrence,' Nick said. 'Vito's partner. Thanks for coming.'

'My pleasure. If you'd take me to where you'd like me to begin, I'll get set up.'

They walked across the field, Jen and Johannsen in front, Vito and Nick trailing far enough behind that they wouldn't be overheard.

'She's not . . . what I expected,' Nick murmured.

Vito huffed a chuckle. He was keeping himself calm, cool, and collected. And would continue to do so. 'That's an understatement.'

'You're sure she's Katherine's friend? She seems very young.'

'I did finally get in touch with Katherine. Johannsen's the real deal all right.'

'And you're sure she can keep this to herself?'

Vito thought of the memory-zapping gun and had to smile. 'Yeah.' Then they came to the grave and he sobered. Now they would know if Jane Doe was a single or one of many.

Johannsen was staring at the grave. Her mouth drooped and he remembered how she'd dropped her eyes, ashamed of the calloused way she'd referred to the body. She hadn't meant it, he knew. That she was so quick to apologize he could respect. She looked over her shoulder and met his eyes. 'You found the woman here?'

'Yes.'

'The field is big. Do you have a preference on where you'd like me to start?'

'Dr Johannsen thinks it will take four or five hours to scan the whole field,' Vito said. 'Let's survey the area to the right and left of the grave and see what we have.'

'That sounds like a plan,' Jen said. 'How long will it take you to get ready?'

'Not long.' Sophie dropped to her knees in the snow and began opening the cases they'd brought, demonstrating the assembly for Jen who looked like a kid at Christmas. 'The unit sends data to the laptop wirelessly and the laptop will store it.' She set the laptop on one of the cases, powered it up, then stood, the scanning portion in her hand.

Nick leaned forward, studying it. 'It looks like a carpet sweeper,' he said.

'A fifteen-thousand-dollar carpet sweeper,' Johannsen said and Vito whistled.

'Fifteen grand for that? You said it was a little one.'

'It is. The big ones start at fifty. Are you all familiar with ground-penetrating radar?'

'Jen is,' Vito said. 'We were going to call for the cadaver dogs.'

'That works, but GPR gives you an image of what's under the ground. It's not a clear image like an x-ray. GPR tells you where and how deep an object is. The colors on the display represent the amplitude of the object. Brighter colors, bigger amplitude.'

Jen nodded. 'Brighter the color, bigger the amplitude, bigger the object.'

'Or the stronger the reflection. Metals will have high amplitude. Air pockets reflect even better. The amount of reflection depends on what you're looking for.'

'What about bone?' Nick asked.

'Not as bright, but visible. Older the bone, the harder it is to see. As bodies decompose, they become like the soil and the reflections don't stand out as much.'

'How old before you can't see the bones anymore?' Jen asked.

'One of my colleagues identified the remains of a twenty-five-hundred-year-old Native American in a burial mound in Kentucky.' She glanced up. 'I don't think you need to worry about age.' She stood up and wiped her palms on her jacket. Her jeans were soaking wet, but she didn't even seem to notice. She'd said she was 'jazzed' and Vito could definitely see the energy in her clear green eyes. 'Let's go.'

She got to work, scanning along the height dimension of the first grave, slowly and precisely. Vito could see why scanning the whole field would take so long. But if they found something, they were in for a lot more man-hours than that.

Jen went still. 'Sophie,' she said, her voice urgent.

Johannsen stopped for a screen check. 'It's the edge of something. The soil changes here, abruptly. It goes maybe three feet deep. Let me get a few more rows.'

She did, then frowned. 'There is something here, but it looks like it's got metal in it. We tend to see that in cemeteries with older, lead-lined caskets. The shape isn't right for a casket, but there is definitely metal here.' She looked up, her eyes questioning. 'Does that make sense?'

Vito thought about Jane Doe's hands. 'Yeah,' he said grimly. 'It does.'

Johannsen nodded, accepting there would be no more answer than that. 'Okay.' She marked the corners with her garden stakes. 'It's six and a half feet by three feet.'

'The same size as the first one,' Jen said.

'I didn't want to be right, Vito.' Nick shook his head. 'Fuck.'

Jen stood up. 'I'll get my tools and the camera, then I'll get the team back and we'll set up floodlights. Give me a hand with the tools, Nick. Vito, you call Katherine.'

'Will do. And I'll call Liz.' Lieutenant Liz Sawyer had not been pleased to hear of the first body. Multiple unmarked graves would not be the news she wanted to hear.

Nick followed Jen, leaving Vito alone with Johannsen. 'I'm sorry,' she said simply, sadness filling her eyes.

He nodded. 'Yeah. Me, too. Let's check the other side.'

As Johannsen continued on, Vito dialed Liz on his cell. 'Liz, it's Vito. We have the archeologist here. There's another one.'

'Not good,' Liz said tightly. 'One or more?'

46

'One at least. She's just getting started and it's going to take a while. Jen's calling for her team and we're going to get as much done as we can tonight.'

'Keep me apprised,' she ordered. 'I'll call the captain and give him the heads-up.'

'Will do.' Vito slid his phone back into his pocket.

Jen and Nick returned with the digging tools and the camera as Johannsen found the edge of the next grave. 'Same length, same depth.' Twenty minutes ticked by before she looked up. 'And another body. But this one doesn't have any metal.'

'We didn't find metal there with the detector,' Nick said.

Vito looked out over the field. 'I know. That means there could be even more.'

Jen was laying plastic sheeting around the first new grave. 'Take a spade, boys.'

They did, and for a while the four of them worked in silence, Johannsen marking the second plot and moving to the left to begin again, Nick, Vito, and Jen digging. Nick reached the body first. Jen leaned forward and with her small brush, removed the loose dirt from the victim's face.

It was a man, young and blond. Decomposition was not yet advanced. He'd been handsome. 'He hasn't been dead long,' Nick said. 'A week maybe.'

'If that,' Vito said. 'Uncover his hands, Jen.' She did, and Vito twisted closer to get a better look at what he didn't understand. 'What the hell?'

'He's not praying.' Nick frowned. 'What *is* he doing?'

'Whatever he's doing,' Jen said, 'his hands are wired just like Jane Doe's.'

The victim's hands were formed into fists, both settled against his naked torso, the right above the left. The right fist was positioned level with the heart and his elbows pointed down. Both fists formed O's. 'He was holding something,' Vito said.

'A sword.' The whispered words came from above them, where Sophie Johannsen stood, her face ghostly pale under the red bandana. Her eyes were wide, horrified, and fixed on the victim. Vito had the sudden urge to pull her face against his chest, shielding her from the decomposing body.

Instead he stood and put his hands on her shoulders. 'What did you say?'

She didn't move, her eyes still fixed on the dead man.

He gave her a gentle little shake and pinched her chin, forcibly turning her face to his. 'Dr Johannsen, what did you say?'

She swallowed, then lifted her eyes, no longer bright. 'He looks like an effigy.'

'An effigy,' Vito repeated. 'As in "hung in effigy"?'

She closed her eyes, visibly steeling herself and Vito remembered that her bodies had been dead for hundreds of years. 'No,' she said, her voice shaken. 'As in a tomb or crypt. Many times tombs would have images of the dead carved in stone or marble. These statues would lie on their backs on top of the crypt. It's called an effigy.'

She'd calmed herself, sounding like a teacher giving a lecture now. Vito supposed it was her way of coping. 'The women usually had their hands folded like this.' She folded her hands beneath her chin, the pose identical to Jane Doe's.

Vito glanced sharply at Nick, who nodded.

'Go on, Sophie,' Nick said quietly. 'You're doing fine.'

'But . . . but sometimes their arms were folded across their breasts.' Again she demonstrated, laying her hands flat. 'Sometimes the man's hands are folded in prayer, but sometimes he's in full armor, holding a sword. Usually he holds the sword at his side, but sometimes the effigy was carved like this.' She balled her trembling hands into fists and laid them on her chest in exactly the way the victim's were posed. 'He'd hold the hilt of the sword in his hands and the blade would lie flat against his torso, straight down his center. It's not as common a pose. It means he died in battle. Do you know who he is?'

He shook his head. 'Not yet.'

'Someone's son or husband,' she murmured.

'Why don't you go sit in my truck? Here are the keys.'

She looked up at him, her eyes bright with unshed tears. 'No, I'm all right. I just came to tell you I didn't find anything to the left of the other plot. I'm going back toward the trees.' She wiped her eyes with her multicolored gloved fingers. 'I'll be fine.'

Nick stood up. 'Sophie, now that you've told us this, I remember seeing pictures in an old history book. This is a medieval custom, isn't it? Placing an effigy on the grave?'

She nodded but she was still very pale. 'Yes. Earliest known carvings date as far back as 1100 and were common practice through the Renaissance.'

'Guys.' Jen was kneeling on the edge of the grave. 'We've got bigger problems than this guy's sword.' She came to her feet, dusting soil from her coveralls.

Vito and Nick looked down into the grave, but Johannsen stayed back. Vito couldn't say he blamed her. What he saw made him want to turn his face away, but he didn't. Jen had uncovered the victim down to his groin and there was a huge hole in his abdomen. 'Sonofabitch,' he muttered.

'What?' Johannsen asked from five feet away.

Jen sighed. 'This man had his intestines removed.'

'Disemboweled,' Johannsen said. 'A torture used throughout history, but definitely used in medieval times.'

'Torture,' Nick murmured. 'Holy shit, Vito. What kind of sicko would do this?'

Vito's gaze swept the field. 'And how many more did he put here?'

New York City, Sunday, January 14, 5:00 P.M.

The pop of a champagne cork brought the noise level to a low roar. From the back of the room, Derek Harrington watched Jager Van Zandt hold the fizzing bottle away from his expensive suit amid the cheers of a host of young, eager faces.

'We used to be happy with a six-pack as long as it was cold.'

Derek glanced up at Tony England, his smile rueful. 'Ah, the good old days.'

But Tony wasn't smiling. 'I miss those days, Derek. I miss your old basement and working all night and . . . T-shirts and jeans. When it was just you and me and Jager.'

'I know. Now we're growing so fast . . . I don't know half these kids.' More than that, he missed his friend. Fame and pursuit of the dollar had changed Jager Van Zandt into a man Derek wasn't sure he knew anymore. 'I suppose success does have a price.'

Tony was quiet for a moment. 'Derek, is it true we're going IPO?'

'I've heard the rumors.'

Tony frowned. 'Rumors? You're the damn vice president, Derek. Shouldn't you have a little better information than *rumors*?'

Derek should, but he didn't. He was saved a reply by Jager, who'd climbed on a chair and held his champagne flute high. 'Gentlemen. And ladies. We're here to celebrate. I know you all are tired at the end of a long convention, but it's over and we did well. Every bit of our production of *Behind Enemy Lines* is committed. We have orders for every video game we can crank out the door. We're sold out, yet again!'

The young people cheered, but Derek stayed silent.

'He sold out, all right,' Tony muttered.

'Tony,' Derek murmured. 'Not here. Not the place or time.'

'When will be the place and time, Derek?' Tony demanded. 'When we're both Jager's yes-men? Or am I the only one who has to worry about *becoming* a yes-man?' Shaking his head, Tony made his way through the crowded room and out the door.

Tony had always been dramatic, Derek knew. Passion often came hand in hand with artistic genius. Derek wasn't sure he had passion anymore. Or genius. Or art.

'Of course you'll all see a nice hefty reward for all those sales in your bonus checks,' Jager was saying and there were more cheers. 'But for now, a sweet reward.' Two waiters rolled in a long rectangular table. On it sat a cake that was easily six feet wide and three feet long and had been decorated with the oRo logo – a golden dragon with a giant R on its chest. The dragon gripped two O's, one in each claw.

He and Jager had chosen the logo with care. Derek had created the golden dragon, and Jager chose the company name. The letters o-R-o were symbolic, tied to Jager's native Dutch. It had never bothered Derek the R was five times bigger than either of the O's. But it bothered him now. Many things bothered Derek now. But, pasting a smile on his face for the benefit of the employees, he accepted a flute of champagne.

'We're entering a new phase of oRo growth,' Jager said, 'and to that end, we have some changes to announce. Derek Harrington is being promoted.'

Stunned, Derek straightened, staring at the smiling Jager. Quickly he re-pasted the smile, unwilling to be seen as out of the loop.

'Derek will now be executive art director.' There were more cheers and Derek nodded, his smile frozen. He now understood what Jager had done, and his expectation was confirmed with Jager's next words. 'And to recognize his incredible contribution to *Behind Enemy Lines*, Frasier Lewis is promoted to art director.'

The employees applauded as Derek's heart sank to his toes.

'Frasier couldn't be here tonight, but he sends his personal regards and good wishes for the next venture. He asked me to make this toast for him, and I quote: "*Enemy Lines* got us into orbit. May *The Inquisitor* launch oRo to the moon!"' Jager lifted his glass. 'To oRo and to success!'

His hand shaking, Derek slipped from the room. There was so much cheering that nobody even noticed he'd gone. In the hall he leaned one shoulder against the wall, his stomach churning. The promotion was a lie. Derek hadn't been promoted up. He'd been pushed aside. Frasier Lewis had brought riches and success to oRo, but his dark methods left Derek afraid. He'd tried to stop Jager, to keep oRo on the high road.

But now it was too late. He'd just been replaced by Jager's yes-man.

Philadephia, Sunday, January 14, 5:00 P.M.

It was worse than she ever could have imagined. What had been excitement for a hunt when she'd first arrived had abruptly become cold dread when she'd looked on the face of the dead man. Her dread became colder as the afternoon waned. She continued to scan and tried to stop thinking about the markers she'd laid. Or the man they'd found. Someone had tortured and killed him. And others. How many others would there be?

Katherine had returned to examine the victim and she and Sophie had exchanged sober nods, but no words. There was an unnatural hush to the site, the small army of cops moving efficiently but quietly as they did their jobs.

Sophie tried to focus on recording the objects under the ground. But they weren't objects. They were people, and they were dead. She tried not to think about that, taking refuge in the routine of the scan, of the precise placement of each stake.

Until she reached into her pocket and found it empty. She'd grabbed two packs from the equipment room before meeting Vito. *A dozen to a pack.* Twenty-four stakes. *Six graves.* She'd located six graves already. The grave the police had located before she got there made seven. *And I'm not finished yet. My God. Seven people.*

Her vision blurred and angrily she rubbed at the tears with the back of her hand. CSU would have something that she could use to mark more graves. She raised her eyes to look for Jen McFain, but a sound behind her made her body freeze. It was a zipper, amplified in the surreal hush. Slowly she met Katherine Bauer's eyes over the body bag she'd just zipped shut, and was hurled back sixteen years. Katherine's hair had been darker then, a little longer.

The body bag she'd zipped had been much smaller.

The hush faded. All Sophie could hear was the drum of her own pulse. Katherine's eyes widened with horrified understanding. She'd looked just like that back then, too.

Sophie heard her name, but all she could see was the body on the gurney, as it had been that day. *So very small.* That day she'd been too late and could only stand in shock as they'd rolled her away. A wave of grief surged, powerful and sudden. Anger followed in its wake, bitter and cold. Elle was gone, and nothing could bring her back.

'Sophie.'

Sophie blinked at the sudden pinch on her chin. She focused on Katherine's face, on the lines sixteen years had wrought and let out a shuddering breath. Remembering where she was, she closed her eyes, embarrassed. 'I'm sorry,' she murmured.

The pressure on her chin intensified until she opened her eyes. Katherine was frowning up at her. 'Go to my car, Sophie. You're white as a sheet.'

Sophie pulled away. 'I'm all right.' She glanced up to find Vito Ciccotelli standing next to the very large body bag, his dark eyes narrowed as he watched her. He'd thought her rude and insensitive before. Now he probably thought she was unstable, or even worse, weak. She lifted her chin and straightened her shoulders, meeting his watchful stare with a flash of defiance. She'd rather be considered rude.

But he didn't look away, just kept those dark eyes fastened to hers. Unsettled, Sophie shifted her gaze away from Vito and took a step back. 'I'm all right. Really.'

'No,' Katherine murmured. 'You're not all right. You've done enough for today. I'll have one of the officers drive you home.'

Sophie's jaw tightened. 'I finish what I start.' She bent to retrieve the GPR's handle which had fallen from her hands as she'd taken her little skip down memory lane. 'Unlike some people.' She started to turn, but Katherine grabbed her arm.

'It was an accident,' Katherine whispered, and Sophie knew the woman honestly believed that to be the truth. 'I thought after all this time you'd have accepted that.'

Sophie shook her head. Her anger lingered, bubbling inside her and when she spoke, her voice was cold. 'You were always too soft on her. I'm afraid I'm not that—'

'Forgiving?' Katherine interrupted sharply.

Sophie huffed a laugh, utterly mirthless. 'Blind. I'll finish the job you asked me to do.' She pulled away from Katherine's grasp and shoved her hand in her empty pocket, then remembered. Stakes. She searched for Jen only to find the small army had gone largely still, watching with blatant curiosity as the scene between her and Katherine unfolded.

She wanted to scream for them to mind their own damn business, but controlled the impulse. She looked for Jen, but it was Vito Ciccotelli's dark eyes she met once again. He'd never looked away. 'I've run out of stakes. Do you have any markers?'

'I'll find something.' He gave her another long look of speculation before turning for the CSU van. When he was no longer watching her, she felt the air leave her lungs in a long sigh and realized she'd been holding her breath for a long time. As the sigh left her body, so did her temper. Now all she felt was weary regret and shame.

'I'm sorry, Katherine. I shouldn't have lost my temper.' She stopped just short of saying she'd been wrong. She'd never lied to Katherine and wasn't about to start now.

The corners of Katherine's mouth lifted in wry acceptance of what Sophie had left unsaid. 'I know. Seeing the victim would have been bad enough, but you had a shock on top of that. I never meant for you to see any bodies. I thought you'd do the scan, then go home. I guess I didn't think that through very well.'

'It's okay. I'm glad you asked me to help.' Sophie squeezed

Katherine's arm and knew the air was clear between them again. *It's a good thing Katherine's more forgiving than me*, she thought ruefully. Then again, it was easier to forgive when one felt the loss less keenly. Elle had not been Katherine's child. *She was mine.* Sophie cleared her throat, and when she spoke, her voice was brusque. 'Now let me get to work so all the cops will stop looking at us.'

Katherine looked over her shoulder, as if realizing for the first time they had an audience. With a single lifted brow, the little woman sent everyone back to their business. 'Cops are the nosiest,' she whispered. 'Worse gossips than girls.'

'Now, that's just mean.'

Sophie's eyes flew up to see Vito standing behind them, clutching a handful of colored flags as if they were flowers.

Katherine smiled up at him. 'No, that's just true, and you know it.'

One corner of his mouth lifted. 'Replace "nosy" with "observant" and we're square.' His words were directed to Katherine, but he looked at Sophie, his eyes just as intent as before. He held out the flags. 'Your markers,' he said. She hesitated before scooping them from his hand, the thought of touching him making her nervous. Ridiculous. She was a professional and she would do the job she'd been brought here to do.

She took the flags and shoved them in her pocket. 'I hope I don't need this many.'

Vito's slight smile disappeared as his gaze swept the field. 'That makes two of us.'

Katherine sighed. 'Amen.'

Dutton, Georgia, Sunday, January 14, 9:40 P.M.

Daniel Vartanian sat on his hotel bed, rubbing his brow behind which the beginnings of a migraine lurked. 'That's the situation,' he finished and waited for his boss to speak.

Chase Wharton sighed. 'You have one fucked-up family. You know that, don't you?'

'Believe me, I know. Well, can I have the leave?'

'Are you sure they're really traveling? Why all the lies?'

'My parents keep up appearances, no matter what.' His parents had covered up many family secrets to preserve the family's 'good name.' *If people only knew.* 'That they didn't want anyone to know about my mother's illness is par for the course.'

'But it's cancer, Daniel, not some awful secret like pedophilia or something.'

Or something, Daniel thought. 'Cancer would be enough to start tongues wagging. My father wouldn't tolerate that, especially since he'd just agreed to run for Congress.'

'You never said your father was a politician.'

'My father was a politician from the day he was born,' Daniel said bitterly. 'He just did it from the bench. But I didn't know he was running. Apparently he'd just agreed to run before he went away.' This he'd heard from Tawny Howard who'd taken his and Frank's dinner order. Tawny had heard it from the secretary of Carl Sargent, the man his father had visited the last time he'd been in town. 'I'm sure he views my mother's cancer as fodder for the opposition. My mother will go along with whatever he says.'

Chase was silent and Daniel could imagine his worried expression.

'Chase, I just want to find my folks. My mother's sick. I . . .' Daniel blew out a breath. 'I need to see her. I have something to tell her and I don't want her to die before I can. We had an argument and I said some harsh things.' He'd actually said them to his father, but the feelings of anger and disgust . . . and shame . . . they'd extended to include his mother as well.

'Were you wrong?' Chase asked quietly.

'No. But . . . I shouldn't have let so many years pass with this between us.'

'Take your leave then. But the minute you suspect anything

other than an ordinary vacation, you back off and we'll set up a proper investigation. I don't want my ass fried because a retired judge is missing and I didn't follow procedure.' Chase hesitated. 'Be careful, Daniel. And I'm sorry about your mom.'

'Thanks.' Daniel wasn't sure where to begin, but was certain clues resided in his father's computer. Tomorrow a pal from the GBI was coming to help him sort through his father's computer records. Daniel only hoped he could deal with what he found.

New York City, Sunday, January 14, 10:00 P.M.

From his chair in the darkness of their hotel suite's sitting room, Derek watched Jager stumble through the door. 'You're drunk,' Derek said with disgust.

Jager jerked upright. 'Goddamn it, Derek. You scared the shit out of me.'

'Then we're even,' Derek said bitterly. 'Just what the hell was that all about?'

'What?' The word was uttered with contempt and Derek felt his temper boil higher.

'You know *what*. Who the hell gave you the right to make Lewis the art director?'

'It's just a title, Derek.' Jager shot him a scathing look as he yanked his tie from his collar. 'If you'd been in the bar celebrating with us instead of up here in the dark, sulking like a little boy, you would have heard the news firsthand. We got a booth at Pinnacle.'

'*Pinnacle?*' Pinnacle, *the* game convention of the year. On the *planet*. This was *huge*. Pinnacle was to game designers what Cannes was to filmmakers. *The* premier event to see and be seen. To have your art admired by the entire industry. Gamers would stand in line for days for a ticket. Booths were awarded by *invitation only*. Pinnacle was . . . the pinnacle. He let out a slow breath, hardly daring to believe it was true. Only in his wildest dreams . . . 'You're kidding.'

Jager laughed, but it was an ugly sound. 'I would never kid about something like that.' He walked to the sideboard and poured himself another drink.

'Jager, you've had enough,' Derek started, but Jager flashed him a furious glare.

'Shut up. Just shut up. I'm so fucking tired of you and your "don't do this" and "don't do that." ' He tossed back a swallow. '*We're* going to Pinnacle because *I* took a risk. Because *I* had the balls to push the envelope. Because *I* have what it takes to succeed.'

Derek cocked his jaw, coldly furious at what had been left unsaid. 'And I don't.'

Jager spread his arms wide. 'You said it.' He looked away. 'Partner,' he muttered.

'I am, you know,' Derek said quietly.

'What?'

'Your partner.'

'Then start acting like one,' Jager said flatly. 'And stop acting like some religious fanatic. Frasier Lewis's art is entertainment, Derek. Period.'

Derek shook his head as Jager headed toward his room. 'It's indecent. Period.'

Jager stopped, his hand on the doorknob. 'It's what sells.'

'It's not right, Jager.'

'I don't see you refusing any paychecks. You act morally repulsed by the violence, but you're in it for the money as much as I am. And if you're not, you need to get out.'

'Is that a threat?' Derek asked quietly.

'No. It's reality. Just contact Frasier and tell him to speed up the fight scenes he's been promising me for a month. I want them by nine Tuesday morning. I need the fight scenes from *Inquisitor* to show at Pinnacle so he needs to light a fire under his ass.'

Stunned, Derek could only stare. 'You already gave him the new game.'

Jager turned, his eyes cold. 'It's an *entertainment venture*,' he said between his teeth, 'and yes, I gave Frasier the design for *Inquisitor* months ago. If I left it to you, we'd end up with the same sorry washed-out graphics we've had for years. He's been researching and working the design for months while you've been sitting on your ass, doodling *cartoons*.' The last was uttered with contempt. 'Face it, Derek, I've moved oRo to the next level. Keep up or get out.' He shut the door with a snap.

Derek stood motionless for a long time, staring at the door. *Keep up or get out. Get out.* He couldn't just *get out.* Where would he go? He'd put all his talent, all his heart into oRo. He couldn't just walk away. He needed his salary. His daughter's college tuition wasn't cheap. *I am a hypocrite.* He'd disagreed so vehemently with using Frasier Lewis's scenes because the killings were so chillingly real. But Jager was right. *I take the money. I like the money.*

He needed to make a choice. If he planned to continue at oRo, he needed to come to terms with his distaste for Frasier Lewis's 'art.' *Either I'm morally opposed or I'm not.*

He sighed. Or he needed to decide if Jager had been telling him the truth, hard as it would be to accept. *The same sorry washed-out look.* That hurt. *Am I jealous? Is Lewis the better artist?* If so, could he accept that, and, more important, could he work with him?

Derek got up and paced the length of the room, stopping at the bar. He poured himself a drink, then sat back down in the dark to consider his options.

Chapter Four

Vito watched as Katherine wheeled away another body in a bag, the third they'd recovered so far. He'd been male, about the same age as the 'Knight' as the first man had been dubbed. The name was inevitable once word had spread among the team that the archeologist said the victim's hands had been posed to hold a sword. The woman they'd uncovered that morning had become the 'Lady.'

He wondered what they would call this last victim. The third victim had lain with his arms at his sides. Well, kind of. One arm lay straight, but the other was mangled at the shoulder, barely attached at the joint and rotated so that the palm faced outward. The man's head was in worse shape. What little that remained was unrecognizable.

'It's late,' Vito said. 'We've got uniforms on guard duty. I say we call it a night.'

'So, we meet back here tomorrow at first light?' Nick asked.

Vito nodded. 'Then we begin to ID the victims. Katherine should have the initial exams done by morning. The autopsies could take days.'

Jen looked around. 'Where is Sophie?'

Vito pointed to his truck where Johannsen sat sideways on the passenger side, her door wide open. She'd been there for about a half hour. He'd worried she'd freeze, then tried to put her out of his mind, figuring she'd have shut the door if she got too cold. But he'd been unsuccessful in pushing her out of his thoughts or his sight. He'd watched her as they'd worked. Seeing the Knight had rocked her. Still she'd worked steadily.

But something else had happened. When Katherine had zipped the body bag shut, Sophie looked like she'd seen a ghost. Whatever memory the body had triggered, it had been substantial enough to send Katherine to her side. And the two had exchanged angry words, that much had been crystal clear.

From then on, he'd watched her even more closely. It was simple curiosity, he told himself. Or perhaps nosiness was more accurate, as Katherine claimed. He wanted to know what had happened, both today and on whatever day she'd been remembering.

But he probably would never find out. He'd take her back and that would be that. Still, the sight of her sitting in his truck tugged at him. She sat with her knees up under her coat, much as she had earlier in the day. She looked young and very much alone.

'Are we finished with her?' Vito asked.

Jen nodded, looking at the printout of Sophie's scan. 'She did an incredible job.' Stakes and flags were arranged in four rows of four plots, every plot the same exact size, rows and columns spaced with military precision. 'We just have to start digging.'

When Vito got close to the truck he noticed she'd loaded and secured the two big cases into the truck bed, all by herself. They'd been heavy when he'd done it earlier. *She must have some muscle under her field jacket*. He thought about how she'd felt those few seconds she'd leaned against him and wondered what else he'd find under her jacket, but again, he'd probably never find out.

When Vito got close to Sophie, his heart squeezed. Tears slid down her cheeks in a steady flow as she stared at the field with its stakes and flags. She'd seen things that rocked most seasoned cops. But she'd stayed the course. He respected that.

He cleared his throat and she turned her head to look at him. She wiped at her cheeks with her sleeve but made no attempt to hide the tears or apologize for them. Vito respected that, too. 'Are you all right?' he asked quietly.

She nodded and drew a shuddering breath. 'Yes.'

'You did good today.'

She sniffled. 'Jen showed you the scan?'

'Yes. Thank you. It's very thorough and very well done. But that's not what I meant. You held up under terribly stressful conditions. Most people wouldn't have.'

Her lips trembled and her eyes filled anew. She swallowed hard as she turned her back to stare at the field, visibly fighting for composure. Patiently he waited and when she spoke, it was in a hoarse whisper. 'When Katherine called me today, I had no idea it would be like this. Nine people. My God. It's unreal.'

'You marked seven of the plots as empty. Are you sure?'

She nodded, her tears slowing. 'The seven empty ones are air pockets. But every one of them is covered with something thick and solid. Probably wood.' She looked at him, her eyes filled with horror and pain. 'My God, Vito. He planned to kill seven more.'

'I know.' The scan had given them not only the lay of the land, but insight into the mind of a killer. Vito knew the insight would be valuable when he'd had enough sleep to consider it. 'I'm beat,' he said. 'You must be, too. Let me take you home.'

She shook her head. 'I have to take the equipment back to the university and get my bike. Besides, you must have plans of your own tonight. A family to get home to.'

He thought of the roses, wilted now. He'd buy another bouquet and go to the cemetery next week. It wasn't like Andrea would care one way or another. The flowers and the visit, he knew, were really for himself. 'I don't have plans.' He hesitated, then let the words come. 'Or anyone waiting for me.'

Their eyes held and he could see she'd taken his words the

way he'd meant them. He watched her throat work as she tried to swallow. 'Well, then I'm ready to go when you are.' She was buckling herself in when he slid behind the wheel, then dug into a pocket and pulled out what, in the shadow of the cab, looked like a cigar. 'Want one?'

He started the engine with a frown. 'I don't smoke.'

'I don't either,' she said glumly. 'Anymore, anyway. But you'd have trouble lighting this. It's beef jerky. Good field food. Doesn't spoil. And surprisingly, overrides the taste that's been in my mouth all day.' She shrugged. 'Temporarily, anyway.'

He took one of the sticks. 'Thanks.'

As he munched, she dug into her pocket again, this time pulling out a drink box, like his nephews packed in their lunchboxes. He glanced over and made a face when the letters on the label registered. 'Chocolate milk? With beef jerky?'

She stabbed the box with a little straw. 'Calcium's good for the bones. Want one?'

'No,' he said firmly. 'That's gross, Dr Johannsen.'

'Don't knock it till you try it.' She paused deliberately. 'Vito.' She stared out the window as she sipped. When she was done, she put the box in a baggie, sealed it, and put it back in her pocket.

'So your field jacket serves as a trash receptacle, too?'

She glanced at him, embarrassed. 'Habit. Can't be leaving litter around the dig.'

'So what other foodstuffs do you keep in your pockets?'

'A couple of Ho Hos, but they're a little squashed. They still taste good, though.'

'You like chocolate, I take it.'

'Duh.' She looked wary. 'Don't tell me you don't. I was just starting to like you.'

He laughed and the sound surprised him. He hadn't thought he had enough energy left to laugh. 'I can take it or leave it. But my brother Tino, he's an addict. Milk, dark, white, chocolate chips to Easter bunnies, Tino inhales it.'

She was smiling at him and once again he found himself mesmerized. Even with eyes red from crying, she drew him. 'You have a brother named Tino? Really?'

He forced himself to focus on driving. 'I have three brothers, but you have to promise not to laugh.'

Her eyes were laughing even as she firmed her mouth sternly. 'I promise.'

'My older brother is Dino and my two younger brothers are Tino and Gino. Our sister is Contessa Maria Teresa, but we just call her Tess. She lives in Chicago.'

Her lips twitched. 'I'm not laughing. I'm not even going to make any Mafia jokes.'

'Thank you,' he said dryly. 'What about you? Any family in the area?'

She went still and he knew he'd touched a nerve. 'Just my grandmother and my uncle Harry. And my aunt Freya, of course.' She'd added her aunt almost in afterthought. 'And a few assorted cousins, but we've never been close.' She smiled again, but it was wistful. 'Sounds like your family is. Close, that is. That's nice.'

She sounded lost and once again his heart squeezed. 'It is nice, although at times it's very noisy. My family's in and out of my house like Grand Central Station. Tino actually rents the apartment in my basement, so he's a permanent fixture. There are some times I pray for silence.'

'I think if you truly had silence, you'd wish for noise,' she murmured.

He stole another look at her. Even in the darkness of the cab he could see the weary loneliness on her face, but before he could say a word she straightened her spine and dug into her pockets for more beef jerky.

'How long before I don't taste . . . *that* anymore?' she asked.

'Hopefully in a few hours. Maybe by tomorrow.'

'You want another one?'

He grimaced. 'No thanks. You wouldn't happen to have a

burger or fries in one of those pockets, would you?' he added lightly and was relieved when she smiled at him.

'Nope. But I do have a cell phone, a camera, a compass, a box of paintbrushes, a ruler, two emergency flares, a flashlight, and . . . a box of matches. I can survive anywhere.'

He found himself chuckling. 'It's a wonder you could walk. Your coat must weigh fifty pounds.'

'Close. I've had this coat for a lot of years. I hope I can get it clean.' Her smile faded and the haunted look returned. '*L'odeur de la mort,*' she said quietly. He wanted to say something to comfort her, but no words came, so he said nothing at all.

Sunday, January 14, 11:15 P.M.

Vito stopped his truck in front of the funky ape sculpture. 'Dr Johannsen.' He gently shook her shoulder. 'Sophie.'

She woke with a jerk and in her eyes he saw an instant of disoriented fear before she realized where she was. 'I fell asleep. I'm sorry.'

'Don't. I wish I could have.'

Shaking herself to full attention, she was out of his truck before he could come around to help her. But her shoulders sagged. He took the two small cases from behind her seat. 'You go on up and open the door. I'll carry these.'

'Normally I carry my own gear, but tonight I'll say thank you.' He followed her up to the door, remembering earlier this afternoon, the long look they'd shared. Her hands faltered as she unlocked the front door and he hoped she was remembering it, too. But she opened the door without mishap this time and flipped on a light switch. 'You can leave the cases there. I can get them downstairs myself.'

'Just show me where to put them, Sophie,' he said. 'And I'll go get the other two.'

There was a fine line between independence and stubbornness, Vito thought as he went back to his truck for the two big cases. It seemed Sophie Johannsen walked the sensible side, although he suspected it was only out of sheer exhaustion. She'd allowed him to take the small cases to a basement storeroom, but was adamant that she had to clean the equipment *tonight*.

He took the two big cases from the back of the truck and set them on the sidewalk. He had no idea how long cleaning the equipment would take, but the campus was deserted and he sure as hell wasn't leaving her here alone. Besides, there were way worse fates than watching Sophie Johannsen, so he'd wait as long as he needed to.

He looked down at his muddy boots. If he had to wait, he could at least be comfortable. Reaching behind his seat, he felt for his shoes – and once again came up with the roses. They gave him pause. At least this time they hadn't pricked him.

He'd bought them for the woman he once thought he could love forever, who died two years ago. Today. He'd waited *two years*. Surely that was long enough. But . . .

Vito sighed. He was attracted to Sophie Johannsen. No man with a pulse wouldn't be. But it wasn't the attraction that was bothering him. It was the need he'd felt all day, at the field, in the truck. He'd watched her work and weep and she made him want. Maybe all that sudden yearning was because it *was* today. He didn't want to think so, but Vito was a careful man. He'd pushed a relationship once before and the results had been disastrous. He didn't make the same mistake twice.

Vito tossed the roses behind the passenger seat and changed into his shoes. He'd take Sophie home, then come back in a few weeks and he'd see if she still made him want. If she did, and if she felt the same, nothing would hold him back.

'I thought you'd gotten lost,' she said when he put the two big cases down inside the storeroom. She was bent over a worktable, scrubbing one of the pieces with a toothbrush. 'This could take a while. Go home, Vito. I'm fine here.'

Vito shook his head. The reason he'd picked her up at the

college in the first place was because she didn't have a car. She rode a bike, Katherine had said. He wasn't about to let her ride her bicycle home at this time of night after working all day. 'No, I'll see you home safely. It's the least I can do,' he added when her mouth set stubbornly. He tried a different tack. 'Look, I've got a sister and I'd want somebody to see her home.' Her green eyes narrowed as she shot him a look of annoyed reproach, so he fell back on the tried and true with a sigh. 'I'm tired. Don't argue with me. Please.'

Her frown relaxed and she chuckled. 'Now you sound like Katherine.'

He thought about the angry words the two had shared that afternoon, then the way Katherine had smoothed the hair from Sophie's face before sending her back to finish her scan. Their relationship ran very deep. 'You've known her since you were a girl.'

'She was the mother I never had. Is,' she corrected herself with a small smile. 'She *is* the mother I never had.'

Her face was dirty and streaked from the tears she'd shed. Her hair was disheveled, a few straggling strands having come loose from the tight ball of braids at her nape. He found himself wanting to smooth the hair from her face, just as Katherine had done.

But not for the same reason. He shoved his hands in his pockets.

Tall and strong, with her green eyes and golden hair, Sophie Johannsen was a beautiful woman with a bright mind and a quick temper. And a soft heart. She intrigued him as no woman had for some time. *Two weeks*, he warned himself. *You wait two weeks, Ciccotelli.*

But because his mind had already cut those two weeks down to one, he forced himself to change mental tracks. The sight of the body bag had triggered her extreme reaction. It didn't take a detective to guess she'd seen one before.

'When did your mother die?' he asked and her hands stilled and her jaw tightened.

'She's not dead,' she finally said, resuming her task.

Surprised, Vito frowned. 'But . . . I don't understand.'

Her smile was quick and flat. 'That's okay. Neither do I.'

It was a nice way of telling him to mind his own business. He was wondering how to probe deeper when she stopped working and began unbuttoning her coat. His brain stopped churning and he realized he was holding his breath, waiting to see what her bulky coat concealed. He wasn't disappointed. She shrugged out of the coat, revealing a soft knit sweater that clung to every curve. He let the breath out as quietly as he could. Sophie Johannsen had a hell of a lot of curves.

She hung her coat on a hook on the back of the door, then turned back to her worktable, rolling her shoulders and he shoved his hands deeper in his pockets to keep from touching her. She glanced up at him before resuming her work. 'You know you really can go. I'm fine here alone.'

Irritation scraped at him, obliterating whatever smooth segue he might have come up with. 'So where is your mother then, if she's not dead?'

Again her hands stilled and she turned only her head to look at him with a mixture of cool amusement and incredulity. 'Katherine was right. You cops *are* nosy.' She said no more, concentrating on cleaning the piece as if she performed brain surgery.

Her dismissal irritated him. 'Well? Where is she?'

She shot him a warning look and blew out an impatient breath. 'So, tell me more about the brother who inhales chocolate. *Him* I can like.'

He'd pushed too far and for the life of him didn't know why he'd done so. He wasn't normally so rude. 'Which translates to mind your own business,' he said ruefully.

She flashed a quick grin. 'You detectives are so smart.' She lifted a brow as she opened the next cases. 'So you and your brother are just bachelors roughing it?'

'You're nosy, too, just more subtle about it,' he said and her warm chuckle told him he was right. It had been a while since he'd done this tango, but he still remembered the steps. She was establishing boundaries, which meant she was interested, too. 'Tino's kind of in between jobs. He was a commercial artist at this fancy advertising company, but they started taking on clients and projects he couldn't morally support. So he quit. He couldn't afford his condo in Center City anymore, so . . .'

'So you opened your home,' she said quietly. 'That was nice of you, Vito.'

Her tone soothed his anger, brushing it away as if it had never been. 'He's my brother. And my friend.' And to Vito, that had always been reason enough.

She considered it for a moment, then nodded. 'Then he's a fortunate man.'

He said no more, warmed by the compliment she'd paid him with such effortless sincerity and a week was suddenly too long. The yearning was far stronger now. He wanted to race, to grab what he needed before it disappeared. *One day, Chick. At least sleep on it.* That he could try.

For now Vito contented himself in watching her go about her work. Finally, she stood and dusted her hands on her jeans. 'I'm done.'

His hands itched to touch so he kept them in his pockets, not even offering to help her with her coat. 'Then let's go get your bike.'

Her brows slightly bent in question as she sensed his shift of mood. But apparently she really wasn't as nosy as he was. 'I'm parked around the back.'

Sunday, January 14, 11:55 P.M.

Sophie cast a wary glance up at Vito Ciccotelli as she locked the door to the Humanities building and led him to the parking lot. He'd watched her with an intensity that made her so nervous that what should have been a fifteen-minute cleaning had taken twice that long.

He'd watched her as a large cat would watch his prey, cautious and intent. She wondered why. Why he was so cautious, that was. She knew why she was the prey. She was accustomed to that look from men. When they got that look they wanted sex.

Sometimes they got it. But only when she needed it, too.

Which hadn't been too often and certainly not recently. For the last six months she'd either been working or sitting with Anna, and before . . . Well, it was hard finding someone on the road and she never dated men on a dig. It was a politically foolish thing to do, career suicide. She ought to know. It only took one foolish, stupid, idiotic . . .

And years later, there was still talk. *Easy, needy . . . desperate.* She'd spent the years since focused on her career, striving to remain as sexless as possible. But she was human. She'd had to find men who'd never come in contact with her colleagues and that took time. So she'd spent the better part of her life alone, damning that one regrettable moment when she'd believed the smooth lies of a man she'd thought was her soul mate.

Not all men were pigs, she knew. Her uncle Harry was a sterling example of a kind, good man. Something inside her wanted to believe Vito Ciccotelli was as well. He obviously cared about people, both living and dead. She respected that.

Pocketing her key, she looked up at him. He was staring straight ahead into the night, his mind clearly elsewhere. Alone, she thought. Right now he looked very alone.

Two alone people might find a way not to be. For a while, anyway. It was something to consider. 'Are you all right?' she asked. 'You look . . . grim.'

'I'm sorry. My mind wandered.' He looked around. 'Let's get your bike and put it in the bed of my truck, then I'll drive you home.'

Sophie lifted her brows. 'My bike in your truck? I don't think so.' She started walking and he followed, his huff of frustration audible.

She stopped next to her bike, and in the light of the

streetlamps she saw his face flatten in surprise. 'This is yours?'

'It is.' She unhooked her helmet from the seat. 'Why?'

Sophie was relieved to see his broodiness had disappeared, replaced by a spark of excitement as he took a slow walk around her motorcycle. 'Katherine said you had a bike. I thought she meant a *bicycle*. This . . .' He ran a hand over the engine reverently. 'This is a real beauty.'

'You ride?'

'Yeah. Harley Buell.'

Fast and sleek. 'Oooh. Racer.'

He looked up from his inspection and grinned. 'Scares my mom to death.'

His delight was infectious so she grinned back. 'You bad boy, you.'

He took another walk around the bike, stopping at the front tire so that he faced her. 'I've never seen this BMW model before.'

'It's a classic – 1974. I got it when I was working in Europe. Zero to a hundred in under ten seconds.' She laughed. 'God, it's a rush.'

He suddenly sobered. 'I *am* a cop, Sophie. You don't speed, do you?'

Her grin disappeared. She wasn't sure if he was serious, but decided to err on the side of caution. 'Oh, I meant a hundred *kilometers* an hour. That's barely sixty.'

He continued to frown for another second, and then his lips began to twitch. 'Nice save. I'll have to remember that one.'

Her chuckle was shaky. 'You do that, Vito.' Setting the helmet firmly on her head, she patted her pockets, then frowned. 'Oh, shit.' Frantically, she dug in each pocket and came up with everything but what she was looking for. 'My keys are gone.'

'You just put it in your pocket.'

'That was the university key. I keep it on a separate ring. I'm only here once a week.' She closed her eyes. 'If I lost my keys at the dig, I mean crime scene . . .'

Vito's hand closed over her shoulder and gently squeezed.

'Calm down, Sophie. If you lost them at the crime scene, they're in the very safest place. We'll be covering every inch of that ground with a fine-tooth comb. We'll find them.'

She made herself breathe. 'That's good, but I kind of need them now. My bike keys, my house keys . . . and the Albright. Goddammit, Ted the Third's gonna shit a ring.'

'The Albright?'

'The museum where I work. Ted the Third's my boss. We don't get along very well.'

'Why not?'

'He plays at being *The Historian*,' she said, dropping her voice dramatically. 'Makes me do these damn tours.' She scowled. 'I have to dress up.'

'And you don't like to dress up?'

'I *am* a historian, dammit. I don't just play at it. At least I didn't.'

'So why did you take the job?'

She sighed, frustrated. 'I needed the money for my gran's nursing home and Ted the First was an archeological legend.'

'Ted the First is your boss's grandfather?'

'Yeah. His collection comprises ninety percent of our exhibits.' She shrugged. 'I thought working with the Albright Foundation would be good for my career. Now I'm just biding my time until something else is available.' She smiled ruefully. 'There aren't many medieval castles in Philly. And my pride won't let me flip burgers at McDonald's.'

'So when was the last time you felt your keys in your hand?' he asked quietly.

She closed her eyes and saw her hand closing over her keys. She looked up to find him watching her with that steady gaze once again. 'That's very good. Redirect my panic and clear my mind. The last time I had my keys was when I first got in your truck. It's what was jangling against the garden stakes. Maybe I dropped them in your truck.'

He dug his own keys from his pocket, then smiled down at her, sending her heart into a Riverdance. 'Let's go look.'

Sophie's mouth went dry and every nerve went zinging and she knew if she wasn't careful she'd give him exactly what he wanted. Because at the moment she more than needed it. For the first time in a long time, she actually wanted it too. She took his keys and stepped back, needing the space. 'No, I'll go. You stay and check out my bike.'

She jogged around the building and past the funky ape to his truck. She patted the passenger seat, the floorboards, but found no keys. She remembered the bumpy access road to the gravesite and stuck her hand under the seat, hoping they'd bounced under. Then she sighed with relief when she felt them. But they were stuck on something.

She reached around behind the seat and winced as thorns pricked her palm. She pulled out a bouquet of wilted roses and frowned. They were obviously for someone, because stuck among the flowers was a white card. Before she could look away, the handwritten words registered.

A – I'll always love you. V

The roses might have been for his mom, she thought, but men didn't say *I'll always love you* to their mothers, not like that. No men she wanted to know anyway.

So he was taken. Fair enough. But betrayal pricked at her heart. He'd watched her all day and he . . . *He what, Sophie?* He'd said he didn't have anyone at home. But that was not necessarily an invitation. *Get a grip. You heard what you wanted to hear, because you were sad and needy. Desperate.* She wanted to cover her ears, but the word echoed inside her head. She forced herself to be reasonable. *He was nice to me.* And in the end, that was all he'd done. He'd made no improper advances. He'd been nothing but a gentleman. So of course he was taken. All the good ones were.

He was straddling her bike when she got back, looking lost in thought again. He blinked when she came close. 'Did you find them?'

She held up her key ring and tossed him his. 'Under the seat.'

'Okay.' He climbed off her bike. 'Sophie, I . . . Thank you. You were a huge help today. I wish we could pay you for your time. But I did promise a pizza.' He lifted his brows. 'I know a place that's open late if you want to get one now.'

Sophie swallowed. *He's taken.* She still wanted him . . . *So what kind of woman am I?* She made herself smile. 'If your department really wants to pay me back, give me a get-outta-jail-free card for the next time I get pulled over for going too fast on my bike.'

Vito frowned. 'I wasn't talking about the department taking you out to dinner. I was talking about me.' He drew a deep breath. 'I'm asking you to go to dinner with me.'

She fastened the strap of her helmet under her chin with a hard yank, her heart sinking. *Please don't be asking me on a date. Please be the nice guy I want to believe you are.* 'Like . . . a-a-a date?' God, he had her stammering now.

He nodded, soberly. 'Yeah. Like a date.' He stepped forward and lifted her chin with his finger until she was looking into his eyes. 'I haven't met anyone like you in a long time. I don't want to just walk away.'

She couldn't move, couldn't breathe, could only stare into those dark eyes, desperately wanting to believe his words, desperately wanting what she knew she couldn't have. His thumb brushed her lower lip, sending shivers down her spine. 'What do you say?' he murmured, his voice smooth and soothing. 'I could follow you home, make sure you get home all right. Pick up a pizza on the way. We can talk some more.'

He moved a hair closer and she knew she was about to be kissed. She knew it would probably be one of the most earth-shattering moments of her existence. 'So how about it?' he whispered and she could feel the warmth of him on her skin.

Yes, yes. The words were on the tip of her tongue. Then her brain finally kicked in, replaying Alan Brewster's voice saying almost the exact same words. Sanity returned like a hammer to her head and she took a lurching step back just as he angled his face to kiss her. '*No.*' Breathing hard, she backed up until the back of her legs touched her bike. She climbed on, furious, but whether she was more furious with him for trying it or for herself for nearly becoming yet another notch in another man's bedpost she couldn't say. 'No thank you. Now if you'll excuse me . . .'

He stepped aside without another word and she stomped on the starter, revving the bike's hundred and ten horses to life. Before turning into the street she glanced at her side mirror and saw he hadn't moved. He stood statue still, watching her go.

Chapter Five

Sunday, January 14, 11:55 P.M.

The ringing of his cell woke him from a sound sleep. With a growl he grabbed it and squinted at the caller ID. Harrington. Self-righteous little has-been prick. 'What?'

'It's Harrington.'

He sat up. 'I *know*. Why the hell are you calling me in the middle of the night?'

'It's not even midnight. You usually work all night, Lewis.'

That was normally true, but he wasn't about to let Harrington have the point. He had nothing but contempt for the man and his rainbow-and-Ziggy view of the world. He wanted to strangle the sonofabitch, just like he'd strangled Claire Reynolds. He still did, every time he heard Harrington's whiny voice.

Harrington had tried to block his art every step of the way, starting with his animation of *Claire Dies*, a year ago. Too dark, too violent. *Too real*. But Van Zandt understood business and what sells. The strangulation of 'Clothilde' stayed in *Behind Enemy Lines* even though Harrington bitched and moaned about it. But Harrington wouldn't bitch and moan much longer.

Van Zandt was systematically shoving Harrington out the door and the idiot didn't even have a clue. 'Goddamn it, Harrington, I was dreaming.' Of Gregory Sanders. His next victim. 'Just tell me what's so important so I can get back to it.'

There was a long pause.

'Hel*lo*. You there, man? I swear to God, if you woke me up for nothing—'

'I'm here,' Harrington said. 'Jager wants you to speed delivery on the fight scenes.'

So Van Zandt had finally told Harrington he was out. *It was about time.*

'He wants them by Tuesday,' Harrington added. 'Nine A.M.'

The sweet pleasure vanished like mist. '*Tuesday?* What the fuck's he smoking?'

'Jager's very serious.' And so was Harrington. It sounded like every word was being dragged from his mouth. 'He says you're a month late.'

'You can't rush genius.'

There was another pause, and he thought he could hear Harrington's teeth grind. It was always such fun to yank the man's chain. 'He wants a fight scene and a cut scene from *Inquisitor* to show at Pinnacle.' Another, harder pause. 'We have a booth.'

'Pinnacle?' A booth at Pinnacle meant prestige among gamers. Respect. Pragmatically it meant national distribution, which meant his audience had just become millions. Abruptly his eyes narrowed. This changed things. Pinnacle wouldn't wait. It was a real deadline. 'If you're shittin' me, Harrington—'

'It's true.' Harrington sounded almost upset. 'Jager got the invitation tonight. He wanted me to tell you to get those scenes completed by Tuesday.'

He'd make it happen, even though he'd barely started on the fight scenes. He'd been busy creating the dungeon scenes. 'You've told me. Now let me go back to sleep.'

'Will you have the fight scenes for Jager?' Harrington pressed.

'That's between me and Van Zandt. But you can tell him I'll be in on Tuesday,' he added in as condescending a voice as he could muster, then hung up. Harrington deserved to be booted out on his ass. He was stagnant and way past passé.

Putting Harrington from his mind, he swung his leg over the side of the bed. Spreading lubricant over his residual, he grabbed his leg and pulled it in place with the unconscious motion brought on by years of practice. Meeting VZ would throw a hitch in his schedule. He'd have to move Greg Sanders from Tuesday morning to late afternoon, but he'd still have his next scream by Tuesday at midnight. He sat down at his computer and composed an e-mail to Gregory Sanders, changing the time and signing it 'Kind regards, E. Munch.'

He knew he couldn't test Van Zandt's patience when it came to fight scenes for Pinnacle. Van Zandt recognized his genius, but even VZ would sacrifice art for an animated clip completed in time for Pinnacle. He needed something to show VZ on Tuesday, even if it was half-done. VZ would be satisfied, because even half-done creations by 'Frasier Lewis' were worlds better than anything Harrington could do.

He considered the video he'd taken of Warren Keyes wielding a sword and that of Bill Melville brandishing the flail. For all his claimed expertise in martial arts, Bill had never really achieved the rhythm of the flail, and in the end he'd had to demonstrate it himself. He'd found that bringing the flail into contact with Bill's human head felt a good deal different from the pigs' heads he'd practiced on. The pigs had been long dead, but Bill . . . He pulled the video from the neatly shelved collection with a smile. The top of Bill's head had sheared right off. It would make for a great 'entertainment venture.'

He'd grab something to eat, turn off his phone and Internet connection to eliminate all distractions, then he'd get to work on a fight sequence that would make VZ happy and would make Harrington look like the two-bit hack he was.

Monday, January 15, 12:35 A.M.

Bone tired, starving, and still utterly confused by Sophie's reaction in the parking lot, Vito walked through his front door and into a war zone. For a moment he simply stood and watched as a barrage of wadded paper balls sailed across his living room. A rather expensive vase was perched precariously close to the edge of an end table, knocked askew by the sofa relocation. He needed no other clues to know he'd been invaded.

Then one of the paper balls hit him squarely in the temple and he blinked, stunned. He picked up the offending wad, frowning when he found one of his fishing sinkers inside. The boys had obviously improved their munitions recently. 'Guys.' The balls continued to be hurled across the room. 'Connor! Dante! Cease and desist. *Now.*'

'Oh, man.' The words came from the kitchen, quickly followed by his eleven-year-old nephew Connor, who looked both annoyed and mildly alarmed. 'You came home.'

'I do that most every night,' Vito returned dryly, then winced as a blur of blue flannel hurled itself at his legs. 'Careful.' He leaned over and pried five-year-old Pierce's arms from around his knees, lifting him with a puzzled squint. 'What's on your face, Pierce?'

'Chocolate frosting,' Pierce said proudly and Vito laughed, a good deal of his weariness dissipated. He swung Pierce to his hip and hugged him hard.

Connor shook his head. 'I tried to tell him not to eat it, but you know how kids are.'

Vito nodded. 'Yeah, I know how kids are. You have frosting on your chin, Connor.'

Connor's cheeks darkened. 'We made a cake.'

'Did you save any for me?'

Pierce made a face. 'Not much.'

'Well, that's too bad, because I'm so hungry I could eat a

cow.' Vito eyed Pierce. 'Or maybe a little boy. You look like you'd be pretty tasty.'

Pierce giggled, familiar with the game. 'I'm all gristle, but Dante's got lots of meat.'

Dante popped up from behind the sofa, flexing his biceps. 'It's muscle. Not meat.'

'I think he's all ham,' Vito whispered loudly, making Pierce giggle again. 'Dante, the battle's over for the night. You guys have to go to bed.'

'Why?' he whined. 'We were just having fun.' At nine he was a big boy, nearly bigger than Connor. He rolled over the back of the sofa, and Vito cringed as the movement sent the vase teetering. Dante rolled off the sofa and caught the vase like it was a football. 'Ciccotelli makes the touchdown,' he crowed. 'And the crowd goes wild.'

'The crowd is going to bed,' Vito said. 'And don't even think about the extra point.'

Dante slid the vase to the middle of the table with a grin, indicating he'd been contemplating exactly that. 'Lighten up, Uncle Vito,' he chided. 'You're way too tight.'

Pierce sniffed him. 'And you smell really bad. Like the dog when he rolls in something dead. Mom always makes us give him a bath outside when that happens.'

Images of the bodies flashed in his mind and he pushed them away. 'I'll give myself a bath. But inside. It's cold out there. What are you guys doing here anyway?'

'Dad took Mom to the hospital,' Connor said, suddenly serious. 'Tino brought us over here. We brought our sleeping bags.'

'But . . .' Vito caught Connor's warning glance at his two brothers and bit back the question. He'd have to get the details later. 'Don't you have school tomorrow?'

'No, 'cause it's Martin Luther King Day,' Pierce informed him. 'Uncle Tino said we can stay up all night.'

'Um, no you can't.' Vito ruffled the boy's dark hair. 'I have to get up early tomorrow and I gotta sleep. So you gotta sleep.'

'Besides,' Connor said. 'Tino didn't say all night. He said till midnight.'

'Which is already past,' Vito said. 'Go brush your teeth and roll out your sleeping bags on the living-room floor. Tomorrow clean up all these cannonballs and put my fishing sinkers back in my tackle box. Okay?'

Dante grinned. 'Okay, but we got some good heft with those sinkers.'

Vito rubbed his temple which still throbbed. 'Yeah, I know. Where's Tino?'

'Downstairs trying to get Gus to sleep,' Connor said, hustling Pierce back to brush his teeth. 'He set up the crib in his living room. And Dominic is downstairs, too, studying for a math test. Dom says he'll sleep on Tino's couch, to take care of Gus.'

Dominic was Dino's eldest and very responsible. Certainly more responsible than Vito had been at the same age. 'I'm going to take a shower and when I come out, I want to see three lumps in sleeping bags, and I want to hear snores, okay?'

'We'll be quiet.' Dante hung his head, a martyr now. 'We promise.'

Vito knew they'd try, but he'd played host to his brother's kids enough times to know their good intentions didn't last too long. He sniffed his shoulder and grimaced. He did smell awful. He had to take a shower or the stench would keep him awake all night.

And even though he'd no longer be sleeping on the urge to ask Sophie Johannsen to dinner, he did have to sleep. He had to be back at the four-by-four matrix of graves in less than seven hours.

Monday, January 15, 12:45 A.M.

Sophie let herself into her uncle Harry's house and quietly closed the door. The television in the living room was on, the volume low, as she'd known it would be.

'Hot chocolate's on the stove, Soph.'

Smiling as she sat on the arm of the recliner, she leaned down and kissed Harry's balding head. 'How do you always know to do that? I didn't tell you I was coming.'

She hadn't planned to. She'd planned to shower, eat, and fall into bed. But Anna's house was too quiet and the ghosts, both old and new, were too close for comfort.

'I could say I'm psychic,' Harry said, not taking his eyes from the flickering TV. 'But the truth is I can hear your bike as soon as you turn onto Mulberry.'

Sophie winced. 'I bet Miss Sparks complains.'

'Sure she does. But I think she'd die if she stopped complaining, so consider it your good deed for the day.'

Sophie laughed softly. 'I like the way you think, Uncle Harry.'

He huffed a chuckle, then looked up with a frown. 'Are you wearing perfume?'

'It's Gran's. Too much, huh?' she asked and he nodded.

'Plus you smell like you're eighty years old. Why are you wearing Anna's perfume?'

'Let's just say I came in contact with something really bad. It was in my hair, even after I washed it. Four times, even. I was desperate.' She shrugged. 'Sorry. But trust me, it's better than the alternative.'

He grabbed the mass of hair twisted on the back of her head and squeezed. 'Sophie, your hair is still soaking wet. You'll catch your death of cold.'

She grinned at him. 'I might smell like Gran, but you sound like her.'

He looked disgruntled. Then he laughed. 'You're right. I do. So why did you come all the way over here with your hair all wet, Sophie? Having trouble sleeping?'

'Yeah. I was hoping you'd be awake.'

'Me and Bette Davis. *Now, Voyager*. Hell of a good flick. They just don't make 'em—'

'Like this anymore,' she finished his sentence fondly, having heard it hundreds of times during her life. Sophie had learned at an early age that her uncle was a chronic insomniac who dozed in his easy chair in front of the television while old movies played. It had been an enormous comfort, knowing that if she ever needed him, he'd be right here in this chair every night, ready to listen and advise. Or sometimes just to be there.

And he had been there for her. Always. 'The first time I came down and saw you sitting here you were watching Bette Davis. It was *Jezebel* that time. Hell of a good flick,' she teased, but his face had changed, sobering.

'I remember,' he said quietly. 'You were four years old and you'd had a bad dream. You looked so cute shuffling down the stairs in your footie pajamas.'

She remembered the dream vividly, remembered the terror of waking up in an unfamiliar bed. The beds had always been unfamiliar up to that point in her life. Harry, Gran, and Katherine changed all that. She owed them a great deal.

'I loved those footie pajamas.' They'd been handed down from her cousin Paula, then again from her cousin Nina. The feet had been mended and the flannel washed a hundred times, but to Sophie they were the most luxurious thing she'd ever owned. 'They were so soft, and I'd never been so warm.'

Harry's eyes flickered and his jaw tightened and Sophie knew he was remembering the threadbare cotton pj's she'd been wearing when she'd been so unceremoniously dumped on his doorstep. It had been a night as cold as this one and Harry had been so angry. Years later, she understood his anger had been fully directed at her mother.

'I didn't even realize you were crying at first. Not until I saw your face.'

She remembered the night she'd first come down the stairs, terrified and trembling from the dream, but more terrified of making noise. 'I was afraid to wake anyone up.' She'd learned never to disturb her mother during the night. 'I was afraid you'd get mad and send me away.' She rubbed her thumb over Harry's forehead to smooth away his frown. 'But you didn't. You just picked me up and sat me on your lap and we watched *Jezebel*.' And just like that, Sophie had found a safe place for the first time in her life.

'Why the walk down memory lane, Sophie? What happened today?'

Where to start? 'I spent the day helping Katherine. I can't tell you the details, but it was in a "professional capacity."' She quirked her fingers, punctuating the air.

'You saw a dead body.' His tone hardened. 'Well, that explains the perfume. That was damn irresponsible of Katherine. No wonder you couldn't sleep.'

'I'm a big girl now, Uncle Harry. I can handle a body. Besides, Katherine didn't think I'd actually see one. She felt bad about that.' Turning to meet his eyes, Sophie drew a deep breath. 'She felt a lot worse when I saw her zipping the body into the bag.'

Harry's shoulders sagged and pain filled his eyes. 'Oh, honey. I'm sorry.'

She forced a smile. 'I'm okay. I just couldn't stay in that house tonight.'

'So you'll stay here, in your old room. I'm off tomorrow. I'll make waffles.'

He sounded like a kid himself and this time her smile was real. 'Tempting, Uncle Harry, but I have to leave early tomorrow. I've got to go back to Gran's and let the dogs out, and then I have to work at the museum all day. But how about dinner?'

'You shouldn't be having dinner with an old man like me. You should have a date, Sophie. You've been home six months. Haven't you found anyone you like?'

Vito Ciccotelli's handsome face popped into her mind and she scowled. She had liked him, dammit. Worse, she'd respected him. Worse still, she'd wanted him, even after she'd known she couldn't have him. Now the thought of him left nearly as bad a taste in her mouth as the dead bodies in the field.

'No. Everyone I've met is either married, dating, or a rat.' Her eyes narrowed. 'And sometimes they even act like they're decent and get you to share your beef jerky.'

He looked alarmed. 'Please tell me *beef jerky* is not a new euphemism for sex.'

Confused, she glared at him, then she laughed so hard she nearly fell off the arm of the chair. Quickly she covered her mouth so as not to wake Aunt Freya. 'No, Uncle Harry. To my knowledge, beef jerky is still beef jerky.'

'You're the linguist. You should know.'

She stood up. 'So what about dinner? I'll take you to Lou's.'

'Lou's?' His mouth bent down as he considered it. 'For cheesesteaks?'

'No, for wheat germ.' She rolled her eyes. 'Of course for cheesesteaks.'

His eyes gleamed. 'With Cheez Whiz?'

She kissed the top of his head. 'Always. I'll meet you at seven. Don't be late.'

She was halfway up the stairs to her old room when she heard his chair creak. 'Sophie.' She turned to find him staring up at her, a sad look on his face. 'Not all men are rats. You'll find someone and he'll be honorable. You deserve the best.'

Sophie's throat closed and resolutely she swallowed. 'I'm too late, Uncle Harry. Aunt Freya got the best. The rest of us just have to settle. See you tomorrow night.'

Monday, January 15, 12:55 A.M.

Tino was sitting at the kitchen table when Vito got out of the shower. His brother pointed to a plate piled with linguini and Grandma Chick's red sauce. 'I nuked it.'

Vito slumped in a chair with a sigh. 'Thanks. I didn't have a chance to eat.'

Tino's eyes narrowed in concern. 'You went to the cemetery?'

Besides Nick, Tino was the only other person who knew what today was and how Andrea had died. Nick knew because he'd been there when it happened. Tino knew because Vito had too much to drink a year ago today and spilled his guts. But his secret was as safe with Tino as it was with Nick.

'Yeah, but not the one you mean.' Today's field was a far cry from the neatly maintained cemetery where two years ago he'd buried Andrea next to her baby brother.

Tino's brows went up. 'What, you found graves today?'

Vito looked around the corner at the boys asleep on the living room floor. 'Sshh.'

Tino grimaced. 'Sorry. Bad case?'

'Yeah.' He devoured two helpings without speaking, then piled a third on his plate.

Tino watched him with mild astonishment. 'When did you last eat, man?'

'Breakfast.' A picture flashed in his mind – Sophie Johannsen, her face streaked with tears, offering to share her chocolate milk, beef jerky, and Ho Hos. 'Actually, that's not true. I had some beef jerky an hour or so ago.'

Tino laughed out loud. 'Beef jerky? You? Mr Picky?'

'I was hungry.' And taking it from Sophie's hand had made the snack far more palatable than he would have guessed. She'd nagged at his thoughts all the way home, but now more urgent matters pressed. He lowered his voice. 'I tried to call Dino, but his cell went right to voice mail. What happened tonight?'

Tino leaned forward. 'Dino called at about six,' he murmured. 'Molly had been having numbness and she just collapsed. They think it was a mild stroke.'

Stunned, Vito stared. 'She's only thirty-seven.'

'I know.' Tino leaned in a little closer. 'Dino sent Dominic to a neighbor's with the kids so they wouldn't see the ambulance take her away, then he called here looking for us, to get us to take the kids. He sounded scared to death. I went over to get them.'

Vito pushed his plate aside, no longer hungry. 'So how is she?'

'Dad called two hours ago. She's stable.'

'And Dad?' Michael Ciccotelli had a very bad heart. This kind of stress wasn't good.

'He was ecstatic that Molly was okay and Mom was nagging him to calm down.' Tino studied him for a moment. 'So you didn't make it to the cemetery.'

'No, but I'm okay. It's not like last year,' Vito added. 'I'm fine. Really.'

'So you've paced your bedroom floor every night for the last week because you're fine.' He lifted a brow when Vito opened his mouth to protest. 'Your bedroom's right over mine, man. I hear every creak of your floorboards.'

'I guess it's only fair then. I hear every "Oh Tino." '

Tino had the grace to pretend to be embarrassed. 'I haven't had a woman in my bed in weeks, and it doesn't look like I will again anytime soon. But it's okay. I had a custom portrait to finish. Thanks to your pacing I've finished Mrs Sorrell's painting ahead of schedule.' He waggled his brows. 'You know the painting I mean.'

'I know,' Vito said dryly. The woman had contracted Tino to paint her portrait from a boudoir photo as a gift for her husband. 'The one with the really nice—' He heard a rustle in the living room. 'Sweaters,' he finished firmly and Tino grinned.

'Hey, I'm just glad I finished before the boys came over

today. That job was decidedly . . . M for mature. Mr Sorrell's a lucky man.'

Vito shook his head, mostly to clear the image of Sophie Johannsen in her snug sweater that had popped up in his mind. 'Tino, you're going to get yourself in trouble one of these days, painting naughty pictures of other men's wives.'

Tino laughed. 'Dante's right, you really are too tight. Mrs Sorrell has a sister.'

Vito shook his head again. 'No thanks.'

Tino sobered abruptly. 'It's been two years since Andrea died,' he said gently.

Since Andrea died was far too sanitized a phrase, but Vito didn't have the energy to argue the point tonight. 'I know how long it's been. Down to the minute.'

Tino was quiet for a long moment. 'Then you know you've paid long enough.'

Vito looked at him. 'How long is long enough, Tino?'

'To grieve? I don't know. But to blame yourself . . . Five minutes was too long. Let it go, Vito. It happened. It was an accident. But you're not gonna accept that until you're ready. I just hope you're ready soon or you'll end up a lonely man.'

Vito had nothing to say to that and Tino got up and pulled a plate from the fridge. 'I saved you a piece of the boys' cake. I supervised the baking, so it's safe to eat.'

Vito frowned at the plate. 'It's all frosting. Where's the cake?'

Tino's lips twitched. 'Not much of the batter made it into the pan.' He shrugged. 'When they got here, they were scared about Molly. I figured what was the harm?'

Startled when his eyes stung, Vito dropped his eyes to the cake, concentrating on peeling off the plastic wrap. He cleared his throat. 'That was nice of you, Tino.'

Tino shrugged again, embarrassed by the praise. 'They're our kids. Family.'

Vito thought about Sophie's praise, sincere and unaffected.

He hadn't felt embarrassed. He'd felt warm and more comfortable than he'd felt in a very long time. From the corner of his eye he saw Tino rise.

'I'm going to bed. Tomorrow will be a better day, all the way around.'

Suddenly the need to speak hit him like a club. Keeping his gaze locked on the frosting-covered plate, he pushed the words out. 'I met someone today.'

From the corner of his eye he saw Tino sit back down. 'Oh? Another cop?'

No. No more cops. Not in a million years. 'No. An archeologist.'

Now Tino blinked. 'An archeologist? Like . . . as in Indiana Jones?'

Vito had to chuckle at the mental picture of Sophie Johannsen slashing through the jungle in a dusty fedora. 'No. More like . . .' He realized a swift comparison was not easily conjured. 'She dug up castles in France. She knows ten languages.' *Three of them deader than the body you just left.* She'd been ashamed at her insensitivity. She'd more than made up for it later. So what had happened in those last few moments?

'So she has a brain. Does she have any other interesting features?'

'She's nearly six feet tall. Angelina lips. Blond hair down to her butt.'

'I think I'm in love already,' Tino teased. 'And her . . . sweaters?'

A slow smile curved his lips. 'Very, very nice.' Then he sobered. 'And so is she.'

'Interesting timing,' Tino said blandly. 'I mean, you meeting her today of all days.'

Vito looked away. 'I was worried I was only interested just because it's today. I'd convinced myself that today wasn't the day to make a fast move. That it could be wistfulness or rebound or something.'

'Vito, after two years, it's not rebound in anybody's dictionary.'

Vito shrugged. 'I told myself I'd come back in a few weeks and see if I felt the same. But then . . .' He shook his head.

'Then?'

Vito sighed. 'But then I walked her to the parking lot. Damn, Tino, she rides a bike. Beemer, zero to a hundred in under ten.'

Tino puckered his lips. 'Stacked girl on a fast bike. Now I know I'm in love.'

'It was a stupid reason to jump the gun,' Vito said, disgusted.

Tino's eyes widened. 'So you asked her out? That is interesting.'

Vito frowned. 'I tried, but I don't think I did it very well.'

'Turned you down cold, huh?'

'Yeah. Then took off on her bike like a bat out of hell.'

Tino leaned across the table and sniffed, grimacing. 'It could be your unique cologne. That must have been some graveyard.'

'It was. And I get to go back tomorrow for round two.'

Tino put the plates in the sink. 'Then you should get some sleep.'

'I will.' But he made no move to rise. 'In a bit. I need to chill a little first. Thanks for nuking dinner.'

When Tino was gone, Vito rested his head against the wall behind him, closed his eyes, and in his mind went over those last few moments with Sophie. He wasn't that rusty at asking a woman to dinner, and frankly he'd never been turned down before. Not like that. He had to admit it had pierced his ego some.

It would be easier to dismiss it as womanly whim, except Sophie didn't seem like the type to change her mood with the wind. She seemed too sensible for that. So something had changed. Maybe something he did or said . . . But he was too tired to work through it anymore tonight. Tomorrow he'd just go ask her. That was wiser than trying to guess the mind of a woman, no matter how sensible she seemed.

He'd gotten up to turn out the lights when he heard the noise, little and snuffling, and coming from the lump in Pierce's sleeping bag. Vito's heart squeezed. They were just babies, really. And they must have been so scared, seeing their mom collapse like that. He hunkered down by Pierce's sleeping bag and ran his hand over the boy's back.

Vito peeled the bag to reveal Pierce's tear-streaked face. 'You scared?'

Pierce shook his head hard, but Vito waited and ten seconds later he was nodding.

Connor sat up. 'He's just a kid. You know how kids are.'

Vito nodded sagely, noticing Connor's eyes were a little puffy as well. 'I know. Is Dante awake, too?' He pulled Dante's bag back far enough to peek and Dante blinked up at him. 'So nobody's sleeping, huh? What would help? Warm milk?'

Connor made a face. 'You're kidding, right?'

'It's what they always do on TV.' He sat down on the floor between Pierce and Dante. 'So what would help, 'cause I can't stay awake all night with you. I have to work in a few hours, and I won't be able to sleep if the three of you are wide awake. Eventually you'd start fighting and wake me up. So how do we resolve this?'

'Mom sings,' Dante mumbled. 'To Pierce.'

Pierce gave Vito a yeah-right look. 'To all of us.'

Molly had a nice soprano, pure and perfect for lullabies. 'What does she sing?'

'The fourteen angels song,' Connor said quietly and Vito knew the song was more than a lullaby – it would be like having Molly here with them.

'From *Hansel and Gretel*.' It had always been one of his favorite operas, his grandfather's, too. 'Well, I'm not your mom, but everybody get settled and I'll do my best.' He waited until they were all snuggled. 'Grandpa Chick used to sing the fourteen angels song to me and your dad when we were your age,' he murmured, one hand on Dante's back and one on Pierce's. And singing it brought back sweet memories of the grandfather he had so loved, who'd fostered his love of all kinds of music from an early age.

> When at night I go to sleep, Fourteen angels watch do keep;
> Two my head are guarding, Two my feet are guiding;
> Two are on my right hand, Two are on my left hand,
> Two who warmly cover, Two who o'er me hover,
> Two to whom 'tis given To guide my steps to heaven.

'You sing it pretty,' Pierce whispered when he'd sung the first verse.

Vito smiled. 'Thank you,' he whispered back.

'He sang at Aunt Tess's wedding and at your christening,' Connor whispered. He swallowed. 'Mom cried.'

'It wasn't all that bad,' Vito teased and was relieved to see Connor's lips curve a little. 'I bet your mom's thinking about you right now. She'd want you to sleep.' He sang the second verse more quietly because Dante was already asleep. By the time he finished, Connor was, too. That left Pierce, who looked so little in that big sleeping bag. Vito sighed. 'You want to bunk with me?'

Pierce's nod was quick. 'I don't kick. Or hog the covers. I promise.'

Vito pulled him into his arms, bag and all. 'Or wet the bed?'

Pierce hesitated. 'Not recently.'

Vito laughed. 'Good to know.'

Monday, January 15, 7:45 A.M.

The ringing of the phone next to his bed yanked Greg Sanders out of a sound whiskey-induced sleep. Groggy, he missed his ear on his first two attempts. 'Yeah.'

'Mr Sanders.' The voice was calmly menacing. 'Do you know who this is?'

Greg rolled to his back, suppressing a moan when the room

spun wildly. Goddamn hangovers. But he'd avoided this as long as he could. It was time to pay the devil his due. Greg didn't want to think about what that 'due' would be, but he was certain it would involve a great deal of pain. He swallowed, but his mouth was dry. 'Yeah.'

'You've been avoiding us, Mr Sanders.'

Greg tried to sit up, leaning his spinning head against the wall. 'I'm sorry. I . . .'

'You what?' The voice now mocked him. 'You have our money?'

'No. Not all of it, anyway.'

'That's not good, Mr Sanders.'

Greg pressed his fingers to his throbbing temple, desperation making his pulse race faster. '*Wait*. Look, I have a job. Tomorrow. Pays five hundred. I'll give it all to you.'

'Please, Mr Sanders. That would be like pissing into a forest fire. Much too little, much too late. We want our money by this evening at five o'clock. We don't care what you have to do to get it. All of it. Or you won't be pissing anywhere because you won't have, shall we say, the necessary equipment? Do you understand?'

Greg's stomach roiled. He nodded, nauseated. 'Yeah. I mean, yes. Yes, sir.'

'Good. Have a nice day, Mr Sanders.'

Greg slumped into the pillow, then reared back and hurled the telephone at the wall. Plaster flew and the ringer clanged and glass shattered as a picture fell to the floor.

The bedroom door burst open. 'What the hell?'

Greg groaned into his pillow. 'Go away.' But he was yanked to his back and flinched when a palm connected with his cheek. Greg's head felt like it had exploded. *By five o'clock today I'll wish it had*, he thought.

'Open your eyes, you bastard.'

Blearily Greg obeyed. Jill was glaring down at him, one hand clutching his T-shirt and the other upraised, palm flat.

'Don't hit me again.' It came out very nearly a whimper.

'You . . .' Jill shook her head in bewildered indignation. 'I let you stay here against my better judgment and only because I once had the stupidity to love you. But you're not the man you were. That was *him*, wasn't it? The guy with the creepy voice that keeps calling for you. You owe him money, don't you?'

'Yes.' He hissed out the word. 'I owe him money. I owe you money. I owe my parents money.' He closed his eyes. 'I owe the credit card companies and the bank.'

'You were somebody.' She released his shirt with a shove of disgust that set the room spinning again. 'Now you're just a dirty drunk. You haven't worked in a year.'

He covered his eyes with his hands. 'So my agent tells me.'

'Don't you get smart with me. You had a career. Dammit, Greg, your face made it into nearly every living room in this city. But you gambled it all away.'

'And this was your life, Greg Sanders,' he sneered.

Jill exhaled on what sounded like a sob and he opened his eyes to find tears in hers. 'They're going to break your legs, Greg,' she whispered.

'That's only in the movies. In real life, they do a lot worse than that.'

She took a step back. 'Well, I'm not picking up the pieces this time and I don't want any more damage to my place.' She turned and walked away, pausing at the door. 'I want you out of here by Friday, understand?' Then she was gone.

I should be angry, Greg thought. But he wasn't. She was right. *I had it all and pissed it away. I have to get it back. I have to pay that debt and start over*. He didn't have a penny, but he still had his face. It had earned him a decent living once before. It would do so again.

With care he climbed from the bed and slid into the chair in front of his computer. By tomorrow he'd have five hundred dollars. But that was barely a tenth of the principal he owed. When he added in the interest . . . He needed more money and fast. But how? From whom? Mechanically he clicked on his e-mail, then with a frown opened the message from E. Munch.

At least the job hadn't been canceled, just moved a few hours. *I can hide until then.* But why was he even bothering? Five hundred really was like pissing on a forest fire. He'd do better to run to Canada, dye his hair, and change his name.

Or . . . another idea came to mind. Munch was prepared to pay five bills, cash, and his first e-mail said he had ten roles to fill. Even hung over, Greg could do that math. Munch's profile said he'd worked in film for more than forty years. He'd be old. Old people hid money all kinds of places. Old people could be dealt with, easily.

No. He couldn't do that. Then he thought about the threat to his . . . equipment. Yeah, he could. And if Munch didn't have all the cash . . . well, he'd cross that bridge when he got there.

Chapter Six

Monday, January 15, 8:15 A.M.

Lieutenant Liz Sawyer sat at her desk staring at the map of the four-by-four matrix of graves, her brow crunched into frown lines. 'This is unbelievable.'

'We know,' Vito said. 'But the archeologist says we have nine bodies buried in that field. She's been right on every one so far.'

Liz looked up. 'You've confirmed these seven are empty?'

'Empty, but covered with plywood, just like Sophie said,' Nick replied.

'So what's our status?'

'Three bodies in the morgue,' Vito said. 'The Lady, the Knight, and the guy that's missing half his head. The fourth body is in transit. Jen's working on the fifth.'

Nick went on. 'The fourth body is male, older. The first three look like they may have been in their twenties. This guy might be in his sixties. No obvious anomalies.'

'No posed hands, missing entrails, or dismembered arms?' Liz asked sarcastically.

Vito shook his head. 'The fourth body appeared to be a garden-variety victim.'

Liz sat back, her chair creaking. 'So what are our next steps?'

'We're going to the morgue,' Nick said. 'Katherine promised to give us priority and we need to identify these people. When we start getting names we might see a pattern.'

'Jen has the lab analyzing the soil,' Vito added. 'She's hoping to find out where it came from. The lab will sift through all the fill dirt to see if they can find anything to point to the perp, but it doesn't look like he left anything behind.'

Liz looked down at the map. 'Why the empty graves? I mean, we could guess he's not finished yet with whatever this scheme is, but why leave these two empty?' She pointed to the two graves on the far end of the second row. 'He's filled the entire first row, then the first two on the second row. Then he skips down to the third row.'

'We have to believe he had a reason,' Vito said. 'He's planned this down to the nth degree. I don't think he'd just skip two graves for kicks, but we need to get all the bodies out of there before we start formulating any theories.'

Liz gestured to her office door. 'Keep me apprised. I'll get to work on freeing up another team to work any leads you come up with. Needless to say, the mayor is chomping at the bit. Don't make me look stupid, guys.'

Vito took the map. 'I'll make you a copy. Try to keep the mayor from going to the press too soon, okay?'

'For now we've been lucky,' Liz said. 'The reporters haven't found out about our secret garden, but it's just a matter of time. Too many bodies showing up to the morgue and too many CSU techs coming in for overtime. One of the reporters is bound to grab the scent. Just stick with "no comment" and leave the rest to me.'

Vito's laugh was grim. 'That's one order we'll be glad to follow.'

Monday, January 15, 8:15 A.M.

The Albright Museum was housed in what had once been a chocolate factory. It had been a definite consideration as Sophie had considered Ted the Third's job offer six months before. It was fate, she'd thought. The museum boasted one of the greatest private collections of medieval European artifacts in

North America and it was in a *chocolate* factory. How could she possibly go wrong accepting?

That had become one of the questions for the ages, she thought darkly as she let herself in the museum's front door. Like the secret of life or how many licks to get to the center of a Tootsie Roll Pop. The world would never know.

Because she had, of course, gone wrong. Accepting Ted the Third's job offer had been one of the stupidest things she'd ever done in her life. *And I've done some really stupid things*, she thought, even more darkly. Vito Ciccotelli's handsome face popped into her mind and she shoved it away. At least she'd found out his cheating ways before she'd done something really stupid, like sleep with him.

'Hello?' she called.

'In the office.' Ted's wife, Darla, sat behind the big cluttered desk, a pencil stuck in her graying hair. Darla managed the books, which meant the most important function of the museum – her paycheck – was in capable hands. 'How was your weekend, dear?'

Sophie shook her head. 'You really don't want to know.'

Darla glanced up, her eyes concerned. 'Did your grand-mother take a turn?'

It was one of the reasons that Sophie liked Darla. She was a nice person who really cared. And she seemed fairly normal, which made her the odd Albright. With the exception of Darla, Ted's family was . . . just plain off.

There was Ted himself with his bizarro-world approach to running a history museum and his son, who Sophie always thought of as Theo Four. Theo was nineteen, a sulky, angry boy who played hooky more than he showed up. That wouldn't have been such an issue, but Theo's new job was to run the knight tour and when he played hooky, the responsibility fell to Sophie who was the only other one big enough to fit the suit. Darla was barely five-two and the Albrights' daughter, Patty Ann, even smaller.

Patty emerged from the ladies' room, wearing a very

conservative blue suit, and Sophie narrowed her eyes suspiciously. 'Patty Ann looks nice today. How come?'

Darla smiled without looking up. 'I'm just glad it's not Wednesday.'

Wednesday was Patty Ann's goth day. Any other day you never knew how she'd show up for work. A struggling actress, Patty Ann hadn't yet found her persona, so she imitated everyone else's. Usually not well.

Sophie questioned the wisdom of assigning her to the reception desk and wondered how many visitors took one look at Patty Ann and went on to the Franklin Institute or some other real museum, especially on Wednesdays. But Sophie kept her mouth shut because as much as she hated doing the tours, she hated the thought of cheerily greeting visitors even more. *I miss my pile of rocks.*

Darla looked up, reluctantly. 'Theo's got a cold.'

Sophie rolled her eyes. 'And we have a knight tour scheduled. That's just great. Dammit, Darla . . . I'm sorry. I really wanted to do some real work today.'

Darla looked distressed. 'The tours will bring in a lot of money, Sophie.'

'I know.' And she wondered if she was whoring herself for that money, participating in an enterprise that cheapened history. But as long as Anna was alive, she needed the money. Sophie hoped she needed the money for a long time. 'So what time am I on?'

'The knight tour is at twelve-thirty, Viking at three.'

Oh joy, oh rapture. 'I'll be there with bells on.'

Monday, January 15, 8:45 A.M.

'You got lucky, boys,' Katherine said as she pulled the knight's body from cold storage. 'This guy has a tattoo. May make identifying him a little easier.' She pulled the sheet away, revealing the man's shoulder. 'Can you guess what it is?'

Vito crouched down and stared at the tattoo through narrowed eyes. 'It's a man.'

'Not just any man. If you look at him as closely as you watched Sophie yesterday, you'll figure it out.'

Vito's cheeks heated. He hadn't realized his scrutiny of Sophie Johannsen had been so obvious. Feeling squirmy, he turned back to the victim's shoulder, but not before he caught Nick's look of amusement. It wouldn't have been so bad had Sophie not turned him down cold. It still stung. 'It's a yellow man,' Vito said flatly.

Nick looked over Vito's shoulder. 'It's Oscar. You know, the movie award statue.'

Vito squinted. 'Not a particularly good rendition, but it could be.' Straightening, he looked at Nick. 'Maybe our knight's an actor?'

Nick shrugged. 'It's a place to start. It'll narrow down the missing persons reports.'

Vito took his notebook from his pocket. 'Cause of death was the hole in his gut?'

'That seems likely. I'll start the autopsies today. So far I've only done external exams on the three victims from yesterday.' She looked back at the knight and sighed. 'But this one suffered, I can tell that right now.'

'Being disemboweled has got to hurt a little,' Nick said sarcastically.

'I can only hope he was dead at least for part of it, but I don't think he was. I'm fairly certain he was alive when every major bone in his body was dislocated.'

Vito and Nick flinched. 'My God,' Vito murmured. 'How would . . . ? He's a big guy.'

'Six feet three, two hundred twenty-five,' Katherine confirmed. 'And he fought hard. There are deep abrasions on his wrists and ankles where he was tied with rope. And yeah, I sent a sample of the rope fiber to the lab, but that's a long shot, kids. Other than the dislocations and an empty abdominal cavity, he appears to have been in good shape.' She held up a hand. 'And yes, I've already started a urine tox. I can't see how he could have been overpowered without being drugged. I don't see any head trauma.'

Nick blew out a breath. 'Anything on the woman?'

'Official cause of death is a broken neck.' She pulled out another drawer, their female victim, the sheet forming a tent over her folded hands.

'You need to see her back.' Katherine lifted the sheet and carefully pushed the woman's hip so that the back of her thigh was visible. 'A pattern of contusions, regularly spaced and very deep.' She looked up, her face grim. 'I'm thinking nails.'

Vito's eyes were already beginning to water. Blinking, he focused on the pattern on the woman's skin. Each hole was round and small. 'Is it only on her legs?'

'No.' Katherine slid the drawer back into the wall. 'It's deepest on the backs of her thighs, but the same pattern is visible on her back, calves and the backs of her arms. From the depth of the thigh punctures, I'd say she was sitting up, all of her body weight driving her down onto the nails.'

Nick's expression became strangely strained. 'A chair of nails?'

'Or something like that. Her gluteus was severely burned. No skin remains.' Katherine cocked her jaw, anger in her eyes. 'And she was alive the whole time.'

Vito's stomach churned as the extent of this killer's cruelty became clearer. 'We're dealing with a creative sadist here. I mean, how the hell would anybody even conceive of a chair of nails?'

Nick sat down at Katherine's computer. 'Come here, Chick. Look at this.'

Vito frowned at the screen. It was the chair he'd envisioned, covered in spikes. Restraints were attached to the chair's arms and front legs. 'What the hell is that?'

'I couldn't sleep last night – kept thinking about the way he'd posed their hands. So I got up and Googled medieval effigies.

Sophie was right, by the way. The poses of our victims are exactly like the tomb effigies I found online.'

Vito didn't want to think about Sophie right now. He'd done enough of that during the night while he tossed and turned. 'That's nice,' he scowled, focusing on the screen. 'But what about the chair? Please don't tell me this is available on eBay.'

Nick looked back at the screen, troubled. 'It might be. But this site belongs to a museum in Europe that specializes in medieval torture.'

'A torture museum?' It was real, then. That chair existed in a museum. One also existed right here in Philly. 'I can't begin to imagine how she suffered. How both of them suffered. And we haven't even started on the others.' He pressed his fingers into the back of his skull, a headache forming there. 'How did you find this site?'

'I thought about what Sophie said about disembowelment being used as torture during medieval times. I Googled 'medieval torture' and this is one of the top results. This chair has over thirteen hundred spikes.'

'That would induce the pattern of injury on the victim,' Katherine agreed tightly.

Vito ran a hand through his hair. 'So we have poses like statues on medieval crypts, a chair of spikes, a disembowel-ment and, what, a stretching on a . . . rack? This is not normal, people.'

'A killer with a theme,' Nick mused. 'Except for the body that's on its way in. It didn't appear to have anything funky like this.'

Katherine stepped back from the computer. 'I thought I'd seen everything on this job, but I keep being proved wrong.' She squared her shoulders. 'I do have two other things so far.' She handed Vito a glass jar containing small white crumbs. 'I scraped it from the wire on the male victim's hands. I found what looks like the same substance on the female victim's wires.'

Vito held it up to the light, then passed the jar to Nick. 'Best guess?'

Katherine frowned. 'I sent a sample to the lab, but it looks like something in the silicone family. I'll let you know when I get the results.'

'What's the second thing you have for us?' Nick asked.

'All three of these victims were washed thoroughly. Blood should have been caked all over the three of them, but there was none. That tells me that originally the two posed victims had a lot more of whatever's in that jar all over them.'

'We'll try Missing Persons to match the knight's tat,' Vito said. 'Thanks, Katherine.'

'Then let's call Sophie,' Nick said when they were out in the hall. 'I want to follow up on those torture devices. If that's what he used, he had to get them somewhere and maybe she can give us an idea of where to start looking. We should have gotten her number from Katherine.'

It was a good idea, Vito had to admit. She'd been right about the posed hands. She obviously knew her stuff. And it might give him a chance to find out what he'd done to earn that flash of fury he'd seen in her eyes just before she'd ridden away. More than that, he just wanted to see her again. 'She works at the Albright Museum. We can go when we're done at Missing Persons.'

Dutton, Georgia, Monday, January 15, 10:10 A.M.

'Thanks for coming down,' Daniel said. 'Especially on your day off.'

Luke's eyes were glued to Daniel's father's computer screen. 'Anything for a pal.'

'And the fact that there's a lake down the road with prize bass didn't hurt,' Daniel said dryly and Luke just grinned. 'Did you find anything?'

Luke shrugged. 'Depends. Before mid-November, there are no e-mails.'

'What do mean, none? You mean they never existed or they were erased?'

'Erased. Now, since November we've got e-mails. Acknowledgments for electronic bill pays, mostly. Aside from the usual spam, most of your dad's legit e-mails have been replies to a guy named Carl Sargent.'

'Sargent runs the union at the paper mill that employs half the town. Dad met with him before he went away. Yesterday I found out Dad was going to run for Congress.'

Luke read the remaining e-mails. 'Sargent keeps asking your father to make his candidacy public, and your father keeps putting him off. This one says he's tied up. This one says he'll schedule a press conference when he finishes some urgent business.'

'With my mother,' Daniel murmured. 'She has cancer.'

Luke winced. 'I'm sorry to hear that, Daniel.'

Once again he was gripped by the need to see her just once more. 'Thanks. Do you see any kind of itinerary? Anything that would give me an idea of where they might be?'

'No.' Luke tapped at the keyboard and brought up the online banking screen. 'When you find your father, tell him not to save his passwords in a Word file on his hard drive. It's like leaving your front door key on a silver platter for the thieves.'

'Like I could tell him anything,' Daniel muttered. Luke's mouth quirked in sympathy.

'My old man's the same. Doesn't look like your dad made any major cash withdrawals, not in the last ninety days. That's all the records they keep online.'

'What I don't understand is why he's doing his e-mail and banking remotely. If he has access to a computer wherever he is, why not just do it from there?'

'Maybe he wanted to access documents on his hard drive from the road.' Luke continued to tap keys. 'That's interesting.'

'What?'

'His Internet history's been wiped.'

'Completely wiped?'

'No. But it's pretty sophisticated.' He typed for another minute. 'This is a surprisingly good wipe. Most computer techs wouldn't know how to get past this.' He looked up, his eyes serious. 'Danny, somebody's been in your dad's system.'

A new wave of uneasiness rippled through him. 'Maybe, maybe not. My dad's a computer person from way back. He was also super-paranoid about security. I can see him being worried about leaving a trail.'

Luke frowned. 'If he was so concerned with security, he wouldn't have left his passwords on his hard drive. Besides, I thought your dad was a judge.'

'He was. Electronics is his hobby – ham radios, remote-controlled rockets, but especially computers. He'd take them apart, build his own upgrades. If anyone would know how to keep his system clean, it would be my father.'

Luke turned back to the screen. 'Funny how some things get passed on and others don't. You don't have a computer bone in your body.'

'No, I don't,' Daniel murmured. All that expertise had been diverted to another branch of the family tree. But it was unpleasant to remember, so he briskly closed the door on that dark corner of his memory. 'So can you get through the wipe?'

Luke looked offended. 'Of course. This is interesting. With all those travel brochures, I expected a few travel websites, but there's nothing like that in his cache.'

'What sites did he go to?'

'The weather forecast for Philadelphia two weeks before Thanksgiving. And . . . a search for oncologists in the Philadelphia area. Was Philly one of the brochures?'

Daniel leaned in for a closer look at the screen. 'No, it wasn't.'

'Well, that's where I'd start if I were you. Looks like they wanted to be prepared in case your mother needed a doctor.' He bent his mouth in sympathy. 'I've got a meeting with a lake and a bass. You want to come?'

'No, but thanks. I think I'm going to look around here a

little more. Check out this Philly angle. Thanks for your help, Luke.'

'Any time. Good luck, buddy.'

Philadelphia, Monday, January 15, 10:15 A.M.

'Oh dear God.' Marilyn Keyes lowered herself to the edge of a faded paisley sofa, every ounce of color drained from her face. 'Oh, Warren.' Pressing one arm to her stomach, she raised a shaking hand to her mouth and rocked herself.

'Then this is your son, ma'am?' Vito asked gently. They'd gotten a hit from the Missing Persons file right away. Their knight was Warren Keyes, age twenty-one. He'd been reported missing by his parents and his fiancée, Sherry, eight days before.

'Yes.' She nodded, her breath shallow. 'That's Warren. That's my son.'

Nick sat next to her. 'Is there someone we can call for you, Mrs Keyes?'

'My husband.' She pressed her fingertips to her temple. 'There's a book . . . in my purse.' She pointed to the dining-room table and Nick went to make the call.

Vito took Nick's place on the sofa. 'Mrs Keyes, I'm so sorry, but we need to ask you some questions. Do you need a glass of water or something?'

She drew a deep breath. 'No. But thank you. Before you ask, Warren has had a drug problem in the past. But he'd been clean and sober for almost two years.'

Vito pulled his notebook from his pocket. It wasn't the question he'd planned to ask, but he'd learned long ago when to go with the flow. 'What kind of drugs, Mrs Keyes?'

'Cocaine and alcohol mostly. He . . . fell in with some bad kids in high school. Started using. But he got clean and since he met Sherry, he's changed.'

'Mrs Keyes, what did Warren do for a living?'

'He's an actor.' She swallowed. 'Was an actor.'

'A lot of actors have second jobs. Did Warren?'

'He waited tables at a bar in Center City. Sometimes he modeled. I can get you his portfolio, if that would help.'

'It might.' He gently caught her arm when she started to rise. 'I have a few more questions. Where did Warren live?'

'Here. He and Sherry . . .' Vito sat quietly as she dropped her face into her hands and wept. 'Who would do this?' she demanded brokenly, her words muffled by her hands. 'Who would kill my son?'

'That's what we're trying to find out, ma'am,' Vito said, still gently. Nick came in from the kitchen, a box of tissues in one hand, a framed photo in the other.

'Mr Keyes is on his way,' he murmured.

Vito pressed a tissue in the woman's hand. 'Mrs Keyes? He and Sherry what?'

She wiped her eyes. 'They were saving up to get married. She's a nice girl.'

'Did you get the idea that Warren was worried or afraid of anyone?' Nick asked.

'He was worried about money. He hadn't had any acting jobs in a long time.' Her lips bent into a painful smile. 'His agent told him if he moved to New York, he could find lots of work, but Sherry's family is here. She wouldn't leave and he wouldn't leave her.'

Nick turned the photo so that it faced Mrs Keyes. 'This is Warren with Sherry?'

New tears flooded her eyes. 'Yes,' she whispered. 'At their engagement party.'

Vito put his notebook back in his pocket. 'We need to go through his room,' Vito said. 'And we'll bring in a finger-printing unit.'

She nodded dully. 'Of course. Anything you need to do.'

He stood, aware that he had no words that would bring her comfort. Before Andrea, he'd have asked if she was all right. But this grieving mother was not all right. She was in pain and would be for some time. When he got to the end of the hall, he looked back. Bowed forward, she clutched the photo of her son to her breast, rocking as she wept.

'Chick,' Nick said softly. 'Come on.'

Vito exhaled. 'I know.' He opened the door to Warren's room. 'Let's get to work.'

They began going through Warren's things. 'Sports equipment,' Nick said from the closet. 'Hockey, baseball.' There was a clunk of metal. 'Lifted some serious weights.'

Vito found Warren's portfolio. 'Handsome guy.' He flipped through the pages of photographs and magazine clippings. 'Looks like he mostly did magazine ads. I've seen this one. It's for a local gym. Keyes was a big, strong guy. I can't imagine he would have been easily overpowered.'

'Chick, look.' Nick had powered up Warren's computer. 'Come and look at this.'

Vito stood behind him, staring at the blank screen. 'What? I don't see anything.'

'That's the point. There's nothing here. When I open his 'My Documents,' nothing. Nothing in his e-mail. Nothing in the recycle bin.' Nick looked up over his shoulder, his brows lifted. 'This computer has been wiped clean.'

Monday, January 15, 12:25 P.M.

'You *sure* Sophie works here?' Nick asked, frowning. He stood next to the front desk of the museum, looking around impatiently. 'I don't think *anybody* works here.'

Vito nodded, his attention on the photographs of the museum's founder on the wall of the lobby. 'Yes, she works here. Her bike was parked at the end of the parking lot.'

'That was Sophie's?'

Vito was a little annoyed at the sudden interest on Nick's face. 'Yeah. So?'

'Just that it's just a nice bike, Chick.' Nick's lips twitched. 'Easy, boy.'

Vito rolled his eyes, but the ringing of his cell saved him from having to reply.

Nick sobered. 'Is that Sherry?' They'd been unsuccessful in contacting Warren Keyes's fiancée after leaving his parents' apartment. She wasn't at her own apartment nor was she due to show up at the factory where she worked until seven.

Vito checked the caller ID and his pulse kicked up a notch. 'No, it's my dad.' He flipped open his phone, praying for good news. 'Dad. How's Molly?'

'Stable. She's got some strength back in her legs and her tremors are less frequent. The doctor's trying to figure out what triggered this attack.'

Vito frowned. 'I thought he said she had a mini-stroke.'

'He's changed his mind. They found high levels of mercury in her system.'

'Mercury?' Vito was sure he'd heard wrong. 'How did she get exposed to mercury?'

'They don't know. They're thinking she was exposed to something in the house.'

His heart skipped a beat. 'What about the kids?'

'They didn't have any symptoms. But he wanted them all to come in for testing, so your mother and Tino brought them in. They were pretty scared, especially Pierce.'

Vito's heart squeezed. 'Poor little guy. How long before we know if they're okay?'

'By tomorrow morning. But the doctor doesn't want any of the boys to go home until they know for sure where Molly got exposed. Dino wanted me to ask you if—'

'For God's sake, Dad,' Vito interrupted. 'You know the kids can stay with me as long as they need to.'

'Well, I told him that, but Molly was worried they were causing you trouble.'

'Tell her they're fine. Last night they made cake and played war in my living room.'

'Tess is coming to help you and Tino take care of them,' his father said and Vito felt a spurt of joy, despite his worry. He hadn't seen his sister in months. 'That way your mother and I can be here for Dino. Tess's flight gets in at seven. She's renting a car so she can get around while she's here, so you don't need to get her at the airport.'

'Is there anything else we can do?'

'No.' Michael Ciccotelli drew a deep breath. 'Except pray, son.'

It had been a long time since he'd done so, but it would hurt his dad to know it. So Vito lied. 'You know I will.' He slipped his phone back in his pocket.

'Will Molly be okay?' Nick asked quietly.

'Don't know. My dad says to pray. In my experience that's never good.'

'Well, if you need to go . . . just go, okay?'

'I will. Look.' Grateful for the diversion of work, Vito pointed to the back wall, where a tall door was opening. A woman appeared and walked toward them. She was petite, in her mid-thirties, and wore a sensible blue suit with a skirt that stopped at her knees. Her dark hair was pulled back in a neat twist, making her look professional and . . . boring, Vito realized. She could use some big hoop earrings and a red bandana. She moved behind the desk, obviously sizing them up.

'Can I help you two gentlemen?' she asked, her accent crisp and British.

Vito showed his badge. 'I'm Detective Ciccotelli and this is my partner, Detective Lawrence. We're here to see Dr Johannsen.'

The woman's eyes took on a speculative light. 'Has she done something wrong?'

Nick shook his head. 'No. May we see her?'

'Now?'

Vito bit his tongue. 'Now would be good.' He looked at her nametag. 'Miss Albright.' Up close Vito realized she was much younger than he'd thought, probably in her early twenties. Apparently his age-guesser needed a tune-up.

The woman pursed her lips. 'She's giving a tour right now. If you'll come this way.'

110

She led them through the tall door into a large room where a small crowd of five or six families had gathered. The walls themselves were dark wood, one covered with a faded tapestry. From the other wall hung large banners. The far wall was the most impressive, however, covered with crisscrossing swords. Below the swords stood three suits of armor, completing a grand effect.

'Sweet,' Vito murmured. 'My nephews would love this.' It would certainly keep their minds off Molly. He decided to bring them here as soon as he could.

'Look.' Nick surreptitiously pointed to a fourth suit of armor, standing toward the right side of the hall. A sour-faced boy about Dante's age stood a foot from the armor, loudly complaining about the wait. He stomped his foot and sneered.

'This is so boring. Crummy suit of armor. I've seen better in a junkyard.' He started to kick at the armor when it abruptly bent at the waist in a clatter of metal. Visibly frightened, the boy scrambled back, his eyes wide and his face pale. The crowd went silent and Nick chuckled softly. 'I saw it move a second ago. Served the brat right.'

Vito was about to agree when a booming voice thundered from inside the armor. It took him a second to realize the knight was speaking French, but it didn't take a linguist to understand the meaning. The knight was royally pissed.

The boy shook his head in fear and took two steps back. The knight drew his sword with dramatic flair and matched the kid step for step. He repeated the question more loudly and Vito realized it was the voice of a woman, not a man. A smile tugged at his mouth. 'That's Sophie in there. She said they made her dress up.'

Nick was grinning. 'My high school French is rusty, but I think she basically said "What is your name, you bad little boy?"'

The boy opened his mouth but no sound emerged.

From a side door a man appeared. The size of a linebacker, he

111

wore a dark blue suit and tie. He was shaking his head. 'Whoa, whoa. What seems to be the problem?'

The figure in the armor regally pointed to the boy and uttered something scathing.

The man looked down at the kid. 'She says you're rude and you're trespassing.'

The kid's face heated in embarrassment as the other children laughed.

The man shook his head. 'Joan, Joan. How many times have I asked you not to scare the children? She's sorry,' he said to the kid.

The knight shook her head emphatically. *'Non.'*

The children's laughter grew louder and all the adults were smiling. The man sighed dramatically. 'Yes, you are. Let's just get on with the tour. *S'il vous plaît.'*

The knight handed the man her sword and lifted the helm from her head, revealing Sophie with her long hair braided in a golden crown around her head. She stuck the helm under one arm and lifted the other to gesture to the walls.

'Bienvenue au musée d'Albright de l'histoire. Je m'appelle Jeanne d'Arc.'

'Joan,' the man interrupted. 'They don't speak French.'

She blinked and stared down at the children who now stared up, mesmerized. Even the rude boy was listening. *'Non?'* she asked, disbelieving.

'No,' the man said and she rattled off another question.

'She wants to know what language you speak,' he told them. 'Who can tell her?'

A little girl of about five with golden curls raised her hand and Vito saw Sophie's jaw tighten, so very slightly that he might have missed it had he not been watching. But she quickly smoothed her expression as the child spoke. 'English. We speak English.'

Sophie grew comically horrified. This was part of her act, but he was certain her expression a moment ago was not and found his curiosity aroused once again. Along with the rest of him. He hadn't realized a woman with a sword would be such a turn on.

'*Anglais*?' Sophie demanded and grabbed her sword in a pretend rage. The little girl's eyes went even wider and the man sighed again.

'Joan, we've been over this before. Don't frighten the guests. When American children come in, you speak English. And no insults this time, please. Just behave.'

Sophie sighed. 'The things I must do,' she said, her words heavily accented. 'But . . . it is a living. Even I, Joan of Arc, must pay my bills.' She looked at the parents. 'You understand bills, do you not? There is the rent and the food.' She shrugged. 'And the cable TV. Essentials of life, *non*?'

The parents were nodding and smiling, and once again Vito found himself intrigued.

She looked down at the children. 'It's just that, well, you see, we are at war with the English. You understand this word *war*, do you not, *petits enfants*?'

The children nodded. 'Why are you at war, Miss of Arc?' one of the fathers asked.

She shot the father a charming smile. '*S'il vous plaît*, call me Joan,' she said. 'Well, it is like this—' It was at that moment she saw Vito and Nick standing off to the side. The smile stayed pasted to her mouth but disappeared from her eyes and Vito felt the frost from half a room away. She looked to the man in the suit and tie. 'Monsieur Albright, we have visitors. Can you help them?'

'What the hell did you do to her, Chick?' Nick muttered.

'I have no idea.' He followed her with his eyes as she rounded the children up and led them to the wall with the banners, starting her tour. 'But I plan to find out.'

The man in the suit approached, smiling. 'I'm Ted Albright. How can I help you?'

'I'm Detective Lawrence and this is Detective Ciccotelli. We'd like to talk to Dr Johannsen as soon as it's possible. When will her tour be completed?'

Albright looked worried. 'Is there some kind of trouble?'

'No,' Nick assured him. 'Nothing like that at all. We're working a case and have some questions for her. History-type questions,' he added.

'Oh.' Albright perked up. 'I can answer them.'

Vito remembered Sophie saying that Albright just played at historian. 'We appreciate it,' he said, 'but we'd really prefer to speak with Dr Johannsen. If the tour will be more than fifteen minutes, we can go have our lunch and come back.'

Albright glanced over to where Sophie was now telling the children about the swords mounted on the wall. 'A tour runs an hour. She should be free after that.'

Nick slipped his shield back in his pocket. 'Then we'll be back. Thank you.'

Chapter Seven

Dutton, Georgia, Monday, January 15, 1:15 P.M.

Daniel sat on his parents' bed. For an hour he'd stared at the floor, telling himself to pull back the floorboard he knew concealed his father's safe. He hadn't checked it yesterday. He didn't want Frank to know about the safe, much less its contents.

He wasn't sure what he'd find inside today. He knew he didn't want to know. But he'd put it off long enough. This was the safe his father thought no one else in the family knew about. Not his wife, and certainly not any of his children.

But Daniel knew. In a family like his, it had paid to be the one to know where the secrets were hidden. And where the guns were kept. His father had many gun cabinets and many safes, but this was his only gun safe. This is where he kept the weapons Daniel suspected had their serial numbers filed off. Certainly they were unregistered.

Arthur's unregistered guns had nothing to do with why they might have gone to Philadelphia or where they went when they got there, but Daniel hadn't been able to find any clues anywhere else he'd looked. So here he sat. *Just do it.*

He pulled away the wood and looked at the safe. He'd found the combination oh-so-cleverly concealed in his father's Rolodex as a birthday of a long-dead aunt. Daniel remembered the aunt and her actual birthday, as it had been close to his own.

He dialed the combination and was rewarded with a click. He was in.

But the guns weren't. The only contents of the safe were a check register and a memory stick for a computer. The check register wasn't from the bank the Vartanians had used for generations. Even before he opened it, Daniel knew what he'd find.

There were a steady progression of withdrawals, all written in his father's hand. Every transaction was written 'to cash' in the amount of five thousand dollars.

It was most certainly blackmail. But Daniel was unsurprised.

He wondered which part of Arthur's past had come back to haunt them all. He wondered what was on the memory stick that his father hadn't wanted anyone else to see. He wondered when the next flight left for Philadelphia.

Monday, January 15, 1:40 P.M.

Sophie ripped at the Velcro that held the armor together. 'Ted, for the third time, I don't know why they want to talk with me,' she snapped. Ted Albright's grandfather was an archeological legend, but somehow not one of those brilliant genes had been passed down to Ted. 'This is a *history museum*. Perhaps they have a *history question*. Can you stop with the third degree and get this off me? It weighs a freaking ton.'

Ted lifted the heavy breastplate over her head. 'They could have asked me.'

Like you'd know Napoleon from Lincoln. Outwardly she gathered her composure and calmly replied. 'Ted, I'll talk to them and see what they want, okay?'

'Okay.' He helped her remove the greaves from her shins and she sat down to yank off the boots that covered her own shoes. Vito 'The Rat' Ciccotelli was waiting outside. That she wanted to see him less than Ted Albright said it all. That they'd seen her in *period garb* made it even worse. It was humiliating.

116

'Next time you schedule a knight tour, make sure Theo is here. That armor really does weigh a ton.' She stood up and stretched. 'And it's hot under there.'

'For someone who claims to love authenticity, you complain a helluva lot,' Ted grumbled. 'Some historian you are.'

Sophie bit back what would have been a nasty retort. 'I'll be back after lunch, Ted.'

'Don't take too long,' he called after her. 'You're a Viking at three.'

'You can take your Viking and . . .' she muttered, then rolled her eyes when she saw Patty Ann leaning across the front desk, flirting shamelessly with the two detectives.

She had to admit they were two fine-looking men. Both tall and broad shouldered, handsome by anyone's standards. With his sandy red hair and earnest face, Nick Lawrence had a country-boy kind of appeal, but Vito Ciccotelli was . . . *Admit it, Sophie. You know you're thinking it.* She let out a weary sigh. *Fine. He's hot, okay? He's hot and he's a rat, just like all the others.*

She stopped next to the desk. 'Gentlemen. How can I help you today?'

Nick flashed her a look of relief. 'Dr Johannsen.'

Patty Ann's look was decidedly more threatening as she arched an overplucked eyebrow. 'They're detectives, Sophie,' she said and Sophie swallowed her sigh. Patty Ann had apparently decided to be British today. The proper blue suit now made more sense. 'Homicide detectives,' she added menacingly. 'They want to *question* you.'

Nick shook his head. 'We'd just like to *talk* with you, Dr Johannsen.'

Because he wasn't a rat, she gave him a smile. 'I was about to get lunch. I can give you thirty minutes.'

Vito held the door open for her. He hadn't said a word, but that probing gaze of his hadn't left her face either. She gave him a glance that she hoped was as menacing as Patty Ann's had been to her. He frowned, so she considered herself successful.

The air outside felt wonderful against her skin. 'If we could make this quick, I'd appreciate it. Ted has another tour scheduled and I have to get dressed.' She stopped at the end of the sidewalk. 'So shoot.'

Vito looked up and down the street. It was midday, and both car and foot traffic was heavy. 'Can we go someplace a bit more private?' The frown on his face had made it into his voice. 'We don't want to be overheard.'

'How about my car?' Nick asked smoothly and led the way, then held open the front passenger door. 'Wouldn't want anyone to get the wrong idea by making you sit in the back,' he said with an easy smile, then quickly slid in the back seat. She watched Vito aim a dirty glare Nick's way before taking the driver's seat next to her. Nick simply raised a brow in response and Sophie knew she was being manipulated.

Annoyed, she grabbed the door handle. 'Gentlemen, I don't have time for games.'

Vito clasped her shoulder, his hand gentle but firm as he held her in place. 'This is no game,' he said grimly. 'Please, Sophie.'

Reluctantly she let go of the handle and Vito let go of her. 'What's this about?'

'First of all, we wanted to thank you for your help yesterday,' Nick said. 'But studying the bodies we've recovered so far has raised more questions.' He leaned one shoulder against the back of the driver's seat and dropped his voice. 'We found a strange pattern of punctures on one of our victims. Katherine believes they were caused by nails or some kind of sharp spikes. The punctures start at the neck and stretch down the back of her body to the middle of her calf. There are similar punctures down the back of her arms. We think the victim was forced to sit on a chair of nails.'

She shook her head in reflexive denial. 'You're joking, right? Please say you're joking.' But the memory of the dead man's face, posed hands, and disemboweled body pushed the denial from her mind. 'You're serious.'

Vito nodded once. 'Very.'

A shiver shook her. 'The inquisitional chair,' she said quietly.

'Nick found a photo on a museum website,' Vito said. 'So the chairs did exist.'

She nodded, her imagination painting horrific pictures. 'Oh yes, they existed.'

'Tell us about them,' Vito said. 'Please.'

She drew a deep breath, hoping her stomach would calm. 'Let's see . . . Well, first, the chair was one of many tools used by inquisitors.'

'Nobody expects the Spanish Inquisition,' Nick murmured grimly.

'The Spanish Inquisition is the one that most people are familiar with, but there were several inquisitions.' It was easier to lecture than to think about the victims. 'The first was the Medieval Inquisition. The chair existed during the later Spanish period and may have existed in the Medieval, but its use is a topic of debate among historians. If it was used, it wasn't used as often as most of the other torture methods or devices.'

Nick looked up from the notes he'd been scratching in his notebook. 'Why not?'

'According to original accounts, the inquisitors got a lot of benefit just by showing the chair to the accused. It's a terrifying sight, more terrifying in person than the picture.'

'You've seen one?' Nick asked.

'Where?' Vito added when she nodded.

'In museums. There are several in Europe with good examples.'

'So, where would someone get an inquisitional chair today?' Vito pressed.

'It wouldn't be that hard to make a simple one, if someone really wanted to. Of course there were more sophisticated models, even in the Middle Ages. Most of the chairs had simple restraints, but some had cranks that could tighten the restraints, forcing the nails deeper. And . . .' She sighed. 'Some had metal sheeting that could be heated, burning the accused's skin as well as puncturing it.' Vito and Nick exchanged a look and she lifted her hand to her mouth, horrified. 'No.'

'Where would someone get such a chair?' Vito repeated. 'Please, Sophie.'

The reality of their request began to sink in and a sense of panic began to crowd the horror. They were depending on her knowledge to find a killer and suddenly she felt totally inadequate. 'Look, guys, my specialty is medieval fortifications and strategic warfare. My knowledge of inquisitional hardware is very basic at best. Why don't I call an expert? Dr Fournier at the Sorbonne is world renowned.'

Both men shook their heads. 'Maybe,' Vito said, 'if we absolutely have to, but we want to keep this limited to as few people as possible. Your basic knowledge may be enough for now.' He fixed his eyes on hers, and the tumult inside her began to calm. 'Just tell us what you know.'

She nodded, forcing her brain to think beyond the rote knowledge they could get off any website. She pressed her fingers to her temples. 'Okay. Let me think. He either made his instruments, or he obtained them already made. If they were already made, they could be crude copies all the way up to original artifacts. What are you thinking?'

'We don't know,' Nick said. 'Keep talking.'

'How even was the pattern of nail punctures?'

'Damn even,' Vito said grimly.

'So he's careful. If he made them, he'd pay attention to detail. Maybe he'd want drawings or even blueprints.'

Nick looked as revolted as she felt. 'There are blueprints?'

Vito leaned forward, his brows crunched. 'Where would he get these blueprints?'

He was so close that the scent of his aftershave tickled her nose and she could see the thick black lashes that rimmed his eyes. Then his eyes narrowed, his gaze growing more intense and she realized she'd leaned toward him, drawn like a moth to a flame. Embarrassed and disgusted with herself, she jerked backward, putting more space between them. 'You said to keep talking. I never promised to say anything worthwhile.'

'I'm sorry,' Vito murmured, leaning back. 'Where would he find blueprints?'

Sophie made herself breathe. 'On the Internet, maybe. I've never looked. The museums with the chairs might have documented the design somehow. Or . . . I suppose he could have used the old texts. There are a few journals kept by inquisitors. They might have drawings. He'd need access to the old texts, though.'

'And he'd get this access how?' Nick asked.

'Rare book collections. And he'd have to be able to read them. Most were written in medieval Latin. A few in Old French or Occitan.'

Nick noted them on his pad. 'You can read these languages?'

'Yes, of course.'

'Of course,' Nick muttered.

Vito still watched her, more intensely than before. 'And if he bought them?'

'If he bought them, he either bought copies or real artifacts. You see copies of armor and other weapons for sale on re-creationist websites all the time. Medieval festivals often have booths where weapons of varying quality are sold. Some are handmade and others are mass manufactured, but all are copies.'

'What kind of weapons?' Nick asked.

'Daggers, swords. Flails and axes. But I've never seen torture weapons sold. Now if they were authentic artifacts . . .' She shrugged. 'You'd be talking private collectors.'

Nick nodded. 'What do you know about them?'

'Like with everything else there are good and bad ones. Legitimate collectors purchase their artifacts privately from other collectors or from auction houses like Christie's. Sometimes 'new' old stuff appears on the legitimate market, but that's rare.'

'Like?' Nick prompted.

'Like the Dordogne swords. In 1977, six fifteenth-century

swords that had been previously unknown came up for auction at Christie's. Turns out they came from a rare find – eighty fifteenth-century swords were discovered at the bottom of the Dordogne River in France in the mid-1970s. They'd been on a barge headed for troops fighting the Hundred Years' War. The barge sank and the swords lay buried for five hundred years. But that kind of find is very rare. Normally, catalogued artifacts change hands. Most of our exhibits come from the private collection of Theodore Albright the First.'

Nick frowned. 'The father of the guy we talked to in there?'

'Grandfather. Ted the First was one of the more famous archeologists of the twentieth century. He got a lot of his items from other collectors, but . . .' She lifted a shoulder. 'Ted the First was digging in the teens and early twenties. Nobody knows for sure, but I'd bet some of the items in his collection are artifacts he uncovered on his digs. If it could be proven, the Albrights might be forced to give them back.'

Nick nodded again. 'So he wasn't always a legitimate collector.'

'No, Albright the First was a good guy. See, that's how it was done back then. You came, you saw, you dug, you carted home your loot. Reality is, museums have artifacts because someone brought them home . . . back then.'

'And now?' Nick prodded.

'Today, most governments have seriously cracked down on artifacts being removed from their countries. It's considered theft and they prosecute.'

'So now they go through the black market,' Vito said.

'There's always been a black market. It's just that the prices have been going up since the crackdowns started. I've heard of private collectors buying art and pottery and documents. Roman mosaic floors, even. But not instruments of torture.'

'But it could be happening,' Vito pushed.

'Of course it could. I don't travel in those circles, so I wouldn't know.' She thought about some of the shadier archeologists she'd known. 'But I could ask around.'

Vito shook his head. 'We'll ask the questions,' he said firmly, then lifted his hand when she lifted her chin with a jerk. 'It's procedure, Sophie,' he sighed wearily, 'just like not telling you about the graves yesterday before you found them.'

'But that was to prevent bias,' she pointed out. 'I know the details now.'

'This is to prevent harm,' Vito returned. 'To you. This isn't some academic project for a thesis. This is a multiple homicide in which the killer dug seven extra graves. I don't want to see you in one of them.'

Sophie shuddered out a breath. 'Good point. I'll make you a list.'

One corner of Vito's mouth lifted and his dark eyes warmed. 'Thank you.'

She found herself smiling back before she realized that once again he'd reeled her in like a fish on a hook. *I'm as gullible as a trout.* Wiping the smile from her face, she dropped her eyes to her watch. 'I really need to go.'

She got out of the car, then stuck her head in the open door. Vito was watching her again, his eyes slightly narrowed and . . . hurt. Her heart pricked, but she hardened it. Deliberately she turned to Nick. 'I'll e-mail you a list of any sources I can come up with. Good luck.' She was halfway to the museum's front door when she heard a car door slam, then Vito calling her name. She kept walking, hoping he'd take the hint and leave her alone, but his footsteps grew louder as he closed the distance between them.

'Sophie. Wait.' He gripped her arm and pulled until she stopped.

'What more do you want, Detective?'

He tugged on her arm. 'I want you to turn around and look at me.'

She complied. His face was inches away, his brows furrowed in a confused frown. From the corner of her eye she saw Nick leaning against his car wearing a similar look of confusion and she felt a spurt of indecision, but the words on the card she'd

123

found with the roses echoed in her mind. *A – I'll always love you. V.* 'Let go of my arm.' He released her but didn't move back, so she did. 'What do you want from me, Detective?'

'What happened? Last night we were talking and you were smiling, then I asked if you wanted to get a pizza and you got mad. I want to understand why.'

'Maybe I just didn't want to have dinner with you.'

'No. If looks could have killed, I would have dropped dead on the spot. I'd like to know why. And I'd like to know why I'm Detective now when I was Vito last night.'

She huffed a flat laugh. He sounded so victimized. 'You guys really are all the same, aren't you? Look, *Vito*, I'm sorry your ego got bruised, but it's time you learned that not all women are going to fall at your feet. I'll get you the information, as quickly as I can. But not because of you, so get that straight now.' She took a step, then stopped. He was still standing there, his dark eyes snapping with anger and suddenly the questions she'd asked herself too many times demanded answers.

'Tell me, *Vito*. When you're on the make, do you *think* about the woman at home?'

'What are you talking about?' he asked, each word deliberately spaced.

'Then I guess the answer is no. What about the target? Do you think she's stupid, that she'll never find out that she's only a conquest? Do you think the woman at home will never find out that she's being betrayed?'

'I don't know where you get your information, but *I have no woman at home.*'

She stomped her foot. 'The 'woman at home' is a *metaphor*. It means you're *taken.*'

His expression didn't change. 'I have no one, Sophie.'

She held his gaze. 'So those roses in your truck . . . weren't yours?'

His eyes flickered. He opened his mouth, but this time no words emerged.

She smiled, but not nicely. Turning on her heel, she walked

124

the rest of the way to the museum without interruption. But when she got to the door she saw his reflection in the window. He stood where she'd left him, watching her go. Just like the night before.

Monday, January 15, 2:15 P.M.

Vito slumped in the passenger seat, ignoring Nick's curious stare. 'Just drive.'

Nick pulled away from the curb into traffic. 'Where to?'

'Let's go to the morgue. Jen should have sent a few more in by now.'

'Happy, happy, joy, joy,' Nick muttered. He was silent for several minutes as Vito stared out the window, thinking about knights and torture . . . and roses.

'We could contact another professor,' Nick finally said quietly. 'Other universities have archeology programs. I checked it out on the Web last night.'

'You checked lots of stuff on the Web last night,' Vito returned, and even he could hear the animosity in his voice. 'Sorry.'

'It's okay. The house is too quiet,' Nick murmured. 'I always hated the way Josie would stay up all night with her music blaring, but now that she's gone . . . I miss it.'

Vito turned only his head to study his partner. 'Do you miss her?'

'I know she cheated, and I know it makes me a fool. But yeah. I miss her.'

It was an open door, Vito knew. Nick didn't like talking about his private life. That he'd been duped by his ex-wife for so long was an especially sore spot. But he'd opened the door so that Vito could talk.

'She saw the roses.'

Nick winced. 'Sheee-it.'

'Yeah. That about sums it up.'

'Did you tell her who the roses were for?'

'That would have been too logical.' Vito huffed a disgusted sigh. 'No, I didn't. I couldn't. So she thought the worst. I guess it just wasn't meant to be.'

'What a crock of bullshit. Vito, do you like her?'

'Don't you?'

'Well, yeah, of course. Even if she does speak Occitan, whatever the hell that is. She's funny and cute and . . .' He shrugged with a rueful grin.

'Hot,' Vito supplied morosely.

'That 'bout sums it up. But more importantly, she might be able to help us with this case.' He glanced over, serious again. 'So even if you don't want to explore her personally, tell her the truth so we can use her "basic knowledge."'

'I don't want to tell her the truth.' *I don't want to tell anybody the truth.*

'Then make up a damn good lie, because if we end up having to pay another expert, Liz'll want to know why. And I'm not taking your whoopin', Chick.'

Vito gritted his teeth. Of course Nick was right. A free resource was too valuable to let get away for personal reasons. 'Fine. I'll stop by the museum tomorrow.'

'Better do it tonight. I've got to go to court tomorrow, so you'll be on your own.'

Vito blinked in surprise. 'Did I know about this?'

'I told you twice and sent you a memo. You've been distracted this week.'

By Andrea. Vito blew out a breath. 'I'm sorry. So why are you in court?'

Nick's jaw tightened. 'Diane Siever.'

Vito winced. Diane had been a thirteen-year-old Delaware girl who'd gone missing three years before. Nick had been the unlucky cop to stumble across her body during a raid on a heroin ring when he'd still been Vice. 'Do you still get cards from her folks?'

Nick swallowed hard. 'Every damn Christmas. I wish they weren't so grateful.'

'You gave her parents closure. At least they know. I can't imagine not knowing.'

'I can't imagine sitting in a courtroom watching the sorry asshole that murdered your daughter strutting up to the stand like a damn peacock.' Nick's knuckles whitened as he gripped the wheel. 'Damn DA deals. Every time I think they're on our side, they go and deal a murderer. Makes me sick.'

The 'sorry asshole,' a junkie with track marks on his track marks, had rolled on his partner, an up-and-coming local drug lord. The DA had wanted the drug lord more than the junkie and had dealt him down. 'Which DA made the deal?'

'Lopez.' Nick nearly spat the name.

Vito frowned. 'Maggy Lopez? *Our* Maggy Lopez?'

'One and the same.'

Maggy Lopez was a recent addition to Liz Sawyer's homicide team, but every time she drew one of their cases, Nick had let Vito handle the communications. Now that made sense. 'You never said one word about her before.'

Nick just shrugged angrily. 'I shouldn't have this time. Call the lab and see if they got anything on Keyes's computer.'

'Okay.' Vito's call was answered by Jeff Rosenburg. 'You guys have a chance to look at that computer we took from Warren Keyes's residence this morning?'

'Dream on, Chick. We've got a line out the door.' Jeff always said that.

'Can you look? It's important.'

'Important,' Jeff finished with him sarcastically. 'What isn't? Hold on . . .' A minute later he was back. 'You lucked out, Chick.' Jeff always said that, too. 'We got to it, but only because one of the techs is working on a special drive – wiping project.'

'So you're saying Keyes's drive *was* wiped?'

'Not totally. It takes a lot to totally wipe a drive, but enough is gone to make it a challenge. The method was very elegant.' Jeff sounded impressed. 'It was a virus, delivered through your vic's e-mail. But it was timed.'

'Like a sleeper?'

'Just like. The tech is still trying to piece together the code to find out how long the virus stayed hidden before leaping to life and gobbling your vic's files. We'll call you if we come up with anything more.'

Vito snapped his phone shut thoughtfully. 'Wiped,' he said. 'But elegantly.' He told Nick what Jeff had said. 'So we have a sadistic OCD killer who digs graves with military precision, who has a sick medieval obsession, and who is a computer wizard.'

'Or who has access to a computer wizard,' Nick countered. 'Or maybe we're dealing with more than one killer.'

'Could be. Let's see what else Jen's dug up.'

Monday, January 15, 3:00 P.M.

They found Katherine studying x-rays. Vito stood behind her, easily able to see over her head. Andrea had been small like that. There had been times Vito was afraid he'd break her. Sophie Johannsen on the other hand . . . she was just a few inches shorter than he was. When she'd confronted him about the roses, those full lips of hers had been about even with his chin. Physically, it would take a lot to break her, but inside was a vulnerability that touched him. *You really are like all the others.* Someone had hurt her. Deeply. *And she thinks I'm just like them.*

That bothered Vito. Deeply. He needed her to know he wasn't like all the others. Even if only for his own peace of mind.

'Who is this guy?' Nick asked with a frown, snapping Vito's attention back to the x-rays at which he'd been blindly staring. 'Did he push our bodies to the back of the line?'

Vito scanned the skull illuminated on the light board. 'He's not one of ours. No evidence of medieval torture. This guy took a bullet right between the eyes.'

'No medieval wounds and he took a bullet,' Katherine

agreed, 'but this is one of your victims, boys.' She extended one hand. 'Meet victim number one-dash-three.'

'What?' Vito said.

'He's ours?' Nick said at the same time.

'What does one-dash-three mean?' Vito added.

'Yes, he's yours. One-three means he comes from the third grave in the first row. He was young, late teens, early twenties maybe. Cause of death was that bullet to his skull. He's been dead perhaps a year. I'll know more after I run some tests.'

She walked to the counter and grabbed a sheet of paper. On it she'd drawn a four-by-four matrix of rectangles and had made notes in all but three of them. 'This is what you have so far. Seven empty graves, nine occupied ones. Jen's recovered six of the nine bodies. She's in the process of excavating the seventh body in row one, grave four, aka one-four.'

'The fourth row is empty,' Nick murmured. 'Three-one, Caucasian male, midtwenties, blunt trauma to head and torso. Trauma with a jagged object to head and right arm. Right arm nearly severed. Time of death, at least two months ago. Contusions on torso and upper arms, circular in shape, approximately one quarter inch in diameter.' He looked up. 'This is the third body we pulled out last night.'

'Exactly. Three-two is the woman with the folded hands.'

'Sophie told us about the Inquisitional Chair,' Nick said, his voice heavy with disgust. 'Our boy has the deluxe model. Spikes and metal plates for heating.'

Katherine sighed. 'This just gets better all the time. Three-three is your knight.'

'Warren Keyes,' Vito said. 'He was an actor.'

'I thought so. I finished his autopsy, by the way.' She handed Vito the report. 'Cause of death was heart failure brought on by blood loss. His abdominal cavity was empty. There were no injuries to his head, but the bones in his arms and legs were all dislocated. The force was shear, not radial.'

'Meaning they were pulled, not twisted,' Vito said, scanning the report.

'Yes.'

'He was stretched on a rack,' Nick murmured.

'I'd say that's a good guess. He was definitely drugged.'

'His mother said he was clean and sober. He'd been in rehab,' Vito said.

'That's entirely plausible. There was damage to his nasal membranes from the coke. I found a lot more of that white mixture up in his nasal cavity.'

'So was the stuff you found silicone grease?' Nick asked.

'Silicone lubricant, yes. The lab's going to try to narrow it to a brand for you. But there was something mixed with the silicone. Plaster. It had filled his sinus cavity.'

Nick frowned. 'Plaster and lubricant? Why?'

But a memory was poking at the edge of Vito's mind. 'One Halloween when we were kids, our boy scout troop made masks by taking plaster casts of our faces. We used cold cream to make the plaster lift off better. He made death masks of Warren Keyes and the woman with the hands.'

'Then he took the cast over most of their body,' Katherine said. 'But why?'

'It has something to do with medieval effigies.' Vito shook his head. 'He made a tomb, maybe? I don't know. None of this makes sense yet.'

Nick had turned back to Katherine's diagram of the graveyard. 'So what about the elderly male they brought in this morning?'

'Ah. Him.' Katherine tapped the second row from the top. 'The second row had two bodies and two empty graves. The bodies were both elderly, one male, one female.' She lifted a brow. 'The female was bald.'

Vito blinked. 'He shaved her head?' he asked but Katherine shook her head.

'She'd had a mastectomy.'

'He killed a woman with breast cancer?' Nick shook his head. 'Good God almighty. What kind of sick bastard kills an old woman with cancer?'

'The same kind that would torture and mutilate his other victims,' Katherine said. 'But he didn't torture her. She had a broken neck, but no additional injuries. Now the old man, he's a very different story.'

'Of course he would be,' Vito muttered as she put up three new x-rays.

'The old man in plot two-two has a broken jaw, massive trauma to his face and torso. He was beaten badly, by a fist, I'm guessing. The jaw is dislocated and the cheekbones are crushed. This was a vicious attack with lots of power behind it.'

'A big fist,' Vito murmured. 'He's a big guy, our killer. He had to have been to haul Warren Keyes's body around, even if he drugged him.'

'I agree. The man has six broken ribs. These femur injuries were made with something bigger and harder. Both femurs were broken.' She turned around, both brows lifted. 'But the pièce de résistance . . .'

'Shit.' Nick sighed. 'What?'

'His fingertips are gone. Sliced clean off.'

Vito and Nick looked at each other. 'Somebody wanted the old man to stay incognito,' Vito said and Nick nodded.

'So he's probably in the system. Were they sliced before or after death, Katherine?'

'Before.'

'Of course,' Vito muttered. 'Time of death?'

'I'd say two months or more. The bodies of the elderly couple were in a similar stage of decomposition to three-one, the man whose right arm is nearly severed.'

'The one with the circular bruises,' Vito murmured. 'Any idea of what they are?'

'Not yet, but I haven't really looked too hard. One of my techs found the bruises and recorded it in the log.'

Nick rubbed the back of his neck wearily. 'And now we have one-three with a bullet in his head. Decidedly postmodern era.'

'Dead for a year, not a few weeks to a few months like the others,' Vito added. 'This doesn't make any sense at all.'

'Not yet,' Nick agreed. 'We won't be able to make any sense of it until we identify more of the victims. We got lucky on Warren Keyes. Was there anything you could readily see that might identify the others?'

Katherine shook her head.

'Shit,' Nick muttered. 'So, we've got six bodies so far, one identified. Four of the six are young, two old. One actor, one cancer patient, one who might be identified if we'd been able to run his prints.'

'Who the killer really hated,' Vito added. 'And *that* breaks with his profile.'

Nick lifted a brow. 'Keep talkin'.'

'He dug all those graves perfectly, all exactly the same. He's obsessive-compulsive. The third-row vics were tortured, but with tools, not his bare hands. The new guy with the bullet – another tool. The old man's injuries say he really let loose. Rage and passion aren't the MOs of an OCD perp.'

'Personal,' Nick agreed thoughtfully. 'If he knew the old man, chances are good that he knew the old woman, too. But he used his hands on her. Broke her neck.'

'But he didn't beat her up.'

Katherine cleared her throat. 'Boys, this is all fascinating, but I've been on my feet all day and I'd like to get out of here before midnight. So leave.'

'Gee, Ma, we like the morgue,' Nick whined and, chuckling, she shooed him out.

'If you want autopsies – then go. I'll call you later. Now go.'

Chapter Eight

Monday, January 15, 4:05 P.M.

Scowling in the mirror, Sophie scrubbed at the last of the theatrical makeup that stubbornly clung to her cheeks. 'Damn Viking tour,' she muttered. 'Paint me up like a ten-dollar hooker.' The employee washroom door opened and Darla appeared, her face a frown of affectionate exasperation.

'You don't have to scrub so hard, Sophie. You're going to take your skin off.' She retrieved a jar from the vanity under the sink. 'How many times have I told you to use cold cream?' She spread a thick layer on Sophie's face and began to dab gently.

'About a million,' Sophie grumbled, flinching at the slimy coldness on her skin.

'Then why don't you use it?'

'I forget.' It was a childish grouse and Darla smiled.

'Well, stop forgetting. It's almost like you think if you take off your skin that Ted's going to stop telling you to use the makeup. I can tell you right now, he's not going to let it go.' She dabbed while she talked. 'You might know history, Sophie, but Ted knows what sells. Without the tours, this museum might close.'

'And your point would be what, exactly?'

'Sophie.' Darla grabbed her chin and pulled her forward until her back hunched. 'Hold still. Close your eyes.' Sophie did so until Darla let her go. 'You're done.'

Sophie touched her skin. 'Now I'm greasy.'

133

'What you are is impossible, and you have been all day. What's wrong with you?'

A sadistic medieval killer and a handsome cop who makes me drool even though he's a cheating rat. 'Vikings and Joan of Arc,' she said instead. 'Ted hired me to be a curator, but I don't have time to work on exhibits. I'm always doing these damn tours.'

Behind them a toilet flushed and Patty Ann emerged from one of the stalls. 'I think it's a guilty conscience,' she said ominously as she bent down to wash her hands. 'Sophie was questioned by two cops this afternoon. One of them nearly dragged her off to the police car.' She glanced slyly at Sophie from the corner of her eye. 'You must have done some slick talking to make him let you go.'

Darla looked alarmed. 'What's this about the police? Here? At the Albright?'

'They had some history questions, Darla. That was all.'

'What about the dark one?' Patty Ann needled and Sophie wanted to throttle her. 'He chased you back to the museum.'

'He did not chase me,' Sophie said firmly, loosening the ties of her bodice. But Vito had done exactly that and her heart beat harder every time she thought about it. There was something about Vito Ciccotelli that drew her, tempted her, which was shameful in and of itself. She needed to get him the information he'd asked for so that she wouldn't have to see him again. Temptation removed. Case closed.

She changed her clothes and escaped to the little storeroom Ted had given her for an office. It was tiny and filled with boxes, but it had a desk and a computer and a phone. A window would have been nice, but at this stage she was choosing her battles.

She sank down in her old chair and closed her eyes. She was tired. Tossing and turning all night had that effect, she supposed. *Focus, Sophie.* She needed to think about shady archeologists and collectors so she could make that list for Ciccotelli.

She considered the people she'd worked with over the years.

Most were ethical scientists who handled artifacts as carefully as Jen McFain had handled the evidence at the crime scene. But inevitably her thoughts wandered to *him*. Alan Brewster. *The bane of my life.* She'd never paid attention to the rich donors who subsidized their digs, but Alan knew everyone. He would be a good contact for the detectives. Except . . .

Except Alan would ask Vito how he'd gotten his name. Vito would say, 'From Sophie,' and Alan would smile like the lying cheating rat he was. She could hear his voice now, smooth, cultured. 'Sophie,' he'd say. 'A most *able* assistant.' That's what he'd say when they'd . . . finished. She'd actually thought he'd meant it affectionately, that she'd been special to him.

Her cheeks heated as shame and humiliation reasserted themselves, as they did every time she remembered. Little had she known, *then*. She knew a hell of a lot more now.

But guilt sidled up to join the shame. 'You're a coward,' she murmured. Nine people were dead and Alan might be able to help, and she was letting her ego get in the way. She wrote his name on her notepad, but just seeing it in black and white left her cold. He'd tell. He always told. It was part of his fun. He'd tell Nick and Vito and then they'd know, too. *What do you care what they think about you?* But she did. She always did.

'Think of somebody else,' she told herself. 'Somebody just as good.' She thought hard until another face came to mind, but not the man's name. He'd been a fellow grad student working that same dig with Alan Brewster. While she'd been 'assisting' Alan, this guy had been researching stolen antiquities for his dissertation. She ran a search, but found no such dissertation. But the guy had a friend . . . Hell.

His name Sophie remembered. Clint Shafer. With a sigh, she searched the white pages and got a number. Before she could change her mind, Sophie dialed. 'Clint, this is Sophie Johannsen. You might not remember me, but—'

He cut her off with a wolf whistle. 'Sophie. Well, well, how are you?'

'Just fine,' she said. *Nine graves, Sophie.* 'Clint, do you remember that friend of yours who was researching stolen antiquities?'

'You mean Lombard?'

Lombard. Now she remembered. Kyle Lombard. 'Yeah, that's him. Did he ever finish his dissertation?'

'No, Lombard dropped out.' There was a pause, then slyly, 'That was after you left the project. Alan was just-devastated.'

There was laughter in his voice and Sophie's cheeks heated as she bit back what she really wanted to say. 'Have you heard from him?'

'Who? Alan? Sure. We chat often. You come up a lot.'

She bit down harder on her tongue. 'No, I meant Kyle. Where is he now?'

'I don't know. I haven't heard from Kyle since Avignon. He dropped out of the program and I signed up to join Alan's team on that Siberian dig. So, you're in Philly?'

Sophie cursed caller ID. 'Family emergency.'

'Well, I'm up in Long Island, but you knew that already. We could . . . get together.'

One stupid mistake and I'm still paying. She forced a brightness into her voice as she baldly lied. 'I'm sorry, Clint. I'm married now.'

He laughed. 'So? So am I. That never stopped you before.'

Sophie exhaled slowly. Then stopped biting her tongue and let it fly. *'Foutre.'*

Clint laughed again. 'Name the time and the place, sweetheart. Alan still calls you one of his most able assistants. I've waited a long time to evaluate you myself.'

Her hand shaking, Sophie carefully hung up the phone. Then she took the sheet of paper on which she'd written Alan Brewster's name and crumpled it into a tight ball in her tighter fist. There had to be *someone else* the police could contact.

Monday, January 15, 4:45 P.M.

'Here. Don't say I never give you anything.'

Vito looked up when a bag of corn chips landed on the missing persons printout he'd been scanning. Liz Sawyer was leaning against the side of his desk, opening her own bag. He looked over to Nick's empty desk where she'd thrown a second bag of chips. 'Nick got barbeque flavor. I wanted barbeque flavor.'

Liz leaned over and switched the bags. 'God, you're worse than my kids.'

Vito grinned and opened the bag of barbeque chips. 'But you love us anyway.'

She snorted. 'Yeah, right. Where's Nick?'

Vito sobered. 'With the DA. He got called down to be prepped for tomorrow.'

Liz sighed. 'We've all had our Siever cases, unfortunately.' Her eyes narrowed. 'You had one, too. A couple of years ago. Right about this time.'

Vito crunched on his chips, keeping his expression bland, even though his gut clenched. Liz was fishing. He knew she'd known something wasn't right about Andrea's death, but she'd never come out and asked. 'Right about.'

She watched him for another few seconds, then shrugged. 'So bring me up to speed on our mass-grave situation. The story broke on the noon news and the phones down in PR have been ringing off the hooks ever since. Right now we're 'no commenting' like there's no tomorrow, but that won't hold water too much longer.'

Vito told her everything they knew, finishing with their visit to the morgue. 'Now I'm combing through missing persons reports trying to match vics.'

'The girl with the folded hands . . . If Keyes was an actor/model, maybe she is, too.'

'Nick and I thought the same thing. When we're through looking through missing persons, we'll canvas the bars where the actors hang out down by the theater district. Trouble is, the vic's face is too decomposed to show her pictures.'

'Get an artist down to the morgue. Have them look at bone structure and do the best they can.'

Vito munched glumly. 'Tried that. Both artists are with live victims. It'll be days before they're freed up enough to sketch a dead victim.'

'Goddamn budget cuts,' Liz muttered. 'Can you draw?'

He laughed. 'Stick figures with a ruler.' Then sobered, thinking. 'My brother does.'

'I thought your brother was a shrink.'

'That's my sister Tess. Tino's the artist. He specializes in faces.'

'Is he cheap?'

'Yeah, but don't tell my mom. She thinks we're all, you know, saints.' He lifted his brows cagily. 'Candidates for the priesthood even.'

Liz laughed. 'Your secret's safe with me. Has your brother done anything like this?'

His mind came back to Tino. 'No. But he's a good guy. He'll want to help.'

'Then call him. If he's willing, bring him down and sign a release. You're getting pretty good at finding free help these days, Chick. Archeologists, artists . . .'

Vito made himself grin carelessly. 'So what do I get for my trouble?'

Liz reached over and snagged Nick's chips and threw them at him. 'Like I said, don't say I never give you anything.'

New York City, Monday, January 15, 4:55 P.M.

'Derek, I need to talk to you.'

Derek looked up from his laptop screen. Tony England stood in the open door of his office, his jaw clenched and sullen fire in his eyes. Derek leaned back in his chair. 'I was wondering when you'd come. Come in. Close the door.'

'I started for your office at least twenty times today. But I was too angry.' Tony lifted a shoulder. 'I'm too angry now.'

Derek sighed. 'What do you want me to do, Tony?'

'Be a man and tell Jager *no for once*,' he exploded, then looked away. 'I'm sorry.'

'No you're not. You've been with oRo since the beginning. You supervised the fight scenes in the last three games. You expected to take my place someday, not be demoted to work for a newcomer.'

'All that's true. Derek, you and I made a great team. Tell Jager no.'

'I can't.'

Tony's lip curled. 'Because you're afraid he'll fire you?'

Derek let him have that shot. 'No. Because he's right.'

Tony's spine went ramrod straight. 'What?'

'He's right.' He waved at his laptop. 'I've been studying *Enemy Lines* next to everything we did before. *Enemy Lines* is stunning. The work we did on the last project is barely mediocre by comparison. If Frasier Lewis can do it—'

'You sold out,' Tony said dully. 'I never believed you . . .' He lifted his chin. 'I quit.'

It was what Derek expected. 'I understand. If you sleep on it and decide to change your mind, it will be like we never had this conversation.'

'I won't change my mind. And I won't work for Frasier Lewis.'

'Then contact me for a recommendation. For whatever it's worth.'

'Once it would have been worth a great deal,' Tony said bitterly. 'Now . . . I'll take my chances on my own. Enjoy the money, Derek, because once Jager forces you out, it'll be all you have left.'

Derek stared at the door Tony quietly closed behind him. Tony was right. Jager was forcing him out. The signs had been there for weeks, but Derek hadn't wanted to see.

'Derek?' his secretary called through the intercom. 'Lloyd Webber is on line two.'

He was not in the mood to speak to any more reporters. 'Tell him no comment.'

'He's not a reporter. He's a parent and wants to talk to you about *Enemy Lines*.'

Nor was Derek in the mood to listen to any more irate parents who found *Enemy Lines* disturbing and violent. 'Take a message. I'll call him back tomorrow.'

Monday, January 15, 6:00 P.M.

His timing had been good, Vito thought as he watched Sophie exit the Albright Museum. *She looks tired*, he thought as she got closer to her bike.

He stepped around his truck as she unhooked her helmet from her seat. 'Sophie.'

She gasped. 'You scared the hell out of me,' she hissed. 'What are you doing here?'

Vito hesitated, now unsure of the words to say. From behind his back he whisked out a single white rose and watched her eyes narrow.

'Is this a joke?' she said, her voice gone low and hard. 'Because it's not funny.'

'Not a joke. It bothered me that you thought I was just like "all the others." I wanted you to know that I'm not.'

For a moment she said nothing, then shook her head and bungeed her backpack to her seat. 'Okay. Fine. You're a prince,' she said sardonically. 'A really nice guy.' She straddled her bike and tucked her braid under her jacket before pulling the helmet onto her head. 'I would have gotten you the list anyway.'

Vito spun the rose between his fingers nervously. She wore a black leather jacket tonight, and she'd exchanged the rainbow-fingered gloves for leather gloves similar to his own. With her forbidding expression and all that black leather, she looked like

140

a dangerous biker chick, not like the eclectically dressed academic he'd met the day before. She tugged the strap under her chin and stood up to start the bike. She was leaving and he had not accomplished his mission.

'Sophie, wait.'

She paused, poised to kick the engine into gear. 'What?'

'The flowers were for someone else.' Her eyes flickered. She obviously hadn't expected him to own up to it. 'They were for someone I cared for who died. I was going to put them on her grave yesterday, but got tied up in the case. And that's the truth.' As much as he was willing to divulge, anyway.

She frowned slightly. 'Most people put carnations on graves in the winter.'

He shrugged. 'Roses were her favorite.' His throat thickened as a picture of Andrea flashed through his mind, burying her face in a bouquet of roses. Blood red, they'd stood out in marked contrast to her olive skin and black hair. The colors mocked him. Her black hair soaking up her red blood as it flowed from the bullet hole in the side of her head – the hole he'd put there.

Abruptly he cleared his throat. 'Anyway, I was getting flowers for my sister-in-law who's in the hospital and I saw the white roses. They made me think of you.'

She was studying him warily. 'Either you're really good or you're telling the truth.'

'I'm not that good. But I've never cheated in my life, and I didn't want you to think I had.' He laid the rose across her handlebars. 'Thanks for listening.'

She stared down at the flower for a long, long moment, then her shoulders sagged. Tugging off one glove, she pulled a folded sheet of paper and a pen from the pocket of her coat. Unfolding the paper, she wrote something at the bottom, then with a hard swallow handed it to him. 'Here's your list. It's not much.'

There was a defeated look in her eyes that startled him even as it squeezed his heart. There were twenty typed names, some with websites. She'd written one more name at the bottom. 'This seems like more than not much,' he said.

She shrugged. 'The top eighteen keep booths at the Medieval Festival that takes place every fall. They sell swords and chain mail and such. Most also sell their goods on the Net. If anyone's been asking questions about torture devices, they might have tried one of these guys first.'

'And the others?'

'Etienne Moraux is my old professor at the university in Paris. I did my graduate research under him. He's a good man, well connected in the archeological world. If someone's found a chair recently, he'll know. If one's been sold or gone missing from any museums or legitimate private collections, he'll know that, too. As for his knowledge of the black market, I doubt it, but you never know if he's heard rumors.'

'And Kyle Lombard?'

'He's a long shot. I don't even know where he is. But ten years ago he was working on his dissertation while we were on a dig in southern France. He was investigating stolen artifacts. He never finished his dissertation, and I couldn't find him in any of the alumni lists, but you have your spy-guy ways.'

'And our memory-zapping guns,' he said, hoping to coax a smile to her lips. Instead, her eyes filled with a sadness that shook him. But she didn't look away.

'Sometimes I think that would be a very useful thing to have,' she murmured.

'I agree. What about this last name? Alan Brewster.'

For a moment her eyes flashed with a rage so intense he nearly stepped back. But it was gone as suddenly as it had come, her anger seeming to fizzle, leaving her looking weary and defeated once again. 'Alan's one of the top archeologists in the Northeast,' she said quietly, 'well connected with wealthy donors that make a lot of digs possible, here and in Europe. If somebody's been buying, he might know.'

'Do you know where I can find him?'

She broke the stem off the rose, then with care pocketed the bloom. 'He's the chair of medieval studies at Shelton College. It's in New Jersey, not too far from Princeton.' She stared at the ground, hesitating. When she looked back up, her eyes were filled with despair and grim acceptance. 'If you could not mention my name, I'd appreciate it.'

So she and Brewster had some bad history. 'How do you know him, Sophie?'

Her cheeks reddened and Vito felt a spurt of jealousy, irrational but undeniable. 'He was my graduate advisor.'

He swallowed the jealousy back. Whatever had happened, it still caused her pain. He made his voice gentle. 'I thought you did your graduate degree under Moraux.'

'I did, later.' The despair in her eyes gave way to a quiet yearning that made him ache. 'You have what you came for, Detective. Now I need to go.'

He had what he'd come for, but not everything he needed. From the look in her eyes, she needed it, too. Quickly he folded the paper and shoved it in his pocket as she tugged her glove back on. 'Sophie, wait. There is one more thing.' Before he could change his mind he straddled her front tire, slipped his hands around her helmet, and covered her mouth with his.

She stiffened, then her hands came up to circle his wrists. But she didn't pull his hands away and for a few precious moments they both took what they needed. She was sweet, her lips soft under his and the scent of her lit a fire in his blood. He needed more. He fumbled with the strap under her chin and managed to jerk it free. Without breaking contact, he pushed the helmet from her head, dropped it on the ground behind him, then tunneled his fingers through the hair at her nape. He'd pulled her closer, perfecting the fit of his lips on hers when she surged into motion and the kiss suddenly changed from slow and sweet to reckless and urgent.

Bracing her hands on his shoulders, she lifted on her toes and ate at his mouth with hot, greedy little bites, a hungry whimper rising from her throat. He'd been right. The thought pushed

143

through the heat as he urged her lips apart and took the kiss deeper. She'd needed this as much as he had. Maybe more.

Her fingers were clenched in the shoulders of his coat and his heart was pounding so hard it was all he could hear. Vito knew this hadn't begun to satisfy what he needed. What he really needed wasn't going to happen standing over her bike in a parking lot. He left the warmth of her mouth, brushing his lips along her jaw, pressing against the underside where her pulse beat hard and fast.

Vito pulled away just far enough to search her face. Her eyes were wide, and in them he saw hunger and need and uncertainty, but no regret. Slowly she lowered to her heels, running her hands along his arms until she reached his wrists. She pulled his hands from her hair, then closed her eyes as she clutched his hands in hers for several beats of his heart. Then carefully she released him and opened her eyes. The look of despair had returned, stronger now, and he knew she'd walk away from him.

'Sophie,' he started, his voice harsh and gravelly. She put her fingers over his lips.

'I need to go,' she whispered, then cleared her throat. 'Please.'

He reached for the helmet he'd dropped on the ground and watched as she strapped it under her chin once again. He didn't want her to leave like this. He didn't want her to leave at all. 'Sophie, wait. I still owe you a pizza.'

She flashed him a forced smile. 'Can't. I've got to visit my grandmother.'

'Tomorrow, then?' and she shook her head.

'I teach a graduate seminar at Whitman on Tuesdays.' She lifted her hand, stopping him before he pressed further. 'Please don't. Vito, yesterday when I met you I was hoping you'd be decent and I was so upset when I thought you weren't. I'm truly glad you are. So . . .' She shook her head, regret now in her eyes. 'So good luck.'

She stood up, kicked the bike into gear and was out of the lot in a roar. As he watched her go, he realized it was the third time in two days he'd done so.

Monday, January 15, 6:45 P.M.

Sophie sat back with a frustrated sigh. 'Gran, you have to eat. The doctor says you'll never get out of here if you don't get your strength back.'

Her grandmother glared at the plate. 'I wouldn't feed that to my dogs.'

'You feed filet to your dogs, Gran,' Sophie said. 'I wish *I* ate as well.'

'They only get filet once a year.' Her chin lifted. 'On their birthday.'

Sophie rolled her eyes. 'Oh, well, as long as it's a special occasion.' She sighed again. 'Gran, please eat. I want you strong enough to come home.'

The defiant spark faded from Anna's eyes, her thin shoulders slumping back against her pillow. 'I'm never going home, Sophie. Maybe it's time we both accepted that.'

Sophie's chest hurt. Her grandmother had always been the picture of health, but the stroke had left her frail and unable to use the right side of her body, and her speech was still too slurred to be understood by strangers. A recent bout of pneumonia had robbed her of even more strength and made every breath she drew painful.

The world had once been Anna's stage – Paris, London, Milan. Opera fans flocked to hear her *Orfeo*. Now Anna's world was this small room in a nursing home.

Still, the last thing Anna needed was pity so Sophie hardened her voice. 'Bullshit.'

Anna's eyes flew open. 'Sophie!'

'Like you haven't said that word a hundred times.' *A day*, she added to herself.

Twin spots of color darkened Anna's pale cheeks. 'Still,' she grumbled, then dropped her eyes back to the plate. 'Sophie, this food is vile. It's worse than usual.' She lifted her left brow, the only one she could lift anymore. 'Try it yourself.'

Sophie did, then grimaced. 'You're right. Wait here.' She went to the door and saw one of the nurses at the station. 'Nurse Marco? Did you get a new dietitian?'

The nurse looked up from her clipboard, her expression guarded. 'Yes. Why?'

Most of the nursing home staff were wonderful. Nurse Marco, however, was a grouch. To say that she and Anna did not get along was putting it mildly, so Sophie tried to ensure her visits coincided with Marco's shifts. Just to keep things civilized. 'Because this food tastes really bad. Could you possibly get Anna something else?'

Marco pursed her lips. 'She's on a controlled diet, Dr Johannsen.'

'Which she will follow, I promise.' Sophie smiled as engagingly as she could. 'I wouldn't ask if it weren't really bad. Please?'

Marco's sigh was long-suffering. 'Very well. It will be a half hour or so.'

Sophie came back to sit at Anna's bedside. 'Marco will bring you a new dinner.'

'She's mean,' Anna murmured, closing her eyes.

Sophie frowned. Her grandmother said things like that increasingly often these days and Sophie was never completely sure what she should believe. Likely it was petulance brought on by the frustration of being helpless and in pain, but she always worried there could be something more.

Sophie seemed worried most of the time these days – about Anna, about bills, about the career she hoped she could some-day reclaim. And today she'd added a new worry – what Vito Ciccotelli would think about her once he met Alan Brewster.

She touched her lips with her fingertips and let herself remember that kiss. Her heart started pounding all over again. She'd wanted more, so much more. And for just a moment, she'd let herself hope that just this once, she could have it.

What a fool you are. She'd finally met a really nice man who might have been everything she wanted – and she'd sent him to the one man who was most likely to paint her as a cheap sex-crazed slut with no moral compass. *Maybe he won't believe Alan.* Hah. Men always believed Alan, because on some level they wanted to believe she was cheap, that she'd fall into bed with anyone who asked.

Nine graves, Sophie. You did the right thing. But why did the right thing always suck so much? With a sigh she settled in her chair and watched Anna sleep.

Monday, January 15, 6:50 P.M.

'So how did your prep with the DA go?' Vito asked as he got into Nick's sedan. They'd met outside the factory where Warren Keyes's fiancée Sherry worked.

'Okay.' Nick tossed him a sub. 'Lopez thinks she can nail the drug dealer.'

'Then there'll be some justice,' Vito said, unwrapping the sandwich. The aroma of meatballs filled the car. 'Some justice is a hell of a lot better than none.'

Nick's shrug said he didn't agree, but wouldn't argue. 'What'd I miss?'

'I went through the missing-persons printouts. Highlighted anyone vaguely matching our vics. Got approval from Liz to bring in an artist to give us something to show.'

Nick whistled. 'She gave you money?'

'Hell, no. I got Tino.'

Nick looked impressed. 'Good thinking.'

'He should be meeting Katherine at the morgue any time now. Then I stopped by the hospital to see Molly. She's doing better.'

'You have been busy. They figure out where Molly got the mercury?'

'Yeah. The state's environmental people found their gas meter had been broken.'

147

'They still make meters with mercury?'

'No, but Dino's house is old and the meter's the old style. Pop said they told him the utility companies have been replacing them, but they hadn't gotten to Dino's neighborhood yet. They found mercury in the mud under the meter.'

'But meters don't just break.'

'They think it was hit by a ball or a rock or something. Pop asked the boys, but none of them knew anything about it. Molly said last Friday the dog came in covered in mud. She bathed him and that's how she came into contact with the mercury. The vet tested the dog and found low levels, but not enough to hurt him. But after she bathed the dog, Molly vacuumed, which sent mercury through the house. They've got to replace all the carpet before they can live there again, so I'll have company for quite a while.'

'Well, I'm glad she's all right. That's the important thing.'

Vito drew Sophie's list from his pocket. 'And . . .' He sighed. 'I went to see Sophie.'

'You really *were* busy.' He scanned the sheet. 'Sellers of medieval novelties, chain mail . . .' He looked up, a light in his eyes. 'The circular bruises on the guy missing half his head. He could have been wearing chain mail.'

Vito nodded. 'You're right. The bruises would be just about that size. Good job.'

'Professor in France,' Nick continued. 'Long-shot Lombard, whereabouts unknown. And Alan Brewster. Why is his name handwritten in?'

'She gave me that one at the last minute. I think there's some bad history there.'

Nick glanced up briefly. 'No pun intended.'

Vito rolled his eyes. 'No. I considered phoning him at home, but thought we might want to visit him in person.'

Nick considered it. 'This guy hurt Sophie, huh?'

'Seems like it. She didn't want me to mention her name.'

'What made her change her mind?'

'I told her the truth. Some of it anyway,' he clarified when

148

Nick's brow went up. He thought about the way she'd so carefully pocketed the rose, and remembered the kiss, which still filled his mind. 'She believed me. Then she gave me the list and added Brewster's name.'

'You're gonna go tomorrow?'

Vito nodded. 'I told Tino to focus on the woman with the folded hands. I want to take whatever he comes up with to the actors that hang around the theaters, but they won't start gathering until late afternoon. I'll have time to visit Brewster in the morning. He may be able to point us in the right direction. If we can find where they're getting the devices, we can follow the money trail.'

'Well, when we're done here I'll go back to the office and run a list of Kyle Lombards. I might as well try to track him down tomorrow while I'm waiting to testify.' Nick straightened abruptly. 'There she is. Sherry Devlin.' He pointed to a young woman getting out of a rusted Chevette. 'She looks beat. I wonder where she's been.'

Vito took Sophie's list back, folded and pocketed it. 'Let's go find out,' he said and the two of them got out of Nick's car and approached Sherry Devlin. 'Miss Devlin?'

She spun to face them, her face freezing in fear.

'Relax,' Vito said. 'We're detectives, Philly PD. We're not going to hurt you.'

She looked from Vito to Nick, her eyes still a little wild. 'Is this about Warren?'

'Where have you been all day, Miss Devlin?' Nick asked, in lieu of an answer.

Sherry's chin lifted. 'In New York. I thought maybe Warren had gone up there to look for work. I figured if the police wouldn't help me look, I'd search for him myself.'

'And did you find anything?' Vito asked gently and she shook her head.

'No. None of the agencies he'd worked for in the past had heard from him in a long time.' There was a tension to her posture that told Vito she knew why they'd come.

'Miss Devlin, I'm Detective Ciccotelli. This is my partner, Detective Lawrence. We have some bad news for you.'

The color drained from her face. 'No.'

'We found Warren's body, Miss Devlin,' Nick said gently. 'We're so sorry.'

'I knew something terrible had happened to him.' She lifted her eyes, numb with grief. 'They said he'd run away, but I knew he'd never leave me. Not voluntarily.'

'Leave your car here. We'll take you home.' He helped her sit in the back seat, then crouched next to her. 'How did you know where to look in New York?'

She blinked slowly. 'From Warren's portfolio.'

'We looked at his portfolio, Miss Devlin,' Nick said, 'We didn't see a list of modeling agencies, just photos.'

'That's his photofolio,' she murmured. 'His résumé is online.'

Vito felt an electric current zip down his spine. 'Where online?'

'At UCanModel dotcom. He had an account there.'

'What kind of account?' Nick asked.

She looked confused. 'For models. They upload their photos and credits, and people who want to hire them can contact them through the site.'

Vito glanced over at Nick. *Bingo.* 'Did Warren ever use your computer?'

'Sure. He was at my place more than he was at his folks'.'

Vito squeezed her hand. 'We're going to want to take your computer into our lab.'

'Of course,' she murmured. 'Anything you need.'

Monday, January 15, 8:15 P.M.

'Sophie, wake up.'

Sophie blinked and focused on Harry's face. She'd fallen asleep in the chair next to Anna's bed. 'What are you doing here?' Then she winced when she remembered. 'Lou's for cheesesteak. I forgot. Dang, and I'm hungry, too.'

'I brought you one. It's out in my car.'

'I'm sorry I stood you up. I had a long day.' She studied Anna's sleeping face. 'Marco must have given her her meds. She's out for the night, so I might as well go.'

'Then come eat your sandwich and tell me about your long day.'

In his car, Sophie stared up at the nursing home while she ate. 'Gran keeps saying that this one nurse is mean to her. Does she say that to Freya?'

'Freya hasn't mentioned it.' Harry frowned. 'Do you think Anna's being abused?'

'Don't know. I hate having to leave her here at night.'

'We have to, unless we get a private nurse and that's expensive. I checked into it.'

'I did, too. But I can barely afford this place, and Alex's money will be gone soon.'

Harry's jaw tightened. 'You shouldn't be using your inheritance for Anna's care.'

She smiled at him. 'Why not? What else would I use it on? Harry, everything I own fits in this backpack.' She nudged it with her toe. 'That's the way I like it.'

'I think that's what you tell yourself. Alex should have provided for you better.'

'Alex provided for me just fine.' Harry always thought her biological father should have done more. 'He paid for my university so that I could provide for myself. Not that I seem to be doing very well with that.' She scowled. '*S'il vous plaît.*'

'Let me guess. You were Joan again today.'

'Yeah,' she said glumly. 'And the only thing worse than being Joan is having somebody I know see me that way.' She'd felt embarrassed when Vito and Nick had seen her in her costume. Of course, she'd be more embarrassed when Vito found out what kind of person she'd been. Alan would be sure to give him an earful.

'I think you make a cute Joan,' Harry said. 'But who saw you?'

'Just this guy. It's nothing.' No, it hadn't been nothing. It had been incredible. She shrugged. 'I thought he was a cheater, but it turns out he's a really nice guy.'

'Then what's the problem, Sophie?' Harry asked gently.

'The problem is that he's about to meet Alan Brewster.'

Harry's eyes flashed dark. 'I'd hoped I'd never hear that name again.'

'Me, too. But we don't get everything we want, do we? I have no doubt that within an hour after talking to Alan that Vito will think I'm trashy, and worse, hypocritical trash because I yelled at him for cheating on a girlfriend he doesn't even have.'

'If he's really a nice man he won't listen to the vile gossip of a snake like Brewster.'

'I hear you, Uncle Harry. I just know better. Men hear about Brewster and I become a different person. I can't seem to make people back here forget.'

Harry looked sad. 'You'll go back to Europe when Anna dies, won't you?'

'I don't know. Maybe. But I don't think I can stay around Philly. Funny thing is, it happened over there, but it's here that the story won't die. Alan and his wife won't let it because I had to be a freakin' hero and try to do the right thing. Confess to the wife. *Merde*. Freakin' idiot is more like it,' she muttered. 'Confession is not good for the soul and there's a damn good reason the wife's always the last to know.'

'Sophie, that's the first time you didn't tell me Anna wasn't going to die.'

Sophie went still. 'I'm sorry. Of course she'll—'

'Sophie.' His admonishment held affection. 'Anna's led one hell of a life. Don't feel guilty because you believe she won't hold on. Or that you'll get your life back once she passes. You gave up a lot to come home. She appreciates that. So do I.'

She swallowed hard. 'How could I have done anything else, Harry?'

'You couldn't have.' He patted her knee. 'You done with your sandwich? Because I have to get rid of the evidence. Freya can't know I went to Lou's. It's not on my diet.'

'She'll smell the onions. I'm sorry, Harry. You're busted.'

'Well, it was worth it. I'll just drive with the windows open on the way home.' He rolled down his window as Sophie gathered her backpack and the trash and got out.

'I'll dispose of the evidence,' she said in a loud whisper. 'See you around, Harry.'

'Sophie, wait.' She turned around and leaned in his window. His face was serious. 'If this Vito is a good man, nothing Brewster says would make him disrespect you.'

She kissed his cheek. 'You're so sweet. Naïve, but sweet.'

He frowned. 'I'm just afraid the right man will come along and you'll be so sure he's going to think the worst that you don't give him an opportunity. I don't want to see you miss your chance, Sophie. I'm not sure how many we get to waste.'

Chapter Nine

Monday, January 15, 9:00 P.M.

'There he is.' Vito studied the photo of Warren Keyes on UCanModel dotcom. He'd logged onto Warren's account from his own PPD computer using the user name and password supplied by Sherry Devlin. Sherry's computer sat in a box on Nick's desk. One of Jeff's computer techs would be coming in to check it out within the hour.

'Spotty résumé,' Nick said, standing behind him. 'He didn't get a lot of work.'

Vito clicked around the statistics section of Warren's account page. 'Looks like he hasn't had a lot of hits lately. Six in the last three months. But look at the last date.'

'January 3. That's the day before the last day Sherry saw him alive. Coincidence?'

'I don't think so.' Vito went to the photo section and clicked through the thumbnails that comprised Warren Keyes's career. 'Look at this one.' It was two photos spliced together, both close-ups of Warren's bicep. One half showed the Oscar tattoo in reasonable detail, on the other half the tattoo had been rendered invisible with makeup. 'There's something about that tattoo that's been bothering me.'

'Oscar? Doesn't seem too uncommon for a young guy who wanted to be an actor.'

'No, that's not it.' Vito shook his head. 'I went to visit Tess in Chicago a while back and she took me to a museum where they were exhibiting the Oscar statues that were going to

154

be given at the Academy Awards that year.' He looked up over his shoulder. 'The company that makes the statues is in Chicago.'

'Okay,' Nick said slowly. 'And?'

Vito visualized the statue and the memory clicked. 'Oscar is a knight.'

'What?'

'Yeah, he's a knight.' Excited now, Vito did a Google search and pulled up a close-up of the Oscar statue itself. 'Look at his hands. Just like Warren's were posed.'

Nick whistled softly. 'Hell's bells. Look at that. He's holding a freaking sword. If Oscar were lyin' down, he'd be the spittin' image of the boy in the morgue.'

'Not a coincidence,' Vito said firmly. 'He picked Warren because of the tattoo.'

'Or he posed Warren because of the tattoo.'

'No, he planned this. He'd posed the woman's hands weeks before. God, Nick. Warren got picked because of his damn tattoo.'

'Shit.' Nick sat down. 'I wonder if the girl's picture is in here too.'

'And the guy without half his head. And the boy with the bullet between his eyes.' Vito checked his watch. 'Tino's been at the morgue since seven. Maybe he's got something we can use.'

As if on cue, the elevator dinged and Tino walked into the bullpen. Vito winced. His younger brother's face was haggard and drawn, his dark eyes stark. 'I shouldn't have asked him to do this.'

'He'll live,' Nick insisted, then stood up. 'Hey, Tino.' He pulled up a chair. 'Sit.'

Tino sat, heavily. 'How do you do it, Vito? Look at those people, every day?'

'It's an acquired skill,' Nick answered for him. 'What d'ya got for us?'

Tino held out an envelope. 'I have no idea if this is anywhere close. I did my best.'

'It's better than we had before,' Vito told him. 'I'm sorry, Tino. I shouldn't have—'

'Stop,' Tino interrupted. 'I'm okay and yes, you should have. It was just more intense than I'd expected.' He made his mouth smile. 'I'll live.'

'That's what I told him.' Nick slid the drawing from the envelope. From the page stared a serious female face and Vito could see his brother had captured the girl's facial structure. But more than that was a poignant sadness that Vito suspected was Tino's own feelings coming through as he'd sketched. It was beautifully done.

Nick hummed his approval. 'Wow. How come you can't draw like this, Vito?'

'Because he sings,' Tino answered wearily. 'And Dino teaches, Gino builds, and Tess cooks like a goddess.' He blew out a sigh. 'And on that note, I'm going home, Vito. Tess should be there with the boys and I'm going to see if she'll make me supper.' He licked his lips with distaste. 'Anything to get this taste out of my mouth.'

Vito remembered Sophie's beef jerky. 'Tell Tess to make it spicy, and save me some. Oh, and tell her to take my room. I'll bunk on the sofa.'

Tino stood up. 'Your ME showed me the other bodies, Vito. I don't think I can do anything for the guy . . .' He grimaced. 'You know. Without a head. And the kid with the bullet is too far gone. Same for the kid with the shrapnel. You'll need—'

'Whoa.' Vito stopped him with a raised hand. 'What shrapnel?'

'Your ME called him one-four.'

Nick frowned. 'Shrapnel? What the hell?'

'Sounds like we have some catching up to do in the morgue,' Vito said grimly. 'I'm sorry, Tino. Go on. We'll need what?'

'I was just going to say you'll need a forensic anthropologist to reconstruct their faces. But the two old people I might be able to do. I can come back tomorrow and try.'

Vito felt a stirring of pride. 'We'd appreciate it.'

Zipping up his coat, Tino shot them a lopsided grin. 'I expect a recommendation. Who knows, I might have found a new career. God knows art doesn't pay anything.'

'Where's that stack of missing-persons reports?' Nick asked when Tino was gone. 'We can search this UCanModel site using the missing-persons names that fit the girl's profile, then compare the photos to Tino's drawing.'

'Sounds like a plan.'

Monday, January 15, 9:55 P.M.

Nick tossed the missing-persons printout to Vito's desk in disgust. 'That was the last one.' He glared at the UCanModel site on the computer screen. 'She's not in there.'

'Or she's not in *there*.' Vito pointed to the printout. 'Maybe she wasn't declared a missing person. Or maybe she's not local. Just because Warren was from Philly doesn't mean she was. I'm not ready to give up yet.'

'Fuck,' Nick grumbled. 'It would have been so sweet to find her fast.'

'Go home,' Vito said. 'I'll keep searching while I wait for Jeff's computer tech to comb Sherry's hard drive. I'll check each model face by face if I have to.'

'There have to be five thousand names in there. You'll be here all damn night.'

'Maybe not.' Vito ran the cursor over all the drop-down menus. 'I can't imagine that photographers looking for models are gonna scroll one picture at a time. They'd want to be able to look at all the blondes or brunettes, short or tall. Whatever.'

Nick sat up a little straighter. 'So you could narrow the field. You know she was a brunette, five-foot-two, with short hair and blue eyes.'

'The eyes and hair are changeable. She could always wear contacts or a wig. But the height doesn't change.' Vito squinted at the screen. 'You can search, then sort by physical character-istics. So we search for five-foot-two and sort by hair color, then eye color.' He filled in the fields and clicked search. 'You go home, I'll stay here.'

'Hell, no. It's just getting interesting again. Besides, you could find some cute girls on this site. They even list their bra size. What more do you want?'

'Nick.' Rolling his eyes, Vito shook his head.

'Hey, I'm single again and I don't have time for bars.' His expression went sly. 'Nor do I have the likes of Sophie Johannsen interested in me.'

She was interested. Vito swallowed hard. If she'd been any more interested he would have needed CPR. But she didn't want to be. She'd turned him down, yet again. Last night it had been a misunderstanding. Tonight he suspected she under-stood all too well, even if he didn't. So he ignored Nick and stared at the screen. 'Only a hundred results. Her being short was good. Most of the models are tall.'

'Like Sophie.'

'Nick,' Vito gritted. 'Shut up.'

Nick gave him a puzzled look. 'You're serious, aren't you? I just assumed—'

'Well, you assumed wrong. And I'm not going to push this time.'

Nick seemed to chew on that for a minute. 'Okay. Then let's work.'

Vito clicked through each model's portfolio, then stopped and blinked. 'God, Tino is good.' The face staring out at them was the exact image of Tino's drawing.

'I'll say.' Nick leaned in for a closer look, very sober now. 'Brittany Bellamy. Hell, Chick. She wasn't even twenty. Click 'contact.''

Vito did, but it was an e-mail form. 'They don't give phone numbers or even geographical info, and I don't want to send an e-mail. If we're right, she won't answer.'

''Cause she's dead,' Nick muttered. 'And if we're wrong,

158

we've given out potentially valuable details on the killer's MO. But you can check with her former clients in the morning.' He stood up. 'I'm going home. I'll call you when I'm outta court tomorrow.'

'Good luck,' Vito said, then dialed Liz Sawyer's home number. 'Hey, it's Vito.'

'What do you have?'

'Possible ID on the girl with the hands.' He filled her in. 'I'll confirm tomorrow.'

'Very nicely done, Vito. I mean it. And thank your brother for me.'

Liz didn't give out praise often. When she did, it felt good. 'Thanks. And I will.'

'I rearranged some schedules and freed up Riker and Jenkins. They'll be available to help you chase leads and IDs as of tomorrow morning.'

Liz had done well. Tim Riker and Beverly Jenkins were good cops. 'Full time?'

'For a few days. It was the best I could do.'

'Appreciate it. I'll ask them to track Brittany Bellamy through her modeling clients tomorrow. I got some names from the archeologist that I want to run down. One of them might be able to help us trace the equipment this guy is using. I want a money trail.'

'Always follow the money,' Liz agreed. 'Schedule a briefing for oh-eight tomorrow.'

'Will do. Hey, I gotta go. Looks like the IT guy is here.'

A young guy carrying a laptop was approaching his desk. 'You Ciccotelli?'

'Yeah. You Jeff's guy?'

One side of his mouth lifted. 'I prefer Brent.' He shook Vito's hand. 'Brent Yelton. And just so you know, calling us "Jeff's guy" won't make you a lot of friends on our floor.'

Vito grinned. 'I'll remember that. The computer's in the box. Thanks for coming out.'

Brent nodded. 'I was the one who checked out the computer

you took from Keyes's room. I told Jeff to call me if anything else came up on this case, that I'd be there.'

Vito scowled. 'I used up a favor to get you here. Jeff's an asshole.'

Brent laughed as he hooked Sherry's computer to his laptop. 'One more reason not to be associated with him.' He sat in Nick's chair and for five minutes worked in silence. Finally he looked up. 'Well, this machine hasn't been wiped. No trace of the virus that took out the victim's computer. Somebody has been fooling with the history, though.'

Vito walked around to stand behind him. 'What do you mean?'

'The wipe on the vic's machine was a virus. This here is totally an amateur effort. Somebody didn't want anybody knowing he visited certain sites and deleted them from the history. But that doesn't delete them from the hard drive.' He glanced up. 'Big mistake people make when they use company computers to surf for porn. They delete the history, but it's still on the drive and any IT person worth a nickel can find it.'

'Good to know,' Vito said wryly. 'So which sites were deleted by our amateur?'

Brent did a little doubletake. 'This is a first for me. Somebody's hiding visits to medievalworld.com, medievalhistory .com, fencing.com . . . here's one for clothing of the Middle Ages, more of the same, yada yada, and . . . Hmm. A site for Caribbean cruises.'

Vito sighed. 'Their honeymoon. Warren and Sherry were getting married. She said he'd dropped some hints about cruises, to see if that's where she wanted to go.'

'And the medieval stuff?'

Vito stared at the list broodingly. 'It all fits. I'm just not sure how.'

'Call me if you come up with any more wiped machines. Gotta say I'm intrigued. That virus had one of the sneakiest codes I've ever seen. Here's my card with my cell.' He grinned as he packed up his laptop. 'That way you don't have to go through Jeff.'

'Thanks, man.' Vito pocketed Brent's card, then dialed Jen McFain's cell.

'McFain.' The connection was bad, but Jen's fatigue came through loud and clear.

'Jen, it's Vito. What's happening?'

'Just sent the eighth body to the morgue, another elderly woman. Nothing funky.'

'Meaning no bullets, no shrapnel, no cancer, no weird bruises or folded hands.'

'Pretty much. We're on the final grave now. First row, first grave.'

'Well we've ID'd the Knight for sure and maybe the Lady.'

'Wow.' She sounded impressed. 'That's fast work.'

'Thanks. You didn't do too badly yourself. Six bodies excavated in one day.'

'We couldn't have without Sophie's map. The real work starts tomorrow when we start sifting through the dirt we took away.'

'Speaking of tomorrow, we're having a briefing at oh-eight. Can you be here?'

'If you bring coffee and crullers from that bakery at the end of your street, then I'm there. Hold on. The team's calling me.' A minute later she was back. 'Last one's uncovered.' Her voice held new energy. 'Young female. And Vito, she's missing a leg.'

Vito grimaced. 'You mean he cut off her leg?'

'No, she's an amputee. And oh, my goodness. If I'm not mistaken . . . Oh, Vito, this is good. Really good. She's got a plate in her skull. Oh man, this is gold.'

Vito blinked hard. 'She has a gold plate in her skull? Jen, that doesn't make sense.'

She huffed in frustration. 'Dammit, Vito, stick with the program here.'

'Sorry. I'm just tired. Try again.'

'Well, it's not like this has been a garden party for me either.

Pay attention. Her skull has decomposed, revealing a metal plate. She obviously had it implanted after an injury or surgery at some point in her life. Now that she's decomposing, it's visible.'

'Oh.' He frowned. 'I'm still missing why this is so good.'

'Vito, an implantable metal plate is a class-three medical device. All class-three medical devices have unique, traceable serial numbers.'

Cognition clicked and he stood up straighter. 'By which we can identify her.'

'And the prize goes to the man who just woke up.'

Vito grinned, almost giddy over this lucky turn. 'I'll call Katherine and have her start with the amputee first thing tomorrow morning. See you at oh-eight.'

Monday, January 15, 10:15 P.M.

Daniel was staring mindlessly at CNN on the hotel television when his cell phone rang. 'Luke? Where have you been?'

'Catching fish,' Luke said dryly. 'That's what usually happens on a fishing trip. I didn't get your message till now. So what's up? Where are you?'

'In Philadelphia. Listen, I found a memory stick after you left this morning. I plugged it into my laptop and all I could see was a list of files with PST at the end.'

'Those are e-mail files. That's probably your dad's backup file since he wiped everything before November.'

Daniel pulled the memory stick from his pocket. 'How can I see what's on here?'

'Plug the stick into your PC. I'll walk you through. It's not hard.'

Daniel did what Luke said to do and was soon looking at his father's e-mails. 'I've got 'em.' Several years' worth, in fact. But Daniel didn't think he wanted Luke to know what had been on the memory stick any more than he wanted Frank Loomis to know about his father's secret safe. 'Let me check it out. Thanks, Luke.'

It took Daniel only minutes to get to the message that stopped his heart. It was from 'RunnerGirl' and was dated July, eighteen months before. It said only, 'I know what your son did.'

Daniel forced himself to breathe, to think. This was not going to be pretty at all.

Tuesday, January 16, 12:45 A.M.

It was damn good. On his computer screen the Inquisitor battled his opponent, the Good Knight. Both characters fought sword in one hand, flail in the other. Each step was smooth, each jab of a sword or arc of the flail a realistic combination of muscular movement. It was a masterpiece.

Van Zandt would be pleased. Soon hundreds of thousands across the world would flock to experience *this*. Van Zandt considered him an animation genius, but he never forgot that the computer animations were merely a means to an end. The end was having his paintings displayed in the best galleries, the very galleries that had rejected him before.

He lifted his eyes to the seventh painting of *Warren Dies*. To the moment Warren Keyes ceased to be. Perhaps those galleries had been right. His work before Claire and Warren and all the others had been generic. Familiar. But these – Warren, Claire, Brittany, Bill Melville as the flail sheared his head away – these were genius.

He stood up and stretched. He needed to sleep. He had a long drive ahead of him tomorrow morning. He wanted to be in Van Zandt's office by nine and out by noon. That would allow him ample time to meet Mr Gregory Sanders at three. By midnight he'd have *Gregory Dies* on canvas and a whole new scream.

He took a few stiff steps, rubbing his right thigh. This old house was too drafty. He'd picked it for its remote location and ease of . . . appropriation, but every gust of winter wind found its way inside. Philadelphia in the winter was hell. Made him long for magnolias and peach blossoms. He clenched his jaw. He'd been exiled from home far too long, but that would soon change. The old man's hold over him was broken.

He chuckled. So was the old man. Broken. He walked to his bed on the far side of his studio. Sitting on the mattress, he focused on the poster board that he'd mounted on the wall next to his bed, positioned so that he could see it every time he woke. The poster board on which he'd drawn the matrix. Four by four.

Sixteen blocks, nine of them filled with still shots of the victim at that crucial moment of death. Well, one was a photo of a painting. He hadn't filmed his strangulation of Claire Reynolds, but in the moments after her death, he had created *Claire Dies* and knew his life had irrevocably changed. In the days thereafter he'd relived the moment he'd ended Claire's life over and over.

In those days, he'd dreamed of doing it again and again. And in those days he'd formulated the plan which was progressing well. Some might attribute his success to luck, but only fools believed in luck. Luck was for the lazy, the undeserving. He believed in intellect, and in skill. And fate.

He hadn't always believed in fate, in the inevitable overlap of one person's destiny with another's. He believed now. How else could he explain walking into Jager Van Zandt's favorite bar a year ago, just hours after the man had received a crushing review on his last game? 'Less exciting than Pong,' the reviewer had proclaimed and Van Zandt had been just drunk enough to pour out every last detail, from his frustration with Derek Harrington to the fear that the game he was ready to launch, *Behind Enemy Lines*, would be equally disastrous.

How else could he explain the sudden appearance of Claire Reynolds with her bold but poorly executed attempt at blackmail the very next day? Those had been fate.

Intellect was being able to combine Claire's unfortunate end and Van Zandt's unfortunate present into a new destiny that would meet his own needs. But none of it could have happened without skill. He had been uniquely gifted to give Van Zandt exactly what he wanted in exactly the form he needed. Few others could create images, worlds, with both pixels and paint. Few others had the computer expertise to imbue them with life.

But I can. He'd created the virtual world of the evil Inquisitor, a fourteenth-century cleric who saw the elimination of heretics as more of a hostile takeover opportunity and the elimination of witches to be the door to great power. The more wealthy heretics and true witches the Inquisitor found and eliminated, the more powerful he would become, until he became the king.

A fanciful tale, but gamers would enjoy the political scheming and lies required to get ahead. Points would be scored by how clever the deceit and how diabolically complex the torture. He'd filled most of the primary roles – the powerful Witch who'd suffered the torture of the chair before revealing the source of her great power, the Good Knight who is vanquished with the flail, the king himself who suffers a most ignominious and . . . gutless end.

Of course all of these subjects had played supporting roles as well. He'd been careful to plan the tortures to get the most use out of each subject, both audio and video. With a few small changes, these additional tortures would be converted to at least twenty additional minor characters that gamers could add to their collection.

Gregory Sanders would play the role of an honest cleric attempting to stop the evil Inquisitor. Of course the cleric would not prevail and Gregory Sanders would meet a most bitter and painful end, after which he would be buried in the final plot on the third row. The third row would be complete.

The first row was already complete, filled with casualties of *Behind Enemy Lines* – Claire and Jared and Zachary. And poor Mrs Crane. Crane was . . . collateral damage, an unfortunate victim of his real-estate acquisition. Regrettable, but unavoidable.

The fourth row was currently empty, reserved for cleanup when *Inquisitor* was complete. The fourth row would hold his resources, the only people capable of proving the images in his medieval fantasy world were more than the product of an active imagination. They were the only people who knew the instruments of torture were indeed real, who knew of his intense interest in the weapons and warfare of the Middle Ages. They would pose a distinct threat when *Inquisitor* hit store shelves, so they would have to be dealt with before that time.

The three vendors of illegal antiquities would give him no pause. They were pompous asses who'd overcharged him too many times. Simply put, he disliked all three. But the historian . . . She would be another regrettable loss. He had nothing against her, per se. On some level he even . . . liked her. She was intelligent and skilled. A loner. *Just like me.*

Still, she'd interacted with him on too many occasions. He could not allow her to live. Like the two old women, he'd make it as painless as possible. Nothing personal. But the historian would die and would be laid to rest in the last block on the fourth row.

He lifted his gaze and stared at the second row of blocks with cold resolve. Two blocks were filled. Two remained. Unlike any of the others, this row, these blocks were very, very personal indeed.

Tuesday, January 16, 1:15 A.M.

Daniel had been staring at the ceiling for hours, putting off what he knew he had to do. It was probably too late, in more ways than one. But she had a right to know, and he had a responsibility to tell her.

She'd be angry. She was entitled. With a sigh Daniel sat up and reached for the phone, dialing the number he'd committed to memory long ago but had never called.

She answered on the first ring. 'Hello?' She sounded awake and alert.

'Susannah? It's . . . me. Daniel.'

There was a long moment of silence. 'What do you want, Daniel?' There was an edge to her voice that made him cringe. But he supposed he deserved it.

'I'm in Philadelphia. Looking for them.'

'In Philadephia? Why would they go there?'

'Susannah, when was the last time you talked to them?'

'I called Mom on Christmas Day, a year ago. I haven't talked to Dad in five years. Why?'

'Frank called me, told me they might be missing, but it looked like they were only on vacation. Then I found e-mails on Dad's computer. They say "I know what your son did." '

Once again he was treated to a moment of silence. 'So what did his son do?'

Daniel closed his eyes. 'I don't know. The only things I know is that one of them did an Internet search for Philadelphia oncologists and that the last person to actually talk to them was Grandma. I'm here looking for them, and I'm prepared to go to every hotel in this city, but it would help to know what number they called Grandma from.'

'Why don't you ask someone from GBI to run it for you?' she asked.

Daniel hesitated. 'I'd rather not. My boss wanted me to initiate a missing-person case. I told him I would when I had evidence that this was more than a simple vacation.'

'Your boss is right,' she said coldly. 'You should do this by the book.'

'I will, once I'm convinced they are missing, and not on vacation. So can you run Grandma's LUDs?'

'I'll do my best. Don't call me again. I'll call you if and when I find something.'

Daniel winced when the phone clicked in his ear. It had actually gone far better than he'd anticipated.

Tuesday, January 16, 1:15 A.M.

The occupants of the second row were completely personal. The old man and his wife were already buried there. Soon the empty plots would hold the old man's spawn. How fitting that the family would spend eternity together . . . *in* my *graveyard.* His mouth curved. How fitting that the only one buried in the family plot behind the little Baptist church in Dutton, Georgia . . . *is me.*

He hadn't asked for the confrontation now. Artie and his wife had brought it to him, right to his doorstep. He'd always planned to wage this war, but after he'd made his mark. After his goals were met. When he had true success to shove down the old man's throat. When he could say, *You said I'd never be anything. You were wrong.*

It was too late for that. He'd never be able to say, 'You were wrong.' Artie started it, but now that he was engaged in battle, he'd finish it, once and for all. The old man had paid dearly for his crimes. His offspring would soon follow.

Artie's daughter would play the final major role in his game – she would become the Queen, the only character standing between the Inquisitor and the throne. She would be, of course, destroyed. Painfully.

Artie's son would play a mere peasant poaching the king's land. A minor role in the game. He stood abruptly. *But his death will close a significant chapter in my life.* He crossed the floor of his studio with a purposeful stride, no longer tired. Opening a cabinet, he carefully drew out the tool that would deliver his vengeance. He'd saved it for years, just waiting for this time. Setting it on his desk, he pried open the jagged steel jaws and set the trap. Hands steady, he lowered a pencil between the jaws and tapped the release. The jaws snapped shut and the shattered pencil flew from his hand.

He gave a hard nod of approval. Artie's son would know pain – intense, excruciating, unimaginable pain. Artie's son would scream for help, for release, and finally for death. But no one would hear him. No one would save him. *I killed them all.*

Tuesday, January 16, 6:00 A.M.

Vito stumbled into the kitchen, lured by the smells of coffee and sizzling bacon. Then smiled at the sight of his sister Tess sitting at the kitchen table, feeding baby Gus in his high chair. Or trying to.

Gus pushed his bowl of oatmeal away. 'Want cake,' Gus said, very distinctly.

'Don't we all?' Tess asked the baby wryly. 'But we don't always get what we want, and I know your mama does not give you cake for breakfast.'

Gus tilted his head, measuring her slyly. 'Tino cake.'

Vito's lips twitched. Cake had been Tino's answer to every child-care calamity since the boys had arrived. 'I guess we're busted.'

She wheeled around, eyes wide. But the startled look quickly gave way to her gorgeous smile as she quickly crossed the small kitchen into his open arms. 'Vito.'

'Hey, kid.' Something was wrong. Her smile had been genuine, but her body was tense as she hugged him. 'What's wrong? Is it Molly?'

'No, she's better this morning. You worry too much, Vito. Sit. I'll get your plate.'

Still wary, he sat. 'I found the snack you left in the fridge last night. Thanks.'

She threw a look over her shoulder as she heaped eggs and bacon on his plate. 'That was an entire ravioli, not a snack. But you're welcome.' She put the plate on the table before him and took the other chair. 'What time did you get home last night?'

'Almost one.' On the way home he'd stopped at the bar where Warren Keyes had waited tables. Interviews with Warren's boss and coworkers had turned up nothing new. No one had noticed anything or anyone out of the ordinary. 'I didn't want to wake you.'

'You didn't. The boys wore me out last night.' She tickled Gus's feet through his socks. 'This one moves fast on these chubby little legs and you've got too many things lying around that he can break. Once I got Gus and the others asleep, I crashed.'

Vito frowned. 'Dante was awake when I got home, crying out on the back porch.'

Tess's eyes widened. 'The back porch? It's freezing cold out there.'

Vito's back porch was enclosed with glass, but it wasn't heated and it *had* been freezing cold. 'I know. He was wrapped up in his sleeping bag, but still. I was scared shitless when I came in and saw he wasn't asleep on the living-room floor. I think I scared him shitless when I found him out there. He said he just wanted to be alone.'

'He was upset about Molly,' Tess said. 'That's understandable.'

Vito had his doubts, but hadn't pressed the boy. 'Maybe. I made him come back in, but keep an eye on him.' He regarded Tess over his cup. 'So what's wrong?'

Her chuckle was wry. 'You're nosy, you know that?'

Sophie came to mind and he felt a sharp stab in his heart. 'So I've been told.'

Tess lifted her brows. 'I'll tell if you tell.'

'I should know better than to probe a shrink. Okay, but you first.'

She shrugged. 'Being around the kids is hard. Aidan and I have been trying to . . .' She looked down. 'Both of us are one of five kids, and we can't even have one.'

'Maybe you just need to give it some time.'

170

She looked up and his heart wanted to break at the sadness in her eyes. 'It's been eighteen months. We're starting to talk doctors and treatment and adoption.'

He reached over and squeezed her hand. 'I'm sorry, kid.'

Her lips curved, still sadly. 'Me, too. So now it's your turn. What's her name?'

He huffed a laugh. 'Sophie. And she's very pretty, very smart and I like her, but she doesn't want to like me. She pretty much asked me to leave her alone and I will.'

'Advisable from the standpoint of not becoming a stalker, but utterly uncharacteristic for you. I don't think I've ever known you to not pursue a female that caught your eye.'

That had been true until Andrea. She'd said no at first, but he'd been infatuated. He'd pursued and she'd eventually changed her mind. It ended up being the worst thing that could have happened to either of them. 'Maybe I've just grown up.'

'Uh-huh.' She nodded, clearly unconvinced. 'Right.'

He stood up. 'Well, right or wrong I have to get out of here. I have to stop at the bakery and the morgue before work.'

Tess made a face. '*Bakery* and *morgue* are two words that should not be used together, Vito. Will you be home for dinner?'

'I don't know.' He dropped a kiss on her forehead. 'I'll call you either way.'

'I've got to get the boys off to school.' She looked around the kitchen. 'Then I think Gus and I will go shopping for curtains. Your windows look sad.'

It was Tess that looked sad, but there wasn't anything Vito could do to fix it any more than he could fix the look of sadness he'd seen on Sophie's face the night before.

Tuesday, January 16, 8:01 A.M.

'Mmmm.' Jen McFain sank her teeth into a sugary cruller. 'Have one.' She pushed the box toward Beverly Jenkins, one of the detectives Liz had assigned to Vito's case.

Beverly cast a baleful eye at the box. 'How do you stay so skinny, McFain?'

'Metabolism.' Jen grinned. 'But if it's any consolation, my mom says my metabolism will come to a screeching halt when I'm forty and every bite I take will land on my ass.'

Beverly's lips twitched. 'Then there is a God.'

Liz came in with Katherine and Tim Riker, Beverly's partner. 'Where are we, Vito?' Liz asked when they'd taken their seats and passed the donut box down the table.

'Liz gave you most of the details yesterday,' Vito said to Riker and Jenkins. 'We have one firm ID yesterday and two more tentative IDs last night,' Vito said. He walked to the whiteboard where he'd recreated Katherine's sketch of the four by four matrix. In each rectangle he'd written in a short description of each victim and their cause and approximate time of death.

'We've ID'd Warren Keyes, and our tentative IDs are on these females.' He pointed to plots three-two and one-one. 'The one with the folded hands could be Brittany Bellamy.' He taped her picture on the side of the board. 'Brittany was a model. Her picture and a list of her clients is in the packet of info I made for each of you. We don't know where she lives. Her name isn't in our missing persons files or in the DMV files. She might not be local.'

'What about the other female?' Liz asked.

'Her name is Claire Reynolds,' Katherine said. 'She's got a metal plate in her head and she's an amputee, right leg, above the knee. I came in at six and contacted the manufacturer of the metal plate. They were able to match the serial number on the plate to Claire Reynolds. The plate was put into Claire's head after a car accident. Claire was living in Georgia at the time and the surgery was done in Atlanta. I assume her leg was damaged in the same accident. I'll know when I get her medical history.'

Vito took up the tale. 'Claire moved to Philly about four years ago. Her last known employment was with one of the branches of the library. Her parents reported her missing about fourteen months ago. Their description matches the body we found.'

'And the timing is consistent with the level of decomposition,' Katherine added. 'I haven't started her autopsy yet, but I did x-ray her while I was waiting for the guy to check his records for her name. Her neck was broken. No other obvious injuries.'

Vito taped her picture to the whiteboard next to the rectangle marking her grave. 'I got this photo from the DMV records. Her parents need to be notified.'

Beverly was taking notes. 'We can take that. We'll also see if we can get a hair sample or anything we can use for a positive DNA ID.'

'You found the woman with the folded hands in the same modeling site that Warren Keyes used,' Tim said. 'Was Claire a model too, and is there any possibility we could find any of these others there?'

'I didn't check to see if Claire was a model. She doesn't really have the look, but that doesn't mean she wasn't. It's worth a check.'

'I doubt the three elderly people were models,' Liz said. 'It's more likely you'll find the three younger men there, the head-wound, gunshot, and shrapnel vics.'

Vito frowned. 'Tino said there wasn't enough of the other young men left for a sketch, and the forensic anthropologist is at a conference until next week.'

Beverly lifted her brows. 'Tino?'

'My brother, aka free consultant sketch artist. He did this sketch of the girl with the folded hands. We used it to locate Brittany Bellamy on the modeling site.' Vito pulled Tino's sketch from his folder and slid it to the middle of the table. 'He thinks he can do sketches of the older couple, but none of the others.'

'He's good,' Tim said, comparing the sketch to Brittany's picture. 'But if he can't get us sketches, we can try to match their physical characteristics to missing persons.'

'It's worth a try,' Vito agreed. 'But first we need to confirm our victim really is Brittany Bellamy. After you notify Claire Reynolds's parents, can you two also call Brittany's clients and see if you can track down an address?'

Jen raised a brow. 'And you'll be doing . . .?'

'I'll be tracking down the equipment he used on the most recent torture-murders. I want to establish a money trail. Sophie Johannsen gave me a list of people who either sell reproductions or may know of the sale of authentic artifacts. I'm looking for a chair, a rack, a sword, and mail.' He looked at Katherine. 'Nick thinks the circular bruises you saw were from chain mail.'

'He could be right. Someone would have had to hit him with a lot of force to cause that kind of bruising,' she said thoughtfully. 'Like maybe with a hammer.'

'But that doesn't explain the other injuries,' Liz said. She pulled the photos of victim three-one closer. 'Whatever hit his head and arm was heavy and sharp. Jagged, even.'

'The blow to his head came from a horizontal angle,' Katherine added. 'It was enough to rip the top of his head off. The blow to his arm was delivered vertically.'

'Warren had held a sword at some point,' Jen suggested. 'Maybe he used that.'

Katherine shook her head. 'We're looking for something blunt, but also sharp.'

'And medieval.' Jen grimaced. 'What about that spiked ball on a chain? If it got whipped around hard enough, it could deliver a blow with that kind of force.'

'A flail,' Tim said and winced. 'God.'

'I'll add a flail to my list,' Vito said. 'Okay. We know Warren got a hit on his résumé the day before he disappeared. The modeling site allows prospective employers to contact the models via e-mail. We don't know who e-mailed him because they sent a virus to wipe his hard drive.'

'Maybe we can get something from Brittany's computer,' Liz said. 'Get it to IT for testing. Also get into her account and see if she got any hits in the last month.'

Beverly nodded. 'Will do. You know, Vito, there's one thing that bothers me.'

'Only one?' Vito asked and she shot him a dry smile.

'The fingertips on the old man. Your report says you think it was the only crime of real passion out of all of these, and that makes sense. But why take his fingertips? Seems like the killer must have known the man could be identified by his prints, but it would have been a threat only if the body were found. He obviously didn't think any of his other victims would be found. He made no effort to disguise any of them.'

'It was part of the assault,' Katherine said. 'The fingerpads were cut off while the old man was still alive. Whoever this guy is, the killer really hated him.'

'Let's let Tino sketch their faces,' Vito suggested, 'then we'll see if anything pops. What about the old lady buried in the first row?'

'Haven't even peeked at her yet. I'll do the autopsy today.' Katherine looked at Jen. 'Did you get anything on the bullet I took from one-three?'

'Yes. The bullet's from a German Luger,' Jen said with a satisfied nod. 'The ballistics guy thinks it's vintage 1940s. He's going to do some checking today.'

Liz shrugged. 'It's a common enough gun, even the vintage ones. It most likely won't be traceable.'

But Tim was nodding. 'Yeah, but it's significant considering he's buried next to a guy with shrapnel in his gut. It's going to be interesting to get a read on the grenade that was used on him. And if the gun is vintage, it's just more data to show that this guy goes for authenticity wherever possible.' Tim looked over at Vito. 'You got two historical themes going on, both warfare related.'

'You're right. We just need to figure out why. Jen, what do we know about the field?'

'Nothing yet. We start sifting dirt today. I sent samples of the fill dirt from each grave along with a sample of the dirt from the field off to the lab. They should have an analysis in a few days.

We can at least see if the fill dirt came from the field.'

'I'd like to know why *that* field,' Liz mused. 'What led him to *that* field?'

'Good point.' Vito jotted it down. 'We'll check out Harlan P. Winchester's aunt. She's deceased, but she owned the land when the first grave was dug. What else?'

'I'm expecting a lab report on the silicon lubricant this afternoon,' Katherine said.

'Good.' Vito rose. 'We're done for now. We all have our list of to-do items. Let's meet back here to debrief at five o'clock. Stay in touch and stay safe.'

Chapter Ten

Patty Ann wasn't at the front desk when Sophie let herself into the museum. Theo Four was, and Sophie was glad to see him. 'You're back. Now you can wear the armor.'

He shook his head. 'Not today. I won't be here for the first tour.'

'*Theo*. You have to stay. That knight tour is a pain.'

'For which my father pays you well,' Theo said stonily.

Sophie wanted to hit him, but Theo was a very large young man, built like a rock. 'I got news for you, kid. Your dad pays—' She broke it off. Her meager salary wasn't an appropriate topic to share with the owner's son. She turned, headed for her office.

'Sophie, you have a package.' Theo gestured to a small box on the desk.

Annoyed with herself for getting angry at the boy, Sophie grabbed the small box from the desk and took it into her office, shutting her door behind her. With short rips she tore the paper from the box and flipped off the lid.

Then dropped the box, muffling her scream with her hand.

A dead mouse rolled out of the box. Its head didn't follow. At the bottom of the box was the mousetrap that had been the mouse's execution device.

Breathing hard, she sank blindly into her chair, her hand still clamped hard over her mouth. Bile rose and she choked it back.

177

She knew exactly who had sent the mouse and why, because she'd received a similar one ten years before.

From Alan Brewster's wife. Amanda Brewster did not like other women sleeping with her husband, even women who'd been tricked into doing so. Clint Shafer must have wasted no time calling Alan to say that Sophie had called last night. Amanda must have been listening.

I should call the police. But she wouldn't today any more than she had the last time, because deep down she knew Amanda Brewster had a right to her anger. So she scooped up the mouse and put the lid back on the box. For a brief second she considered tossing it in the Dumpster, but knew she couldn't any more than she could keep Alan's name to herself last night. She'd bury it later.

Tuesday, January 16, 9:15 A.M.

Daniel Vartanian had ripped the listings of hotels from the phone book he'd found in his hotel nightstand drawer. Armed with pictures of his parents, he planned to hit the hotel chains in which they normally stayed first, then work his way down.

He was tying his tie when his cell rang. It was Susannah. 'Hello.'

'It was an Atlanta area code,' Susannah said without greeting. 'A cell phone, registered to Mom.'

It should have made him feel better. 'So she called Grandma on her own phone to say she was coming to see you. Do you know where the phone was physically located when the call was placed?'

Susannah was quiet for a long moment. 'No, but I'll try to find out. Good-bye.'

He hesitated, then sighed. 'Suze . . . I'm sorry.'

He heard Susannah's careful exhale. 'I'm sure you are, Daniel. But you're about eleven years too late. Keep me apprised.' And with that she was gone.

She was right of course. He'd made so many mistakes. He went back to tying his tie, his hands unsteady. Maybe this time he could get something right.

Tuesday, January 16, 9:30 A.M.

Dr Alan Brewster's office was a mini-museum, Vito thought as Brewster's assistant showed him in. Brewster's assistant, on the other hand . . . well there was nothing mini about her. She was tall, blonde, with Barbie-doll proportions, and Vito instantly thought of Sophie. Obviously, Brewster liked them young, tall, blonde, and beautiful.

This year's model was Stephanie, who oozed sex with every step. 'Alan's coming. He said to make yourself comfortable,' she added with a knowing smile that invited Vito to make himself very comfortable indeed. 'Can I get you anything? Coffee? Tea?' An amused confidence in her eyes left the *Me* unsaid, but strongly implied.

Vito kept his distance. 'No thanks. I'm fine.'

'Well if you change your mind, I'm just outside.'

Semi-alone, Vito took in the understated opulence. Brewster's mahogany desk was about an acre wide and neat as a pin, with only a single framed picture of a woman with two teenaged boys to clutter its glossy surface. Mrs Brewster and the kids.

One wall was lined with shelves filled with knickknacks from all over the world. Another wall was covered with photos. On closer inspection Vito could see that nearly every one contained the same man. *Dr Brewster, I presume.* The pictures spanned twenty years, but Brewster always looked trim, tanned, and sophisticated.

Many of the photos were taken on digs, labeled with the place and date. Russia, Wales, England. In every photo Brewster stood next to a tall, blonde, beautiful girl. Then Vito stopped at the photo labeled 'France,' because Sophie was the girl. Ten years younger, she stood next to Brewster, wearing her army camouflage field coat and red bandana. And a smile that went far beyond joy of the job. She'd been in love.

And Brewster had been married. Vito wondered if she'd known, then dismissed the thought. Of course she hadn't and now her words from the day before made perfect sense. A slight noise behind him made him glance up and in the reflection of the glass covering the photo he saw Brewster standing behind him, watching silently.

Vito looked at the France photo for another few seconds, then went on to give equal time to photos from Italy and Greece as if he still believed himself to be alone. Finally Brewster cleared his throat and Vito turned, widening his eyes. 'Dr Brewster?'

Brewster closed the door behind him. 'I'm Alan Brewster. Please sit down.' He gestured to a chair, then took his place behind the massive desk. 'How can I help you?'

'First, I have to request that you keep what I'm about to ask in confidence.'

Brewster spread his hands, then steepled his fingers. 'Of course, Detective.'

'Thank you. We have a case in which we suspect that stolen goods have changed hands,' Vito began and Brewster's brows rose.

'And you suspect one of my students? Are we talking TVs, stereos? Term papers?'

'No. The objects we've recovered appear to be artifacts. Medieval, actually. We Googled history and archeology professors and yours is one of the names that came up as an expert in this field. I'm here to get your professional opinion.'

'I see. Then let's proceed. What kind of objects are you talking about?'

Vito weighed his options. He didn't like Brewster, but then he hadn't liked him before he walked in the door. Just because the man cheated on his wife didn't mean he wouldn't be a good resource. 'We have various weapons. Swords, flails, for example.'

'Easily copied, of course. I'd be happy to authenticate anything you've found. Weaponry and warfare are my areas of expertise.'

'Thank you. We may take you up on that.' Vito hesitated, considering. He had to ask about the chair sometime. Might as well be now. 'We also found a chair.'

'A chair,' Brewster repeated with a hint of disdain. 'What kind of chair?'

'One with spikes. Lots of spikes,' Vito said and watched Brewster's face flatten in what might have been genuine shock before the color rose in his tanned cheeks.

The man quickly recovered his poise. 'You think you've found an inquisitional chair? You have it in your possession?'

'Yes,' Vito lied. 'We were wondering how someone might have come by it.'

'Artifacts like that are very rare. What you have is most certainly a copy. We'd have to authenticate. If you brought it to me, I'd be happy to help.'

On a cold day in hell, Vito thought. 'But if it *is* authentic, where would it come from?'

'Europe, originally, but few survive. Rarely do they come up for sale or auction.'

'Dr Brewster, let's cut through the bull, shall we? I'm talking about the black market. If someone wanted to buy an artifact like a chair, where would he go?'

Brewster's eyes flashed. 'I haven't the faintest idea. I don't know anyone who deals in illegal merchandise, and if I did, I would report them immediately to the authorities.'

'I'm sorry,' Vito said and watched the fire in Brewster's eyes bank. If he was an actor, he was very good. Vito thought of Sophie. Brewster must be one hell of an actor. 'I didn't mean to imply you'd be involved in anything illegal. But if one of these chairs were to suddenly surface, would you hear about it?'

'Most assuredly, Detective. But I have not.'

'Do you know of any private collectors who might have interest in such items, were they to come up for legal auction?'

Opening his desk drawer, Brewster took out a pad and jotted down a few names. 'These men are of the highest ethics. I'm sure they will be as unable to help you as I.'

Vito slipped the paper into his pocket. 'I'm sure you're right. Thank you for your time, Dr Brewster. If you do hear anything, please call me. Here's my card.'

Brewster swept the card into the drawer with his notepad. 'Stephanie will see you out.' Vito was at the door when Brewster added, 'Please tell Sophie I said hello.'

Controlling his surprise, Vito turned, forcing confusion to his face. 'I'm sorry?'

'Please, Detective. We all have our sources. I have mine and you have . . . Sophie Johannsen.' He smiled, a sly gleam in his eye that made Vito want to poke the man's eyes out. 'You're in for a real treat. Sophie was one of my most able assistants.'

Vito lifted a shoulder, barely controlling the pagan urge to leap across that mahogany desk and rip Brewster's face off. Instead he shook his head. 'I'm sorry, Dr Brewster. You really do have me at a loss. Maybe this Sophie Johnson—'

'Johannsen,' Brewster corrected smoothly.

'Whatever. Maybe she talked to my boss, but . . .' Vito shrugged. 'Not to me.' He made himself smile conspiratorially. 'Although it appears I missed something special.'

Brewster's eyes narrowed slightly. 'That you did, Detective. That you did.'

Tuesday, January 16, 10:30 A.M.

It had been, Vito conceded, a professionally unproductive trip. Brewster hadn't provided anything of real use and Vito didn't believe the names he'd been given would be of any use either. He'd pursue the leads though, and see what more he could learn.

His cell buzzed, Riker's number on the caller ID. 'Vito, it's

Tim. We just left Claire Reynolds's parents' place. Her parents had all of Claire's things boxed in their basement. Bev got some hair from Claire's old brush so we can get DNA. Her parents said they went to her apartment just before Thanksgiving a year ago when she hadn't returned their calls, but she hadn't been there in a long time. Then they checked her job and found the library where she'd worked received a letter of resignation fifteen months ago. The mother insists the signature isn't Claire's. We'll bring the letter in, too.'

'Huh. Somebody didn't want anyone to investigate her as missing.'

'That's what we thought. But that's not the best part. In the box with all her belongings were two prosthetic legs, one for running and one for water sports. And . . .' he paused dramatically, 'one bottle of silicone lubricant.'

Vito sat up straighter at that. 'Really? Isn't that interesting?'

'Yeah.' There was a triumphant smile in Riker's voice. 'This one had never been opened. Claire's mother said she used the lubricant to put on her leg and that she kept bottles in her apartment, her car, and her gym bag. The family didn't find the car or the gym bag, so Claire may have had a few bottles on her when she was killed.'

'A very practical souvenir for our killer.'

'Yeah. We'll have the lab match it to the samples Katherine took from the two vics.'

'Excellent. What about Claire's computer?'

'Her parents say she didn't have one. When we're done at the lab we'll get on the phones and see if we can find Brittany Bellamy.'

'Then we'll be three down, six to go. I got a few names of personal collectors from the professor I visited this morning and I'll run those down. After hearing the Luger was vintage, I'm more convinced our guy is going for the most authentic weapons he can find. But just in case, I'm going to visit a few of the dealers that sell reproductions at the medieval festivals. We'll see what shakes out. Keep in touch.'

Vito closed his phone and sat with it clenched in his fist, staring at the little shop in front of which he'd parked. Andy's Attic was the only seller on Sophie's list that had a physical shop. All of the others sold through Internet sites. For now, Vito wanted to confine his interviews to people he could see so that he could watch their reactions.

Like he'd watched Brewster. Slimy little sonofabitch. But how had Brewster known Sophie was his source? She wasn't supposed to have made any calls, just given him names. Frowning, he dialed Sophie's cell.

She answered, her tone guarded. 'This is Sophie.'

'Sophie, it's Vito Ciccotelli. I'm sorry to bother you again, but . . .'

She sighed. 'But you just talked to Alan Brewster. Did he give you anything?'

'The names of three collectors he insists are ethical and legitimate. But Sophie, he knew you'd given me his name. I tried to evade my way out of it, but someone had told him before I got there. Who else did you talk to?'

She was quiet for a moment. 'A guy who was a grad student with me the summer I worked for Brewster. His name is Clint Shafer. I didn't want to call any of them, but I couldn't remember Kyle Lombard's name and back then Kyle and Clint were friends.'

'Did you call anyone else?'

'Only my old graduate advisor, the one I put on the list. I called Etienne before I saw you last night and left him a voice mail saying he should talk to you when you called. He called me back late last night.'

She'd changed graduate programs after she left Brewster, he thought. Her tone had become defensive, as if she expected him to be angry, so he kept his voice gentle. 'Did your old advisor say anything useful?'

'Yeah.' Some of the tightness in her tone eased. 'I sent it to you in an e-mail.'

So she wouldn't have to talk to him again. She'd known what

Brewster would tell him and still she'd given his name. 'I haven't checked my mail yet. What did he say?'

'It's all rumor, Vito. Etienne heard it at a cocktail party.'

He took out his notepad. 'Sometimes rumor is true. I'm ready.'

'He said that he heard one of their donors, Alberto Berretti, had died. This guy lived in Italy and had a big collection of swords and armor, but it had been whispered for years that he also collected torture items. His family put his collection up for auction recently, but less than half of the swords and none of the rumored torture items were offered up for sale. Etienne said he'd heard a few people discreetly inquired, but the family denied finding anything other than what they auctioned.'

'Did your teacher believe the family?'

'He said he didn't know them, and wouldn't speculate. But the important thing is, there are some artifacts out there, somewhere. They may or may not relate to your case. Sorry, Vito, that's all I know.'

'You've helped a great deal,' he said. 'Sophie, about Brewster.'

'I need to go now,' she said tightly. 'I have work to do. Good-bye, Vito.'

Vito looked at his phone for a full minute after she hung up. He should listen to her. The last time he'd pursued a woman, it had gone so wrong. It could go wrong again.

Or it could go right and he'd get the only thing he'd ever wanted. Someone who waited for only him at the end of a long day. Someone to come home to. Maybe that would be Sophie Johannsen and maybe it wouldn't. But he'd never know unless he tried. And this time he'd have to make sure it went right. Into his cell he punched in a number with single-minded intent. 'Hey, Tess, it's Vito. I need a favor.'

New York City, Tuesday, January 16, 10:45 A.M.

'Wow.' Van Zandt's eyes never left the computer screen as his character battled the Good Knight, sword in one hand, flail in the other. Van Zandt's knuckles were white as he gripped his game controller, his face a study in concentration. 'My God, Frasier, this is amazing. This will put oRo right up there with Sony.'

He smiled. Sony was the company to catch. Sony games were present in millions of households. Millions. 'I thought you'd like it. This is the final fight. By this point, the Inquisitor has become all-powerful and has stolen the queen herself for his own. The knight will die trying to win her freedom. Because he's . . . you know, a knight.'

'The wonderful myth of chivalry.' A muscle in VZ's jaw twitched as he struggled. 'Artificial intelligence is superb. This knight is damned hard to kill. So die already,' he said through clenched teeth. 'Come on. Die already. Die for me. Yes.' The knight collapsed to his knees, then onto his chest as VZ dealt the killing blow with the flail.

VZ frowned. 'But it's . . . so . . . anticlimactic. I was hoping for a little more . . .' He gestured broadly. '*Pah.*'

Expecting just such a reaction, he pulled a folded sheet of paper from his pocket and tossed it across Van Zandt's desk. 'Here. Try it this way.'

His eyes sparkling like a kid's, Van Zandt entered the code, opening the alternate gameplay he'd created. '*Yes,*' he hissed when the Good Knight's head sheared away, sending bone and brain flying. '*This* is what I was hoping for.' He glanced from the corner of his eye. 'Pretty smart, making it an Easter egg. If the gamers haven't guessed the code within six months after release, we'll let it "slip." Within two hours it will be all over the Net and we will have ourselves some very effective, cheap publicity.'

'Then mothers and preachers and teachers will get whipped into an uproar, objecting to the senseless violence pervasive in our society.' He smiled. 'Which just makes their kids go out and buy more copies.'

Van Zandt grinned. 'Exactly. You could throw a few nude scenes in, too. If the violence does not whip them into frenzy, a little nudity will. Explicit sex is even better.'

He considered the scenes he'd constructed using Brittany Bellamy. She was fully nude. There was no sex, but the violence was so raw, he knew VZ would be pleased. He hadn't planned to show the dungeon to Van Zandt today, but the time seemed right. He pulled a CD from his laptop case. 'You want a peek at the dungeon?'

Van Zandt stuck his hand out, greedy anticipation all over his face. 'Give it to me.'

He leaned forward with the CD and VZ snatched it from his hand. 'This is the way the dungeon will look by the end,' he explained as VZ inserted the CD. 'The Inquisitor starts out small, accusing landowners of witchcraft, then taking their assets once he's arrested them and killed them with conventional weapons, his sword, dagger, et cetera. With the money, he buys bigger and better torture toys.'

As the sequence started, the camera wound through mist, coming to the cemetery on the grounds of a church, a perfect copy of a French abbey outside Nice.

Van Zandt shot him a surprised look. 'You put the dungeon in a *church*?'

'Under it. A medieval 'up-yours' to the establishment. Which was the Church.'

Van Zandt's lips twitched. 'I do not want to stand next to you in a lightning storm.' The camera entered the church and passed through the crypt. Van Zandt whistled softly. 'Very nice, Frasier. I especially like the tomb effigies. Very authentic.'

'Thanks.' The plaster casts had given him a nice model to work from. Except now he needed to order more lubricant for his leg. He'd gone through Claire's stash and had to use some of his own. The camera descended the stairs into the cave where Brittany Bellamy awaited her fate. 'This woman is

Brianna. She's an accused witch. But the Inquisitor knows she really is a witch and wants her to share her secrets. She will be a most stubborn captive.'

'Be quiet. Let me watch.' And he did, his expression changing from amusement to horror as the Inquisitor placed the screaming woman on the inquisitional chair. 'My God,' he whispered as Brianna's screams tore the air. 'My God.' Like Warren, Brittany Bellamy had suffered well, her screams a beautiful thing to hear. He'd simply imported the sound file of her screams into his computer-generated animation.

When the Inquisitor put a flame to the chair, Brittany shrieked in pain. Van Zandt actually paled. When the scene ended on a close-up of Brianna's eyes at that moment of death, Van Zandt collapsed back in his chair, sweat beading on his forehead. He stared at the screen which had faded to the oRo dragon.

When a full minute of silence had passed, he drew a breath, prepared to defend his art. 'I'm not going to change it, VZ.'

Van Zandt held up his hand. 'Quiet. I'm thinking.'

Five full minutes passed before Van Zandt swiveled to face him. 'Split the scenes.'

He could feel his temper start to boil. 'I'm not cutting up my scenes, VZ.'

Van Zandt rolled his eyes. 'Have you no patience? We will include the chair scene with the main release, but keep it hidden. We will release the code for the more gruesome knight scene as free publicity. We will follow that free publicity by announcing the availability of the execution code for the chair . . . but at a price. Unlocking this part of the dungeon will cost our customer another $29.99.'

The base release was priced at $49.99. Van Zandt's plan would add more revenue with no extra cost, increasing profits by four hundred percent. 'You capitalist, you,' he murmured and Van Zandt lifted his eyes, his gaze piercing.

'Of course. That is why the R is the biggest letter in oRo.'

He remembered the small print on the logo below the dragon's claws. *'Rijkdom?'*

Van Zandt's smile was razor sharp. 'It is Dutch for "wealth." It is why I am here. It should be why you are here as well.' He stretched out his hand. 'Give me the rest.'

He shook his head, suddenly hesitant. 'I gave you enough for the Pinnacle show.'

'So Derek told you about our Pinnacle opportunity?'

His lip curled. 'Yeah.'

Van Zandt's brow lifted. 'You do not like Pinnacle?'

'I do not like Derek.' He spaced each word, mimicking Van Zandt's heavy speech.

'Derek has served his purpose, but he will not move with us to the next level. You, Frasier, I have high hopes for.' He hadn't moved his hand. 'Give me the rest. Now.'

Cocking his jaw, he slapped another CD into Van Zandt's hand. 'This is King William. When the good knight is defeated, William attempts a final rescue of his queen. But by this point the Inquisitor is a very strong sorcerer. Even the king himself cannot defeat his dark magic and is captured.'

Van Zandt's smile grew sharp. 'And what does the Inquisitor do to King William?'

He thought about Warren Keyes, the way he'd screamed. It still sent shivers down his spine. 'He stretches him on the rack, then disembowels him.'

Van Zandt laughed softly. 'Remind me never to make you angry, Frasier Lewis.'

Chapter Eleven

Philadephia, Tuesday, January 16, 11:30 A.M.

'This still isn't right,' Vito muttered as he ran his finger over the chain mail Andy had spread out on his counter. It was way too big. Andy's Attic was an all-purpose costume store. Vito imagined their killer would sneer at such poor recreations.

'I've shown you all the mail I have,' Andy said stiffly. 'What are you looking for?'

'Something smaller. About a quarter inch in diameter.'

'You should have said so when you first came in,' Andy grumbled. 'I don't keep that quality here in the store, but I can order it for you.' He thumbed through a catalog. 'What you're talking about is much better quality, but pricier.' He found a picture of a man wearing a mail hood and shirt. 'This hauberk-and-coif set runs eighteen hundred.'

Vito blinked. 'Dollars?'

Andy looked offended. 'Well, yeah. It's SCA approved. You know, Society for Creative Anachronism. You don't know anything about this stuff, do you? Is this a gift?'

Vito coughed. 'Yeah. So this set is eighteen hundred. How much for just the shirt?'

'The hauberk is twelve-fifty.'

'Do you ever sell these out of your store?'

'Not usually. Usually I sell 'em off my website.'

'Have you sold any recently? Like before Christmas?'

'Yeah. I sold nine hauberks before Christmas. But I sold twenty-five last summer, about a month before the Medieval

Festival. Serious jousters like to get the feel of the mail before the event.' Andy closed the catalog and handed it to Vito. 'Detective.'

Vito winced. Busted. 'I'm sorry.'

Andy's smile was rueful. 'I won't say anything. I kind of figured it when you first walked in. My uncle was PPD, thirty years. What else are you looking for, Detective . . .?'

'Ciccotelli. A sword, about this long, with a hilt this big.' Vito gestured. 'And a flail.'

Andy's eyes widened. 'Holy shit. Well, let's see what we can find out.'

Tuesday, January 16, 11:45 A.M.

Van Zandt locked the CDs in his desk drawer. 'This is good work, Frasier.'

He stood up. 'Since you're set for Pinnacle, I'll be leaving. I've still got lots to do.'

Van Zandt shook his head. 'I have a few more things to discuss. Please sit.'

With a frown, he complied. 'Like what?'

'You must learn patience, Frasier. You're still young. You have lots of time.'

Why did old people always equate youth with the need for patience? Just because he *had* lots of time didn't mean he wanted to *wait* lots of time. 'Like what?' he repeated, this time through his teeth. He had Gregory Sanders to meet at three o'clock.

Van Zandt sighed. 'Like the queen. Have you designed her face?'

He thought of the old man's daughter. 'Yes.'

'And? What will she look like?'

Her face flashed in his mind. 'Pretty. Petite. Brunette. Similar to Bri— Brianna.' *Shit.* He'd very nearly said Brittany. *Focus.*

'No, I don't think that type of character has a dramatic

191

enough beauty. Your queen should be stately. Bigger. Your Brianna looks little more than one and a half meters.'

Brittany Bellamy had been five-two. He'd chosen her because of her small stature. His chair was on the small side and he wanted it to look larger with respect to the woman sitting in it. 'You want a different queen?'

'Yes.' Van Zandt had lifted his brows, as if expecting dissent.

He considered it. Van Zandt had an eye for what worked. What sold. He could be right. This was going to be messy. He'd be filling the third row in the field with Gregory Sanders, and the fourth with his resources, and the old man's spawn still had to die. If he used any more models for this game, he'd need to start another row. Well, the field was big. 'I'll think about it.'

'You'll do it,' Van Zandt corrected mildly, and although challenge burned his tongue Frasier didn't oppose him. For now, he still needed him. 'Next, the flail scene.'

He narrowed his eyes. 'What about it? It's done.'

'No, it's not. The scene you have in there is so sedate. He just . . . falls. It's anticlimactic. Why not make the basic scene the head-coming-apart scene, then for the hidden scene make it even more exciting? Maybe his head could completely explode, or he could be decapitated entirely. It's—'

'No. That's not how it happens. The skull doesn't explode and the entire head doesn't come off.' He'd been very disappointed to discover this truth.

Van Zandt's eyes had narrowed. 'How do you know?'

Be careful. 'I've researched it. Talked to doctors. That's what they say.'

Van Zandt shrugged. 'So what? What does it matter what really happens? It's all fantasy anyway. Make the base injury more exciting.'

He counted to ten inside his head. *Remember, this is a means to an end. It is not forever. Soon you can walk away and not have to think about Van Zandt or oRo Entertainment ever again.* 'Okay. I'll spice it up.' He stood up but VZ stopped him.

'Wait. One more thing. I'm thinking about your dungeon. Something's missing.'

'What?'

'An iron maiden.'

Oh, for God's sake. How amateurishly *trite.* His opinion of Van Zandt was rapidly deescalating. *'No.'*

'For God's sake, Frasier, why not?' Van Zandt asked, exasperated.

'Because that is not period. Maidens didn't even appear until the fifteen hundreds. I'm not putting an iron maiden in *my* dungeon.'

'Every one of our gamers will expect to see a maiden in *his* dungeon.'

'Do you know how long it'll take to—' He drew a breath. He'd nearly said 'build.' There were no iron maidens to be had. If he wanted one, he'd have to build it himself and there was no way he'd do that. 'Jager, I'll find a new queen. I'll spice up the flail scene, but I won't put a fraudulent piece in *my* dungeon.'

His eyes darkening, Van Zandt leaned to one side and picked a sheet of letterhead out of his inbox. 'I see my name on this letterhead as president. I do not see your name, Frasier. Anywhere.' He tossed the sheet back in the inbox. 'So just do it.'

Gritting his teeth, he snatched his laptop case from the floor. 'Fine.'

Tuesday, January 16, 11:55 A.M.

'Excuse me!'

Derek paused on the steps that led from the street to oRo's office building, a bag lunch from the deli in his hand. A man was getting out of a taxi with a small suitcase. Although he was well dressed, it looked like he hadn't slept in days. 'Yes?'

'Are you Derek Harrington?'

'Yes. Why?'

The man started for the steps, weary desperation on his face.

'I just need to talk to you. Please. It's about my son and your game.'

'If you're upset your son's playing *Behind Enemy Lines*, that's out of my hands.'

'No, you don't understand. My son isn't playing your game. I think my son is *in* your game.' He pulled a wallet-sized photo from his pocket. 'My name is Lloyd Webber. I'm from Richmond, Virginia. My son Zachary ran away a little more than a year ago. His note said he was going to New York. We never heard from him again.'

'I'm sorry, Mr Webber, but I don't understand what that has to do with me.'

'Your game has a scene where a young German soldier gets shot in the head. That boy looks exactly like my Zachary. I thought he'd modeled for your artists, so I looked up your company. Please. If you have a record of the models you've used, please see if he was one of them. Maybe he's right here, in New York.'

'We don't employ models, Mr Webber. I'm sorry.' Derek started to move away, but Webber sidestepped him, blocking his path.

'Just look at his picture. Please. I tried to call you but you wouldn't accept my calls. So I got up this morning and bought a plane ticket. *Please.*' He held out the photo and with a sigh for the man's pain, Derek took it.

And felt every breath of air seep from his lungs. It was the same boy. *The exact same face.* 'He's . . . he's a handsome boy, Mr Webber.' He looked up to find Webber's eyes filled with tears.

'Are you sure you haven't had him in your studio?' he whispered.

Derek felt light-headed. He'd known from the minute he'd laid eyes on Frasier Lewis's work that it possessed an element of realism that crossed the lines of decency, but the thoughts that were running through his mind right now . . . 'Can I take your son's photo, Mr Webber? I can show it around to the staff. We don't employ models, but maybe one of them saw him somewhere. In a restaurant or maybe on a bus. We get our ideas for characters from so many places.'

'Please. Keep the picture – it's a copy and I can get you more. Show it to anyone you think can help.' He extended a business card in a trembling hand and, his own hand shaking, Derek took it. 'My cell phone number is on there. Please call me at any time, day or night. I'll stay in town for a few days, just until you know one way or the other.'

Derek stared down at the photo and the business card. Frasier Lewis was still here, inside, talking to Jager. He could ask him point-blank. But he wasn't sure he wanted the answer. *Be a man, Derek. Take a goddamn stand for something.*

He looked up and nodded. 'I'll call you one way or the other. I promise.'

Gratitude and hope shone in Webber's eyes. 'Thank you.'

Tuesday, January 16, 12:05 P.M.

His simmering fury came to a full boil when he saw Derek Harrington waiting for him by the building exit. His fist clenched around the handle of his laptop case. He'd much rather his fist be engaged in more satisfying pursuits, such as breaking Harrington's face. But there was a time and place. *Not here, not yet.* Without a word of greeting or acknowledgment of any kind, he walked past Harrington and out the door.

'Lewis, wait.' Harrington followed him out. 'I need to talk to you.'

'I'm late,' he gritted out and started down the steps to the street. 'Later.'

'No, now.' Harrington grabbed his shoulder and he teetered dangerously, nearly losing his balance and falling down the steps. He caught himself, leaning against the iron handrail. Fury erupted and he shoved Harrington's hand out of the way.

'Get your hands off me,' he said, his roar barely contained.

Derek took a step back so that he was two steps higher. They now stood eye to eye. There was something new in Harrington's eyes, something defiant.

'Or what?' Derek asked quietly. 'What would you do to me, Frasier?'

Not here. Not yet. But the time would come. 'I'm late. I have to go.'

He turned to go, but Derek followed, passing him on the steps so that he waited at the bottom. 'What would you do to me?' he repeated, with more force. 'Hit me?' He climbed one step and looked up out of the corner of his eye. 'Kill me?' he murmured.

'You're crazy.' He started down the stairs again, but Harrington grabbed his arm. This time he was prepared and stood steady, his good leg taking his weight.

'Would you kill me, Frasier?' Harrington asked in that same low voice. 'Like you killed Zachary Webber?' He took a photo from his coat pocket. 'The resemblance to your German soldier is amazing, wouldn't you agree?'

He looked at the photo and kept his expression impassive, even as his heart began to beat more rapidly. For staring back from the photo was Zachary Webber's face as it had been the day he'd picked him up off I-95 outside of Philly, hitchhiking. Zachary had been on his way to New York, to be an actor. His father had told him he was too young, that he should finish high school. Zachary had scorned his father. *I'll show him*, he'd said. *When I'm famous, he'll eat every damn word.*

The words had echoed in his mind that day. They had been his own, at Zachary's age. Meeting Zachary was fate, just like Warren Keyes's tattoo.

'I don't see it,' he said carelessly. He got to the street and turned to look Derek in the eye once again, as the older man still stood on the steps. 'You should be careful before making accusations of that nature, Harrington. It could come back to haunt you.'

Tuesday, January 16, 1:15 P.M.

Ted Albright was frowning. 'You were flat today, *Joan.*'

Sophie glared at Ted Albright as she pulled the armored boots from her feet. 'I told you to get Theo to do the knight tour. My back is killing me.' So was her head. And her pride. 'I'm going to get some lunch.'

Ted grasped her arm as she walked away, his grip surprisingly gentle. 'Wait.'

Slowly she turned, prepared for another argument. 'What?' she snapped, but stopped when she saw the look on his face. Marta was right, Ted Albright was a very handsome man, but right now his broad shoulders were slumped and his face was haggard. 'What?' she said, much more softly than she had the first time.

'Sophie, I know what you think of me.' One corner of his mouth lifted when she said nothing. 'And believe it or not, I respect that you're not denying it right now. You never actually met my grandfather. He died before you were born.'

'I read all about his archeological career.'

'But none of the books tell what he was really like. He wasn't a dry *historian.*' His voice dropped low on the word. Then he smiled. 'My grandfather was . . . fun. He died when I was a kid, but I still remember that he loved cartoons. Bugs Bunny was his favorite. He gave me pony rides on his back and he was a huge Stooges fan. He loved to laugh. He also loved the theater and so do I.' He sighed. 'I'm trying to make this a place children can come and . . . *experience*, Sophie. I'm trying to make this a place my grandfather would have loved to visit.'

Sophie stood there a moment, uncertain of what to say. 'Ted, I think I have a better idea of what you're trying to do, but . . . hell. I *am* a dry historian. Asking me to dress up. It's humiliating.'

He shook his head. 'You're not dry, Sophie. You don't see the faces of the kids when you start to talk. They love to listen to you.' He let out a breath. 'I have tours scheduled every day for weeks. We need that income. Desperately,' he added quietly. 'I have everything I own invested in this building. If this museum fails, I'll have to sell the collection. I don't want to do that. It's all I have left of him. It's his legacy.'

Sophie closed her eyes. 'Let me think about it,' she murmured. 'I'm going to lunch.'

'Don't forget you're leading the Viking tour at three,' Ted called after her.

'I won't,' she muttered, torn between guilt and what she still considered justified ire.

'Yo, Soph. Over here.'

The greeting came from Patty Ann who stood at the lobby desk smacking gum, loudly.

Sophie crossed the lobby with a sigh. Patty Ann was trying to be from Brooklyn today, but she sounded more like Stallone's Rocky. Sophie leaned against the desk and said, 'Don't tell me. You're going out for *Guys and Dolls*.'

'I got the part locked, and you got a package.' Patty Ann nudged it to the edge of the counter. 'That's two packages in one day. You're getting mighty popular.'

Sophie went instantly on edge. 'Did you see who left the package?'

Patty Ann's smile was coy. 'Sure I did. It was a dame.'

Sophie bit back the urge to strangle the girl. 'Did this *dame* have a *name*?'

'Sure she did.' Patty Ann blew a bubble. 'A really long one. Ciccotelli-Reagan.'

Relieved and stunned at once, Sophie blinked. 'No kidding?'

'Cross my heart.' Patty Ann's smile went sly. 'I asked if she was any relation to a big hunky cop and she said he was her brother. Then she asked if I was Sophie.'

Sophie cringed. '*Please* tell me you said no.'

'Of course I said no,' Patty Ann huffed, indignant. 'I want to play interestin' roles. No offense, Sophie, but you ain't that interestin'.'

'Ah . . . thank you, Patty Ann. You've made my day.'

The girl tilted her head thoughtfully. 'Funny. That's what she said, too. The dame.'

Sophie liked Vito's sister already. 'Thanks, Patty Ann.' When she got to her dark little office, she closed the door and chuckled. Patty Ann wasn't a bad kid. Too bad she didn't fit the armor. She'd make a great Joan. Still smiling, she sat at her desk and opened the package. Then stared. *What the hell?* It was a pen. *No, it wasn't.*

The smile on her face faded as she realized exactly what she was looking at. She took the silver cylinder out of the box and hit a tiny button on its side with her thumb. The top sprang up, a blue light strobed, and a tinny little siren screeched.

It was a toy reproduction of the *Men in Black* memory zapper, and her eyes stung as she realized exactly what it meant. Vito Ciccotelli had once again offered her a do-over.

A note was tucked in the box. The handwriting was feminine, but the words were not. *Brewster's an ass. Forget him and go on. V.* Sophie had to smile at the PS. *Don't forget to take off your purple sunglasses before you zap yourself or it won't work.* A squiggly arrow pointed to the other side of the paper so she turned it over. *I still owe you a pizza. The place two blocks from your building at Whitman College makes a good one. If you still want to collect, I'll be there after your class tonight.*

Sophie put the note and the toy back in the box, then sat, thinking hard. She'd collect on the pizza. But she owed Vito Ciccotelli a great deal more. She checked her watch. Between the Viking tour and the evening seminar she taught she didn't have a lot of time, but she'd do what she could.

Vito hadn't gotten anything out of Alan Brewster. Sophie had known he wouldn't. Giving his name was more to soothe her own conscience than for any real benefit Alan would be to Vito's investigation. But Etienne Moraux had given her a good lead. Missing artifacts were floating around the world somewhere. They were probably still in Europe. But what if they weren't? What if they were right here?

Etienne hadn't known the man who died or any of the other

main players in the European world of arts patronage. He wasn't the type to notice wealth and influence any more than she was. But she knew people who did.

Sophie thought about her biological father. Alex had been well connected on a number of social and political levels, although she'd always been nervous about using his position and influence. Some of her reticence stemmed from her stepmother's obvious dislike of her husband's bastard American child. But most of her hesitation was wrapped up in the whole bizarre tangle of Anna and Alex and the rest of her family tree, and so she only called on the family when it was vital.

But this *was* vital. This was justice. So she'd use her father's influence once again. She'd like to think he would have approved. Alex's friends might know the man who'd died, whose collection was now AWOL. They might know the man's family, his connections. If there was one thing she'd learned the hard way over her life – never underestimate gossip. Good or bad.

She opened her phone book to the page where Alex Arnaud had written his friends' numbers so that Sophie would not 'be alone' in Europe when he was gone. By that point in his illness, his handwriting had become spidery and weak, but she could still make out the names and numbers. She'd known all of these people since she was a child, and all had offered their assistance countless times. Today she'd accept.

Tuesday, January 16, 1:30 P.M.

His heart was still pounding as he drove south toward Philly, along the same stretch of I-95 where he'd met Zachary Webber the year before. He was rattled and that made him angry. This day had not gone the way he'd planned.

First Van Zandt's unreasonable demands. Iron maidens, new queens, and exploding heads. He'd thought Van Zandt understood the value of authenticity. In the end, the man was just like everyone else.

Then Harrington. Where the hell had he gotten that picture? Ultimately it didn't matter. No one could prove he'd ever met Zachary Webber, much less held a 1943 German Luger to the boy's head and pulled the trigger. Harrington had taken a lucky guess, but he was shooting blanks.

Nevertheless, the whiny bastard was probably in VZ's office this very moment, trying to convince him . . . To do what? *Fire me? Report me to the cops?* Van Zandt would never do either. He had a Pinnacle invitation and he couldn't show up empty-handed. *He needs me.* Unfortunately, he also needed Van Zandt. For now.

Harrington, on the other hand, needed to be dealt with, and soon. He'd whine to Van Zandt but would eventually take his story elsewhere, to someone who actually might listen. Van Zandt had said that Harrington had outlived his usefulness.

He chuckled. Van Zandt had no idea how prophetic his words would become. He'd deal with Harrington, but for now he had an appointment to keep.

Tuesday, January 16, 1:30 P.M.

An hour and a half had passed before Derek had been summoned to Jager's office and he'd used that time to plan how he would confront his partner with his suspicions about Frasier Lewis without sounding like a lunatic. When he'd finished, Jager's forehead bunched in a frown. But in his eyes Derek saw bored indifference.

'What you are suggesting, Derek, is very serious indeed.'

'Of course it's serious, Jager. You can't sit there and tell me you don't see any resemblance between that missing boy and the character in Lewis's animation.'

'I don't deny a resemblance. But that's a far cry from accusing an employee of cold-blooded murder.'

'Lewis didn't even acknowledge the resemblance. He's a cold bastard.'

'What did you expect him to say? You'd just accused him of murder. Perhaps you expected him to say, "You are correct. I kidnapped Zachary Webber, held a gun to his head, blew out his brains, then made him a character in a video game."' He tilted his head, bemused. 'Does that sound sane to you?'

It didn't, not when explicitly spelled out like that. But there was something wrong. Derek could feel it in his gut. 'Then how do you account for this?' He tapped the photo. 'This kid is missing, then just happens to show up in *Behind Enemy Lines*.'

'He saw him somewhere. Hell, Derek, where did you get your inspiration?'

Did. Past tense. Something desperate rose in Derek's chest. 'You don't even know anything about Lewis. What were his production credits before you hired him at oRo?'

'I know what I need to know.' Jager tossed a paper across his desk.

Derek stared at the picture of a confident Jager with the headline: *oRo SCORES A COUP – Up and comer earns a seat at Pinnacle.*

'So you've arrived,' Derek said dully.

'Yes, *I* have.'

The personal pronoun had been carefully enunciated. 'You want me to quit.'

Jager lifted his brows, maddeningly calm. 'I never said that.'

Suddenly the desperation eased and Derek knew what he needed to do. Slowly he stood. 'Well, I just did.' He stopped at the door and looked back at the man whom he'd once called his closest friend. 'Did I ever really know you?'

Jager was calm. 'Security will walk you to your desk. You can pack your things.'

'I should say good luck, but I wouldn't mean it. I hope you get what you deserve.'

Jager's eyes went cold. 'Now that you're no longer with the company, any move to discredit any of my employees will be considered slander and prosecuted with zeal.'

'In other words, stay away from Frasier Lewis,' Derek said bitterly.

Jager's smile was a terrible thing to see. 'You do know me after all.'

New Jersey, Tuesday, January 16, 2:30 P.M.

Vito drove through the quiet little neighborhood in Jersey, following Tim Riker's directions. He'd left Andy from Andy's Attic sorting through receipts of sales of swords and flails to join Tim and Beverly who were waiting for him on the sidewalk.

'Brittany Bellamy's house?' he asked when he got out and Beverly nodded.

'Her parents live here. The only address Brittany listed with all her jobs was a PO box in Philly. If she doesn't live here, hopefully her parents can tell us where.'

'Have you talked to her parents?'

'No,' Tim said. 'We were waiting for you. One of the photographers on her résumé said he'd hired Brittany to do an ad for a local jewelry store last spring.'

'The ad was for rings.' Beverly's eyes grew dark. 'Only her hands were in the shot.'

'Nick and I think the killer chose Warren for his tattoo. That Brittany was a hand model could have drawn him, since he posed her hands. Was she reported missing?'

'No,' Tim said with a frown. 'So this might not be our vic.'

'Then let's go find out.' Vito led the way to the door and knocked. A minute later a girl opened the front door. She was perhaps fourteen and about the same size as their victim, her hair the same dark brown. In her hand was a box of tissues.

'Yes?' she asked, her nose stuffy, her voice muffled through the storm door glass.

Vito showed her his shield. 'I'm Detective Ciccotelli. Are your parents home?'

'No.' She sniffled. 'They're both at work.' Her heavy eyes narrowed. 'Why?'

'We're looking for Brittany Bellamy.'

The girl's chin came up and she sniffled again. 'My sister. What's she done?'

'Nothing. We'd just like to talk to her. Can you tell us where she lives?'

'Not here. Not anymore.'

Beverly stepped forward. 'Can you tell us where she does live then?'

'I don't know. Look, you should talk to my parents. They'll be home after six.'

'Then can you give us your parents' phone number at work?' Beverly pressed.

The sleepy look in her eyes was replaced by fear. 'What's happened to Brittany?'

'We're not sure,' Vito said. 'We really need to talk to your parents.'

'Wait here.' She closed the door and Vito could hear the deadbolt clicking. Two minutes later the door opened again and the girl reappeared with a cordless phone. She handed the phone to Vito. 'My mom is on the phone.'

'Is this Mrs Bellamy?'

'Yes.' The woman's voice was both frantic and angry. 'What's this about the police? What's Brittany done?'

'This is Detective Ciccotelli, Philly PD. When was the last time you saw Brittany?'

There was a moment of tense silence. 'Oh my God. Is she dead?'

'When was the last time you saw her, Mrs Bellamy?'

'Oh, God. She is dead.' The woman's voice was becoming hysterical. 'Oh God.'

'Mrs Bellamy, please. When—?' But the woman was weeping too loudly to hear him. The young girl's eyes filled with tears and she took the phone from Vito's hand.

'Ma, come home. I'll call Pop.' She disconnected and held the phone against her chest with both fists, much like Warren Keyes had held the sword. 'It was after Thanksgiving. She and my dad had a big fight because she dropped out of dental school to be an actress.' She blinked, sending the tears down her face. 'She left home, said she'd make it on her own. That's the last time I saw her. She's dead, isn't she?'

Vito sighed. 'Do you have a computer?'

She frowned. 'Yeah, it's brand-new.'

'How new, honey?' Vito asked.

'A month or so.' She faltered. 'Right after Brittany left the old one crashed. My dad was so mad. He didn't have a backup.'

'We're going to need to get your parents' permission to search her room.'

She looked away, lips quivering. 'I'll call my pop.'

Vito turned to Beverly and Tim. 'I'll stay here,' he murmured. 'Go back to the precinct and start searching for the third victim in that row on UCanModel dotcom.'

'Flail guy,' Tim said grimly. 'But we can't count on his name being in the missing person reports. Even if Brittany had been reported missing, she might not have ended up in the Philly reports, being way down here in Jersey.'

'The database allows you to search by physical attribute. If you can't figure it out, call Brent Yelton in IT. Tell him I sent you. Also, see if he can get a listing of everyone who got hits the same days Warren and Brittany's résumés were viewed. I'm betting this guy didn't just get lucky with the first model he contacted. Maybe we can find somebody who talked to him that's still alive and still has their computer intact.'

Bev and Tim nodded. 'Will do.'

The girl had come back to the storm door. 'My pop's on his way.'

A Catholic shrine rested against the house. 'Do you have a priest?' Vito asked.

She nodded, dully. 'I'll call him, too.'

Tuesday, January 16, 3:20 P.M.

Munch was late. Gregory Sanders glanced at his watch for the tenth time in as many minutes, feeling way too visible sitting in the bar where Munch had promised to meet him. He knew only to look for an older man who'd be walking with a cane.

The waitress stopped at his table. 'You can't stay here if you don't order nothin'.'

'I'm waiting for someone. But bring me a G&T.'

She tilted her head, studying him closer. 'I've seen you before. I know I have.' She snapped her fingers. 'Sanders Sewer Service.' She grinned. 'I loved that ad.'

He held a polite smile firmly in place as she walked away. He'd done sophisticated ads for national campaigns, but everybody who'd grown up in Philly remembered him in that stupid commercial that his father had forced his six sons to do. He would never be taken seriously by anyone who knew about that commercial. And he needed to be taken seriously. He needed Ed Munch to hire him for this job.

Greg fingered the switchblade he'd slid up his sleeve. What he really needed was to catch the old man unaware so he could rob him blind. But he couldn't sit out here in the open for much longer. Those guys wanted their money, and they wanted it now.

His cell buzzed in his pocket and he quickly looked around, wondering if he'd been discovered. But his cell was a throw-away and only Jill had his number. 'Yeah?' Jill was crying and he sat up straighter. 'What?'

'Damn you,' she sobbed into the phone. 'They were here, in my place. They trashed everything, looking for you. They put their hands on me.'

She was hysterical, screeching so high it hurt his ears. 'What did they do?' he asked, dread clutching at his gut. 'Dammit, Jill, what did those sonsofbitches do?'

'They hit me. Broke two of my teeth.' She quieted suddenly.

'And they said tomorrow they'd do worse, so now *I* have to find a place to hide. So help me God, you'd sure as hell better hope they find you, 'cause if I find you first, I'm gonna kill you myself.'

'Jill, I'm sorry.'

She laughed harshly. 'Yes, you are. Sorry. Just like my father always said. And yours.' She hung up and Greg exhaled, long and heavy. If they found him, they'd beat him, too. And if by some miracle he survived, his face would be so messed up that he wouldn't be able to work for weeks. He had to get some money. Today.

Munch was nearly a half hour late. The old man wasn't coming. Greg stood up and walked out of the restaurant, not sure where he'd go next, only sure that he had to get that money. Thinking about knocking off convenience stores, he walked to the curb to catch the next bus. Where he'd go, he had no clue. Away from Philly, most certainly.

'Mr Sanders?'

Greg spun, his heart in full throttle. But it was just an old man with a cane. 'Munch?'

'I'm so sorry, Mr Sanders. I ran late. Are you still interested in my documentary?'

Greg sized the old man up. At one time he'd been a good-sized guy, but now he was stooped and brittle. 'Are you still paying cash?'

'Of course. Do you have a car?'

He'd sold it long ago. 'No.'

'Then we'll take my truck. I'm parked on the next block.'

Once he got his money, he could steal the old man's truck and fly. 'Then let's go.'

Tuesday, January 16, 4:05 P.M.

Sophie's office phone was ringing when she got back after the Viking tour. She ran to answer it. It was after ten in Europe. The men she'd called would just be finishing their dinner about now. 'Hello?'

'Dr Johannsen.' It was a haughty, cultured voice that she'd heard before.

Sophie drew a breath. Not Europe. It was Amanda Brewster. 'Yes.'

'Do you know who this is?'

She glanced at the box with the mouse and new rage hit her like a wave. She planned to give the poor animal a decent burial after her shift. 'You are a sick bitch.'

'And you have a poor memory. I told you once to stay away from my husband.'

'And you have poor hearing. I told you that I don't want your husband. I don't ever want to see him again. You do not need to worry about me, Amanda. In fact if I were you, I'd be more worried about your husband's new blonde assistant du jour.'

'If you were me, you'd have Alan,' she said smugly and Sophie rolled her eyes.

'You need to get some professional help.'

'What I need,' Amanda gritted through clenched teeth, 'is for every little whore to keep their hands off my husband. I told you the last time I caught you that—'

'You didn't catch me,' Sophie said in exasperation. 'I came to you.' Which, after trusting that Alan Brewster had really loved her, was Sophie's second big mistake. She stupidly had thought the wife of a philanderer should know, but Amanda Brewster hadn't listened then and she wasn't going to listen now.

'—that I'd ruin you,' Amanda continued as if Sophie had not said a word.

The woman hadn't needed to ruin her then. Alan and his posse had accomplished that on their own, with their sexual innuendo. And they'd started it again.

Which really pissed her off. She picked up the toy Vito had sent her, wishing it would work through the phone, wishing she could wipe the entire incident off the face of the planet. But that wasn't going to happen and it was time she dealt with it. She'd run from Alan ten years ago, ashamed of what she'd done and scared of Amanda's threats to her career. She was still ashamed, but she wasn't running anymore.

'Get some help, Amanda. I'm not afraid of you anymore.'

'You'd better be. Look at you now,' Amanda screeched. 'You're working in a third-rate museum for an idiot. You think your career's in the toilet now.' She laughed, not a little hysterically. 'You'll be digging sewer trenches by the time I'm done with you.'

Sophie huffed a surprised chuckle. 'Digging sewer trenches' were the same exact words Amanda had used ten years before. At twenty-two, Sophie had believed her. At thirty-two, she recognized the ranting of a mentally imbalanced woman. She probably should pity Amanda Brewster. Maybe in another ten years she would.

'You're not going to believe anything I say about Alan, but you can believe this. Send me another package like you did this morning and I *will* call the police.'

She hung up and looked around her tiny windowless office. Amanda was right about one thing. Sophie *did* work in a third-rate museum.

But it didn't have to be. Amanda was wrong about one other thing. Ted wasn't an idiot. Sophie had watched the faces of the tour group this afternoon. They'd had fun, and they'd learned something. Ted was right. He was keeping his grandfather's legacy alive the best way he knew how. *And he hired me to help him do that.* So far she hadn't been a lot of help.

Because she'd spent the last six months feeling sorry for herself. Big important archeologist forced to leave the dig of a lifetime. 'When did I become such a snob?' she wondered out loud. Just because she wasn't digging in France didn't mean she couldn't do something important here.

She looked at the boxes that filled her office, stacked floor to ceiling. Most of them were filled with pieces of Ted the First's collections that Ted and Darla hadn't been able to find room for in the main museum. She'd find a place for them.

She looked at her hand and realized she still clenched Vito's memory zapper. Carefully she returned it to its box. She'd put her personal life back on track when she met Vito for dinner. She'd start putting her professional life back on track right now.

She found Ted in his office. 'Ted, I need some space.'

His eyes narrowed. 'What kind of space? Sophie, are you leaving us?'

Her eyes widened. 'No, I'm not leaving. I want more exhibit space. I've got some ideas for new exhibits.' She smiled. 'Fun ones. Where can I put them?'

Ted smiled back. 'I have the perfect place. Well, it's not perfect yet, but I have every confidence you'll whip it into shape.'

Tuesday, January 16, 4:10 P.M.

Munch had spent the first half hour of their drive telling Greg Sanders about the documentary he was making. It was a fresh look at daily life in medieval Europe.

God, Greg thought. *What a yawner.* This would have been worse for his career than Sanders Sewer Service. 'How about the other actors?'

'I begin shooting them next week.'

Then they'd be alone. And Munch hadn't paid anyone else yet. He should have a lot of cash in his house. 'How much farther out is your studio?' Greg demanded. 'We must have gone fifty miles.'

'Not much farther,' Munch replied. He smiled and Greg felt a cold shiver burn down his back. 'I don't like to bother my neighbors, so I live out where no one can hear me.'

'How would you bother them?' Greg asked, not so sure he wanted the answer.

'Oh, I host medieval reenacting groups.'

'You mean like jousting and shit?'

Munch smiled again. 'And shit.' He turned off the highway. 'That's my house.'

'Nice place,' Greg murmured. 'Classic Victorian.'

'I'm glad you approve.' He pulled into the driveway. 'Come in.'

Greg followed Munch, impatient that the old man took so long walking with the damn cane. Inside he looked around, wondering where the old man kept his money.

'This way,' Munch said and led him into a room filled with costumes. Some were on hangers, while others were worn by faceless mannequins. It looked like a medieval department store. 'You'll wear this.' Munch pointed to a friar's robe.

'Pay me first.'

Munch looked annoyed. 'You'll be paid when I am satisfied. Get dressed.' He turned to go and Greg knew it was now or never.

Do it. Quickly he flipped out his blade, moved in behind the old man and hooked his arm around Munch's neck, pressing the sharp edge against his throat. 'You'll pay me now, old man. Walk slowly to wherever you keep your money and you won't get hurt.'

Munch went still. Then in an explosion of movement he grasped Greg's thumb and twisted. Greg yelped with pain and his knife clattered to the floor. His arm was whipped behind his back and a second later he was on the ground, Munch's knee in his back.

'You slimy little sonofabitch,' Munch said and it was not the voice of an old man.

Greg could barely hear him over the pounding in his head. The pain was excruciating. His arm, his hand. They were burning. *Pop.* Greg screamed as his wrist snapped. Then moaned when his elbow did the same.

'That was for trying to rob me,' Munch said, then grabbed a handful of Greg's hair and smashed his head into the floor. 'That was for calling me old.'

Nausea rolled through him when Munch stood up and pocketed his blade. *Get help*. He slipped his hand into his pocket and fumbled his cell open with his left hand. He had time only to push one button before Munch's boot came crashing against his kidneys.

'Hands out of your pockets.' He shoved his boot into Greg's stomach and flipped him to his back. Greg could only stare in horror as Munch pulled off his gray wig. Munch wasn't old. He wasn't gray. He was totally bald. Munch pulled off his goatee and put it next to the wig. The eyebrows were last and Greg's stomach clenched as panic gave way to cold hard fear. Munch had no eyebrows. He had no hair of any kind.

He's going to kill me. Greg coughed and tasted blood. 'What are you going to do?'

Munch smiled down at him. 'Terrible things, Greg. Terrible, terrible things.'

Scream. But when he tried, all that came out was a pathetic croak.

Munch threw his arms wide. 'Scream all you want. No one can hear you. No one will save you. I've killed them all.' He bent down until all Greg could see were his eyes, cold and furious. 'They all thought they suffered, but their suffering was nothing compared to what I'm going to do to you.'

Chapter Twelve

Tuesday, January 16, 5:00 P.M.

Sober-faced, they'd reassembled to debrief. Vito sat at the head of the table, Liz on his right, Jen on his left. Next to Jen were Bev and Tim. Katherine sat next to Liz, her expression drawn. Vito thought about her having to do autopsies on all those bodies. She probably had the worst job of them all.

Although informing a family that their nineteen-year-old daughter was dead had been no picnic either. 'Nick's on his way from court,' he told Liz. 'They just adjourned.'

'Did he testify?'

'Not yet. ADA Lopez thinks it'll be tomorrow.'

'Let's hope so. Well, bring me up to speed so we can get out of here.'

Vito checked his watch. 'I'm also expecting Thomas Scarborough.'

Jen McFain's brows went up. 'Nice. Scarborough's a great profiler. But how did you get him so quickly? Last I heard he had a client list months long.'

'You can thank Nick Lawrence for that.' A tall man with linebacker's shoulders and wavy chestnut hair came into the room and from the corner of his eye Vito saw both Beverly and Jen sit a little straighter. Dr Thomas Scarborough wasn't what Vito thought most women called movie-star handsome, but he had a presence that filled the room. He leaned over and shook Vito's hand. 'You must be Chick. I'm Scarborough.'

Vito shook his hand. 'Thanks for coming, Dr Scarborough.'

'Thomas,' he said and took a seat. 'ADA Lopez introduced me to your partner outside court this morning. We were waiting to testify. Nick asked me about perps who use torture, and I was intrigued.'

Vito introduced everyone, then went to the whiteboard where he'd drawn the grave matrix that morning. 'We've confirmed that the woman with the folded hands is Brittany Bellamy. We compared prints from her bedroom to the vic's. They're hers.'

'So we've identified three of the nine,' Liz said. 'What do they have in common?'

Vito shook his head. 'We don't know. Warren and Brittany were on the modeling website, but Claire was not. Warren and Brittany were tortured. The killer broke Claire's neck, but did no more. There was at least a year between their murders.'

'The one thing they do have in common is that they were all buried in that field,' Jen said. 'I didn't think the fill dirt was from the field and I was right. The field is mostly clay. The fill dirt used in all the graves is sandier. It probably came from a quarry.'

Tim Riker sighed. 'And Pennsylvania is full of quarries.'

Liz frowned. 'But why use fill dirt from somewhere else? Why not use the dirt he dug from the hole in the first place?'

'That's actually an easy question to answer,' Jen said. 'The soil from the field gets clumpy when it gets wet. The quarry soil is sandy, so it doesn't absorb water the same way. It flows. It would be easier to pack a body in sand rather than clumpy clay.'

'Can we identify where exactly the soil came from?' Beverly asked her.

'I've called in a geologist. His team is looking at the breakdown of the minerals to give us an idea of where that soil naturally occurs. But it's going to take a few days.'

'Can we get them to move any faster?' Liz asked. 'Get them to up their resources?'

Jen lifted her hands. 'I tried to push it, but so far everyone is telling me that is the fastest they can work, and that is with the maximum resources. But I can try again.'

Liz nodded. 'Then do. The nature of his burial pattern indicates he's not finished. He could be working on a new victim right now. Two days could make a big difference.'

'Especially since we've disrupted his routine,' Thomas said quietly. 'This killer is incredibly obsessive-compulsive. He's left one open space at the end of the third row, and if his current pattern holds, he'll be looking for a new victim any time now. When he finds you've discovered his carefully planned burial site . . . It's going to throw him. He's going to be angry, maybe disoriented.'

'Maybe he'll make a mistake,' Beverly said.

Thomas nodded. 'It's possible. It's also possible that he'll retreat, go under and regroup. He went almost a year between the first murders and these recent ones. He could wait another year. Or more.'

'Or he could find another field and dig another matrix of graves,' Jen said flatly.

'That, too,' Thomas acknowledged. 'What he does next may depend on why he's doing this at all. Why he kills. What got him started? And why a year between sprees?'

'We were kind of hoping you could help us with that,' Vito said dryly.

Thomas's smile was equally dry. 'I'll do my best. One of the things we need to establish is how he chooses his victims. The last two came from the modeling website.'

'Maybe the last three,' Tim Riker said. 'I ran a search on all the male models at UCanModel that have the same height and weight as Flail Guy.'

'Stop calling him that,' Katherine snapped, then pursed her lips hard. 'Please.'

There was a raw desperation in her voice that made everyone turn to look at her.

'I'm sorry, Katherine,' Tim said. 'I didn't mean to be disrespectful.'

She nodded unsteadily. 'It's okay. Let's just call him three-one, for his grave. I just finished that man's autopsy. Brittany Bellamy and Warren Keyes suffered horribly, but there's every indication their ordeal was no longer than a few hours. Three-one was tortured over a period of days. His fingers and thumbs were broken. His legs and arms were broken, his back flayed open.' She swallowed. 'And his feet were burned.'

'The soles of his feet?' Liz asked gently.

'No, his whole foot. The scarring is total and has a clear delineation. Like a sock.'

'Or a boot,' Nick said grimly, coming in the door. He squeezed Katherine's shoulder reassuringly before taking the seat next to Scarborough. 'It was one of the torture devices on the websites I found. The inquisitors would pour hot oil down into a boot, usually one foot at a time. It was a very effective method of getting people to say anything they wanted them to say.'

'But what could our killer have possibly wanted these people to say?' Beverly asked, frustration in her voice. 'They were models, actors.'

'Maybe he didn't want them to say anything. Maybe he just wanted to see them suffer,' Tim said quietly.

'Well, they suffered,' Katherine said bitterly.

Vito closed his eyes and forced himself to visualize the scene, horrible as it was. 'But Katherine, something doesn't make sense. The way his head had sheared off, he had to have been sitting up. If he'd been lying down, I would think the skull would crush, not shear. If this guy was in such horrible shape before he was hit with a flail – or whatever – how did he even sit up to receive the blow?'

Katherine's lips thinned. 'I found rope fibers in the skin of his torso. I think he was tied so that he was vertical. The pattern of circular bruising was on top of the fibers.'

There was a moment of silence as everyone digested this latest horror. Vito cleared his throat. 'What did you find when you searched the UCanModel database, Tim?'

'A hundred names, roughly, but knowing about his feet being burned helps. Brittany Bellamy had been a hand model and the killer posed her hands. Warren had the tattoo of Oscar holding the sword and his hands were posed the same way.' Tim pulled a sheaf of papers from his folder and began scanning the list. 'There are three that were foot models.' He looked up at Katherine. 'What size were the victim's feet?'

'Ten and a half.'

Rapidly Tim thumbed through the pages, then stopped and focused. 'Yes.' He looked up again, triumphant. 'But only one has size-ten-and-a-half feet. William Melville. Goes by Bill. He did a shoot for a foot spray ad last year.'

Vito's pulse picked up some speed. 'Good work, Tim. Really good work.'

Tim nodded soberly, then looked at Katherine. 'Now he has a name.'

'Thank you,' she murmured. 'That means a lot.'

'When we break, we'll need to confirm it,' Vito said briskly. 'Nick and I will take finding an address for Bill Melville and checking him out. Tim, I'd like you and Beverly to keep working that database. I still want to know who our killer attempted to hire and couldn't. I also want to know who he's contacted lately. We need to find him and stop him before he finishes out that row.'

'We're meeting Brent Yelton from IT when we're done here,' Beverly said. 'He said he'd try working through the user side but that he'll probably need help from the website hosts themselves.' She grimaced. 'And for that we'll need a warrant.'

'You get me the details,' Liz said, 'and I'll get a warrant.'

'So each of the last three victims was chosen based on a physical attribute,' Thomas said, musingly. 'Using the modeling database, he could search for the attributes he wanted. There's also a certain drama about posing hands, et cetera. Models are accustomed to playing roles in front of a camera.'

Nick frowned. 'Could this guy be filming all this?'

217

'It's a thought.' Vito jotted it on the whiteboard. 'Let's leave it as a thought for now and go on. Computers. Warren's hard drive was fried. The Bellamy family's was also fried. But Claire didn't have a computer.'

'So he didn't meet her through the website.' Tim said. 'Unless she used a public computer. She did work at a library.'

Vito sighed. 'An Internet session on a public computer fifteen months ago will be hard to trace. That could be a dead end.'

'What did you find out about where he could have gotten his tools?' Nick asked. 'Were Sophie's contacts any help?'

'Not much.' Vito sat back down. 'The chain mail was high quality. A mail shirt with links that small runs over a thousand bucks.'

'Whoa,' Nick said. 'So our boy has some funds.'

'But the mail is available through a number of Web stores.' Vito shrugged. 'As were the sword or the flail. It'll be hard to trace a single purchase, but that's what we'll need to do. Sophie did tell me that one of her professors heard that a collection of torture artifacts had gone missing. I'll follow up on that tomorrow. It was in Europe, so I'll have to involve Interpol.'

'Which will add time,' Liz grumbled. 'Can't your archeologist dig some more?'

Jen winced. 'No pun intended.'

'I'll ask her,' Vito said. *If she meets me tonight.* If she didn't . . . He supposed he'd have to walk away, but he wasn't sure he could. She drew him in a way no woman had in a very long time. Maybe ever. *Please, Sophie. Please come.* 'Jen, what more have you found at the crime scene?'

'Nothing.' She lifted a brow. 'But that's something, in a way. We're still sifting fill dirt and will be for days, but something is missing from the site.'

'The dirt he took from the graves initially,' Beverly said and Jen touched her nose.

'We've combed those woods and haven't found any evidence of dirt he removed.'

'He could have spread it out,' Tim said doubtfully.

'Could have, and he might have, but that would have required a lot of work. Sixteen graves is a lot of dirt. It would have been easier for him to just pile it off to one side.'

'Or remove it. He has to have a truck,' Vito said.

'Or access to one. We might be able to tell what kind. We got a tire print from the access road leading to the field. It's at the lab.' Jen bent her lips down as she thought. 'That resignation letter Claire's parents gave Bev and Tim was just a copy. We need to get the original. Who has it?'

A cell phone rang and everyone instantly checked their own phones. Katherine held hers up. 'Mine,' she said. 'Excuse me.' She got up and moved to the window.

'The library where Claire worked had the letter,' Tim said. 'We requested it today, but they said they had to 'go through channels.' They hoped to have it tomorrow.'

Jen's smile was sharp. 'Good. Let's see if we can get some decent prints.'

Katherine slapped her phone shut, then turned to the group, her eyes bright again. 'That silicone lubricant you found with Claire's things?'

'The lubricant for her prosthetic leg,' Vito said warily. 'What about it?'

'It matches the sample I took from the wire on Brittany's hands.'

Vito pounded his hand on the table. 'Excellent.'

'But,' Katherine nearly sang, 'it doesn't match the sample we took from Warren. The lubricant found on Warren's hands was close in formula, but not exact. The lab called the manufacturer, and they said they had two main formulas but often create custom blends for clients with allergies.'

Vito looked at the table, processing. 'So the sample found on Warren's hands is a custom blend.' He looked up. 'Did Claire buy a custom blend, too?'

Katherine lifted her brows. 'Not in the manufacturer's records.'

'So it belonged to somebody else?' Beverly asked.

'She could have bought it somewhere else, or somebody may have bought it for her,' Liz cautioned. 'Don't assume until you know.'

Katherine nodded. 'True. The manufacturer said her orders came through a Dr Pfeiffer. You can ask him if she bought anything special. But if she didn't, either she got it from somebody else or the killer did.'

Vito rubbed his hands together. 'We're starting to get somewhere. Thomas, after all you've heard, what are your thoughts on this killer?'

'And are we talking just one?' Nick added.

'Very good point.' Thomas leaned back in his chair, arms folded across his chest. 'But my gut says he works alone. He's younger, almost certainly male. Intelligent. He has a dispassionate capacity for cruelty. It's . . . mechanical. He is obsessive, obviously. This would spill into other areas of his life – occupation, relationships. His knack with creating computer viruses is consistent. He'd be more comfortable with a machine than with people. I'd bet he lives alone. He will have some record of violence in his adolescence, anything from being a schoolyard bully to abusing animals. He's . . . process oriented. And he's efficient. He could have just killed two people to use for his effigies, but he combined them with whatever torture experiments he needed to do first.'

'So an anal, obsessed, cold loner who measures twice and cuts once,' Jen said sourly and Thomas chuckled.

'Nicely summarized, Sergeant. Add dramatic to it and you've got it covered.'

Vito stood up. 'Well, Nick and I and Bev and Tim have things to do. Thomas, can we bring you in as needed?'

'Absolutely.'

'Then we reconvene tomorrow at eight,' Vito said. 'Be careful and stay safe.'

Tuesday, January 16, 5:45 P.M.

Nick sank into his chair and propped his feet on his desk. 'I swear, waiting outside court makes me more ragged-out than if I'd worked a whole damn day.'

'Did you make any progress finding Kyle Lombard?'

'No. I must've called seventy-five Kyle Lombards while I was waiting outside the courtroom today. I got nothin' but a dead cell phone battery. No dice.'

'You can try again tomorrow.' Vito picked a note on his desk. 'Tino was here. He went to the morgue to sketch the old couple from the second row.'

'Hopefully he can work another miracle,' Nick said.

'He sure hit the nail on the head with Brittany Bellamy.' Vito sat down at his computer and pulled up the UCanModel website and found Bill Melville's résumé and photo. 'Come over here and meet Mr Melville.'

Nick came around their desks to stand behind him. 'Big, brawny guy like Warren.'

'But other than size, no resemblance.' Warren had been fair, while Bill was dark and forbidding looking. 'He has martial arts experience.' Vito looked up at Nick. 'Why the hell would the killer purposely choose a victim that could beat the shit out him?'

'Doesn't seem too smart,' Nick agreed. 'Unless he thought he'd need those skills. Warren searched fencing sites and was posed with a sword. Bill was killed with a flail.' Nick sat on the edge of Vito's desk. 'I didn't get lunch. Let's grab some chow before we check out Melville's last known address.'

Vito checked his watch. 'I have dinner plans.' *I hope.*

Nick face broke into a slow grin. 'Dinner plans?'

He felt his cheeks heat. 'Shut up, Nick.'

Nick's grin just broadened. 'No way. I want details.'

Vito glared up at him. 'There are no details.' *Not yet, anyway.*

'This is even better than I thought.' He snorted a laugh when

Vito rolled his eyes. 'You're no fun, Chick. Okay then, what did you find out from that Brewster guy?'

'That he's an asshole who likes tall blonde girls and cheats on his wife.'

'Oh. Well, now Sophie's reactions to the flowers make sense. You said he gave you some names of potential collectors.'

'All pillars of society and every one of them over sixty years old. Hardly able to dig sixteen graves and move around big men like Keyes and Melville. I checked financials as much as I could without a warrant and came up with nothing suspicious.'

'What about Brewster himself?'

'Young enough, I guess. His office looks like a museum, but it's all out in the open.'

'He could have a stash.'

'He could, but he was out of the country the week Warren went missing.' Vito shot Nick a rueful look. 'I Googled him when I got back from the Bellamys'. The first thing that popped up was a conference he'd spoken at in Amsterdam on January 4. Airline records show Dr and Mrs Alan Brewster flew first class from Philly to Amsterdam.'

'First class is pricey. Professors don't make that much. He could be dealing.'

'Wife's loaded,' Vito grumbled. 'Gramps was a coal baron. I checked that, too.'

Nick's lips twitched in sympathy. 'You really wanted it to be him.'

'A whole hell of a lot. But unless he's an accomplice, Brewster's only guilty of being an asshole.' Vito brought up the DMV database on his computer. 'Melville was twenty-two years old, last known address was up in North Philly. I'll drive.'

Tuesday, January 16, 5:30 P.M.

Sophie was up to her butt in sawdust in the old warehouse that sat at the back of the factory area they'd converted to the museum's main hall. Ted was right, the warehouse wasn't perfect, but Sophie could see the potential. And, there were still some places she could smell chocolate if she sniffed hard enough. It had to be fate.

She looked around the future site of her hands-on 'dig.' She hadn't been so content in a long time. Well, maybe *content* was the wrong word. She was energized and aware, thinking of all the wonderful things she could do with this huge empty space with its thirty-foot ceilings. Her brain was firing like a machine gun.

And her nerve endings were firing, too. She was meeting Vito Ciccotelli tonight. She was keyed. Needy. And feeling the edge of her self-imposed sexual suppression all too keenly. She'd never allowed another relationship with a colleague, which meant finding a man outside the dig, in the city. By nature those relationships were surface only, really no more than a way to scratch her itch when it got too hard to handle. But 'one night stand' always came to her mind afterward and she hated herself. Vito would be different. She just had a feeling. Maybe the drought would soon end.

All in good time. For now, she was anxious to explore the contents of the crates she'd dragged from her office. She'd already uncovered some incredible treasures.

Working in her dark little office, she'd been surrounded by medieval reliquaries and hadn't even known it. Using a crowbar, she opened a crate and scooped more sawdust onto the floor until she got down to the smaller box inside.

She heard footsteps behind her a heartbeat before the voice. 'You can't have it.'

With a gasp she whirled, swinging the crowbar high above her head. Then she exhaled. 'Theo, I swear to God, I'm going to hurt you one of these days.'

Theodore Albright the Fourth stood looking at her from the shadows, his jaw stern. Stiffly he crossed his arms over his broad chest. 'You can't have these things. Children will come in here. They'll break them.'

'I don't plan to put anything valuable out in the open. I'm going to have plastic copies made, and break the copies in pieces – to hide in the dirt for people to find. The way we'd find broken pottery in a dig.'

Theo looked around the room. 'You're going to make it look like an authentic dig?'

'That's my plan. I know your grandfather's treasures are precious. I won't let anything happen to them.'

His wide shoulders relaxed. 'I'm sorry I scared you.' His eyes dropped to her hand and she realized she still held the crowbar. Bending at the knees, she laid it on the floor.

'It's okay.' Amanda Brewster's little gift and phone call had left her shakier than she'd thought. 'So . . . did you need something?'

He nodded. 'You have a phone call. It's some old guy from Paris.'

Maurice. 'Paris?' She was already taking him by the arm and guiding him out the door. 'Why didn't you tell me?' she demanded as she locked the room behind them.

In her office, she shut the door, grabbed the phone and let her mind relax back into French. 'Maurice? It's Sophie.'

'Sophie, my dear. Your grandmother. How is she?'

She heard the fear in his voice and realized he thought she was calling with bad news about Anna. 'She's holding her own. That's actually not why I called. I'm sorry, I should have told you so you didn't worry.'

He let out a breath. 'Yes, you should have, but I can't be angry that you're not calling with bad news, I suppose. So why did you call?'

'I'm doing some research and was hoping you could give me information.'

'Ah.' His voice perked up and Sophie smiled. Maurice had always been one of the biggest gossips of her father's crowd. 'What kind of information?'

'Well, it's like this . . .'

Tuesday, January 16, 8:10 P.M.

'So the victim is Bill Melville?' Liz asked on the phone as Vito turned his truck onto his street.

'His prints match the ones Latent lifted from his apartment. Nobody had seen him since Halloween. Kids in his building said he always dressed up and handed out candy.'

'Sounds like a nice guy.'

'I don't know about that. He dressed like a ninja. The kids thought he did it to let them know he could handle weapons. Nunchucks, staffs. It was his way of maintaining security. But he did give out good candy, so everybody seemed happy.'

'Why hadn't someone gone in his apartment before?'

'Melville's landlord did but didn't find anything. We got lucky. The landlord already filed an eviction notice. Another two days and all of Melville's stuff would have been in the Dumpster.'

'Was his computer fried?'

'Yep. But,' Vito smiled grimly. 'Bill printed out a few of the e-mails. Left them on the printer. He was contacted by a guy named Munch to do a history documentary.'

'Did you get his e-mail address?'

'No. The printed e-mail only said 'E. Munch.' If we had the actual e-mail on his machine we could have clicked on the name to get his e-mail address, but the files are wiped. The good thing is, we have a name to use when we question all the models on the UCanModel website who got hits on their résumés the days around our victims.'

'So Beverly and Tim were able to get into the website's records?'

'Yeah. The owners of the site are cooperating fully. They don't want all their clients pulling off the site because of a killer. They haven't handed over any blanket lists, but they will work with Bev and Tim on a person-by-person basis. Bev and Tim are going to start contacting the models who were contacted by Munch tomorrow.'

'Although it's not likely to be his real name. Are you headed back to the office?'

'No, I'm home.' He'd parked behind Tess's rental and beside a car he'd never seen before. 'My nephews are staying with me and I've hardly spent five minutes with them. I'm going to help my sister get everyone tucked in, then go grab some dinner.' And if he was lucky . . . His mind wandered to that single kiss. It had tormented him all day, distracting him, derailing his thoughts. What if she didn't come? What if he had to walk away? What if he never got to taste her full lips again? *Sophie, please come.*

Vito got out of his truck and looked in the window of the strange car and saw the back floorboards strewn with McDonald's trash and ratty old sneakers. Teenager, he guessed. When he opened his front door, he saw he was partially right.

Multiple teens were gathered around a computer someone had set up in his living room. One kid sat in Vito's easy chair, feet up as he faced the monitor, a keyboard on his lap. Dominic stood behind the chair, a frown on his handsome face as he looked on.

'Hey,' Vito called as he closed his front door. 'What's all this?'

Dominic's eyes flickered. 'We were working on a school project, but took a break.'

'What kind of project?' he asked.

'Science,' Dominic said. 'Earth–space,' he clarified.

The kid with the keyboard looked up with a cynical sneer. 'We had to create life,' he said drolly and the others snickered.

Except for Dom, who frowned. 'Jesse, cut it out. Let's get back to work.'

'In a minute, choir boy,' Jesse drawled.

Dom's cheeks flushed a dark red and Vito realized his oldest nephew had been taking ribbing for his clean-cut ways. He moved to Dom's side. 'What's the game?'

'*Behind Enemy Lines*,' Dom told him. 'It's a World War II fighting game.'

The screen was filled with the interior of an ammunitions

bunker, in which eleven soldiers with swastikas on their arm-bands already lay dead. The camera looked out over the barrel of a rifle. 'This guy is an American soldier,' Dom explained. 'You can choose your character's nationality and your weapon. It's the newest rage.'

Vito studied the screen. 'Really? The graphics look two or three years old.'

One of the boys eyed him warily. 'You play?'

'Some.' He'd held the community record for Galaga when he was fifteen, but didn't think divulging that fact would do more than make him look like a dinosaur. He lifted a brow. 'Maybe I'll learn a few things about taking out the bad guys or fast car chases.'

The boy who'd just spoken grinned good-naturedly. 'Well, you won't learn anything from this game. It's just average.'

'That's Ray,' Dom said. 'He's a gamer. So is Jesse.'

'So what's the big deal with this game?' Vito asked.

Ray shrugged. 'Everything in the game part's a rehash from this company's last five games. Game physics, environments, AI . . .'

'Artificial intelligence,' Dom murmured.

'I know,' Vito murmured back. 'So I repeat, what's the big deal? The characters are flat and the AI really sucks. I mean, Jesse here just took out a dozen bad boys with arm-bands and not one of them winged him. What's the challenge in that?'

'We're not playing it for the game,' Jesse said, apparently unoffended. 'We're playing it for the cut scenes.' He laughed softly. 'Fuckin' unbelievable, man.'

Dom looked around, frowning. '*Jesse*. My little brothers are here.'

'Like they don't hear it from your old man,' Jesse said, bored.

Dom gritted his teeth. 'They don't. Look, let's get back to work.'

'Just a minute,' Vito said softly, his eyes on the screen. He'd let this play out because he was curious, both about Dom's classmates and what kids were playing these days. He never knew when knowing current kid-speak would come in handy in the interview room. He'd caught many a teen off guard pretending to share their interests. But as soon as Vito's curiosity was sated, Jesse would be out on his ass.

On the screen, the American soldier reloaded his weapon and muttered, 'This was a trap. She betrayed me, the whore.' He cocked the rifle. 'She'll come to regret that move.' The scene changed and the soldier was at the door of a small French cottage.

'So what's the story here?' Vito asked Ray.

'This is . . . the cut scene.' He said it like it was the Sistine Chapel or something. When Vito frowned, Ray looked disappointed. 'A cut scene is—'

'I know what a cut scene is,' Vito interrupted. The cut scene was the animated movie clip where the main character talked to people, learned secrets, or simply got free stuff. 'Most of the ones I've seen have been boring and just kept you from the game. What I was asking was, what's special about this one?'

Ray grinned. 'You'll see. This is Clothilde's house. She claimed to be French Resistance, but she gave our soldier up. That's why he was ambushed back there at the bunker. It's payback time. Jesse's right. This really is unbelievable.'

On the screen, the door opened to the inside of the cottage as the game flowed into the cut scene. The graphics abruptly changed. Gone were the grainy characters and choppy motion. When the American soldier walked through the door and began to search the cottage, it looked real. The solder finally found Clothilde hiding in a closet. He yanked her out of the closet and up against a wall. 'You bitch,' he snarled. 'You told them where to find me. What did they give you? Chocolate? Silk stockings?'

The busty Clothilde sneered up at him, although her eyes were wide with fear.

'Watch her eyes,' Ray whispered.

'Tell me.' The soldier shook the woman's shoulders violently.

'My life,' Clothilde spat. 'They said they would not kill me if I told. So I told.'

'Five of my buddies died back there. Because of you.' The American put his hands around her throat and Clothilde's eyes grew wider. 'You should have let those German bastards kill you. Now I will.'

'No. Please no!' As she struggled the screen filled with her face and his hands. The fear in her eyes . . .

'Amazing,' Ray whispered beside him. 'The artist is truly amazing. It's like watching a movie. It's hard to believe somebody created this.'

But someone had. Disturbed, Vito felt his jaw tighten. Somebody had drawn this. And kids were watching it. He nudged Dom aside. 'Go check on your brothers.'

From the corner of his eye, Vito could see Dom's face relax in relief. 'Okay.'

On the screen, Clothilde was sobbing and begging for her life. 'Are you ready to die, Clothilde?' the soldier mocked and she screamed, loud and long. Desperate. Too real. Vito winced and looked at the kids' faces as they watched transfixed. Eyes wide, mouths slightly open. Waiting.

The scream ended and there was a long moment of silence. Then the soldier laughed softly. 'Go ahead and scream, Clothilde. No one can hear you. No one will save you. I killed them all.' His hands tightened, his thumbs moving to the hollow of her throat. 'And now I'll kill you.' His hands tightened further and Clothilde began to writhe.

Vito had seen enough. 'That's it.' He leaned forward and hit the power button on the monitor and the screen went dark. 'Show's over, kids.'

Jesse whipped the recliner down and stood up. 'Hey. You can't do that.'

Vito pulled the computer's power cord from the wall. 'Hey. Watch me. You can play that crap in your parents' house, but you're not playin' it here. Pack it up, buddy.'

Jesse weighed his options. Finally he turned away in disgust. 'Let's get out of here.'

'Dude.' One of the boys winced. 'Without Dom's science project, we got nothin'.'

'We don't need him.' Jesse tucked the computer under his arm. 'Noel, get the monitor. Ray, get the CDs.'

Noel shook his head. 'I can't fail again. You might not need Dom's project, but I do.'

Jesse's eyes narrowed. 'Fine.' The others followed, leaving Ray and Noel.

Ray grinned at Vito. 'His parents wouldn't let him play the game at home either.'

Vito looked over his shoulder. 'Will Jesse cause any problems for Dominic?'

'Nah. Jesse's no match for Dom. Dom's the captain of the JV wrestling team.'

Vito bent his mouth, impressed. 'Wow. He never told me that.'

'Dominic can take care of himself,' Ray said. 'Sometimes he's just too nice.'

Dominic came back down the hall, Pierce riding on his back. The five-year-old had just gotten out of the bath and his hair was wet, and his pj's were Spiderman. Vito was glad he'd turned off that filth before the little ones had seen it.

Dom looked at the remaining two teenagers. 'Jesse's gone?'

Ray grinned again. 'Sheriff here ran him out of town on a rail.'

'Thanks, Vito,' Dom said quietly. 'I didn't want him watching that stuff here.'

Vito presented his back to Pierce, who took a flying, screeching leap. 'Next time, just tell him to leave.'

'I did tell him to leave.'

'Well, then . . . toss him out on his ass, if you have to.'

'Awwww,' Pierce said. 'Uncle Vitoooooo. You said the donkey word, Uncle Vito.'

Vito winced. He'd forgotten 'ass' was on the swear-word list.

'Sorry, pal. You think Aunt Tess'll wash my mouth out with soap?'

Pierce bounced. 'Yes, yes!'

'Yes, yes,' Tess said from the hall. Her hair hung in damp waves. Obviously as much water had landed on her as on Pierce. 'Vito, watch your mouth.'

'Okay, okay.' He gave a final nod to Dom. 'You did fine, kid. Next time you'll do even better.' He jogged back to Tess, giving Pierce a ride.

'Well? Did she get it?' She was referring to the present she'd left for Sophie.

'Don't know. She gets out of class soon. I guess I'll find out then. But thanks for picking it up. Where did you find a memory neutralizer toy anyway?'

'Party store on Broad Street. Guy advertises he's got every Happy Meal toy ever sold. The neutralizer was a pretty popular one when the movie came out.' She lifted a brow. 'You owe me two hundred bucks for the toy and the curtains.'

Vito nearly dropped Pierce. '*What?* What kind of curtains did you buy? Gold?'

She shrugged. 'The curtains were only thirty bucks.'

'You paid a hundred and seventy dollars for a Happy Meal toy?'

'The toy was in its original wrapper.' Her lips twitched. 'I hope she's worth it.'

Vito blew out a breath. 'Me, too.'

Chapter Thirteen

Tuesday, January 16, 9:55 P.M.

'Is something wrong, Dr J?'

Sophie looked up to see Marta walking across the parking lot behind the Whitman humanities building. 'My bike won't start.' She got off and huffed a weary sigh. 'It was running just fine right before class. Now it tries to start and just sputters.'

'Bummer.' Marta bit her lip. 'You do have gas in the tank, don't you? The last time my car wouldn't start I got all upset till I realized I'd forgotten to get gas.'

Sophie bit back her impatience. Marta was trying to help. 'I filled up this morning.'

'What's wrong?' Spandan had joined them, along with most of the other students in her Tuesday night graduate seminar. This semester she was teaching Fundamentals of the Dig to a packed classroom, and while she normally would have hung around to answer questions, she'd bolted right after class tonight. Vito was waiting for her at Peppi's Pizza and all she'd been able to think about during class was that kiss.

'My bike won't start and now I'm late.'

Marta looked interested. 'For a date?'

Sophie rolled her eyes. 'If I don't get there soon, no.'

The door behind them opened again and John came down the wheelchair ramp. 'What's wrong?'

'Dr J's bike's busted and she's late for her date,' Bruce said.

John steered his chair around the crowd and leaned forward

to peer at her engine. 'Sugar.' He tapped her gas tank with one gloved finger.

'What?' Sophie leaned forward to immediately see that he was right. A dusting of sugar crystals around the gas tank sparkled in the light of the street lamps. 'Dammit,' she hissed. 'I swear to God that woman's going to pay this time.'

'You know who did this?' Marta asked, wide-eyed.

That the saboteur had been Amanda Brewster was almost certain. 'I have an idea.'

Bruce had his cell phone in his hand. 'I'm calling campus security.'

'Not now. I will report this. Don't worry,' she added when Spandan tried to protest. She unbungeed her backpack from the seat. 'But I'm not going to wait around for them to come right now. I'm really late. It's a good fifteen-minute walk to the restaurant.'

'I'll drive you.' John asked. 'I've got my van.'

'Um . . .' Sophie shook her head. 'Thanks, but I'll walk.'

John's chin went up. 'It's equipped with hand controls. I'm a good driver.'

She'd offended him. 'It's not that, John,' she said hastily. 'It's just . . . I'm your teacher. I don't want to appear improper.'

He angled her a look up through his ever-shaggy hair. 'It's a ride, Dr J. Not marriage.' One side of his mouth lifted. 'Besides, you're not my type.'

She laughed. 'Okay. Thanks. I'm going to Peppi's Pizza.' She waved to the others. 'See you Sunday.' She walked alongside his chair until they came to the white van he drove. He opened her door, then activated the lift for his chair. Capably, he swung his body out of the chair and behind the driver's seat.

He saw her watching and his jaw tightened. 'I've had lots of practice.'

'How long have you been in the chair?'

'Since I was kid.' His tone was clipped. She'd offended him again. Saying no more, he pulled the van out of the parking lot.

Unsure of what to say next, Sophie went for something she

hoped was more neutral. 'You missed the first part of class tonight. I hope nothing was wrong.'

'I got tied up at the library. I was so late that I almost didn't come at all, but I needed to ask you about something. I tried to catch you after class, but you rushed out.'

'So you had an ulterior motive for offering me a ride.' She smiled. 'What's up?'

He didn't smile back, but then John rarely smiled. 'I have a paper due tomorrow for another class. It's almost done, but I was having trouble finding primary references for one piece of it.'

'What's the topic?'

'Comparison of modern and medieval theories on crime and punishment.'

Sophie nodded. 'You must be taking Dr Jackson's medieval law class. So what's the question?'

'I wanted to include a comparison of the medieval practice of branding with contemporary use of sex offender registration. But I couldn't find any consistent information on branding.'

'Interesting topic. I can think of a few references that might help.' She dug in her backpack for her notebook and started writing. 'When is your paper due?'

'Tomorrow morning.'

She grimaced. 'Then you'll need to use the online references unless the librarians work later than they used to. I know some of these are available online. The others might only be available through old-fashioned books. Oh, Peppi's is right around the corner.' She ripped out the page and handed it to him as he pulled into the restaurant's parking lot. 'Thanks, John. Good luck on your paper.'

He took the sheet with a sober nod. 'See you on Sunday.'

Sophie stood still as he drove away, then held her breath as she scanned the lot for Vito's truck. Slowly she let the breath out. He was still here.

This was it. She'd walk into that restaurant and . . . change her life. And suddenly she was scared to death.

Tuesday, January 16, 10:00 P.M.

Daniel sat on the edge of his hotel bed, exhausted. He'd been to more than fifteen hotels since breakfast and he was no closer to finding his parents. His parents were creatures of habit, so he'd started with their favorite hotels, the expensive ones. He'd gone on to the big chains. No one had seen them, or remembered them if they had.

Wearily he toed off his shoes and fell back against the mattress. He was tired enough to fall asleep like this, his tie still knotted and his feet still on the floor. Maybe his parents hadn't come to Philadelphia after all. Maybe this had been a wild goose chase. Maybe they were already dead.

He closed his eyes, trying to think past the pounding in his temples. Maybe he should call the local police and check the morgues.

Or the doctors. Perhaps they'd been to one of the oncologists on the list he'd printed from his father's computer. But no doctor would tell him anything. Patient confidentiality, they'd say.

The ringing of his cell phone startled him out of a near doze. Susannah.

'Hello, Suze.'

'You haven't found them.' It was more a statement than a question.

'No, and I've walked all over town today. I'm beginning to wonder if this is really where they came.'

'They were there,' Susannah said, little inflection in her tone. 'The call from Mom's cell phone to Grandma's was placed from Philadelphia.'

Daniel sat up. 'How do you know that?'

'I called in a marker, had it traced. I thought you should know. Call me if you find them. Otherwise, don't. Good-bye, Daniel.'

She was going to hang up. 'Suze, wait.'

He heard her sigh. 'What?'

'I was wrong. Not to leave. I had to leave. But I was wrong not to tell you why.'

'And you're going to tell me now?' Her voice was hard and it pricked his heart.

'No. Because you're safer if you don't know. That was my only reason for not telling you then . . . and now. Especially now.'

'Daniel, it's late. You're talking in riddles and I don't want to listen.'

'Suze . . . You trusted me once.'

'Once.' The single word rang with finality.

'Then trust me again, please, just on this. If you knew, you'd be compromised. Your career would be compromised. You've worked too hard to get where you are for me to drag you down for the simple purpose of unloading my guilty conscience.'

She was quiet so long he had to check to see if they were still connected. They were. Finally she murmured. 'I know what your son did. Do you know, Daniel?'

'Yes.'

'And you want me to forgive you?'

'No. I don't expect that. I don't know what I want. Maybe to hear you call me Danny again.'

'You were my big brother, and I needed your protection then. But I learned how to take care of myself. I don't need your protection now, Daniel, and I don't need you. Call me if you find them.'

She hung up and Daniel sat on the edge of a strange hotel bed, staring at his phone and wondering how he'd allowed everything to become so completely fucked up.

Tuesday, January 16, 10:15 P.M.

'Honey, if you're not going to order, you have to leave. Kitchen closes in fifteen.'

Vito checked his watch before looking up at the waitress.

'How about a large with everything?' he said. 'And just bring it in a box. I'll take it with me.'

'She's not coming, huh?' the waitress said sympathetically, taking his menu.

Sophie should have been there a half hour ago easily. 'Doesn't appear so.'

'Well, a man like you should have no trouble finding somebody better.' Clucking, she went back to the kitchen to place his order, and Vito leaned his head against the wall behind his booth and closed his eyes. Tried not to think about the fact that Sophie hadn't come. Tried to focus on the things he could really change.

They'd identified four of the nine victims. Five more to go.

Roses. He smelled roses and felt the booth shake as someone slid into the other side. She'd come after all. But he stayed where he was, eyes closed.

'Excuse me,' she said and he opened his eyes. She was sitting across from him wearing her black leather jacket. Huge gold hoops hung from her ears and she'd pulled her hair over one shoulder. 'I'm waiting for somebody, and I think you might be him.'

Vito chuckled. She'd taken them back to the moment they'd met. 'That memory zapper works better than I thought. Maybe I should try it.'

She smiled at him and he felt some of his stress ease. 'Hard day?' she asked.

'You could say that. But I don't want to talk about my day. You came.'

She lifted a shoulder. 'It's hard to resist movie swag. Thank you.'

Her hands were grasping each other so tightly that her knuckles were white. Taking a breath, he reached across the table and pulled her hands apart, then held each one. 'It was hard for you to give his name, but you did it anyway, to help us.'

Her hands tensed as her eyes skittered away from his. 'And

all those mothers, wives, husbands, and sons. I didn't want you to talk to Alan because I was ashamed. But I was more ashamed at not telling you.'

'I meant what I said in the note. Brewster is an ass. You should forget him.'

She swallowed. 'I didn't know he was married, Vito. I was young and very stupid.'

'Everything made sense when I met him. I think you knew it would.'

'Maybe.' She looked up, resolutely, he thought. 'I brought you something.' She pulled a folded sheet of paper from her pocket and handed it to him.

Vito unfolded it and laughed. She'd drawn a four-by-four matrix. Across the top she'd written *French, German, Greek,* and *Japanese.* Down the side were *damn, shit, hell,* and *fuck.* In the boxes she'd filled in what he assumed were translations. 'I like this four-by-four matrix a lot better than the one I've been staring at for two days.'

She was grinning at him and he felt even more weight roll from his shoulders. 'I promised to teach you some new swear words. I wrote the phonetic spelling, too. I wouldn't want you pronouncing them wrong. It spoils the effect.'

'It's great. But you're missing 'ass.' I got busted by my nephew for that one tonight.'

Brows lifted, she took the paper from his hands and pulled a pen from yet another pocket, then wrote the offending word and all its translations. She handed it back and he folded the paper and slipped it in his pocket. 'Thank you.' Then he took her hands in his again and was relieved to find her relaxed. 'I wasn't sure you were coming.'

'I had trouble with my bike. I had to catch a ride with one of my students.'

He frowned. 'What kind of trouble with your bike?'

'It wouldn't start. Somebody put sugar in my tank.'

'Who would do that?' His eyes narrowed when her lips pursed. 'Who's been bothering you, Sophie?'

'Oh, Brewster's wife. She's a nut case. Sent me a threatening . . . note. Kind of.'

'Sophie,' he warned.

She rolled her eyes. 'She sent me a dead mouse, then called to tell me to keep my hands to myself. She must have heard Alan talking to Clint. The woman's certifiably crazy. She thinks all the women are throwing themselves at Alan.'

'His current assistant probably is.' He sighed. 'But I'm sorry she thinks you did.'

'It's okay. Really. I've been tiptoeing about dealing with Alan for a long time, and this forced me to deal. It's all good.' She scowled. 'Except my bike. That pisses me off.'

It was an opening he couldn't pass up. 'I can take you home.'

His words came out deeper and more suggestive than he'd planned. Her cheeks heated and she looked down, but not before he saw her eyes darken with desire, sending a wave of lust singing through his system.

'I'd appreciate it,' she said quietly. 'Oh, I almost forgot.' She tugged her hand free and pulled out another folded sheet from her pocket. 'I got a little more information for you on that guy who died in Europe. Alberto Berretti.'

This sheet listed the names of Berretti's children and their attorneys. It also listed names of the man's household and business staff and his key debtors. It would be a very good start when he talked to Interpol the next day. 'Where did you get this?'

'Etienne – you know, my old professor? He didn't even know any more than Berretti's name and the rumor. But my father's old friend knows lots of rich people, and if not personally, he knows someone who does. I called him, and he got the information.'

Vito pushed back his irritation. 'I thought you agreed not to call anyone else.'

'I didn't call anyone I thought was dealing or buying.' She was irritated and didn't bother pushing it back. 'I've known Maurice since I was a little girl. He's a fine man.'

'Sophie, I'm grateful. I just don't want you hurt. If you know him, he should be fine.'

'He is,' she said stubbornly. But she didn't pull the hand he held away and Vito saw that as a good sign. He took her free hand again and once again she relaxed.

'So . . . your father. Is he still alive?'

She shook her head sadly. 'No, he died about two years ago.'

She'd liked her father, then. Unlike her mother. 'It must have been hard on him, having you so far away in Europe for so long.'

'No, he lived in France. I was able to see him more at the end of his life than when I was growing up.' She looked at him sideways. 'My father's name was Alex Arnaud.'

Vito crunched his brows. 'I know I've heard that name before. No, don't tell me.'

She looked amused. 'I'd be very surprised if you knew him.'

'I've seen his name fairly recently.' The memory clicked and he stared at her. 'Your father was Alexandre Arnaud the actor?'

She blinked. 'I'm impressed. Not many Americans know his name.'

'My brother-in-law is a film buff. Last time I was visiting them, he was on a French film kick and a few of them weren't too bad. No offense.'

'None taken. So which one did you see?'

'Do I get a bonus prize for getting the movie title, too?' Again her cheeks heated, and he realized there was as much shyness as desire in her eyes. This was new for her, flirting, like this, and that was an even bigger turn-on than anything else. Almost anything, he amended. He knew what lay under the black jacket was more than enough of a turn-on on its own. 'I'm glad I have a good memory,' he teased, then reluctantly released her hands when the waitress set the pizza on the table with a knowing grin.

'You still want this to go?' the waitress asked. 'I can bring the box.'

'I'm starving,' Sophie confessed. 'Are you closing soon?'

The waitress patted her hand and gave Vito a wink. 'When you're done, honey.'

Vito snapped his fingers. '*Soft Rain*,' he said. 'Your father's movie.'

Sophie stopped chewing, her eyes wide. 'Wow. You're good.'

Vito put a slice on his plate. 'So what's my bonus prize?'

Her eyes shifted, changed, nerves giving way to anticipation. He could see her pulse flutter at the hollow of her throat as she caught that full bottom lip between her teeth. 'I don't know yet.'

Vito swallowed hard, his own pulse kicking into overdrive. He barely restrained the urge to drag her away from the table and bite her lip himself. 'Don't worry. I'm sure I can think of something. Just do me a favor and eat fast, okay?'

Tuesday, January 16, 11:25 P.M.

It was good. Damn good. Not as good as *Warren Dies*, but still better than ninety-nine point nine percent of the drivel that made it into galleries.

He looked back at the stills, then at his own painting of the moment of Gregory Sanders's death. There was something about Sanders's face. Even in death it looked better on film than in reality. His lips quirked. The boy probably could have been a star.

Well, if he had anything to say about it, Gregory would. For now, he had a bit of cleaning up to do. He'd hose off the body in the studio below ground. His dungeon. Gregory had been suitably impressed. Suitably terrified.

As well he should have been. 'Try to steal from me,' he muttered. The young man had begged forgiveness. For mercy. There had been none.

He'd be able to get several good scenes from the Gregory footage. Thievery had been a common crime in the Middle

Ages, with a variety of punishments. It hadn't been the torture he'd planned, but it had worked, all in all.

He'd head out to bury the body at first light, then get back here to work on the game. By morning he should have some responses to the e-mail he'd sent to the tall blonde from UCanModel before meeting Gregory this afternoon. He'd devise an end fit for a stately queen to please Van Zandt. Then he'd make the knight's damn head explode. He wasn't sure exactly how he'd accomplish it, but he'd figure it out.

Tuesday, January 16, 11:30 P.M.

Sophie's hands shook as she tried to get her key in the lock in Anna's front door. They'd said nothing as he'd driven her home, save her clipped directions. Through it all he'd held her hand, at times so hard she nearly winced. But it was welcome pain, if there was such a thing. For the first time in a long time, Sophie felt alive. And clumsy. She cursed softly when the key bounced off the lock for the third time.

'Give me the keys,' he ordered quietly. He managed the door on the first try, bringing the dogs, barking shrilly. The look on his face would have been comical had she not been so impatient. He was staring down at Lotte and Birgit with mild horror.

'What the hell are those?'

'My grandmother's dogs. My aunt Freya lets them out at noon, so they're impatient by now. Come on, girls.'

'They're . . . colored. Like your rainbow gloves.'

Sophie looked at the dogs with a wince. 'It was an experiment. I need to let them out. I'll be right back.' She took the dogs out through the kitchen and stood on the back porch, arms wrapped around herself, toes tapping, while they sniffed the grass and each other. 'Hurry up,' she hissed at them. 'Or you're both getting dry dogfood for a month.'

242

The threat seemed to work, or maybe they just got cold, because they finally hurried. Sophie scooped them up and nuzzled each fuzzy head against her cheek before putting them down in the kitchen. She locked the deadbolt, then turned and sucked in a breath. Vito had materialized inches away, his eyes dark and reckless and her knees went weak. He'd shed his coat and gloves and made quick work of hers.

His gaze dropped to her breasts, still covered by layers of clothing. He lingered there for a few beats of her heart before lifting his eyes to hers and for a few more hard beats it was as if she couldn't breathe. Her breasts were tight, her nipples almost painfully sensitive and the throbbing between her legs had her wishing he would hurry.

But he didn't. With maddening care, he traced her lower lip with his fingertips until she shuddered. His lips curved, his smile sharp. Predatory. 'I want you,' he whispered. 'I'd be lying if I said anything different.'

She lifted her chin, wishing he'd touch her. Nervous that he didn't. 'Then don't.'

His eyes flashed and for another long moment he stared, as if he waited for her to say something more. Then in a blur of motion his hands were in her hair and his mouth was on hers and she moaned because it felt so good. His kiss was reckless and hot and demanding and she wanted more of it. She wanted more of him.

She flattened her hands against his chest, feeling his rock-hard muscles through his shirt, nearly moaning again when those muscles flexed against her palms. She curled her fingers into his shirt, pulling him closer. Needing to feel that hard chest pressed against her aching breasts. She wound her arms around his neck and lifted herself the few inches she needed to align their bodies, needing to feel his hardness all over.

He didn't disappoint, and in seconds he'd pressed her back against the door, the hard ridge in his jeans thrusting where it felt the very best. The door against her back was ice cold, but Vito burned hot against her front as she strained against him.

His hands finally took her breasts, his fingers plucking and teasing until she moaned again.

His hips and hands came to an abrupt halt and he ripped his mouth from hers.

'No.' It was a whimper, but she was too turned on to care.

'Sophie. Look at me.' She opened her eyes. He was so close she could see every eyelash. 'I told you what I wanted. I need you to do the same. Tell me what you want.'

He would make her say it. 'You.' The single syllable emerged rusty. 'I want you.'

He shuddered out a breath. 'It's been a long time for me. I can't go slow this time.'

This time. 'Then don't.'

He nodded slowly, then dropped his hands to the hem of her sweater and yanked, pulling it over her head. Then he laughed breathlessly when it got tangled in her hair. Together they freed her, and he sobered, staring at the wispy white lace of her bra.

He swallowed hard. 'God, you're pretty.' He skimmed his fingertips down the scalloped edges and under the fullness of her breasts, narrowly, but purposely missing her nipples which now strained against the lace. But his hands were shaking.

Her heart was going to pound right out of her chest. 'Touch me, Vito. Please.'

Again his eyes flashed and in another blur of movement he'd dispensed with the lace by ripping the front clasp. She had only a moment to feel the cold air against her skin before he'd covered one breast with his warm palm, the other with his even warmer mouth. She threaded her fingers through his wavy dark hair and held him close, then closed her eyes and let herself feel. And it felt so good. So necessary.

Too soon he straightened. 'Sophie, look at me.'

She opened her eyes. His mouth was wet, his eyes live coals. 'Where's your bed?'

Another shudder shook her and she lifted her eyes to the ceiling. 'Up.'

His grin was quick and wicked. 'Up it is.' He leaned in to kiss her again and her fingers stumbled over the buttons on his shirt, his over the zipper on her slacks. They backed out of the kitchen, frantically dropping clothes as they made their way to the stairs. He stopped at the first step and pressed her into the wall. She was naked, but he still wore his boxers. His eyes took an appreciative ride from her face down her body. His chest rose and fell, as if he jerked each breath from his lungs. 'You're beautiful.'

She'd heard the words before. She so wanted to believe them now. But words were just that. Words. It was the action that counted. A little desperately she pulled his head down and kissed him hard. With a deep growl he took control of the kiss, deepening it, running his hands down her back. He kneaded her butt, pulling her against him. She felt his erection pulse against her and she gyrated her hips, rubbing closer, but she needed more. 'Vito, please. Now.'

A shiver wracked his body, even though his skin burned against her hands and she knew he was as close as she was. He backed away and took her hand to lead her up the stairs but she slipped her hands beneath the elastic of his boxers and pushed them down his hips. Once again he did not disappoint and she wrapped her hand around him and squeezed, dragging a ragged groan from his lungs.

'Sophie, wait.'

'No. Here. Now.' She leaned against him and bit at his lip, her hand in the center of his chest, pushing at the rock hard wall of muscle. She held his gaze, on solid ground. This was sex. This she knew. 'Now.'

She pushed him, straddling his hips as he sank to the steps.

'Sophie, not like—'

She cut off his words by covering his mouth with hers and lowered herself, taking him into her body. He was hot and hard and huge and she closed her eyes against the sensation of being filled. 'You want me.'

'Yes.' His hands gripped her hips, his fingers dug deep.

'Then take me.' She arched her back, forcing him deeper,

opening her eyes to watch his slowly close, his dark stubbled jaw clench, his beautiful body go completely rigid. Then she began to move, slowly at first, then hard and fast as she felt her own climax coming.

With a cry she came and slumped forward, catching her hands on the step above him. She kissed him hard and he groaned into her mouth as his hips jerked wildly. Then his back went rigid and he thrust with staccato beats of motion as he found his own peak.

Breathing like he'd run a race, he collapsed back against his elbows and let his head fall back against the stairs. For a few seconds neither of them said anything, then Sophie rolled away to sit on the step below him, feeling relaxed and . . . damn good. She lightly patted his thigh, but he stiffened, drawing away. Twisting to look at him, she found him staring at her, not with sated pleasure, but raw anger.

'What,' he said harshly, 'the hell was that?'

Chapter Fourteen

Wednesday, January 17, 12:05 A.M.

Sophie's mouth fell open. 'What?'

'You heard me.' He twisted to his feet, leaving her sitting naked on the step staring up at him. He grabbed his boxers and pulled them on, then disappeared into the kitchen. When he came back he was wearing his pants and carrying her clothes. He tossed them to her but she made no move to catch them.

Her whole body was numb, but no longer with pleasure. 'Why are you so mad?'

He stared down at her, fists on his hips. 'You're kidding.'

'You wanted me. You had me.' A wave of fury made it past the numbness and she lurched to her feet. 'What is your problem anyway? Wasn't it good enough for you?' The last she added with a sneer, because hurt was moving in, pushing her anger aside.

'It was damn good. But *that*—' he pointed to the steps, 'wasn't what I wanted. That was . . .' His mouth flattened and so did his voice. 'That was fucking.'

The crudity hit her hard. 'And you feel so used? You got what you came here for, Vito. If the delivery wasn't to your liking, well, at least it was free.'

He faltered. 'Sophie, I didn't come here for . . . I came here to . . .' He shrugged, uncomfortable. 'To make love to you.'

The very words mocked her. 'You don't love me,' she said bitterly.

He swallowed hard and seemed to be choosing his words.

'No. No, I don't. Not now. But someday . . . Someday I could. Sophie, have you never made love?'

She lifted her chin, tears dangerously close. 'Don't you dare make fun of me.'

He exhaled. Then leaned over and picked up her underwear. 'Put them on.'

She swallowed the lump that had taken over her throat. 'No. I want you to leave.'

'And I'm not going to until we talk.' He was gentle again. 'Sophie.' He shook his head and held out her underwear. 'Put them on, or I'll put them on you myself.'

She had no doubt that he would so she snatched them from his hand. She jerked them up around her hips and held out her hands, still nude except for the panties. 'Satisfied?'

He narrowed his eyes. 'Not even close.' He pulled the sweater over her head like she was five years old. She elbowed his hands away.

'I can do it,' she gritted. She pushed her arms through the sleeves and pulled on her pants. 'I'm all dressed now. Now get the hell out of my house.'

He pulled her across the living room. 'Stop fighting me.' He pushed her to the sofa.

'Stop being an asshole,' she shot back. Then she crumpled and the floodgates crashed, letting the tears come. 'What the hell did you want from me?'

'Obviously not what you know how to give. Not yet anyway.'

Furiously she wiped her cheeks. 'I haven't been with a lot of men. Surprised?'

He still stood, fists back on his hips. He was still angry, but now his anger no longer seemed directed at her. *Big fucking deal.* Hers was still directed at him.

'No,' he murmured. 'I'm not surprised.'

'But no *customer* has ever been dissatisfied with the sex. Until you.'

He winced at that. 'I'm sorry. I wanted you and it had been a long time and . . . Sophie, what we just did was incredible. But it was . . . just sex.'

She drew a deliberate breath. 'And you expected *what*? Moonlight? Music? To *hold* me afterward and murmur promises you don't intend to keep? No, thank you.'

His eyes flashed. 'I don't make promises I don't intend to keep.'

'How gallant of you.' Then she dropped her head against the sofa, suddenly so weary. 'You said you wanted it fast, so I did it fast. I'm sorry if you were disappointed.'

He sat beside her and she flinched when his thumb caressed her cheek. 'I said I couldn't go slow.' He slid his fingers through the hair at her nape and tugged her to face him. The smooth timbre of his voice had her heart pounding again, but she refused to open her eyes. 'That's different from racing to the end because that's all there is.' He kissed her eyelids, then both corners of her mouth. 'There were so many things I wanted to do with you. For you.' His mouth covered hers, sweet. Patient. 'To you.' She shuddered and felt him smile against her lips. 'Don't you want to know what all those things are?' he teased and every nerve ending buzzed.

'Maybe,' she whispered and he chuckled, rich and deep.

'Sophie, any two people can just have sex. I like you. A lot. I wanted more.'

She swallowed hard. 'Maybe I can't give you any more.'

'I think you can,' he whispered. 'Sophie, look at me.' She forced herself to look up, dreading what she'd see. Sarcasm and scorn she could take. This she knew. Pity would be harder to swallow. But her breath caught in her throat because what she saw in his eyes was desire, tempered with tenderness and even a little self-deprecating humor. 'Let me teach you the difference between fucking like minks and making love.'

Deep down she'd known there had to be something more, that she'd never really shared what people in real relationships had. Deep down she'd always known she'd only . . . she winced. Fucked like a mink. Somehow it had always been simpler to keep it to that. But deep down, she'd always wanted to know the difference.

He nibbled at her lower lip. 'Come on, Sophie, you'll like it better.'

Sophie eyed the stairs. 'Better than *that*?'

He smiled, sensing victory. 'I guarantee it.' He stood and held out his hand.

She eyed his hand. 'What if I'm not completely satisfied?'

'I don't make promises I don't intend to keep.' He pulled her to her feet. 'If you're not satisfied, then I guess I'll have to keep working until you are.' He cupped her jaw, his lips grazing hers. 'Come to bed with me, Sophie. I have places to take you.'

The breath she drew was unsteady. 'Okay.'

Wednesday, January 17, 5:00 A.M.

Vito crept from Sophie's bed, where she slept curled up like a kitten. A very beautiful, teachable kitten. He moved his shoulders. With claws. Which she'd dug into his back that last time, when he'd taken her so high . . . The memory made him shudder. He'd like nothing better than to feel those sharp claws once more. But he had to get home and change and get on with his day.

Another day of identifying bodies. Of notifying grieving families. Of trying to stop a killer, before there were any more bodies or grieving families. Vito pulled on his clothes, then pressed a kiss against Sophie's temple. At least he'd satisfied one customer.

He looked around for something to write on. He didn't want to leave without saying good-bye. He got the impression she'd gotten enough of that over the years, from men who'd taken what they'd wanted and gone on, leaving her to believe that's all there was.

She had no paper on her nightstand, unless he counted the

candy wrappers, which he did not. But a framed picture caught his eye. He carried it to the window and held it to the light from the streetlamps. It was a young woman with long dark hair and big eyes, taken sometime in the fifties. She sat sideways, looking over the back of a chair, in front of what looked like a dressing room mirror. Vito thought about Sophie's father, a French film star with whom she hadn't spent much time until the end of his life. He wondered if this was her mother, but doubted she'd keep her picture next to her bed.

'My gran.' He looked over to see her sitting up in bed, knees pulled to her chest.

'She was an actress, too?'

'Of a fashion.' She lifted a brow. 'Double bonus prize if you know who *she* is.'

'I liked the bonus prize from before. Are you going to give me a hint?'

'Nope. But I will make you breakfast.' She grinned. 'I figure it's the least I can do.'

He grinned back, then picked up another photo, turning on a lamp. It was the same woman, with a man he did recognize. 'Your grandmother knew Luis Albarossa?'

Sophie poked her head out of a sweatshirt, her face stunned. 'What is it with you? You know French actors and Italian tenors, too?'

'My grandfather was an opera fan.' He hesitated. 'So am I.'

She'd bent at the waist to pull on a pair of sweats and paused, her hair a curtain over her face. She parted it with one hand and glared out. 'What's wrong with opera?'

'Nothing. It's just that some people don't think it's very . . .'

'Manly? That's just macho bullshit inherent in a patriarchal society.' She yanked at the sweats and pushed her hair from her face. 'Opera or Guns-N-Roses, neither makes you less of a man. Besides, I'm the last person you need to prove your manhood to.'

'Tell that to my brothers and my dad.'

She looked amused. 'What, that you give great sex?'

Startled, he laughed. 'No, that opera is manly.'

'Ohhh. It's always good to be clear. So gramps was an opera aficionado?'

'Every time it came to town he'd get tickets, but nobody would go to the concerts except me. We heard Albarossa do *Don Giovanni* when I was ten. Unforgettable.' He narrowed his eyes. 'Give me a hint. What was your grandmother's last name?'

'Johannsen,' she said with a smirk. 'Lotte, Birgit! Time to go out.' The dogs scrambled from one of the bedrooms, yapping. She headed down the stairs and he followed.

'Just a hint, Sophie.'

She just smirked again and went out the back door with the two ridiculously colored dogs. 'You know too much already. You should have to work for a double bonus.'

Chuckling, Vito wandered into the living room and investigated there. A double bonus prize was nothing to sneeze at. Plus, he admitted to himself, he was nosy. Sophie Johannsen was a damn interesting woman on her own, but it appeared her family tree had some unique knots and forks.

He found what he was looking for and carried it to the kitchen. She was back from outside and pulling pots and pans from the cupboard.

'You cook?' he said, surprised again.

'Of course. Woman cannot live by beef jerky and Ho Hos alone. I'm a good cook.' She looked at the framed program he held and sighed dramatically. 'So who is she?'

Vito leaned against the refrigerator, both smug in the knowledge that the double bonus was now his and awed. 'Your grandmother is Anna Shubert. My God, Sophie, my grandfather and I heard her sing *Orfeo* at the Academy downtown. Her *Che faro . . .*' He sobered, remembering the tears on his grandfather's face. In his own eyes. 'After her aria there wasn't a dry eye in the house. She was remarkable.'

Sophie's lips curved sadly. 'Yeah, she was. *Orfeo* here in Philly was her last performance. I'll tell her you knew who she was. It'll make her day.' She nudged him out of the way, taking eggs and a carton of cream from the fridge and setting them on the counter. Then her shoulders sagged. 'It's so hard to watch her die, Vito.'

'I'm sorry. My dad's got heart disease. We're grateful for every day he's with us.'

'Then you understand.' She blew a sigh up her forehead. 'If you want, there are a few photo albums in the living room. If you like opera, it'll be a treat.'

Eagerly he brought them to the table. 'These albums have to be worth a mint.'

'To Gran, yeah. And to me.' She set a cup of coffee next to his elbow. 'That's the Paris Opera House. The man standing next to Gran is Maurice. He's the one who gave me the information about the dead collector,' she added before going back to the stove.

Vito frowned. 'I thought you said Maurice was your father's friend.'

She winced. 'He was Alex's friend, too. It's kind of complicated. Sordid, really.'

She called her father by his first name. Interesting. 'Sophie, stop teasing me.'

She chuckled. 'Maurice and Alex went to university together. Both were wealthy playboys. Anna was in her forties and at the peak of her career, touring Europe. She'd been a widow a long time by then. I guess she was lonely. Alex had had a few small movie roles. Maurice worked for the opera house in Paris which is where he met Anna. The opera threw a party and Maurice invited my father, introduced them, and' – she lifted a shoulder – 'I'm told the infatuation was instantaneous.'

Vito grimaced. 'Your grandmother and your father? That's . . . ew.'

She whipped the eggs with a wire whisk. 'Technically she wasn't my grandmother and he wasn't my father. Not yet anyway. I wasn't in the picture yet.'

'Still . . .'

'I told you it was sordid. Well, they had a grand affair.' She frowned into the pan as she poured the eggs in. 'Then she found out he was married. She tossed him aside.'

Vito was beginning to see a pattern here. 'I see.'

She shot him a wry look. 'Alex didn't. Anna was born in Hamburg, but she was raised in Pittsburgh. I'm told he was quite devastated when Anna left.'

'Who told you all this?'

'Maurice. He's quite the gossip. That's why I knew he'd be able to get all the good stuff on Alberto Berretti.'

'So how did you . . . come into the picture?'

'Ah. It gets even more sordid. Anna has two daughters. Freya the Good and Lena.'

'The Bad?'

Sophie just shrugged. 'Suffice it to say Lena and Anna didn't get along. Freya was older and already married to my uncle Harry. Lena was seventeen, headstrong and rebellious. She wanted a singing career of her own. She got mad when Anna wouldn't give her entrée. They had quite a falling-out. Then Anna broke up with my father.'

She dished eggs onto two plates and put them on the table. 'Like I said, Alex was devastated and he spent a lot of time drunk. Not an excuse, but . . . One night he got approached in a bar by a young woman who seduced him. Lena.'

'Lena seduced him just to get back at her mother? She really was Lena the Bad.'

'It gets worse. Lena and Anna had it out. Lena ran away, and Anna came home to Pittsburgh to lick her wounds. I think Anna really loved Alex and expected to marry him.' She toyed with the food on her plate. 'Nine months later, Lena came home with a bundle of joy.' She twirled her fork. 'Voilà. And that's how I came into the picture.'

'A child of an illicit affair conducted because of another illicit affair,' Vito said quietly. 'Then you met Brewster and unwittingly did what your mother and Anna had done.'

'I'm not that hard to figure out. But I am a good cook. Your food's getting cold.'

She'd closed the door on her life again, but each time it stayed open a little longer. He still didn't know what happened to her mother or how Katherine Bauer had come to be the 'mother she'd never known' or the significance of the body bag, but Vito could be patient. He pushed his clean plate aside. 'What will you do about your bike?'

'I'll get it towed. Can you give me the name of your mechanic?'

'Sure, but you should report it to the police, along with the dead mouse. Brewster's wife can't just get away with terrorizing you like that.'

She made a scoffing noise. 'You can bet your double bonus I'll report it. That woman bullied me once, but I'm done with her.'

'Good girl. How will you get to work this morning?'

'I can use Gran's car until my bike is fixed.' She wrinkled her nose. 'It's an okay car, it just smells like Lotte and Birgit.'

At their names, the dogs came running, wagging their rainbow butts as they begged for handouts. Vito laughed softly. 'Lotte Lehman and Birgit Nilsson. Opera legends.'

'Gran's idols. Naming these girls after them was the biggest honor she could think of. These dogs are like Gran's children. She spoils them rotten.'

'Did she color them?'

Sophie put their plates in the sink. 'No, that was my mistake. I brought Gran home from rehab after her stroke – before she got pneumonia and had to go to the nursing home. She'd sit at the window and watch the dogs play outside, but her eyes were bad. Then it snowed and they were white and she couldn't see them at all.' She trailed off. 'It seemed like a good idea at the time. It was just food coloring. It's actually faded a lot.'

Vito laughed. 'Sophie, you're incredible.' He walked to the sink, pushed her hair aside and ran his lips down the back of her neck. 'I'll see you tonight.'

She shivered. 'I'm going to sit with Gran tonight. It's Freya's bingo night.'

'Then I'll go with you. How often can I meet a legend?'

Wednesday, January 17, 6:00 A.M.

Something was different. Wrong. He drove the highway to his field, Gregory Sanders's body in a plastic bag under the tarp in the bed of his truck. Normally he never passed another car on this road. But he'd passed two cars already. Sheer instinct had him driving past the access road without slowing down, and what he saw as he passed stopped his heart. There should have been untouched snow where the access road met the highway, but instead he saw the crisscross of tire ruts, indicating repeated access by multiple vehicles.

Bile rose in his throat, choking him. *They'd found his graveyard.*

Somehow, someone had found his graveyard. *But how? And who?* The police?

He made himself breathe. Most certainly the police.

They'll find me. They'll catch me. He made himself breathe again. *Relax. How can they catch you? There's no way they can identify any of those bodies.*

And even if they did, there was no way to link any of the bodies to him. His heart was pounding hard and he wiped a shaky hand across his mouth. He needed to get out of here. He had Gregory Sanders's body in a plastic bag in his truck. If for any reason he was stopped . . . Even he couldn't explain a dead body away.

So breathe. Just breathe. Think. You have to be smart about this.

He'd been so very careful. He'd worn gloves, ensured none of his own body came in contact with the victims. Not even a hair. So even if they identified every damn one of the victims, they couldn't link them to him. He was safe.

So he breathed. And thought. His first step was to get rid of Gregory. Next, he had to find out what the cops knew and how they'd found out. If they were close, he'd bolt.

He knew how to disappear. He'd done it before.

He drove for five miles. No one followed him. He pulled off the road, behind some trees. And waited, holding his breath. No police cars drove by. No cars of any kind.

He got out of the truck, for the first time grateful for the chill of a Philadephia morning on his heated skin. The land beyond the edge of the road sloped sharply down into a gulley. This was as good a place as any to dump Sanders.

Quickly he lowered the tailgate, pulled away the tarp and grabbed the plastic bag in his gloved hands. He heaved the bag into the snow, shoving with his foot until it started to slide. The bag hit a tree, then rolled the rest of the way down. There was a visible path in the snow marking its descent, but if he was lucky it would snow again tonight and the cops wouldn't find Gregory Sanders before the spring thaw.

He'd be long gone by then. He got back behind the wheel and turned in the direction he'd come, wondering if he'd done the right thing.

Then he knew that he had. Two police cruisers sat at the entrance to his access road where none had been before, one pointed in, one out. *Shift change*, he thought. He'd slipped through their shift change by the skin of his teeth. An officer got out of one of the cruisers as he approached.

His first inclination was to hit the accelerator and take the cop out, but that would be foolish. Satisfying, but ultimately foolish. He slowed to a stop. Made himself frown in polite puzzlement as he rolled his window down.

'Where are you headed, sir?' the officer asked with no smile.

'To work. I live down this road.' He squinted, pretending to try to see past the cruiser. 'What's going on over there? I seen cars comin' and goin'.'

'This is a restricted area, sir. If you can take another route, then do.'

'Ain't no other route,' he said. 'But I reckon I can keep my eyes to myself.'

The officer took his notepad from his pocket. 'Can I get your name, sir?'

This was where long-term planning paid off, and he settled into his seat, confident now. 'Jason Kinney.' It would be the name registered to his license plate, because he'd filed the change in title with the DMV himself a year ago. Jason Kinney was just one of the driver's licenses he had in his wallet. It always paid to be thorough.

The officer made a big show of walking to the rear of the truck and writing down the license plate. He checked under the tarp before coming back and touching the tip of his hat. 'Now that we know you're a resident of the area, we won't need to stop you again.'

He nodded. Like he'd ever come this way again. *Not*. 'I appreciate it, Officer. Have a nice day.'

Wednesday, January 17, 8:05 A.M.

Jen McFain frowned. 'We seem to have a problem, Vito.'

Vito slid into his seat at the head of the table, still a little breathless from his mad morning dash. After leaving Sophie's he'd raced home, showered, and apologized profusely to Tess about staying out all night without calling. Then he'd headed in to work, only to be accosted at the precinct door by a horde of reporters with flashing cameras.

'I've had all kinds of problems this morning, Jen. What seems to be yours?'

'No crullers. What kind of meeting are you trying to run anyway?'

'Yeah, Vito,' Liz said. 'What kind of meeting starts out without crullers?'

'You never brought food,' Vito said to Liz and she grinned.

'Yeah, but you did, on the first day. First rule of team

leadership – never set a precedent you don't intend to keep.'

Vito looked around the table. 'Anybody else have nuisance demands?'

Liz looked amused, Katherine impatient. Bev and Tim looked tired. Jen just scowled at him. 'Cheapskate,' she muttered, and Vito rolled his eyes.

'We now have one more victim ID confirmed. Bill Melville is victim three-one. I've noted him on the chart. We also have a name. E. Munch. Nick came back from Melville's apartment last night and ran it through the system, but came up with nothing.'

'It's not like he'd use his real name anyway,' Jen said. 'But I'll bet you dollars to *donuts*' – she glared at him meaningfully – 'that the name means something.'

'You could be right. Any ideas, besides the obvious *Munch* connection to food?'

Jen's lips twitched. 'Very funny, Chick. I'll give it some thought.'

'Thank you.' He turned to Katherine. 'What's new on your end?'

'We autopsied the old couple from the second row last night. We didn't find anything new that would help you ID them. But Tino did some sketches. My assistant said he didn't leave the morgue until after midnight.'

Vito felt a sharp spear of gratitude for his brother who'd jumped in with both feet to help. When this was all over he'd find a way to thank him. 'Yes, and we'll compare his sketches to missing-persons files.' From his folder Vito pulled copies of the sketches he'd found on his desk that morning. He passed them to Liz. 'This is what Tino came up with. He made a few of the woman with different hairstyles. It's hard to picture what she might have looked like without seeing some hair.'

'Me next,' Jen said. 'We got two new pieces of news last night. First, an ID on the tire tread print we took from the scene that first day. Our boy drives a Ford F150, just like yours, Vito.'

'Terrific,' Vito muttered. 'So nice to have something in

common with a psycho killer. Let's get the description out there. It's a long shot, but at least we can be keeping our eyes open. Did you get any footprints with that tire tread?'

'None that were usable. Sorry. Now the second thing is the grenade we took out of the gut of the last victim on the first row. It's a vintage MK2 pineapple grenade, made sometime before 1945. Tracing it would be nearly impossible, but it's one more piece of the puzzle. This guy uses the real thing.'

'And speaking of the real thing.' Vito told them about Sophie's inquiries the day before. 'So we have one possible source for his medieval weapons. I was going to call Interpol before I checked out Claire Reynolds's doctor and the library where she worked. And I still need to locate Bill Melville's parents. They don't know he's dead.'

'Give me Interpol,' Liz said. 'You take the doctor and the parents.'

'Thanks.' Vito looked over at Bev and Tim. 'You guys are quiet.'

'We're tired,' Tim said. 'We were up most of the night going through records with the owners of UCanModel. Then the attorneys got involved.'

'Shit,' Vito murmured.

'Yeah.' Tim scraped his palms down his unshaven cheeks. 'The owners want to cooperate, but their attorneys are telling them they have a privacy notice for all subscribers. So it's slow going. We broke at three a.m. and went home to sleep.'

'The owner has to contact all the models who were sent e-mails before we can talk to them.' Bev sighed. 'We're supposed to get on a call with them in an hour.'

Vito hadn't gotten to sleep until three a.m. himself, but the reason was very different and he was pretty sure he'd get no sympathy. 'Katherine, what will you do next?'

'Autopsies on the final four. You have a preference on where I start? Old, young, bullet, or grenade?'

'Start with Claire Reynolds. I'll get with you as soon as I talk to her doctor. Then work on the old lady. She's the one body that doesn't fit with any of the others.' Vito stood up. 'We're done for this morning. Let's meet again at five tonight. Stay safe.'

Wednesday, January 17, 9:05 A.M.

She'd died. The old Winchester woman had died. He sat back, frowning at his computer. She'd died and left her property to her nephew who'd been nearly as old as she was. Who knew who'd found the bodies? But knowing she was dead made more sense. If her nephew planned to sell the property someone might be inspecting it, or perhaps they'd already sold it and somebody was building on it.

The bodies could have turned up that way. He assumed the cops had found them all. Only one person could have been identified by his prints, and those prints he'd erased. All the others . . . it would take the cops weeks to find their own asses with a flashlight. That they could identify the other bodies more quickly was ludicrous.

He felt better now. But still he had loose ends. One of the bodies in that field was the Webber kid and somehow Derek had obtained the kid's photo. He'd deal with Derek today. He needed to—

His cell phone rang and he reflexively checked the caller ID. It was his . . . antiques dealer, for lack of a better description. 'Yeah,' he said. 'What do you have for me?'

'What the *fuck* have you done?' came the furious reply.

His own temper began to sizzle. 'What are you talking about?'

'I'm talking about an inquisition chair. And the fucking cops.'

He opened his mouth, but for a moment no words formed. Quickly he regained his composure. 'I truly have no idea of what you're talking about.'

'The cops have a chair.' Each word was spaced deliberately. 'In their possession.'

'Well, it's not mine. My chair is with my collection. I saw it just this morning.'

There was a pause on the other end. 'Are you sure?'

'Of course I'm sure. What is this all about?'

'A cop asked questions yesterday. He was researching stolen artifacts and black market sales. Said he had a chair with spikes. Lots of spikes. He was a homicide cop.'

His heart began racing for the second time that day, but he kept his cool. He knew they'd found his graves. That the police would connect Brittany's body to an inquisitional chair was not a leap he'd expected them to make. He injected enough confusion in his voice to be believable. 'I'm telling you I don't know what you're talking about.'

'You don't know anything about a massive graveyard in a field north of town? Because the same cop who made the visit is the one leading that case.'

Fuck. He laughed, incredulously. 'I don't know anything about a graveyard either. All I know is that my artifacts are in my possession. If the cops have a chair, it's probably handmade by one of those idiots from the reenactment group. But I must admit to a certain curiosity. How did the police know where to go to ask questions?'

'They have a source. An archeologist.'

That made sense. That was, after all, how he'd located his dealer in the beginning. 'What's his name, this archeologist?'

'*Her* name is Sophie Johannsen.'

His heart skipped a beat, then fury roared, sending his pulse skyrocketing. 'I see.'

'She teaches a class on Tuesday nights at Whitman College in Philly. She also works during the day at the Albright. I have her address at home, as well.'

So did he. He knew she lived alone with two colored poodles who posed no threat at all. Still he scoffed, pretending to be offended. 'I don't want to find her, for God's sake. I was just curious.'

There was a pause, and when the man spoke again it was

calmly, yet the menace of his words rang loud and clear. 'If I were you, I'd be more than curious. As for us, we don't plan to be implicated in anything you've done, and if push comes to shove, we will protect our interests. Don't call us anymore. We no longer want your business.'

There was a click, then silence. He'd been hung up on. He put his cell on his desk, rattled. He had to plug the leaks in the dyke. And quickly. Damn. He'd wanted to keep her available for research purposes until he was finished with his game.

He'd just have to find another source.

Wednesday, January 17, 9:30 A.M.

'Dr Pfeiffer's with a patient right now, Detective.' Receptionist Stacy Savard was frowning at him from her side of the glass that separated the office from the waiting room. 'You'll have to wait or come back later.'

'Ma'am, I'm a homicide detective. I only show up when people are dead when they shouldn't be. Could you please have the doctor see me as soon as possible?'

Her eyes had widened. 'H-homicide? Who?' She leaned forward. 'You can tell me, Detective. He tells me everything anyway.'

Vito smiled at her as patiently as he could. 'I'll just wait over there.' A few minutes later an elderly man came to the doorway.

'Detective Ciccotelli? Miss Savard told me you were here to see me.'

'Yes. Can we talk privately?' He followed the doctor back to his office.

Pfeiffer shut the door. 'This is very distressing.' He sat down behind his desk. 'Which of my patients is the subject of your investigation?'

'Claire Reynolds.'

Pfeiffer flinched. 'I'm sorry to hear that. Miss Reynolds was a lovely young woman.'

'You'd known her for a long time then?'

'Oh, yes. I've been seeing Claire for . . . must be five years now.'

'Can you tell me what kind of person she was? Outgoing, shy?'

'Very outgoing. Claire was a paraolympian and active in the community.'

'What kind of prosthetic devices did Claire use, Dr Pfeiffer?'

'I don't remember off the top of my head. Wait one moment.' He pulled a folder from a file drawer and flipped through the pages.

'Thick file,' Vito commented.

'Claire was part of an experimental study I'm conducting, an upgrade to the microprocessor in her artificial knee.'

'Microprocessor? Like as in a computer chip?'

'Yes. Older prosthetic legs aren't as stable when the patient is walking up and down stairs or walking with a big stride. The microprocessor is constantly evaluating stability and making fine adjustments.' He tilted his head. 'Like antilock brakes in your car.'

'That I can understand. How is it powered?'

'By a battery pack. Patients charge it overnight. Most can get up to thirty hours' use before the battery dies.'

'So Claire had an upgraded microprocessor in her knee?'

'She did. She was supposed to be coming in for regular checks.' He looked down, ashamed. 'I hadn't realized how long it had been since I'd seen her until just now.'

'When was the last time she came in for an appointment?'

'October 12, a year ago.' He frowned. 'I should have missed her sooner. Why didn't I?' He shuffled through some more paper, then sat back, relieved. 'Oh, here's why. She moved to Texas. I got a letter from her new physician, Dr Joseph Gaspar in San Antonio. Her chart shows we forwarded a copy of her records the following week.'

That was the second letter someone had received in reference

264

to Claire Reynolds's disappearance. First the library's resignation letter, now this. 'Can I have that letter?'

'Of course.'

'Doctor, can you tell me about silicone lubricants?'

'What do you want to know?'

'How are they used? Where do you get them? Are there different ones?'

Pfeiffer took a shampoo-sized bottle from his desk and handed it to Vito. 'That's a silicone lubricant. Go ahead, try it.'

Vito squeezed a few drops onto his thumb. It was odorless, colorless, and left a slick residue on his skin. The samples Katherine had pulled from Warren and Brittany had been white because they'd been mixed with plaster. 'Why is it used?'

'Above-the-knee amputees like Miss Reynolds generally use one of two different methods to achieve suspension – that means attaching the limb. The first is using a liner. It looks like this.' Pfeiffer reached into his drawer and pulled out what looked like a giant condom with a metal pin at the end. 'The patient rolls this liner over the residual limb – you get a very tight fit. Then the metal pin attaches down into the socket of the prosthesis. Some patients use the silicone lubricant under the liner, especially if they have sensitive or broken skin.'

'Did Claire Reynolds use this method?'

'Sometimes, but usually younger patients like Claire use the suction method. It is what it sounds like – the artificial limb is held on through suction and is released using an air valve. This puts the skin in direct contact with the plastic of the prosthesis. Most everyone who uses the suction method uses lubricant.'

'Where would your patients get this?' Vito asked handing him back the bottle.

'From me or directly from the distributor. Most distributors have online stores.'

'And formulas? Are there a lot of them?'

'One or two main ones. But a lot of cottage industries offer special blends, herbs and things.' He took a magazine from his desk and flipped to the back. 'Like these.'

Vito took the magazine and scanned the ads. 'Can I keep this?'

'Certainly. I can have Miss Savard get you a sample of the lubricant, as well.'

'Thank you. Doctor, I know it's been more than a year since you've seen Miss Reynolds, but I was wondering if you could remember her frame of mind. Was she happy or sad, angry or worried maybe? Did she have a boyfriend?'

Pfeiffer looked uncomfortable. 'No, she didn't have a boyfriend.'

'Oh. I see. Well, a girlfriend then?'

Pfeiffer's discomfort increased. 'I didn't know her that well, Detective. But I know she often marched in activist parades. She mentioned it several times when she came in to get her leg checked. I think she was just trying to get me to react, honestly.'

'Well, then, how about her mood?'

Pfeffer steepled his fingers under his chin. 'I know she was worried about money. She was nervous that she wouldn't have enough for the microprocessor upgrade.'

'I'm confused. I thought she was in your study and already had the new processor.'

'She was and she did, but when the study was completed she was going to have to buy it. The maker offers the micro-processor at their cost, but it was still more than Claire could afford. This upset her a great deal.' His expression grew very sad. 'She thought having the upgrade would give her an edge in the paraolympic games.'

Vito stood. 'Thank you, Doctor. You've been a huge help.'

'When you find who did this, will you let me know?'

'Yes. I will.'

'Good.' The doctor rose and opened his office door. 'Stacy?' The receptionist came to his office quickly. 'Stacy, the detective is here about Claire Reynolds.'

Stacy's eyes widened as she placed the name. 'Claire? But . . .' She leaned against the door, her shoulders sagging. 'Oh, no.'

'Did you know Miss Reynolds well, Miss Savard?'

'Not *well* well.' She looked up at Vito, shocked and upset. 'I chatted with her when she would come for her fittings. Congratulated her when she won a race or something. She was always up.' Stacy's eyes filled with tears. 'Claire was a sweet person. Why would anyone hurt her?'

'That's what I have to find out. Doctor?' Vito looked at the file in the man's hand.

The doctor shook himself. 'Oh, yes. Stacy, make a copy of the letter we received from Dr Gaspar in Texas for Detective Ciccotelli.'

'Actually, I need the original.'

Pfeiffer blinked. 'Of course. I wasn't thinking. Stacy, just keep the copy for our files and assist the detective in any other way we can.'

Chapter Fifteen

Wednesday, January 17, 11:10 A.M.

'Bye! Bye!' The class of eight-year-olds waved as they were herded out the door.

'That was wonderful.' Their teacher beamed at Sophie and Ted the Third. 'Normally the kids get irritable and bored at museums, but you made it fun, what with the costume and acting and the ax. And your hair! It all looks so real.'

Sophie adjusted the battle-ax she'd rested on her shoulder after brandishing it early in the Viking tour. The kids' eyes had nearly popped from their heads. 'The hair is real,' she smiled back. 'The rest is . . . fun. We're here to bring history to life.'

'Well, I'll certainly be sure to tell the other teachers.'

'We certainly appreciate the support,' Sophie said warmly.

Ted's glance was wary. 'You should see her Joan of Arc. I think it's even better.'

'He's just trying to sweet-talk me because the armor is heavy. Please come back.'

'You were nice to them,' Ted said when the teacher was gone. 'What's wrong?'

Sophie winced. 'I guess I had that coming. I had an epiphany yesterday, Ted. You do a good thing here. And I haven't been very nice.'

He looked over, his brows arched. 'I thought it was part of the act,' he said dryly. 'You mean you really *did* want to cleave me in two with your ax?'

Sophie's lips twitched. 'Only sometimes.' She sobered. 'I'm sorry, Ted.'

'We were happy you came to work here, Sophie,' Ted said, serious as well. 'You have great respect for my grandfather's work. I know you don't believe it, but so do I.'

'Yes, Ted, I do believe that. That was part of my epiphany.'

He looked through the glass where the last of the children was getting on a yellow bus. 'I didn't know you spoke Norwegian. It's not one of the languages on your résumé.'

That's all he would say on the subject, she realized. They'd just go on. 'I don't. But then, neither do they.' She chuckled. 'I only know Norwegian cuss words because my gran used to say them. I think that's all she picked up from my grandfather.'

Ted's eyes popped wide. 'You used Norwegian cuss words with *children*?'

'Good God, no.' She was miffed that he even considered it. 'I speak a little Danish and some Dutch. The rest was pure Swedish Chef.' Her lips quirked. 'Bork-bork-bork.'

Ted looked both relieved and touched. 'We might make a thespian out of you yet, Sophie Johannsen.' He walked away. 'Don't forget, you're Joan at noon.'

'That armor is still too heavy,' she called back after him, but with considerably less rancor than before. She headed for the washroom to get the makeup off her face before she broke out in hives. That was not how she wanted to be seen by Vito tonight.

She shivered, despite the sweat trickling down her back from the heavy costume. Vito had certainly made good on his word, more than once during the night. There was a big difference between making love and fucking like minks. She imagined it would be even better if she ever were to actually fall in love. She considered asking Uncle Harry, then laughed out loud picturing the horror on his face.

'Excuse me, miss.'

Still smiling, Sophie stopped next to the old man who'd been studying the photos of Ted the First in the front lobby, hunched over his cane. 'Yes, sir?'

'I overheard part of your tour. It was fascinating. Do you do private tours also?'

There was something in his eyes that bothered her. *Horny old bastard, trying to pick me up.* Eyes narrowing, her fist tightened on the battle-ax handle. 'How private?'

He looked confused, then shocked. 'Oh, my. No, no, no. I live at a retirement home where the diversions are often boring, so I've taken it on myself to become something of the social coordinator. I was wondering if we could schedule a tour.'

Sophie laughed in embarrassed relief. 'Of course, I'd be glad to. I know how bored my gran gets with nothing to do all day.'

'Your grandmother is certainly welcome to join us.'

Sophie's smile dimmed. 'Thank you, but no. She's not well enough to come on a tour. You can reserve a time with the girl behind the desk.'

He frowned. 'The one dressed in black? She looks a bit dangerous.'

'Patty Ann goes goth on Wednesdays. Kind of her own tribute to Wednesday Addams. She's really quite nice. She'll be happy to set you up with a tour. Now if you'll excuse me, I have to get this makeup off my face or I'll bloat up like Pugsly.'

He watched her go, his eyes noting every fluid step she took. He'd known her for months, but he'd never really seen her until today. He'd never even suspected the magnetism she'd possessed until he'd seen her like *this* – a six-foot-tall blonde swinging a two-handed battle-ax over her head, green eyes flashing like some mythical Valkyrie. She'd held the small crowd of children and their teachers in thrall for over an hour.

And me, as well. Forget about the models on the website. He'd found his new queen. Van Zandt would be ecstatic. And Dr Sophie Johannsen would no longer be a loose end. It was so cool when he could kill two birds with one stone.

DIE FOR ME

Barbara Mulrine, librarian and Claire's former boss, slid an envelope across the counter. 'This is the original of the resignation letter we received from Claire Reynolds.'

Marcy Wiggs nodded. She was about Claire's age and seemed to be taking the news of Claire's death harder than her fifty-something, pragmatic boss. 'We had to request it from the main office since she was out of our system for more than a year.' Marcy's lip trembled. 'That poor sweet girl. She wasn't even thirty.'

From the corner of his eye Vito watched Barbara roll her eyes and was instantly more interested in the older woman's take. He opened the envelope and looked inside. The letter was printed on ordinary paper and he suspected they'd get nothing of value in terms of prints, but still he asked. 'Can you get me a list of anyone who's handled this?'

'I can try,' Barbara said while Marcy sighed.

'We all feel so terrible that this happened. We should have suspected something at the time, should have made a phone call, but . . .'

Vito slid the envelope in his folder. 'But?'

'But nothing,' Barbara said sharply. 'You shouldn't have suspected anything, Marcy. And Claire was not a sweet girl. You're just saying that now because she's dead.' She looked at Vito, vexed. 'People always remember the dead as better than they were, especially when they get murdered. And when they're murdered and have a handicap . . . well, you might as well call the Pope and request a canonization.'

Marcy's lips thinned, but she said nothing.

Vito looked from one woman to the other. 'So Claire was not a nice person?'

Marcy looked up out of the corner of her eye petulantly and Barbara blew out a sigh of frustration. 'No, not really. When we got her resignation letter, we had a party.'

'Barbara,' Marcy hissed.

'Well, we did. He's going to ask around and anybody'll tell him it's true.' Barbara looked back at Vito. 'The party part and the not-nice part.'

'What did she do that wasn't nice?'

'It was just her attitude,' Barbara answered wearily. 'We wanted to like her, all of us did. But she was abrupt and rude. I've worked here for over twenty years. I've had employees with all kinds of abilities and disabilities. Claire wasn't nasty because she was an amputee. She was nasty because she liked to be.'

'Was she into drugs or alcohol?'

Barbara looked appalled. 'Not that I ever saw. Claire's body was her temple. No, this was more a sense of entitlement. She'd come in late, leave early. Her work was always done, but only what I asked and nothing more. This was just a job for her.'

'She was a writer,' Marcy said. 'She was working on her novel.'

'She was always working on that laptop,' Barbara agreed. 'Her novel was about a paraolympian, semiautobiographical I guess.'

Marcy sighed. 'Except that the protagonist was nice. Barbara's right, Detective. Claire wasn't that nice. Maybe I just wanted her to be.'

Vito frowned. 'You say she had a laptop?'

The women looked at each other. 'Yeah,' Barbara said. 'A nice new one.'

Marcy bit her lip. 'She got the new one about a month before she . . . died.'

'Her parents didn't find a laptop,' Vito said. 'They said she didn't have one.'

Barbara made a face at that. 'There were lots of things Claire didn't tell her parents, Detective Ciccotelli.'

'Like?' Vito asked, but he thought he knew.

Marcy pursed her lips again. 'Now, we weren't judgmental, but—'

'Claire was a lesbian,' Barbara broke in, matter-of-factly.

'Her parents wouldn't have approved?'

Barbara shook her head. 'No. They were very conservative.'

'I see. Well, did she mention a partner or a girlfriend?'

'No, but there was this photograph,' Barbara said. 'In the paper. It was a picture taken at one of the gay pride marches – Claire in a lip-lock with another woman. Claire got really upset. Figured her folks would see it and all hell would break loose and they'd stop paying her rent. She called the paper and complained.' She grimaced. 'And now you're going to ask me which paper it was, and I don't remember. I'm sorry.'

'That's okay. Was it a local community paper, or big like the Philly *Inquirer*?'

'I'm thinking a local paper,' Marcy said uncertainly.

Barbara sighed. 'I was thinking a big one. I'm sorry, Detective.'

'Don't be. You've been a lot of help. If you remember anything else, please call me.'

Wednesday, January 17, 12:30 P.M.

Vito stopped his truck in front of the courthouse and Nick jumped in. 'Well?'

Nick tugged at his tie. 'It's done. I was the last witness for the prosecution. Lopez wanted me to go last to paint the picture of the murdered girl so that the final thing the jury would remember that it wasn't just the drugs, but that a girl had died at their hands.'

'Sounds like a good strategy. I know you have your issues with Lopez, but she's a damn good DA. Sometimes you have to deal with a demon to bring down the devil. It's not pretty, but it's the big picture that counts. I hope the girl's parents understood that.'

Nick pulled his palms down his face wearily. 'Actually, they were the ones to tell me that very thing. I was ready to apologize for Lopez pleading their daughter's killer down to manslaughter so she could get the drug dealer, and they said that the way Lopez handled it, both men would pay and the dope dealer would never touch anyone else's child. They were very grateful.' He sighed. 'And I felt about an inch tall. I owe Maggy Lopez an apology.'

'I'd just be happy to have her work this case. After we nail this sonofabitch, that is.'

'Speaking of,' Nick said, 'where are we going?'

'To tell Bill Melville's parents that he's dead. You get to tell them.'

'Gee thanks, Chick.'

'Hey, I told the Bellamys. It's only fair—' His cell buzzed. 'It's Liz,' he told Nick. He listened, then sighed. 'We're on our way.' Vito turned his truck around.

'Where are we going?'

'Not to the Melvilles',' Vito said grimly. 'We're going back to Winchester's field.'

'Number ten?'

'Number ten.'

Wednesday, January 17, 1:15 P.M.

Jen was already at the scene, coordinating. She walked over to Vito and Nick when they got out of the truck. 'The officer on guard got the APB on the F150 and realized he'd stopped a truck just like it this morning. When he ran the plates, he saw the name the guy gave matched, but when he called the phone number listed for the address, it didn't match. He drove down this road until he saw the tire tracks in the snow.' She pointed down at an opaque bag lying in the gully. 'He saw that and called it in.'

'He knows we're on to him,' Nick said. 'Damn, I was hoping we'd have more time.'

Vito was shoving his feet into his boots. 'Well, we don't. You check it out yet, Jen?'

'It's a man.' She started down the slope. 'I haven't opened the bag. He ain't pretty.'

The sight that greeted them at the bottom of the slope would linger in Vito's mind for a long, long time. The plastic had pulled taut over the man's face, so that it appeared he was straining to break free. The opacity of the bag clouded everything but the man's mouth which yawned grotesquely, as if frozen in a scream that no one would hear.

'Hell,' Nick whispered.

Vito shuddered out a breath. 'Yeah.' He crouched by the body and did a quick visual. The body was not wrapped in a single bag, but two. 'One bag for the head and torso, another for the feet and legs. Tied together.' He pulled at the knot with gloved fingers. 'Simple knot. You want me to open him up?'

Jen crouched on the other side of the body with a knife and carefully sliced the plastic next to the knot so that the bags separated, but the knot itself was preserved. She then sliced up the front of the bag and drew a breath. 'Grab an edge, Chick.'

Together they pulled the plastic apart and Vito had to swallow back bile. 'Oh my God.' He dropped the plastic back down and turned his face away.

'Branded,' Nick said.

'And hanged,' Jen added. 'Look at the ligature marks on his throat.'

Vito looked down. Jen still held her side of the plastic, exposing the left side of the victim's body and face where the left cheek bore a brand of the letter T. Steeling himself, he pulled his side of the plastic back all the away, exposing the right side.

'His hand,' was all he could mutter. *Or the lack thereof.*

'Oh, my . . . Oh . . .' Jen sucked in a sharp breath between her teeth.

'Shit.' Nick lurched to his feet. 'What the fuck is with this guy?'

Vito pursed his lips and glanced down the length of the bag, knowing it would get worse. 'Cut the lower bag away, Jen. All the way down to his feet.'

She did, and then she and Vito stood up, each holding a piece of the plastic in one hand. 'He cut off his foot, too,' she said quietly.

'Right hand, left foot.' Vito carefully lowered the bag. 'It means something.'

She nodded. 'Just like E. Munch means something.'

Sonny Holloman, Jen's photographer, came skidding down the slope. 'Hell.'

'Yeah, we got that,' she said wearily. 'Get him from all angles, Sonny.'

For a few minutes the only sound was the clicking of Sonny's shutter.

Jen turned her gaze to the dead man's face. 'Vito, I know this guy. I know I do.'

Vito squinted, concentrating. 'So do I. Shit. It's right there, on the edge of my mind.'

Sonny lowered his camera. 'Shit,' he repeated hollowly. 'Sanders Sewer Service. It's the Sanders kid. The oldest one, who stood at the end looking miserable.'

Jen's eyes widened with the horrified realization she was looking at someone she knew. 'You're right.'

'What the hell are you talking about?' Nick said but Jen shushed him.

'Let me think. Sid Sanders's sewer service sucks septic systems—'

'Spankin' spotless,' Vito and Sonny said together, grimly.

'What the *hell* are you *talking* about?' Nick demanded.

'You didn't grow up around here,' Vito said, 'so you wouldn't know. This guy was in a commercial.'

Jen shook her head. 'Not just any commercial. This was a . . .'

'Pop culture phenomenon,' Vito supplied. 'Nick, didn't you have a commercial that was so bad that everybody in your town knew it, remembered it?'

276

'Made fun of it?' Sonny added.

'Yeah. We had Crazy Phil who sold cars like a hillbilly auctioneer on crack.' Nick frowned. 'Turns out he *was* on crack. So this guy is your Crazy Phil?'

'No, this guy had the bad fortune to be Crazy Phil's son,' Vito said. 'Sanders had a septic cleaning service and wanted to advertise, but was too cheap to hire models.'

'So he lined up all six of his sons.' Jen sighed. 'They had to say the slogan and pretend to be happy about it. I always felt sorry for them. Especially the oldest one. He was a really cute guy and could've had any girl he wanted except for that stupid commercial . . . wait. This guy isn't old enough to be the oldest Sanders kid. The oldest one's our age. He's got to be one of the younger kids.'

'Well, they all did look alike,' Sonny said. 'Like the Osmonds.' He looked down, pity etched into his face. 'Six Sanders sons. Sid really went in for the alliteration.'

'Did you actually know these kids?' Nick asked and Jen shook her head.

'Hell, no. A lot of people on the outskirts had septic systems. Sid Sanders made a lot of money. They lived in the pricey district, and the boys went to prep schools and everything. The Sanders slogan became this huge deal and people were seeing how fast they could say it. Young, old, in restaurants and the grocery store . . .'

'Especially at keg parties,' Sonny said, then shrugged. 'Hey, I got an older brother who was in a fraternity at the time. I just listened to the war stories afterward.'

'I wonder if our guy knew this was one of the Sanders kids,' Nick said thoughtfully. 'I mean, would he have killed him and left him out here if he thought he'd be so easily recognized? It took the three of you less than ten minutes to ID him.'

Jen's eyes gleamed. 'So E. Munch may be an out-of-towner.'

Vito sighed. 'At least we know where to go to notify this guy's folks.'

Nick met his eyes. 'What about the brand? And the hand and foot?'

Vito nodded. Sophie would know what it meant. 'I know where to go for that, too.'

Wednesday, January 17, 2:30 P.M.

Sid Sanders sat holding his wife's hand. 'You're sure?' Sid asked hoarsely.

'We'll need you to make a formal ID, but we're pretty sure,' Vito murmured.

'We know this is difficult,' Nick added quietly, 'but we need to see his computer.'

Sid shook his head. 'It's not here.'

His wife lifted her face. 'He probably hocked his computer a long time ago.'

Her voice was bleak, but underneath Vito also heard guilt. 'Why?' Purposely he looked around the lavish living room. 'Did he need money?'

Sid's jaw tightened. 'We'd cut him off. Gregory was an addict. Booze, drugs, gambling. We helped him as long as we could, got him out of more scrapes than we should've. Finally we had to cut him loose. It was the worst day of our lives. Until today.'

'So where was he living?' Nick asked.

'He had a girlfriend,' Mrs Sanders murmured. 'She threw him out too, but called me a month ago to say she'd taken him in until he could dry himself out. She didn't want us to worry.'

Vito noted her name on his pad. 'So you liked his girlfriend?'

Mrs Sanders's eyes filled. 'We still do. Jill would have made a good daughter-in-law, and even though we were sad when she broke it off, we knew it was the best thing for her. Gregory was pulling her down.'

'We gave that boy everything, but he always wanted more.' Sid closed his eyes. 'Now he's got nothing.'

Wednesday, January 17, 3:25 P.M.

Nick stood in the middle of Jill Ellis's living room, taking in the destruction. 'Looks like a hurricane tore through here.'

Vito slipped his phone into his pocket. 'Jen's sending a CSU team.' He looked at the landlord, who'd let them in with his master key. 'Have you seen Miss Ellis recently?'

'Not since last week. She kept this place neat as a pin. This ain't good, Detective.'

'Can you get us her rental app?' Nick asked. 'Maybe there's a number we can call.'

'Sure. I'll be back in ten minutes.' He stopped at the door, his eyes angry. 'It was that good-for-nothing boyfriend of hers. Richie Rich.'

Vito met the man's eye. 'You mean Gregory Sanders?'

The landlord scoffed. 'Yeah. Spoiled rich kid. Jill worked hard, and once she even tossed him out on his ass. But he came back, begging her for another chance. I told her to slam the door in his face, but she said she felt sorry for him.'

'You say "worked." Do you think she's come to harm?' Vito asked.

The man hesitated. 'Don't you?'

Vito studied his face. 'What do you know, sir?'

'I saw some guys leaving here yesterday, about three. I was outside putting kitty litter on the sidewalk. Didn't want anyone slipping on the ice and suing me.'

'So these guys?' Nick prodded gently and the landlord sighed.

'There were two of them. They got into a car that was all pimped up – neon, hydraulic shocks. I started to go up, to check on Jill, but I got a call from Mrs Coburn in 6-B. She's old and she'd fallen down, hurt her hip. By the time I got home from getting her to the emergency room, it was late.' He looked away. 'I forgot about Jill.'

'You sound like you take pretty good care of your tenants,' Vito said kindly.

The landlord eyes were full of guilt. 'Not as well as I should have. I'll get that app.'

When the landlord was gone, Nick sat down at Jill Ellis's computer. 'This day just keeps gettin' better.' He clicked the mouse. 'Wiped clean as a baby's butt.'

'I didn't expect anything else. Looks like she got a phone call yesterday afternoon. Her answering machine's blinking.' Vito hit play. Then frowned. 'Come here, Nick.'

Nick was halfway back to the woman's bedroom, but came back. 'What is it?'

'I don't know.' Vito rewound, then hit play again, turning up the volume to full. 'It's a man talking, but it's muffled.'

'That sounded like a moan.' Nick rewound, this time putting his ear to the speaker before hitting play. 'Sounds like he's saying, "Terrible, terrible things."'

'Like what?'

Nick looked up. 'That's what he's saying.' He put his ear back to the speaker. 'There's the moan . . . *Scream all you want. No one can hear you. No one will save you. I've killed them all.*' Grim, Nick straightened, just as the voice grew loud enough to be heard on its own. They stared at the machine. Then they heard him.

The voice was sneering but refined. And decidedly southern.

'They all thought they suffered, but their suffering was nothing compared to what I'm going to do to you.'

There was silence, followed by a slurred voice. The words were hard to understand, but the tone was not. The second man was frantic. Terrified. *'No, please no. I'm sorry. I'll do anything. Just . . . Oh, God. No.'* There was another moan, then a laugh followed by a dragging sound, and the southern voice became muffled.

Once again Nick put his ear to the speaker. 'Let's take a ride, Mr Sanders. I call it my time machine. Now you'll see what happens to thieves.'

Nick looked up, his face as stunned as Vito felt. 'Meet E. Munch.'

Wednesday, January 17, 3:00 P.M.

Daniel Vartanian had stopped for a Philly cheesesteak for lunch. It would probably be the high point of his day, because he'd had no success in his search. The locals, he'd learned, took their cheesesteak with Cheez Whiz. The food was delicious and steaming hot, which was good because he was starving and freezing cold.

He didn't think he'd ever been so cold. He didn't know how Susannah had adapted to winters in the North, but he knew she had. They hadn't talked in years, but he'd followed her career. She was an up-and-comer in the New York DA's office. His smile was grim. Together they were Law and Order. It didn't take a shrink to figure out why.

I know what your son did. Daniel had dedicated his life to making up for what Arthur Vartanian's son had done and for what Arthur had not. Susannah had done the same. His mother had been caught in the middle, but she'd made her choices. Wrong ones.

His cell phone rang. It was Chase Wharton. His boss would want an update. He'd be honest. Mostly. 'Hey, Chase.'

'Hey. Did you find them?'

'Nope, and Philadelphia has a hell of a lot of hotels.'

'Philadelphia? I thought you were going to the Grand Canyon.'

'My dad's PC showed he'd searched for oncologists in Philadelphia. I figured they'd come up here to start their vacation.'

'Your sister is only a few hours away,' Chase said quietly.

'I know.' And he knew what Chase was intimating. 'And, yes, they'd be two hours away and not drop in on either of us. Like you said, I have a fucked-up family.'

'But no sign of foul play?'

I know what your son did. 'No, Chase, I've found no evidence of foul play. If and when I do, I'll blast my way to the local cops faster'n you can say Cheez Whiz.'

'All right. Be careful, Daniel.'

'I will.' Daniel hung up, sick with himself, sick with this whole situation. Quite possibly he was sick with his whole life. He wrapped his sandwich and tossed it in the paper sack. He'd lost his appetite. He'd never lied to Chase. Never lied to any of his bosses. *I know what your son did*. He'd just never told the whole truth.

And if he found his folks . . . alive . . . well, then, he wouldn't have to start. He started his car and headed to the next hotel.

New York City, Wednesday, January 17, 3:30 P.M.

Derek Harrington stopped at the steps to his walk-up apartment, miserable. He'd had a life. A career he loved, a wife he adored, a daughter who looked at him with pride in her eyes. Now he couldn't even look himself in the eye. Today he'd sunk to a new low. He'd walked past the police station five times but hadn't gone in. According to his contract, Derek would get a settlement should he ever choose to quit. That settlement would pay his daughter's college tuition. His silence would ensure his daughter's future.

Lloyd Webber's son would never have a future. He knew the boy was dead, just as he knew he'd have to tell the police his suspicions about Frasier Lewis. But the power of gold was strong and had him firmly in its grip. *The power of gold*. He started up the stairs. oRo. He and Jager had named their company well. He had his key in the door when he flinched at the sharp jab to his kidney. *A gun*. Jager or Frasier Lewis? Derek didn't think he wanted to know.

'Don't speak. Just obey.'

Derek now knew who held the gun. And he knew he was going to die.

Philadelphia, Wednesday, January 17, 4:45 P.M.

Vito jogged from his truck up the stairs to the library. This better be good, he thought. He'd had to move the five o'clock meeting to six and now he'd be late meeting Sophie at her grandmother's nursing home.

But the call he'd received from librarian Barbara Mulrine sounded like it could be another big break. He'd dropped Nick off at the precinct with Jill Ellis's answering machine. Nick was going to get the electronics guys to clean up the tape before six.

Barbara was waiting with Marcy at the desk. 'We tried to get him to come in, but he wouldn't,' Barbara said, bypassing any greeting.

'Where is he?' Vito asked.

Marcy pointed to an elderly man sweeping the floor. 'He's afraid of the police.'

'Why?'

'He's from Russia,' Barbara said. 'He's here legally, I'm sure of that. But he's been through a lot. His name is Yuri, and he's been in the U.S. for less than two years.'

'Does he speak English?'

'Some. Hopefully enough.'

It took Vito less than five minutes to realize that 'some' wasn't nearly enough. The old Russian had talked to 'a man' about 'Miss Claire.' After that, what they had was a failure to communicate bilingually. This was going to take longer than he thought.

'I'm sorry,' Barbara said softly. 'I should have told you to line up an interpreter.'

'It's okay. I'll take care of it.' Vito sighed. Getting a Spanish interpreter took long enough. Getting a Russian one could take hours. It didn't look like he'd be meeting any archeologists or opera legends tonight. He'd have to take the old man in while they waited for the interpreter. At least he could get other work

283

done. 'Sir, I need you to come with me.' He held out his hand and the old man's eyes widened in fear.

'No.' Yuri's hands clutched the handle of his broom and it was then Vito saw his misshapen knuckles. The man's hands had been broken, years ago it appeared.

'Detective,' Barbara murmured. 'Please don't do this to him. Don't make him go.'

Vito held up both hands in surrender. 'Okay. You can stay here.'

Yuri looked at Barbara and she nodded. 'He's not going to make you go anywhere, Yuri. You're safe here.'

Warily, Yuri turned away and went back to sweeping.

'You wouldn't get him to talk to you if you forced him to go to the station,' Barbara said. 'You can leave, and I'll stay here with him until you can get an interpreter.'

Vito smiled ruefully. 'That might take hours. You've been here all day.'

'I don't mind. I didn't like Claire Reynolds, but I don't want whoever killed her to get away with it. And I promised Yuri a long time ago that he'd be safe here.'

Vito's opinion of the librarian climbed another notch. 'I'll do my best to help you keep that promise.' He dug his cell from his pocket. 'Now I have to break a date.'

She made a sad face. 'That's a shame.'

Vito thought of his double bonus prize. 'You have no idea.' He walked to the window and dialed Sophie's cell. She answered right away. 'Sophie, it's Vito.'

'What's wrong?'

He'd thought he'd stripped the stress from his voice. 'Nothing. Well, yeah, something. Look, I may have a break in this case and I have to stick with it. I may be able to meet you later, but it's not looking good.'

'Can I help with anything?'

My double bonus prize, he thought, but made himself focus. 'Actually, you can. We're going to want you to tell us about medieval punishments for theft.'

'I can do that. Do you need me to come to the station?'

Vito turned around and looked at the old man. 'Maybe. I'm stuck somewhere else for a while, waiting . . .' A thought struck. 'Sophie, do you speak Russian?'

'Yes.'

'Very well or just the cuss words?'

'Very well,' she said cautiously. 'Why?'

'Can you come to the Huntington Library?' He gave her the address. 'I'll explain when you get here. Bye.' He hung up and called Liz and updated her.

'You got another free consultant,' Liz chuckled. 'You realize everyone is going to expect you to do this from now on. You're never going to get any budget money again.'

'Technically, Sophie counts as the same consultant,' he said dryly. 'Tell the team I'll be there when I can, but it'll be after six. Also, can you have Katherine print a photo of the brand on the Sanders kid's cheek? I'll bring Sophie in when she's done here to look at it. She's already seen one body. I don't want her to have to go to the morgue.'

'Will do. Hey, I heard back from Interpol. We may have a hit.'

Vito straightened. 'Great. Who?'

'I'm waiting on a fax with a picture. Hopefully I'll have it when you get here. I'll keep everyone on standby for the six o'clock debrief.'

'Thanks, Liz.'

Chapter Sixteen

Wednesday, January 17, 5:20 P.M.

Sophie was breathing hard as she rushed into the library. Vito was across the lobby, talking with a woman in a dark sweater. He looked up and smiled and her heart shot off like a rocket. She managed to cross the lobby with some decorum, when she really wanted to launch herself into his arms and take up where they'd left off that morning.

From the flash of his dark eyes, he was thinking the same thing. 'So, what's the big mystery?' she asked with what she hoped wasn't the dazzled smile of a teenaged fan-girl.

'I need you to translate for me. Sophie, this is Barbara Mulrine, the librarian here.'

She nodded to the woman. 'It's nice to meet you. What do you need translated?'

Barbara pointed to an old man washing windows. 'Him. His name is Yuri Chertov.'

'He's a witness,' Vito said. 'Make sure he knows he's not in trouble.'

'Okay.' She approached the old man, noticing his hands right away. *Oh, no.* Still she kept her smile respectful as she switched her brain to Russian. 'Hello. I'm Sophie Alexandrovna Johannsen. How are you?'

He looked to Barbara who gave him an encouraging smile. 'It's all right,' she said.

'Do you have an office with a homey sofa or someplace that

at least doesn't look like an interrogation room?' Sophie asked the librarian.

'Marcy, mind the desk for a while. This way.' She led them to the back.

When the four of them were in Barbara's office, Sophie switched back to Russian. 'Let's sit down,' she said. 'I don't know about you, but I have had a long day.'

'As have I. This is my second job. When I have finished here, I will go to a third.'

His Russian was of the higher class. This man was very educated. Sophie could only guess at the path that had brought him to work three menial jobs. 'You work hard,' she said, choosing her dialect more carefully. 'But hard work is good for the soul.'

'Very good for the soul, Sophie Alexandrovna. I am Yuri Petrovich Chertov. Tell your detective to ask his questions. I will answer to the best of my ability.'

'Ask him if he knew Claire Reynolds,' Vito said when she told him to begin.

The man nodded, his eyes darkening. 'Claire was not a good person.'

Sophie relayed it and Vito nodded. 'Ask him why not?'

Yuri frowned. 'She treated Barbara with disrespect.'

'And you as well, Yuri Petrovich?' Sophie asked him, and his eyes darkened more.

'Yes, but I was not her employer. Barbara is a kind person, very loyal. Claire often took advantage of Barbara's trust. I once saw her take money from Barbara's purse. When Claire saw that I'd seen, she threatened to turn *me* in to the police for the theft.'

As Sophie translated, Barbara's mouth fell open. 'How did she know how to threaten you, and why were you afraid?' Vito asked. 'Barbara says you're here legally.'

Sophie translated Vito's question, but the librarian's shock needed none. Yuri looked down at his hands. 'Claire had her computer with her and used one of the translation websites to translate her threat. It was a very rough translation, but still I understood. As for fear of the police . . .' He shrugged. 'I take no chances.' He looked at Barbara sadly when Sophie had finished. 'I am sorry, Miss Barbara,' he said in English.

Barbara smiled. 'It's all right. It can't have been much money. I didn't miss it.'

'Because I replaced it,' Yuri said when Sophie told him what she'd said.

Barbara's eyes grew moist. 'Oh, Yuri. You shouldn't have done that.'

Vito looked touched as well. 'Ask him about the man he spoke with.'

Sophie did. 'He was about my age,' Yuri answered. 'I am fifty-two.'

Sophie's eyes widened before she could stop herself. *Fifty-two.* He looked as old as Anna, who was almost eighty. Sophie's cheeks heated when his brows lifted. She dropped her eyes. 'I am very sorry, Yuri Petrovich. I didn't mean to be rude.'

'It is all right. I know I look much older. This man you seek was nearly two meters tall, perhaps one hundred kilos. Thick gray hair that waved. He had robust health.'

Sophie looked at Vito. 'About six-four, two-twenty, mid-fifties. Thick gray wavy hair. And . . . healthy.' She turned back to Yuri, curious. 'Why did you notice his health?'

'Because his wife looked ill. Near unto death.'

Vito's eyes flashed as she relayed that information. He drew two sketches from his folder. Sophie remembered Vito saying his brother Tino had sketched some of the victims' faces. Sophie knew she was looking at two of the nine victims right now. 'Are these the people he saw?' Vito asked.

Yuri awkwardly took the sketches in his gnarled hands. 'Yes. Her hair was different. Longer and darker, but the faces are very similar.'

'Ask him when they came in, what they said, and if they gave him their names.'

'They were here before Thanksgiving,' Yuri said when she

translated. His smile was wry. 'They said quite a lot, but I understood very little. The man did all the talking. The woman sat. He asked about Claire Reynolds. Had I seen her? Did I know her? He had an accent. How do you say . . .' He said a word Sophie didn't know.

'Wait.' She pulled her Russian dictionary from her backpack. She found the word, then looked back up at Yuri, puzzled. 'He had a *dangerous* accent?'

'Not dangerous.' Yuri blew a frustrated breath. 'He said *Yawl*. Like . . . Daisy Duke.'

Sophie blinked, then laughed. 'Hazardous. Oh, like the *Dukes of Hazzard*.'

Yuri nodded, a gleam in his eye. 'I saw the movie. You're far prettier than that Jessica Simpson.'

Sophie smiled. 'You're very kind.' She looked up at Vito. 'They were southerners.'

'Did they give their name?'

Yuri frowned. 'Yes. It was like D'Artagnan from *The Three Musketeers*, but with a *V*. He said his name was Arthur *Vartanian*, from Georgia. I remembered that clearly because I am also from Georgia.' He lifted an ironic brow. 'Small world, is it not?'

One corner of Vito's mouth lifted as he wrote down the man's name and the state of Georgia. Yuri's Georgia was, of course, half a world away, both geographically and philosophically. 'A very small world indeed,' she said to Yuri. 'Please, pardon my rudeness, but would you tell me what you did in Georgia?'

'I was a surgeon by profession. But in my heart I was a patriot, and for this I spent twenty years in Novosibirsk. When I was released I came to America, with the help of sponsors like Barbara.' He lifted his broken hands. 'I paid a high price for my freedom.'

Sophie's throat closed and she found she had no words. Novosibirsk was the site of several Siberian prisons. She couldn't imagine what he'd endured.

He saw her distress and awkwardly patted her knee. 'And what do you do, Sophie Alexandrovna, that you have such an expert command of my language?'

I'm an archeologist, a linguist, a historian. But what came out was none of those things, because in her mind she suddenly saw the rapt faces of the children as she'd taught them medieval history through Ted's tours. This man's history was every bit as relevant. No, she thought looking at his hands. *More.*

'I work in a museum. It's small, but we get good attendance. We try to bring history to life. Would you come and talk to people about your experiences?'

He smiled at her. 'I would like that. Now, your detective looks eager to leave.'

Sophie kissed both his cheeks. 'Stay well, Yuri Petrovich.'

Vito shook Yuri's hand, gently. 'Thank you.'

'The two people,' Yuri said in English, pointing to Vito's folder. 'They are not well?'

Vito shook his head. 'No, sir. They're not well at all.'

Wednesday, January 17, 6:25 P.M.

Vito waited as Sophie parked her grandmother's car in the precinct lot. When she got out, he slipped a hand through her hair and kissed her the way he'd been wanting to since she'd crossed the library lobby. When he lifted his head, she sighed.

'I was afraid I'd imagined this.' She leaned up and kissed him lightly. 'You.'

They stole a few moments to just look at each other, then Vito forced himself to step away. 'Thank you. You saved me hours waiting for a translator.' He took her hand and led her toward the precinct entrance.

'It was my pleasure. Yuri Petrovich said he would come and talk at my museum.'

Vito looked down at her, surprised. 'I thought it was

290

Albright's museum and you were just biding your time till you could leave,' he said, and her lips curved.

'Things change. You know, Vito, interpreters get paid good wages. Overtime even.'

'I'll try to find some money in the budget.' *If I can't, I'll pay her myself.*

She frowned at him as they walked. 'I said helping you was my pleasure.' Her brows winged up. 'I was hoping my payment would also be.'

Vito chuckled. 'I'm sure I can think of something. So tell me about your day, Sophie Alexandrovna. Any more nasty gifts from Brewster's wife?'

'No.' Her expression grew thoughtful. 'It was actually a very nice day.'

'So tell me.' She did, and her stories of her tours had him chuckling again as the elevator opened to his floor. 'Hey,' Vito said to Nick as he and Sophie came into the bullpen. 'We hit the jackpot with the library. We were able to get an ID on the old couple.'

'Good,' Nick said, but there was no energy in his voice. 'Hey, Sophie.'

'Hello, Nick,' she said warily. 'Good to see you again.'

Nick tried to smile. 'I see you're official this time. The badge,' he added.

Sophie looked at the temporary badge they'd issued her at the downstairs desk. 'Yeah, now I'm part of the club. I get to know the password *and* the secret handshake.'

'That's good,' Nick said quietly and Vito frowned.

'Please don't tell me there's another body. That would totally ruin my day.'

'No, not that we know of anyway. It's that answering machine tape, Chick. It's bad.'

'Bad like you can't hear it?'

'No. Bad like you can,' Nick answered heavily. 'You'll hear it soon enough.' He sat up, forced a smile. 'So, don't keep me in suspense. Who are two-one and two-two?'

Vito had been on the phone with Records as he drove back from the library. 'Arthur and Carol Vartanian, from Dutton, Georgia. And get this – he's a retired judge.'

Nick blinked. 'Whoa.'

'Sit,' Vito said to Sophie, pulling out his desk chair for her. 'I'll see if we have that photo of the brand on the victim's cheek. Then you can go to your grandmother.'

She caught the sleeve of Vito's coat as he pulled away. 'And then?'

Nick perked up, genuinely. 'And then?' he repeated cagily.

Vito smiled down at Sophie and totally ignored Nick. 'Depends on how late I get out of here. I still want to meet your grandmother if I can.'

'Meeting the grandmother,' Nick said. 'Does that have some double meaning?'

Sophie laughed. 'You sound like my uncle Harry.'

Liz came out of her office. 'You're back. And you must be Dr Johannsen.' She shook Sophie's hand firmly. 'We're very grateful for all you've done.'

'Please call me Sophie. I was glad to help.'

'Did you get the photo of the victim's cheek, Liz?'

'No, Katherine said she'd bring it to the meeting. They're all waiting for us in the conference room, so let's go. Sophie, can you wait for us in the cafeteria? It's on the second floor. Hopefully Vito can keep this meeting short. My sitter's on overtime.'

'Sure. I have my cell, Vito. Call me when you're ready to show me the pictures.'

Sophie went down the elevator and Liz glanced up at Vito with what might have been a smirk. 'You never said she was so young.'

'And pretty,' Nick teased in a singsong.

Vito wanted to scowl, but found he could only grin. 'Yeah, she is, isn't she?'

DIE FOR ME

It had been a gratifying day. Perhaps he'd had a rocky start, but the end was looking quite fine. He'd started the day with loose ends. As of this moment, he'd snipped all but one. Only one person could keep a secret, a truth his antique dealer had illustrated with dazzling clarity that morning. He didn't regret utilizing the dealer's services. After all, one couldn't just walk into Wal-Mart and buy an authentic broadsword, circa 1422. Special purchases required special connections. Unfortunately his dealer had a supply chain, which increased his exposure considerably.

And since only one man could keep a secret, the whole chain had to go. They'd gone nicely and without much fuss. Now, should the police continue asking about chairs with lots of spikes, they would find no answers. His dealer had been silenced.

'How are you doing back there, Derek?' he called to the back of his van, but there was no reply. If Harrington was awake, it would be a miracle. In hindsight he probably should have cut Derek's dose. He'd given him the same amount he'd given Warren and Bill and Gregory, and they'd all been twice Derek's size. He did hope Derek wasn't dead. He had plans for him.

Just as he had for Dr Johannsen. He definitely didn't want to kill her, at least not at the outset. She'd die, but at a time and method of his choosing. She was big enough that he didn't need to worry about the dose. By midnight he'd have all his loose ends snipped, his queen secured, so that he could focus on what was important.

Finishing the game. Making oRo, and by extension himself, a household name. His dreams were finally within his grasp.

Wednesday, January 17, 6:45 P.M.

'Sorry, everyone,' Vito said, closing the door behind them. They were all there, Jen, Scarborough, Katherine, Tim, and Bev. Brent Yelton from IT had also joined them, which Vito hoped meant good news. 'Thanks for waiting.'

Jen looked up from her laptop. 'Did you get an ID for the couple?'

'Yeah, finally.' Vito went to the whiteboard and wrote their names in the first two blocks of the second row on the grave diagram. 'Arthur Vartanian and his wife, Carol. Ages fifty-six and fifty-two. Come from a small town in Georgia called Dutton.'

'And he's a freakin' judge,' Nick added, slumping into the chair beside Jen.

'Interesting,' Scarborough said. 'Arthur Vartanian was the one murder of passion. Maybe he sentenced the killer to prison.'

'But why did he kill them here and not in Dutton, Georgia?' Katherine asked. 'And why leave those two empty graves?'

Vito sighed. 'We'll add those questions to the list. Let's cover the tape first.'

'That's why I'm here,' Scarborough said. 'Nick wanted me to hear it.'

Nick handed Jen a CD and she put it in her laptop, positioning the small speakers she'd connected and turning the laptop to Nick. 'I've listened to this four or five times already,' Nick said. 'There are periods of dead tape, so we'll fast-forward through those. Electronics cleaned it up as best they could. Part of the static is that it's a cell phone. The other part is that the phone is covered, probably in a pocket or something.'

'We checked Jill Ellis's LUDs.' Jen said. 'She made a call to Greg's cell phone at 3:30 yesterday afternoon. She received this call at 4:25.'

Nick hit play and the CD began with a ragged moan that made everyone flinch.

'*Scream all you want. No one can hear you. No one will save you. I've killed them all.*' It went on, the killer promising to make Greg suffer and Greg pleading pitifully. '*It's time for your ride in my time machine. Now you'll see what happens to thieves.*'

Nick fast-forwarded. 'He drags him for a minute, then there's a bang, like a door being opened too hard. And then this.' He hit play and they heard squeaking that echoed softly. 'There's about five minutes of dead space. And then . . .' He hit play.

There was a scraping sound, then the killer's voice. '*Welcome to my dungeon, Mr Sanders. You will not enjoy your stay.*'

Another thud, then the volume dropped. 'We think he took off Greg's coat and dropped it next to him. Greg's cell phone's still connected, but it gets hard to hear in some places.' Nick's jaw tightened. 'In others it's way too loud.'

'*You are a thief and . . . subject to penalties . . . law.*' More dragging and crashing and fevered pleas from Greg Sanders that nauseated Vito. Then more squeaking.

'He's rolling something,' Nick said, then closed his eyes tight, waiting.

The scream left sweat beading on Vito's forehead. 'What the hell was that?'

'Don't worry,' Nick said grimly. 'You'll get to hear it again.'

And they did, as Greg Sanders screamed again. '*You bastard. You fucking bastard. Oh, God.*' A big crash, then Greg's screams became moans.

'*See what you've made me do. What a mess. Sit up. Sit up.*' There was scraping and more dragging and the labored breathing of exertion. '*Now we can proceed.*'

'*You . . . you bastard.*' It was Greg's voice, very faint. '*My hand . . . My . . .*' A broken sob of anguish.

'*And . . . foot. See, you . . . common thief . . . stole . . . church . . . special punishment.*'

More words followed. Vito leaned forward to hear them, but jerked back when Greg shrieked again. It was a hideous wail, part agony, part terror. It didn't sound human.

Liz lifted her hands. 'Nick, turn it off. That's enough.'

Nick nodded and stopped the CD, leaving a thick silence broken only by the sound of their own heavy breathing. 'It pretty much ends there,' Nick said. 'Greg screams some more, then I think he passes out. After five minutes of dead space the tape ends. One of the guys in Electronics is trying to place the sounds, the squeaks and bangs.'

Scarborough exhaled quietly. 'I've been a psychologist for twenty years. I've never heard anything like this. Your killer showed no remorse, and beyond the slamming and banging, I heard no real rage in his voice. There was only disdain and contempt.'

Jen took her hand from her mouth where it had been clamped throughout most of the tape. 'He said "Stole . . . church,"' she said unsteadily. 'Greg stole in a church, from a church? Maybe he killed Greg in a church?'

'Before he started cutting his foot, he was chanting. I heard "*ecclesia*,"' Tim said.

'I heard it, too. It's Latin for "church,"' Vito said. 'I was an altar boy,' he added when Nick looked surprised. 'Really. I was.'

Tim dabbed at his forehead with his handkerchief. 'Same here. I heard that word more than enough times during mass. The question is, why did he use it?'

'I'd like to know what he did with Gregory's hand and foot,' Katherine said quietly. 'They weren't with the body.'

'Or anywhere near the scene,' Jen added. 'I even brought in cadaver dogs.'

Vito looked at Thomas. 'He said Greg was going to ride on his time machine, then welcomed him to his dungeon. Is he crazy?'

Thomas shook his head forcefully. 'In a clinical sense, almost certainly not. He's acquired instruments of torture, whether he bought them or made them himself. He's lured his victims with planning and forethought. He's not crazy. I think the time machine reference is part of his . . . fun.'

'Fun,' Vito said bitterly. 'I can't wait to find this guy.'

'I suppose it's too much to hope that Greg's phone had a GPS,' Liz said.

Nick shook his head. 'Throwaway. His old cell was disconnected for nonpayment.'

Beverly cleared her throat. 'He found Greg through the model site. Greg's résumé is posted, but his Septic Service ads aren't listed. I guess he wasn't proud of them.'

'So Munch didn't know he was a local icon,' Nick said. 'Coupled with his *charmin' drawl*' – Nick accentuated his own – 'we can assume he's not from 'round here.'

Vito nodded. 'Munch has a southern accent, as did the Vartanians. Coincidence?'

'At the risk of making myself a suspect,' Nick said dryly, 'no, not a coincidence.'

'The Vartanians were from Georgia,' Katherine said, her brows crunched in thought. 'So was Claire Reynolds.'

'You're right,' Vito agreed. 'Again, not a coincidence. In fact, it's our first solid link between victims other than the UCanModel website. Perhaps the Vartanian family can tell us if Claire and Arthur and Carol knew each other. How about the autopsy reports?'

'I autopsied Claire Reynolds and the elderly lady on the first row. I got nothing more to help you identify the old woman. She had a broken neck, just like Carol Vartanian and Claire. I did get the final report from the lab on the silicone spray. It's a special blend. They didn't know who made it.'

From his folder Vito pulled the magazine that he'd gotten from Dr Pfeiffer that morning. 'Claire's doctor said companies advertise their lotions in the back. Claire definitely would have used lotion, but her doctor said she bought it from him.'

Jen took the magazine. 'She could have bought it from one of these, too. I'll work on tracking the special formula to one of these manufacturers.'

'Thanks. Here are the Claire letters. One's from Pfeiffer, the other from the library.'

Jen took the letters, as well. 'I'll get them to the lab, along with examples of Claire's handwriting. We'll see if anything shakes.'

'Good. Bev and Tim, what did you find at UCanModel dotcom?'

'Nothing for a while,' Bev said. 'We were searching models who'd either gotten hits on their résumé or e-mails from E. Munch. Interestingly, Munch only e-mailed four people – Warren, Brittany, Bill, and Greg. Nobody else.'

Vito frowned. 'That's hard to believe. How could he be sure they'd accept?'

'It's like he knew something else,' Nick mused. 'Blackmail?'

'More like financials,' Brent Yelton said. 'All the victims had overdrawn checking accounts, owed thousands on their credit cards, and had credit scores in the toilet.'

'So we still have nothing,' Nick said darkly, but Beverly was smiling.

'No, we said he didn't e-mail anybody else as Munch,' she said, 'but we kept thinking about what Jen said this morning. That E. Munch meant something. So we Googled and came up with this.' She pulled an art book from under the printouts. It was open to a painting Vito recognized.

It was a surreal, ghoulish-looking character whose mouth yawned open hideously. Just like Greg Sanders's had this afternoon. 'The Scream,' Vito said.

'Edvard Munch,' Scarborough added. 'How apropos, given the way he made Gregory scream. This guy is one scary, very thorough sociopath.'

Beverly flipped to another picture, an even scarier one in a medieval style, with demons wreaking havoc on lost souls in grisly, macabre ways. 'This is Hieronymus Bosch's Garden of Earthly Delights. A model named Kay Crawford got an e-mail from one H. Bosch yesterday afternoon. She hadn't answered the e-mail yet.'

'And we got her computer before it fried,' Brent added with satisfaction. 'Bosch wanted to hire her for a documentary.'

'She's agreed to help us,' Tim said. 'We could set a trap for this bastard.'

A smile started across Vito's face. 'I like it. A lot. I think her help will mainly be her silence, but let's get her in here first thing tomorrow morning. In the meantime, if you've got her computer, can you answer the e-mail and say you want the job?'

Brent nodded. 'I made a full sector image of Kay Crawford's hard drive, so if the virus's timer is triggered by a reply like I think it is, then we'll have a backup.'

'Excellent. And Liz.' Vito turned to her. 'You said you'd gotten a hit from Interpol.'

'It might mean nothing to us.' She slid some faxed pictures from an envelope. 'Apparently the guy in Europe who died, Alberto Berretti? He owed huge back taxes to the Italian government and they were watching his assets at the time of his death. They expected his children to try to divert some of his collection for their own private sale. They've had agents watching Berretti's grown children for quite some time. This is one of Berretti's sons with an American of unknown identity.'

Vito looked at the pictures. 'His face is clear enough, but until somebody recognizes him it doesn't help us. But it's a start.'

Bev and Tim gathered their printouts. 'Vito, we're calling it a night,' Tim said. 'We got no sleep last night, and we're seeing double from all these printouts.'

'Thanks. Can you leave that art book? I want to look at it later.'

'I'll write up a detailed profile for you,' Thomas said. 'This killer used some very specific language. I'll see if any patients like this have been documented.'

'And I'll do the gunshot, the shrapnel, and Greg Sanders's autopsies tomorrow,' Katherine said. 'Oh, here's the photo you wanted of the brand on Sanders's cheek.'

Vito took it and put it on the table. 'Thanks, Katherine. I didn't want Sophie to have to go to the morgue.'

''Cause he likes her,' Nick said slyly, and Katherine smiled.

'Of course he does. She's my little girl.' She slanted a look up at Vito. 'Remember that, Vito. She's my little girl.' With that warning, Katherine left with Thomas.

'I'll get Sophie back up here so she can look at the picture, then we're headed out,' Vito said. He went to the door and stopped short. 'Oh, shit.'

Wednesday, January 17, 7:10 P.M.

Sophie and Katherine sat side by side on a bench outside the conference room.

Vito crouched in front of Sophie, who looked pale. 'What happened?'

She looked down at him, her eyes stark. 'I was on my way to the cafeteria and got a call on my cell, something you needed to know. When I came up to knock on the door . . .' She shrugged fitfully. 'I heard the screams. I'm all right now. Just shaken up.'

Vito took her hands, found them cold. 'I'm sorry. That was a terrible thing to hear.'

Katherine urged her to her feet. 'Come on, honey. I'll take you home with me.'

'No, I need to see Gran.' She saw the others watching and scowled, embarrassed. 'Stop it. I was just shocked. Where's the picture you wanted me to look at?'

'Sophie, you don't need to do that tonight,' Katherine said.

'Stop it, Katherine,' Sophie snapped. 'I'm not five anymore.' She caught her temper and sighed. 'I'm sorry, but don't treat me like a child. Please.' She pulled away and went into the conference room, leaving Katherine looking hurt and forlorn.

'It's hard when your babies grow up,' Liz murmured and Katherine chuckled weakly.

'Maybe I do treat her like she's five, but that's how I remember her best.' She looked at Vito. 'I have sharp implements at my disposal. Don't make me use them.'

Vito winced. 'Yes, ma'am.' He went to the conference room

where Sophie was looking at the photo from Interpol. 'That's not Sanders.' He started to move the Interpol photo from the table, but her hand came down to clamp his wrist like a vise.

'Vito. I know him. This is Kyle Lombard. Remember Monday night, when I gave you Brewster's name, I gave you Lombard's, too.'

'I know. We've been searching for him but haven't found him yet. Liz,' he called, 'come here, please. Are you sure, Sophie?'

'Yes. And it's also why I came up to talk to you. I got two calls, actually. The first was from Amanda Brewster. She was screaming that she knew Alan was with me. Apparently he didn't come home for dinner. I hung up on her. Then not two minutes later, my cell rings again. This time it's Kyle's wife.'

'*Kyle's* wife?'

'Yes.' Sophie sighed. 'She accused me of having an affair with Kyle.'

Vito narrowed his eyes. 'What?'

'She said she'd heard Kyle on the phone, talking about me, and said she'd be damned if she let me steal her husband like I tried to steal Amanda Brewster's.' She shrugged when he lifted his brows in question. 'Amanda was very vocal about the hussy who tried to break up her happy home. There, um, weren't a lot of people who didn't know. Kyle's wife said that Amanda had called yesterday to tell her I was back in the picture. They've circled the wagons to protect their happy marriages.'

'I guess Kyle and Clint learned a lot more from Alan Brewster than archeology,' Vito said dryly, and was rewarded with a wry smile from Sophie.

'I talked to Clint Shafer on Monday. You saw Alan on Tuesday. Tonight Kyle didn't show up for dinner, so his wife checked his caller ID and saw he'd talked to Clint. She called Clint's wife, who went through his caller ID and gave Kyle's wife my number at the museum. Incidentally, Kyle's wife says Clint didn't come home for dinner either.'

'But both wives called you on your cell.'

She frowned. 'You're right. How did she get my cell? Well,

you'll figure that out. My point is, now you have a photo of Kyle Lombard taken . . . where?'

'Bergamo, Italy, was what Interpol said,' Liz answered from behind him.

'That's less than a half hour by train from where Berretti lived. You now have Kyle's photo, who doesn't come home two days after I asked a question. Coincidence?'

'No.' Vito looked at Nick and Liz. 'Let's get an APB for Clint Shafer in—'

'Long Island,' Sophie supplied.

'And one for Kyle Lombard wherever the hell he is.'

'His wife called me from an 845 area code,' Sophie said. 'But if you can't find Kyle through his wife's number, maybe you can find him through Clint's phone records.'

Vito nodded hard. 'Good, Sophie. Very good.'

'No, Vito.' Nick shook his head. 'Bad. Very bad. If Lombard traces to Sophie and Lombard traces to Berretti of the missing medieval torture artifacts, *and* if Lombard isn't out cattin' around on his wife but maybe lying in a gulley somewhere?'

Vito's blood ran cold. 'Shit.'

Sophie sat down hard. 'Oh, no. If Kyle's involved and he's really missing . . .'

'This killer could know about you,' Vito said grimly.

'We'll have to get you protection, Sophie,' Jen said.

Liz nodded. 'I'll take care of it.' She squeezed Katherine's arm. 'Breathe, Kat.'

Katherine lowered herself into the chair next to Sophie. 'I should never have—'

'Katherine,' Sophie gritted through her teeth. 'Stop.'

'*I can't.* This has nothing to do with you being five or fifty-five. This is you being in the sights of the monster who did *this.*' She grabbed the photo of Sanders as tears rolled down her cheeks. 'Who tortured and murdered nine other bodies in my morgue.'

Sophie's expression changed in an instant and she put her arms around Katherine as the ME's shoulders shook. Vito and

Nick looked at each other, stunned. They'd never seen Katherine shed a tear in the past, no matter how bad the bodies got.

But this wasn't a body. This was her little girl and Vito understood her terror.

Sophie patted Katherine's back. 'I'll be fine. Vito will watch out for me. And I have Lotte and Birgit.' She looked up at Vito. 'On second thought, I think you're it.'

Katherine shoved her away, furious. 'This is not funny, Sophie Johannsen.'

Sophie wiped at Katherine's tears. 'No, it's not. Nor is it your fault.'

Katherine grabbed Vito's shirt and yanked him down with a strength that surprised him. 'You'd better not let anything happen to her, too, or so help me God . . .'

Vito stared at the woman he thought he'd known so well. Katherine stared back, serious and very angry. *Too.* She knew about Andrea, what he'd done. He pried her fingers from his shirt and straightened. 'Understood.'

Katherine took a deep shuddering breath. 'Just so we're clear.'

'Crystal,' Vito bit out.

Sophie was staring at them both. 'Did you just threaten him, Katherine?'

'Yeah,' Vito said. 'She did.'

Chapter Seventeen

Wednesday, January 17, 8:30 P.M.

Sophie got out of her car in the nursing home's lot and waited for Vito to park. He'd been silent, brooding, and angry as they'd left the precinct. When he'd followed her to the nursing home, he'd kept so close to her rear bumper that he'd have plowed into her if she'd had to stop suddenly. She'd gone over Vito's and Katherine's confrontation in her mind all the way over, which was a hell of a lot less unnerving than thinking that a killer might be watching her. Something had happened to someone Vito was supposed to have protected. Sophie remembered the roses. Her gut told her they were related.

Vito slammed his truck door and came around to take her arm.

'You are going to tell me what that was all about,' she said.

'Yeah. But not now. Please, Sophie, not now.'

She studied his face in the soft glow of the streetlights. There was pain in his eyes, in the set of his jaw. And guilt. She understood about guilt. She also knew Katherine would never have allowed her to leave with Vito had she not been convinced he could indeed take care of her. 'All right. But calm down. You're going to frighten Anna, and she doesn't need that right now.' She threaded her fingers through his. 'Neither do I.'

He drew several deep breaths and had schooled his features

to calm by the time they got to the desk. Sophie signed them in. 'Miss Marco. How's Gran been today?'

Nurse Marco frowned. 'Same as always. Mean and ornery.'

Sophie frowned back. 'Thanks so much. It's this way, Vito.' She led him back through the sterile halls, aware of the curious stares of the nurses. *Curious nothing*. They were leering. Drooling, even. 'Don't make eye contact,' Sophie murmured, 'or they'll be on you like white on rice. They don't get eye candy like you every day.'

He chuckled, breaking the tension. 'Thanks, but not a picture I wanted in my mind.'

'Don't mention it.' She stopped outside Anna's room. 'Vito, she doesn't look anything like she did before. You need to know that.'

'I understand.' He squeezed her hand. 'Let's go.'

Anna was dozing. Sophie sat next to her and touched her hand. 'Gran, I'm here.'

Anna's eyes fluttered open and one side of her mouth trembled in a smile. 'Sophie.' Her eyes looked up, and up again until she saw Vito's face. 'Who is this?'

'This is Vito Ciccotelli. My . . . friend. Vito loves the opera, Gran.'

Anna's eyes changed, softened. 'Ahh. Sit, please,' she slurred.

'She wants you to sit.'

'I can understand her.' Vito sat and took Anna's hand in his. 'I heard you in *Orfeo* at the Academy downtown when I was a kid. Your *Che faro* made my grandfather weep.'

Anna regarded him steadily. 'And you? Did you weep?'

Vito smiled at her. 'Yes. But let's keep that our secret, okay?'

Anna smiled back, slowly. 'Your secret is safe with me. Talk to me, Vito.'

Sophie's throat thickened as Vito talked about the opera and brought a light to Anna's eyes that hadn't been there in a long time. Way too soon, Nurse Marco intruded.

'She needs her evening medication, Dr Johannsen. You should go.'

Anna breathed out a petulant breath. 'That woman.'

Vito still held Anna's hand. 'She's just doing her job. It was so nice to meet you, Miss Shubert. I'd love to come again.'

'You can, but only if you call me Anna.' Her good eye narrowed slyly. 'Or Gran.'

Sophie rolled her eyes. 'Gran.'

But Vito just laughed. 'My grandfather would have been so jealous of me tonight, sitting with the great Anna Shubert. I'll come again, as soon as I can.'

Sophie leaned over and kissed Anna's cheek. 'Be nice to Nurse Marco, Gran. Vito's right, she's only trying to do her job.'

Anna's lips thinned. 'She's mean, Sophie.'

Sophie shot a worried glance at Vito and saw he'd tilted his head pensively.

'How so, Anna?' he asked.

'She's mean and hateful. And cruel.' It was all Sophie had ever gotten her to say.

Sophie controlled the sudden tremble of her hand. That Vito hadn't laughed it off bothered her a great deal. 'Sleep, Gran. I'll see what I can do about Nurse Marco.'

'You're a good girl, Sophie.' Anna's mood shifted again and she smiled her half smile. 'Come soon, Sophie, and bring your man here.'

'I will. I love you, Gran.' She kissed Anna's other cheek and hurried out, not stopping until she got to her car, Vito never more than a step behind her.

'You didn't talk to the nurse,' he said quietly.

'What am going to say? Are you abusing my grandmother?' Sophie heard the hysteria creep into her voice and sighed, forcing herself to calm. 'She'd just say no.'

'Have you found evidence of abuse?'

'No. Gran's always clean and seems to get her medicine when she needs it. She's kept on a cardiac monitor and a few of the nurses have ICU experience. This is a good nursing home, Vito. I researched it so carefully, but . . . She's my grandmother.'

'You could . . .' He hesitated.

'I could what?'

'You could use a camera,' he said slowly.

'Like a nanny-cam?' Sophie asked, and his lips quirked up.

'In this case a granny-cam,' he said and she laughed, feeling a little better.

'Do you know anything about cameras like that?'

He winced. 'Yeah, I do. My brother-in-law Aidan knows more. I'll ask him.'

'Thanks. If I can get an affordable camera, I'd put it in her room in a heartbeat, just to give me and Harry peace of mind.' She smiled at him. 'And thank you for that, in there. You made Gran so happy. I wish I'd thought of it before, bringing in people who would talk to her about her music. Now I have to go home. When will I see you again?'

Vito blinked at her, incredulous. 'Like, every time you look in your rearview mirror. I'm not leaving you tonight, Sophie. Didn't you hear us? Munch or Bosch or whatever the hell his name is may be watching you.'

'I heard you. And I listened. But I don't expect a twenty-four-hour bodyguard, Vito. That's just not practical.'

Vito's eyes flashed and she thought he'd argue. Then his eyes went as sly as her Gran's had. 'You owe me a double bonus prize for this morning.'

'Yeah, but *you* owe *me* for translating.'

He grinned. 'I think this is what they call compound interest.'

She swallowed, her body already tingling in anticipation. 'See you at the house.'

Wednesday, January 17, 9:25 P.M.

She had an escort, which was most unfortunate. He frowned as he watched Sophie Johannsen drive away in her grandmother's car, followed closely by the truck driven by the man who'd walked her out. He'd have to wait until she was alone.

He'd known she'd show up here. Long ago he'd checked her financials and found the checks she'd written to the nursing home. She paid them a lot of money. He'd heard health care costs were on the rise, but even he'd been surprised. He'd never pay so much for his parents. But then, he no longer had parents, so the point was moot.

He wished he'd been able to hear what they'd been saying. Next time he'd be better prepared. He'd wanted to snip all his loose ends in one fell swoop, but that wasn't going to happen tonight. No matter. He had other diversions. He put his van in gear, then glanced over his shoulder to where Derek Harrington lay, bound and gagged.

'You wanted to know how I got my inspiration,' he said. 'You're about to find out.'

He'd return for Sophie Johannsen tomorrow.

Thursday, January 18, 4:10 A.M.

Vito woke slowly. He'd slept well, exhausted by four long days of work and two short nights of teaching Sophie the fine art of making love. She was a fast learner, capable of assimilating all he'd shown her into moves that left him utterly spent. But now he'd recharged and he wanted her again. He reached . . . and patted an empty bed.

Vito's eyes snapped open. She was gone. He jumped from her bed, his heart knocking in his chest. He stopped in the bedroom doorway and listened, relieved at the low murmur of the TV downstairs. He pulled on his pants and forced himself to take the stairs two at a time instead of in one big leap.

She was curled on the sofa, cradling a mug in her hands. Sleeping at her feet were the dogs, looking for all the world like rainbow-head wigs. Her head jerked around when she heard him. She'd been jumpy, too. 'I woke up and you weren't there,' he said.

'I couldn't sleep.'

He stopped at the coffee table on which he'd left his folder and Bev's art book. The book was open to *The Scream*, and Sophie was watching him.

'I didn't mean to pry. I didn't know it was a book for your case. I was trying to take my mind off . . . Anyway, the page was marked. It goes with the screams, doesn't it?'

Guilt speared him. He'd been sleeping like a baby while the sound of those horrific screams kept her awake. 'We think so. I'm sorry, Sophie. I never would have wanted you to hear what you've heard or see what you've seen.'

'But I have heard and I have seen,' she said quietly. 'And I'll deal with it.'

He sat next to her, stretching his arm across her shoulders, gratified when she snuggled against him. They sat in silence, watching the movie on the TV. It was in French and she was watching without the English subtitles, so after a minute he lost interest in the flick and sniffed at the mug in her hands. 'Hot chocolate?'

'Good German cocoa,' she confirmed. 'Shubert family recipe. Want some?'

'Maybe later. Is this one of your father's movies?'

'*En Garde*. It's not nearly as good as *Soft Rain*, the one you saw.' Her mouth lifted sadly. 'Alex wasn't a great actor, but he got a lot of screen time in this movie. It's a swashbuckler flick, and he fenced competitively when he was in school. There he is.'

Alexandre Arnaud walked across the screen, sword in hand. He was a tall man with golden hair and Vito immediately saw the family resemblance. 'You needed to see him.'

'I told you I'm not that difficult to figure out. I don't like to be alone in this house. If you hadn't been here, I'd be at Uncle Harry's watching Bette Davis movies with him.'

In this house. She sounded morose when she said it, but every time she'd spoken about her uncle it was with affection, so he thought Harry was a good place to begin. He made his voice casual. 'Did you live here or at your uncle's when you were a kid?'

Her wry look said that she'd seen right through his ploy. 'Mostly here with Gran. I started out with Harry and Freya, but they had four kids, and here I got my own room.'

'But you said you didn't like to be alone.'

She pulled back and leveled him a long look. 'Are you interrogating me, Vito?'

'No. Yes. Kind of. I'd prefer you keep thinking of me as nosy. It sounds less harsh.'

'So it does. I lived with my mother until I was four, but she got tired of me and dumped me on Uncle Harry. Harry gave me the first real home I ever knew.'

'An even better reason to hate your mother than her affair with your father.'

Her voice cooled. 'Oh, no. I have much better reasons to hate my mother, Vito.' She turned her eyes to the TV, but she wasn't watching it. 'Anna was still touring that first year, but when she was home I stayed with her in Pittsburgh. When she was gone I stayed with Harry. When I started kindergarten, Gran sold her place in Pittsburgh and moved here so I wasn't shuttled back and forth.'

The picture of a little Sophie being passed around with no roots squeezed at his heart. 'Did Freya not want you?' he asked and her eyes widened.

'Nothing gets past you. Freya hated Lena so much. Having me around was hard.'

How selfish, Vito thought, but kept it to himself. 'So what about your father? Alex.'

'Alex didn't know about me for a long time.'

'Anna didn't tell him.'

'She'd broken up with him less than a year before I was born and she still hurt, according to Maurice. According to Harry, she was terrified my father would take me away.'

'So how did you eventually meet him?'

'I always asked about my father, but nobody ever talked about him, so one day I took a bus to the courthouse, went up to the counter and asked for my birth certificate.'

'Industrious. Did they give it to you?'

'Considering I was only seven, no.'

Vito stared at her. 'Seven? You were riding around on a city bus *alone* at seven?'

'I was trading empty beer bottles to the nearest corner store for Ho Hos and beef jerky when I was four,' she said flatly. 'Anyway, the lady at the courthouse asked for my next of kin. The next thing I knew Uncle Harry was there, so upset. He told Gran I had a right to know my father. Gran said over her dead body, and Harry stopped arguing. I thought that was that. I was plotting a new plan to get my birth certificate when one day Harry shows up at my school with passports and two tickets to Paris.'

'He just up and took you to *France*?'

'Yep. He left a note with Freya so she could tell Anna. I think Uncle Harry slept on the sofa for a long time after he got back for that one. He still does, come to think of it.'

'So what happened when you got to France?'

'The taxi dropped us off at a front door that was fifteen feet tall. I held Uncle Harry's hand so tight. All I'd wanted was to know my father, and all of a sudden I was terrified. Turns out, Harry was too. He was afraid Alex would shun me, or worse, keep me. What happened was a formal visit, but with an invitation to come back over the summer.'

'Did you?'

'Oh, yes. The invitation was issued by the Arnaud family attorney straight to Gran. It was basically a threat that if she didn't send me for the summer, Alex would claim his custodial rights. So I spent my summers in a French mansion, with a tutor and a cook. The cook taught me the art of French cuisine. The tutor was to teach me to speak French, but I picked it up quickly so he moved on to German, then Latin and so on.'

'And the linguist was born,' he said and she smiled.

'Yes. Staying with Alex was something out of a fairy tale. Sometimes he'd take me to see his film friends. The summer I was eight, they were making a film at the ruins of a castle, and I got to go.' The memory of it sparkled on her face. 'It was incredible.'

'And the archeologist was born.'

'I guess so. Alex helped me over the years, with introductions, connections.'

'But did he love you?' The excitement ebbed from her face and his heart squeezed.

'In his own way. And over the summers I grew to love him, but not the way I love Harry. Harry is my true father.' She swallowed hard. 'I'm not sure I ever told him so.'

He started to ask how Katherine factored in, but bit the question back. Mention of Katherine would bring up the confrontation they'd had at the precinct. Similarly he held off asking what the other reasons for hating her mother were. He figured Sophie would want *quid pro quo* in the secret sharing department.

Instead, Vito pointed over to the corner of the room, where CDs and vinyl albums were haphazardly stacked where they had not been before. 'Having a yard sale?'

She frowned. 'No. After seeing you with Gran tonight, I thought she might like to hear some of her old favorites. Anna has an extensive record collection. Very valuable. But they're all gone, along with every recording of Anna in concert. Even *Orfeo*.'

'Could your aunt or uncle have moved them?'

'Maybe. I'll ask them before I get all excited about it. I did so want to take her something to listen to tomorrow, but I'll find something, even if it's off eBay.'

Vito thought of his own record collection – most of which he'd inherited from his grandfather. He suspected there might be an Anna Shubert vinyl in his box, but he didn't want to get Sophie's hopes up, so he closeted that thought away.

Sophie got up. 'I'm going to get some more cocoa. Do you want some?'

'Sure.'

She paused at the doorway. 'I know the other questions you have, Vito. And I think you know mine. But we'll leave things as they are for now.' She left without waiting for a reply and suddenly restless again, Vito got up and paced.

He always came back to the open book on the coffee table, though. Finally he sat down with the book and closed his eyes and let himself remember.

Go ahead and scream. No one can hear you. No one will save you. I killed them all. Then the words echoed in another voice. *Are you ready to die, Clothilde?*

'*Shit.*' Vito lurched to his feet as the pieces connected. 'Holy fucking shit.'

'What?' Sophie ran back, a mug in each hand. 'What's wrong?'

'Where's the phone?'

She pointed with the mug. 'In the kitchen. What is it?'

But he was already in the kitchen dialing Tino's cell. 'Tino?'

'*Vito?* Do you know what time it is?'

'Wake Dominic up. It's important.' He looked at Sophie. 'It's a fucking *game.*'

She said nothing, instead sitting at the table and sipping cocoa while he paced like a wild man. Finally Dom came to the phone. 'Vito?' His voice was scared. 'Is it Mom?'

He felt a pang of guilt for worrying the boy. 'She's fine. Dom, I need to talk to that kid who came to the house last night. The rude one with the game. Jesse something.'

'*Now?*'

'Yes, now. Do you have his number?'

313

'I don't hang with him, Vito. I told you that. Ray might have it, though.'

'Then give me Ray's number.' Vito wrote it down, then placed his next call to Nick.

'What?' Nick was whiny when he was wakened from a sound sleep.

'Nick, last night some kids came to my house. They were playing this World War II video game and there was a scene where this woman is strangled. Nick, listen carefully. The guy who does the murder says "No one can hear you. No one will save you."'

'Oh my God. You're tellin' me this is a *game*?'

'If not, they're connected somehow. Meet me at the precinct in an hour. I'm going to try to get a copy of the game. Call Brent, Jen, and . . . Liz. Have them meet us there.'

Hanging up with Nick, he planted a hard kiss on Sophie's mouth, then licked his lips. 'That chocolate tastes good. Remind me where we left off later. For now, get dressed.'

'Excuse me?'

'I'm not leaving you here alone with those two rainbow wigs for protection.'

She sighed heavily. 'You owe me big-time, boy.'

Vito slowed down long enough to give her a respectable kiss that left them both breathing hard. 'Compound my interest. Now get dressed.'

Thursday, January 18, 7:45 A.M.

'The game is *Behind Enemy Lines*,' Vito explained to Liz, Jen, and Nick while Brent played the game to get them to the strangulation scene. They'd gathered around Brent's computer in the IT bullpen, which was a very different environment from the homicide bullpen. Vito had counted no fewer than six *Star Trek* action figures on as many desks as he'd walked to Brent's

314

cubicle. Brent himself had the set of the original crew of the Starship *Enterprise*. Mr Spock was still in his original box. Brent was very proud of that.

Vito found that very disturbing, but he focused now on the game. 'It's a World War II first-person shooting game. You're an American soldier who's trapped behind enemy lines. The objective is to get from Germany, through occupied France, to Switzerland.'

'This is a very popular game,' Brent commented. 'My kid brother was trying to get one at Christmas and the stores were all sold out.'

Jen made a face. 'The graphics suck. How nineties.'

'Kids don't buy it for the game play,' Brent said. 'I've got it ready to go, Vito.'

Vito pointed to the screen. 'At this point you've decimated a bunker, then searched for the woman who betrayed you. When Brent kills the last Nazi, it'll go to the cut scene.'

Brent fired the final shot and the scene went to the one Vito had watched with the teenagers Tuesday night. On screen, the American had his hands around the French woman's throat and the woman fought for her life.

'No. Please no!' She struggled, and the screen filled with her face and his hands as she sobbed and begged for her life. The fear in her eyes gave Vito a chill. It had been far too real for comfort the first time he'd seen it. Now he knew why.

Jen sucked in a breath. 'My God. It's Claire Reynolds.'

'Are you ready to die, Clothilde?' the soldier mocked and she screamed, chillingly. The soldier laughed. 'Go ahead and scream, Clothilde. No one can hear you. No one will save you. I killed them all. And now I'll kill you.'

His hands tightened further and Clothilde began to writhe. The hands lifted until her feet no longer touched the floor. Her hands grabbed at his, her nails scoring his skin. Panic lit her eyes and she began to gasp for breath.

Then her eyes changed, horror combined with the certainty

that she would die. Her hands clawed, her mouth gaping open as she desperately fought to breathe. Finally she stiffened, then her eyes went abruptly blank, her hands limp on the soldier's now bloody wrists. The soldier gave her a final vicious shake, then tossed her to the floor. As her body lay crumpled in a heap, the camera focused on her eyes. Wide open and dead.

'Clothilde is Claire,' Jen repeated quietly. 'We just saw Claire die.'

'There's a scene where the soldier shoots a young man in the head with a Luger,' Vito told them. 'And another where he blows up a man with a grenade.'

Liz sat heavily. 'He killed all those people for this game?'

'Not all of them,' Vito said. 'At least not for this game. But you should see what this company's coming out with next. Brent, go to their website.'

Brent typed and the screen filled with a gold dragon soaring across a night sky. The dragon landed on a mountain and the letters O-R-O circled the dragon. The R landed on the dragon's scaled chest while the dragon caught the two O's in its front claws.

'Wow,' Nick said. 'Impressive.'

'This is oRo's website,' Brent said. 'They were a not-quite-B-list game designer that was facing bankruptcy before *Behind Enemy Lines* came out. They've doubled their net worth three times in the last six months.' He clicked a button and the face of a barrel-chested man in his forties filled the screen. 'Meet Jager Van Zandt. Pronounce it with a Y, not like "jogger." Jager is the president of oRo and its principal owner. Born in Holland, he's lived in the U.S. for about thirty years.' Brent clicked again and the thin face of another man appeared. He was the same age as Van Zandt, but easily a third smaller. 'This is Derek Harrington, oRo's VP and art director.'

'*He* did the art?' Jen said in disbelief. 'He doesn't look big enough to be our killer.'

'Harrington did the flying dragon,' Brent said. 'He's good at cartoon characters and flashy dragons. He doesn't do faces worth shit. Harrington didn't do those cut scenes.'

'Maybe he'll know who did,' Nick said grimly.

'They're headquartered in New York City,' Vito said. 'When we're done here, I say we take a little trip. Show them the press release, Brent.'

Brent clicked and sat back. 'Front and center.'

' "oRo's next game announced at the New York Gaming Expo," ' Liz read aloud. ' "behind enemy lines continues to exceed sales projections," stated President Jager Van Zandt at the conclusion of a standing-room-only presentation of their breakout game. "Our next endeavor is *The Inquisitor*, a game of swords and sorcery and medieval justice. Very prominently featured will be the dungeon, where gamers earn bonus points for originality and effective use of their weapon arsenal." ' Liz blew out a controlled but angry breath. 'Find these guys and squash them like bugs.'

Vito's smile was fierce. 'That will be a pleasure.'

'So, Brent,' Jen said, 'how do you know all this about oRo?'

'I'm a gamer from way back, so I keep up with all the new companies. My kid brother is *really* good. He's majoring in game design at Carnegie-Mellon.'

Liz looked dumbfounded. 'You can major in game design?'

'One of the hottest new majors out there. My brother and I have been watching the industry because he graduates next year and is looking for places to send his résumé. oRo moved to the top of his list after *Behind Enemy Lines* came out, because they're hiring.'

'Your brother's a computer artist?' Vito asked.

'No, he's into the game physics – how to make the characters move fluidly, which is Jager's department, incidentally. But last year Jager must have finally admitted that his game physics sucked, because he lured one of the big physics experts from one of the other companies. I'm always watching the industry for investment opportunities. Rumor has it that oRo's going IPO soon. But now I couldn't buy their stock.'

'If they're arrested, it'll be worthless,' Liz said. 'You'd lose your shirt.'

'If both Harrington and Van Zandt are involved, yes. But if it's just one of them, their stock will go to the moon. I could retire at forty, but I couldn't live with myself.' He took the CD out of his computer. 'People were murdered for this. I couldn't profit from that.'

That gave them all pause, then Vito squared his shoulders. 'We have to keep anyone from profiting from that, so let's get moving. I'm expecting the fashion model that hadn't responded to Munch's e-mail to come in around ten. Liz, can you meet with her since we're going to New York? Tell her to stay quiet and out of her e-mail.'

Liz shook her head. 'I've got a press conference at ten and meetings with the brass before and after.'

'I'll meet her,' Brent said. 'I won't profit from oRo, but I wouldn't mind meeting a model. Besides, I've already talked to her, with Bev and Tim yesterday.'

Liz chuckled. 'Your priorities are commendable, Brent. But I have to wonder – if Harrington and Van Zandt live in New York City, why are all the victims from Philly?'

'Neither Harrington nor Van Zandt had the personal capability to do this work,' Brent said. 'Somebody who worked for them did, and that person doesn't have to work from their headquarters.' He picked up the CD case. 'Where did you get a copy of this game in the middle of the night, Vito? It's like gold right now until oRo puts out more.'

'A kid from my nephew's school had it at my house Tuesday night. Last night his parents found and confiscated it and were only too happy to give it to me. They wanted it out of their house – they've got other younger children and didn't want them seeing it.'

Liz frowned. 'I don't want our interest in this game leaked, Vito.'

'The kid's dad is a reverend. I don't think he wants anyone to know what his kid was into any more than we want him to tell.'

She nodded. 'Good. I don't want *Jogger* to get wind of our investigation and flee. While you're headed up to their office, I'll give NYPD a heads-up that you're coming. Maybe they can help us shave off some time if we need a warrant. I'll tell them to contact you directly, Vito. Nick, are you all finished with the Siever case – no more court?'

'I'm done. I can't think that Lopez would need to call me back.'

'I'll alert her anyway.' Liz clapped her hands. 'Well, don't just stand there. Go.'

Chapter Eighteen

Thursday, January 18, 8:15 A.M.

Sophie drew an appreciative breath when Vito came through the bullpen door, sending every nerve in her body sizzling.

He smiled at her as he and Nick crossed the room. 'You're not mad at me anymore?'

'Nah. I'll live. Which I imagine was the point.' Which she was smart enough to concede without argument. 'Where are you going?' she added when he put on his coat.

'New York City,' Vito answered. 'It's about the game.' He put the game CD on his desk and she picked it up. 'Be careful with that. Brent says that game's gold.'

She tilted her head looking at the back cover. 'So is the company.'

Nick was watching her. 'Brent meant you couldn't find the game in the stores.'

'I don't know anything about that. But the company's name is Oro. It means 'gold' in both Spanish and Italian.' Sophie squinted. 'Oro is an acronym. Under their logo are little words, but the font's too small. Do you have a bigger picture of their logo?'

Vito opened the company's website on his computer and Sophie leaned close to the screen as the dragon soared. 'These words aren't Spanish or Italian. They're Dutch.'

'Makes sense,' Vito said. 'Their president's from Holland. What do they mean?'

'Well, the *R* is *rijkdom*. It means wealth. The bigger of the two

320

*O*s is *onderhoud*, which is . . . entertainment or fun. The smallest O . . .' She frowned. '*Overtreffen*. To go over, do better.' She looked up at Vito. 'Maybe to transcend, become more.'

'*R* is the biggest letter,' Vito observed. 'I guess we know what oRo's priorities are.'

'How long will you be gone?' she asked.

He was looking through his files. 'Just for the day probably.'

'What should I do while you're gone? I can't stay here all day.'

'I know,' he muttered, but offered no suggestions as he stacked folders.

'I'm Joan of Arc at ten,' she added wryly. 'And the Viking queen at one and four-thirty.'

'You need a new repertoire,' Nick said, zipping up his coat. 'You're gettin' stale.'

'I know. I'm thinking Marie Antoinette, before she lost her head, of course. Or maybe Boudiccea, Celtic Warrior Queen.' She sucked in a cheek. 'She fought topless.'

Vito's hands froze on the folders. 'That is so not fair, Sophie.'

'Yeah,' Nick echoed faintly. 'Really so not fair.'

She laughed. 'Now we're even for making me come in so early.' She sobered. 'Vito, I don't want to be stupid, but I have responsibilities. I'll be careful. I'll call before I leave and when I get there. But I can't sit here all day.'

'I'll ask Liz to get you an escort to the museum. Wait until she can. Please, Sophie, just until we locate Lombard or his pal Clint.'

'Or Brewster,' she murmured. 'It could have been either of them.'

Vito kissed her hard. 'Just wait for Liz, okay? Oh, and if you get a chance, Liz has that picture of the Sanders kid. He had a brand on his cheek. A letter T.'

'Okay.' Then she frowned. 'You're the second person in two days to ask me about branding.'

Vito had walked halfway to the door, but stopped and slowly turned. 'What?'

She shrugged. 'It's nothing. One of my students asked me for some research sources on branding, for a paper he was writing.'

She watched Vito and Nick look at each other. 'What's this student's name?'

Sophie shook her head. 'No way. His name's John Trapper, but . . . no way. I've known John for months. And he's a paraplegic in a wheelchair. There is no way he could have done this.'

Vito's mouth went flat. 'I don't like coincidences, Sophie. We'll check him out.'

'Vito . . .' She sighed. 'Okay. It'll be a waste of your time, but I know you have to.'

Vito clenched his jaw. 'Promise me you won't go anywhere without an escort.'

'I promise. Now go. I'll be fine.'

Thursday, January 18, 9:15 A.M.

'This is so embarrassing,' Sophie muttered.

'Better to be embarrassed than to be dead,' Officer Lyons said mildly.

'I know. But driving me here in a *cruiser*, and now you're walking me to the door . . . Everybody's going to think I'm in trouble,' she grumbled.

'Lieutenant Sawyer's orders. I could write you a note, if that would help.'

Sophie laughed. She *had* sounded like a disgruntled first grader. 'That's okay.' She stopped at the door of the Albright and shook Lyons's hand. 'Thank you.'

He touched his hat. 'Call Sawyer's office when you want to come back.'

Patty Ann's eyes widened as Sophie came in. 'You were with the cops?'

Goth Wednesday was over. Patty Ann was Brooklyn again,

322

and Sophie remembered the tryouts for *Guys and Dolls* were tonight. 'Good luck on the audition, Patty Ann.'

'What's wrong?' Patty asked in what might have been her normal voice. It had been so long since she'd heard it, Sophie wasn't sure. 'Why are cops bringing you to work?'

'Cops?' Ted came out of his office, frowning. 'Were the police here again?'

'I was helping them with a case,' she said, then wished she'd taken Lyons up on the note when Ted and Patty Ann did not look convinced. 'I'm dating one of the detectives and I had car trouble, so he had an officer give me a ride.' Kind of true.

Patty Ann relaxed and her eyes went sly. 'The dark one or the redhead?'

'The dark one. But the redhead is too old for you, so forget about him.'

She pouted. 'Shoot.'

Ted was still frowning. 'First your motorcycle and now your car? We need to talk.'

She followed him into his office and he shut the door, then sat behind his desk. 'Sit down.' When she had, he leaned forward, his expression worried. 'Sophie, are you in trouble? Please be honest with me.'

'No. Both of the things I said were true. I'm helping the police and dating one of the cops. That's all, Ted. Why is this such a big deal?'

He looked grim. 'I got a call last night. From a police officer in New York. She said they needed to get in touch with you. That it was official business.'

Lombard's wife had called from a New York area code. 'You gave her my cell.'

Ted's chin lifted. 'I did.'

Sophie flipped open her phone and found the log of the call from Lombard's wife. 'Is this the number that called you last night?'

Ted took her phone, compared the number to his caller ID. 'Yes.'

323

'She wasn't the police. You can call the New York police and check if you want.'

Ted started to relax. He handed her back the phone. 'Then who was she?'

'It's a long story, Ted. She's a jealous wife who thinks I'm stealing her husband.'

His suspicion became indignation. 'You wouldn't do that, Sophie.'

She had to smile. 'Thanks. Now, listen, I have some ideas before the tour this morning that I wanted to run by you.' She leaned forward and told him about Yuri. 'He said he would come and talk to a tour group. I'm thinking we could add an exhibit on the Cold War and communism. It's not the period your grandfather studied, but—'

Ted was nodding, slowly. 'I like it. A lot. Not enough people think of that as history.'

'I'm not sure I did until yesterday. It was his hands, Ted. Made me think.'

Ted studied her carefully. 'You seem to be thinking a lot lately. I like that, too.'

Uncertain how to respond to that, Sophie stood up. 'You know, we had a visitor yesterday who said he was from a retirement home and looking for an interesting outing for his fellow residents. Seems to me that they'd be more than willing to come in and talk to school groups. Don't limit it to wars. Have them talk about radio programs and TV and inventions and how they felt when Neil Armstrong stepped on the moon.'

'Another good idea. Did you get the man's name?'

'No, but he said he was going to book a tour with Patty Ann. She'd have his name.' Sophie opened the door, then paused, her hand on the doorknob. 'How do you feel about adding some more tours? Joan and the Viking queen are gettin' kind of stale.'

Ted looked happily puzzled both at the suggestion and the twang she'd borrowed from Nick Lawrence. 'Sophie, you always say you're an archeologist, not an actress.'

Sophie grinned. 'But acting is in my blood. My father was an actor, you know.'

Ted nodded. 'I know. And your grandmother was an opera diva. I've always known.'

Sophie's grin faded. 'You never said anything.'

'I was hoping you would,' Ted said. 'It's nice to finally get to know you, Sophie.'

Sophie felt both welcomed and chastised. 'How do you feel about Marie Antoinette?'

Ted smiled at her. 'Before or after she lost her head?'

New York City, Thursday, January 18, 9:55 A.M.

'Damn traffic,' Nick grumbled. 'I hate New York.'

They were finally moving after having inched their way out of the Holland Tunnel. 'This wasn't the best hour to come,' Vito agreed. 'We should have taken the train.'

'Shoulda coulda,' Nick said sourly. 'What the hell is that?'

Vito pulled his chirping cell phone from his pocket. 'Stop grumbling. It's just my cell. I have messages.' He looked over his shoulder. 'I must have lost the signal in there.' Then he frowned. 'Liz called four times in twenty minutes.' He called back, his pulse starting to race. 'Liz, it's Vito. What's happened? Is it Sophie?'

'No.' Liz sounded exasperated. 'I had an officer drive her to her museum and walk her to the door. I have two minutes before my press conference. I need Tino's number.'

'Why?'

'An hour ago, a woman came to the precinct looking for whoever was leading the Greg Sanders investigation.' Liz was talking fast as she walked. 'She said she was a waitress and saw Greg on Tuesday. He was waiting in her bar for a man.'

'Munch. *Yes.* Did she see the man?'

'She saw *a* man. She said Greg left without paying for his drink. Then an old man who'd been sitting at the bar followed him. The waitress followed them both, but when she got to the corner, they were driving away in a truck. I called for the department artist but she's off shift. I don't want to wait so long this witness forgets the old man's face. So . . . damn. I'm late. You call Tino. Ask him to come in as soon as he can.'

Thursday, January 18, 11:15 A.M.

'Mr Harrington is not here. Mr Van Zandt is in meetings and can't be disturbed.'

Vito carefully placed his palms on Van Zandt's secretary's desk and leaned forward. 'Ma'am, we are homicide detectives. He really does want to see us. Now.'

The woman's eyes widened, but her chin came up. 'Detective . . .'

'Ciccotelli,' Vito said. 'And Lawrence. From Philadephia. Call his office again. Tell him we'll be knocking in sixty seconds.'

Her lips thinned and she picked up her phone, then bent over it, cupping the receiver, as if at eighteen inches away Vito couldn't hear every word anyway. 'Jager, they say they are police detectives. . . . Yes, homicide. They're very insistent.' She nodded briskly. 'He'll be out momentarily.'

The door to Van Zandt's office opened, and out walked the man, looking just like his picture. He was big and brawny and for a moment Vito thought *perhaps* . . .

But then he spoke. 'I am Jager Van Zandt,' he said and his voice sounded nothing like the voice on the tape. 'How can I help you?' He regarded them with a cool detachment that Vito sensed was more defensive than arrogant. But arrogant, too.

'We're interested in your game, Mr Van Zandt,' Vito said. *'Behind Enemy Lines.'*

There was no reaction in the man's eyes or face as he inclined his head in a nod. 'Come into my office.' He closed the door behind them and gestured to two chairs that sat before a huge desk. Vito was reminded of Brewster's office. 'Please, sit.'

Jager sat behind his desk and inclined his head, waiting for them to speak.

By previous agreement, Vito and Nick had decided not to reveal the "No one can hear you" line they'd heard on the tape. Instead Vito showed him a printout of the French woman who'd been strangled in the game.

Van Zandt nodded. 'Clothilde.'

'She's strangled in that scene,' Vito said.

'Yes.' Van Zandt lifted a brow. 'You are perhaps offended at the violence? Or that the violence was perpetrated by an American? In the game, of course.'

'Well, yes, we are offended at the violence,' Nick said. 'But that's not why we're here. Who drew that picture, Mr Van Zandt?'

Van Zandt remained impassive. 'My art director is Derek Harrington. He can give you information on any of the artists.'

'He didn't come in today,' Vito said. 'Your secretary said so. Any idea why?'

'We are business partners, Detective. Nothing more.'

Blessing Brent, Vito smiled. 'I read that you've been friends since college.'

'D'y'all have a fallin'-out?' Nick drawled, and for the first time Van Zandt showed a flicker of response. Just a small flash of anger in his eyes, extinguished immediately.

'We have not agreed in recent days. Derek's tastes have become . . . violent.'

Vito blinked. 'Really? He looks so nice in his picture on your website.'

'Appearances can be deceiving, Detective.'

Vito drew another photo from his folder. 'Yes, they can. Perhaps you can help us clear something up.' He slid the picture of Claire Reynolds next to the screenshot of Clothilde. But there was nothing. Not even a flicker to indicate Van Zandt was impacted in any way. Surprise would have been the natural response, but there was nothing.

'The resemblance is uncanny, wouldn't you agree?' Nick asked.

'Yes. But they say everyone looks like someone.' One side of his mouth lifted. 'They say I look like Arnold Schwarzenegger.'

'It's just the accent,' Vito said and Van Zandt's smile disappeared. 'We'd like to find Mr Harrington. Can your secretary give us his address?'

'Of course.' He picked up the phone. 'Raynette, please get Derek's home address for the detectives. Then please show them out.' He said all that while holding Vito's gaze in defiant coldness. 'Is there anything else, Detective?'

'Not right now. Will you be here if we have more questions before we go home?'

He glanced down at the calendar on his desk. 'I will be here. Now, if you'll excuse me.' He stood and opened his office door. 'My secretary will help you now.'

Vito stood up, intentionally leaving the photo of Claire Reynolds on Van Zandt's desk. The door closed at their backs with a firm click. Van Zandt's secretary was glaring at them. 'Mr Harrington's address.' She held a piece of paper in her hand.

Vito slid the paper in his folder. 'When was Mr Harrington last in the office?'

'Tuesday,' she said stonily. 'He left right after lunch and didn't return.'

Vito said nothing more until he and Nick were out on the sidewalk. 'What a snake.'

'Everybody looks like somebody,' Nick mimicked in his best Arnold imitation.

'He was expecting us,' Vito said as they started for Nick's car.

'You caught that, too? His secretary didn't say we were homicide when she announced us, just that we were detectives, but then she said "Yes, homicide."'

'Like he'd asked her first,' Vito mused. 'I wonder who Van Zandt thinks is dead.'

'First round of drinks when we're done says we don't find Derek at that address.'

'Sucker bet, Nick,' Vito said as Nick slid behind the wheel.

'Shit. I was hoping now that you're blinded by love I could slide that one right past.'

Vito chuckled. 'Just drive, okay?'

Nick pulled away from the curb, one brow raised. 'You didn't disagree. So what's the deal, you and Sophie? *Are* you blinded by love?' The last was said in a teasing tone that didn't hide the more serious question underneath.

You don't love me. Her bitter words following that first disastrous, unforgettable . . . mating came back to hit him in the head and now he thought he understood them a little better. Vito wondered if anyone had really loved her other than Anna and her uncle. Her mother was abusive, her father rather cold. Her aunt was selfish and her first lover a cheating snake. Quite a cast of characters.

'Vito?' Nick's voice cut through his thoughts. 'I asked you a question.'

'And I'm trying to answer. Sophie's . . . She's . . .'

'Smart, funny, sexy as hell?'

Yes. All of those things. *But more than those things.* 'Important,' Vito finally said. 'She's important. Harrington lives west of here, so turn left at the corner.'

Thursday, January 18, 11:45 A.M.

Philadelphia had a lot of hotels. After showing his parents' picture to staff at more than thirty hotels, Daniel Vartanian finally found a desk clerk who remembered his mother.

'She was sick, man,' Ray Garrett said. 'I thought Housekeeping would find her dead in the bed. She should have been in a hospital.'

'Can you check the dates they stayed?'

'Against policy. I wish I could help, but without seeing a badge, I'd lose my job.'

I know what your son did. He wasn't on duty, but Daniel pulled his shield from his pocket anyway. 'I'm with the Georgia Bureau of Investigation,' he said. 'I'd appreciate any help you can give me. The woman is sick, and she needs to see her doctor.'

Ray looked at him for a long moment. 'She's your mother, isn't she?'

Daniel hesitated. He closed his eyes briefly. 'Yes.'

'Okay. What name were they registered under?'

'Vartanian.' Daniel spelled it.

Ray shook his head. 'We have no records of a Vartanian. I'm sorry.'

'But you saw her.'

'I'm pretty sure. It's hard to forget a woman that sick. Sorry, man.'

'Can you check Beaumont?' It was his mother's maiden name.

'Nothing. Sorry.'

So close. 'Can I talk to your staff? Maybe one of them remembers something.'

Ray's eyes were kind. 'Wait here.' In a few minutes he was back with a small Hispanic woman in a maid's uniform. 'This is Maria. She remembers your mother.'

'Your mother was very sick, no? But she was nice to us. Tried not be a problem.'

'Do you remember what you called her?'

'Mrs Carol.' She shrugged. 'Her husband called her this too.'

Ray was already typing. 'Here it is. Mr Arthur Carol.'

It was a simple yet elegant ruse, Daniel thought. Carol was his mother's first name. 'Thank you, Maria,' Daniel said. 'Thank you so much.' When she was gone, Daniel turned to Ray. 'Can you tell me when they checked in?'

'Checked in November 19, out December 1. Paid in cash. Is there anything else?'

He thought of the floor of his parents' bedroom. 'Do you have a safe?' Ray's eyes flickered. 'They had articles in the safe, didn't they?'

Ray shrugged. 'Still do. According to this, they didn't get the items they'd stored in the safe when they checked out. We have a policy of ninety days or we pitch it.'

'Can you at least check? That way I'll know if I need to get a warrant.'

'Okay, but this is it.' Two minutes later Ray came back with an envelope, surprise on his face. 'There was a letter in there addressed to you.'

On the envelope was written 'For Daniel or Susannah Vartanian.' The handwriting was his mother's. Daniel drew a breath. 'Thank you, Ray.'

'Good luck,' Ray said quietly.

When he got to his car, Daniel opened the envelope. It was a single sheet of hotel stationery with an address and a box number, written in his mother's hand. Daniel took out his cell phone and dialed. His sister answered on the third ring, her voice brisk.

'District Attorney's office. Susannah Vartanian.'

'Suze, it's Danny.'

Susannah let out a breath. 'Did you find them?'

'No, but I found something else.'

Thursday, January 18, 12:00 P.M.

Johannsen was still being careful. She had surrounded herself with people all morning long. Dragging her anywhere was going to be difficult, because the woman was a veritable Amazon. He planned to get her near his vehicle then disable her quickly. But he needed to get her alone first. He'd planned to wait until she broke for lunch to make his move.

He'd timed it well. Her Viking tour had just finished. He was approaching her when the door opened and another old man came in, winding his way through the children who'd taken the tour. Hands extended in welcome, Johannsen rushed to the old man, who, he was surprised to see, wasn't really old either. He wasn't in disguise, but he wasn't that old. His body had been damaged, likely from repeated abuse. The man's broken hands confirmed the assumption.

He wondered how much torture the man had sustained and how long it would take to wreak that kind of damage. He'd like to paint that man's eyes. He imagined he'd have a hell of a pain threshold and would last a lot longer than any of the models had.

Johannsen and the old man began to speak to each other in what sounded like Russian. As she walked the Russian to the front door, he stepped forward.

Then his cell phone rang. Several people looked up and he turned his face away quickly, hunching over his cane. Drawing attention to himself was not part of his mission. He hurried out of the museum as quickly as he thought an old man should and opened his cell phone when he got far enough away. It was Van Zandt's direct number. Frowning, he dialed back. 'It's Frasier Lewis.'

'Frasier,' Van Zandt said. 'I need to meet with you.'

'I can come up in a few days. Maybe next Tuesday.'

'No. I need to speak with you today. Frasier, Derek quit yesterday.'

He certainly had. In more ways than one. 'Really? Why?'

'Didn't want to give up artistic control. I have a contract for you to sign. I'll be in Philadelphia later this afternoon. Meet me for dinner at seven. You can sign it and I'll be on my way.'

'Executive art director?' he asked and Van Zandt laughed.

'That's what it says on the contract. I'll see you then.'

New York City, Thursday, January 18, 12:30 P.M.

'Told you it was a sucker bet,' Vito muttered under his breath.

Nick nodded, arms crossed over his chest as the two of them

watched a pair of NYPD detectives check anyplace a man could hide. Or be hidden. 'Now what?'

'Put out an APB, I guess. Looks like they're done here.'

The two NY cops came back to the living room. They were Carlos and Charles. Almost as good as Nick and Chick, Vito thought, but not quite.

'He's not here,' Carlos said. 'Sorry.'

'Thanks,' Vito said. 'We didn't think we'd find him here, but . . .'

Charles nodded. 'You guys have ten bodies down there. We'd have looked, too.'

'So what do you boys want to do?' Carlos asked. 'Is this guy a suspect?'

'We don't think he's our killer,' Nick said, 'but he might have an idea of who is.'

'We can put out an APB for you,' Charles offered.

'We appreciate it.' Vito picked up a framed photo, Harrington with a woman and teenaged girl. 'He's married with a kid. Can we find the wife?'

'We'll call it in,' Carlos said. 'Anything else?'

Nick shrugged. 'Maybe recommend a good deli where we can get lunch?'

Philadelphia, Thursday, January 18, 2:15 P.M.

'Can I help you?' The boy behind the counter looked barely old enough to shave.

I certainly hope so, Daniel thought. The address his mother had left on the hotel stationery was a mailbox store on the other side of town.

He'd sat outside for some time, debating whether he should call his boss and make this an official investigation. But 'I know what your son did' continued to haunt him. So here he was, about to use his badge to bypass the law again. 'I need to check a box.'

The boy nodded professionally. 'Can I see your ID?'

Daniel handed him his shield and watched the boy's eyes grow wide.

'I'll look it up . . . Special Agent Vartanian.'

The boy was so impressed with his being an agent he didn't wait to see which box Daniel wanted. The kid typed in his name, then looked up. 'Just a minute, sir.'

Wait was on Daniel's lips, but he bit it back. His name was in their computer. He'd never set foot in this city before this week. Heart pounding, he waited. In a minute the boy returned with a thick manila envelope that had been folded sideways.

'Just this, sir,' the kid said.

'Thank you,' Daniel managed. 'But that's not the only reason I came in. I'm working a case and one of the leads is a box here at this store. I took the responsibility for following up since I had to come by anyway. Can you tell me who owns box 115?'

It was way too easy. Both to utter the lie and to fool the boy. But he got what he needed. 'It's registered to Claire Reynolds. Do you need her address?'

'Please.'

The boy wrote it down, and Daniel once again went out to his car with an envelope in his hand. He carefully sliced the top with his pen knife, then drew out the contents.

For a moment he could only stare in horror and total disbelief. Then the years yanked him back like a riptide. 'Oh, God,' he whispered. 'Dad, what did you do?'

This was worse than his worst fear. *I know what your son did.* Now Daniel knew what his father had done as well. He wasn't sure he could ask why.

When he could breathe again he called Susannah.

'Did you find them?' she asked without preamble.

He forced his mouth to speak the words. 'You need to come.'

'Daniel, I can't . . .'

'Please, Susannah.' His voice was harsh. 'I need you to come. *Please*.' He waited, his heart stuck in his throat.

Finally she sighed. 'All right. I'll take the train. I'll be there in three hours.'

'I'll pick you up at the station.'

'Daniel, are you all right?'

He stared at the papers he held. 'No. I'm not.'

New York City, Thursday, January 18, 2:45 P.M.

'Harrington's either gone under or he's dead,' Vito told Liz on the phone. 'We checked his office, his apartment, and his wife's apartment. Nobody's seen him. His car isn't in its space. We visited his wife who says she hasn't seen him in six months. They have a daughter at Columbia University who said she hasn't seen him either.'

'Why do he and his wife have separate apartments?'

'She said they'd separated. He'd become increasingly depressed and "melancholy" she said, but never violent. NYPD's put out an APB and now we're sitting in front of oRo eating lunch. We're about to go back up to see if we can get an employee list from Van Zandt, or hang outside until one of the employees talks to us. Brent said Harrington didn't do the art, but somebody there did. We just need one person willing to finger him.'

'Good. Stick with it. I have some news on the Vartanians. I called the sheriff in Dutton, Georgia. The Vartanians haven't been seen since before Thanksgiving.'

'That's consistent with what Yuri said last night.'

'I know. There's more. The sheriff informed the Vartanians' son that his parents might be missing last weekend. The son is with the Georgia Bureau of Investigation, and the daughter is with the New York DA's office. Neither of them is in their office. Daniel, the GBI guy, has been on leave since Monday. His sister, Susannah, just took leave this afternoon. I've left word with their supervisors to have them call me.'

But there was more, Vito could tell, and it was worse. 'Just tell me, Liz.'

'The police in White Plains, New York, found Kyle Lombard in his antique store.'

Vito's heart skipped a beat. 'Dead?'

'Bullet between his eyes. Looks like it came from a German weapon, vintage. They're sending the bullet to us so we can match it against the one from the kid on the first row. The local police searched his store and found all kinds of illegally obtained medieval goodies hidden under his floor. Your Sophie would have a field day.'

Vito's willed his stomach to settle. *His Sophie* was now officially in danger. 'What about the other two. Shafer and Brewster?'

'Shafer was riding shotgun with Lombard. So to speak. Also had a bullet between the eyes. Both were tied to chairs and shot there in the store. Brewster's still missing.'

'If Lombard was dealing, let's see if we can check his sales records. Maybe we can find a tie to our guy.'

'Not gonna happen. Lombard's computer was wiped and his paper files were strewn all over the office. And to wrap it in pretty red tape, the store and Lombard's inventory have been seized by the Feds. Even though they were sixty to six hundred years old, Lombard was smuggling weapons. I expect we're going to get leaned on to hand this case over to the Feds sooner or later.'

Vito frowned. 'You won't let that happen, right?'

'To the extent of my authority, no. But were I your boss, and I am, I'd be telling you to get back here and wrap this one up quick or you'll be getting help you don't want.'

'Fuck.' Vito drew a breath. 'Does Sophie know about Lombard and Shafer?'

'I called and told her. She's a smart woman, Vito. She said she wouldn't go out alone and would call one of us to pick her up when she's done for the day.'

'Okay. That's good.'

'Are *you* okay?' Liz asked.

'No. Not really. But if she's careful . . . we just have to catch this guy.'

'So do it. See you soon.'

Scowling, Vito hung up and stared up at the building that housed oRo. 'Lombard and Clint Shafer. Luger, between the eyes.'

'Shit,' Nick muttered. 'I guess that snips off those loose ends.'

Vito started to get out of the car. 'Let's go have another little talk with Van Zandt.'

But Nick stopped him. 'First, you need to eat. Second, you need to calm down. If you spook him, we'll lose him, and like I said before – I ain't takin' your whoopin'.'

'Fine.'

'Maybe I should do the talking this time,' Nick said.

Vito ripped the plastic wrap from his sandwich angrily. 'Fine.'

New York City, Thursday, January 18, 3:05 P.M.

'Mr Van Zandt isn't here.'

Vito gaped at the prune-mouthed secretary. 'What?'

Nick cleared his throat. 'Mr Van Zandt said he'd be available this afternoon.'

'He had an unexpected call from a client. He had to leave.'

'So . . . what time was this?' Nick asked.

'About noon.'

Nick nodded. 'I see. Well then, could you provide us with a list of your employees?'

Vito was biting his tongue. He knew neither of them thought the envelope she handed them with such nasty satisfaction would have the information they wanted.

Nick pulled out a letter on oRo letterhead, its message short and sweet. '"Get a warrant,"' Nick read. 'Signed "Jager A. Van Zandt." Well, then, that's what we'll do.' He pulled a sheet of blank paper from her printer. 'Could you write your name for me please? I want to be sure we spell it correctly on the warrant. Then sign it.'

She was suddenly not so defiant. Still she wrote her name and handed him the page. 'You know the way out.'

'Same way we came in,' Nick said with an easy smile. 'Y'all have a nice day, now.'

Outside on the curb Nick folded the secretary's paper and put it and the envelope in his pocket. 'Handwriting samples,' he said. 'To compare against the Claire letters.'

'Good work. Thanks, Nick. I was too mad to be effective.'

'You've covered for me enough times. I'd say we're good.'

'Excuse me.'

A man was hurrying toward them, his face anxious. 'Have you been in oRo?'

'Yes, sir,' Vito answered. 'But we don't work there.'

'I've been trying to see Derek Harrington since yesterday, but they say he's not in.'

'Why were you trying to see Harrington?' Nick asked.

'It's about my son. He promised he'd show a picture of my son to the other artists.'

Vito's heart sank as his apprehension rose. 'Why, sir?'

'My son is missing and someone in that building saw him. They used him as a model. I want to know when and where. Then I'll least know where to start looking.'

Vito slid his shield from his pocket. 'I'm Detective Ciccotelli, and this is my partner, Detective Lawrence. What's your name, and do you have a photo of your son?'

The man squinted at his shield. 'Philadelphia? I'm Lloyd Webber.' He handed Vito a picture. 'This is my son, Zachary.'

It was the young man who got shot in the head. 'One-three,' he murmured.

'What? What does that mean?' Webber demanded.

'I'll call Carlos and Charles,' Nick said quietly and moved away to use his phone.

Vito met Webber's eyes. 'I'm sorry, sir. But I think we might have your son's body.'

Denial warred with bitter reality in Webber's eyes. 'In Philadelphia?'

'Yes, sir. If this is the boy we think it is, he's dead and has been for about a year.'

Webber deflated. 'I knew. I just didn't want to believe. I need to call my wife.'

'I'm sorry,' Vito said again.

Webber jerked a nod. 'She's going to ask how he died. What should I tell her?'

Vito hesitated. Liz would want to keep as much of this contained as possible, but this father deserved to know what had happened to his son and with that he was sure Liz would agree. 'He was shot, sir.'

Webber flashed a hot furious glance up at the building. 'In the head?'

'Yes, but if you could keep that to yourself for now, we'd appreciate it.'

He nodded, numb. 'Thank you. I won't tell her where he was shot.'

Vito watched as he walked ten feet away and called his wife. Then swallowed hard when Webber's shoulders began to heave. 'Fuck,' Vito viciously whispered, hearing Nick behind him. 'I really want him. Bad.'

'I know. Charles and Carlos asked us to wait here while they get a warrant. They're going to try to seize all oRo's records.'

A car door slammed behind them and Vito and Nick turned. A man got out of a cab, his face grimly determined. 'Are you the detectives from Philly?'

'Yeah,' Nick answered. 'Who wants to know?'

The man stopped in front of them, his hands shoved in his coat pockets. 'My name is Tony England. Until two days ago I worked for oRo. Derek Harrington was my boss.'

'What happened?' Nick asked.

'I quit. Derek was being steamrolled by Jager into doing things he didn't agree with. That *I* didn't agree with. I couldn't stand by and watch Jager destroy it all.'

'How did you know we were here?' Vito asked.

'oRo's a small company. Everyone knew you were there

thirty seconds after you walked in the door. An old friend called, told me you were here asking about Derek. I came down right away, but you were gone.' England's eyes narrowed at Webber, who'd finished his call, but stood with his back to them, quietly weeping. 'Who is he?'

Vito looked at Nick and Nick gave him a little nod. Vito held out the photo. 'The father of this boy. His name is Zachary. He's dead.'

Every drop of color drained from England's thin face. 'Fuck. Holy fuck. That's . . .' He stared in horror at the picture. 'Oh, my God, what have we done?'

'Do you know who drew this boy into the game, Mr England?' Nick asked softly.

England's eyes narrowed. 'Frasier Lewis. I hope you fry his ass and he rots in hell.'

Chapter Nineteen

Philadelphia, Thursday, January 18, 5:15 P.M.

She looked the same, Daniel thought as she passed through the train station's revolving door. Petite and fragile. The men in their house had been big, the women small. *I needed your protection then.*

He'd believed he was protecting her. Obviously he'd been remiss. He got out of his rental car and stood, waiting until she saw him. Her step slowed, and even from where he stood he could see the stiffness in her shoulders.

He walked around and opened her door. She stopped in front of him and lifted her eyes. She'd been crying. 'So you know,' he murmured.

'My boss called me on my cell after I'd already boarded the train.'

'My boss called me, too. The lieutenant who called him was Liz Sawyer. I have the address for her office.' He sighed. 'I was too late.'

'But you know something that will help find who did this?'

He lifted a shoulder. 'Or destroy us both. Get in.'

He slid behind the wheel and put his key in the ignition, but she put her hand over his. Her gray eyes were huge and flashed fire. *'Tell me.'*

He nodded. 'All right.' He gave her the envelope that had been waiting for him at the mailbox store and waited as she slid the contents to her lap.

She gasped, then slowly, mechanically looked at each page.

'Oh my God.' She looked up at him then. 'You knew about these?'

'Yes.' He started up the car. ' "I know what your son did," ' he quoted softly. 'Now you know, too.'

Thursday, January 18, 5:45 P.M.

Sophie stood in the middle of her warehouse, fists on her hips. She'd unpacked a dozen crates since Lieutenant Sawyer's call that afternoon. Keeping herself busy had kept her from dwelling on the fact that Kyle and Clint were dead.

That Kyle and Clint were connected to the killer was without doubt. They'd been killed with the same gun used to murder one of the nine she'd found in the graveyard.

That the killer knew about her had been a possibility this morning when she'd allowed herself to be driven to the museum by a cop with a gun. Now it was more than a possibility, but still it wasn't an eventuality. However she chose to balance nuance with her carefully chosen words, it was still damn scary. So she'd kept busy until Liz could free up an armed body to take her back to the precinct. To Vito.

She hoped he'd had success today. Now more than ever.

'Sophie.'

With a gasp she wheeled, pressing her hand to her heart. Once again in the shadows stood Theo Four. In his hand he held an ax, as effortlessly as if it had been a feather. Controlling her breathing she fought the urge to take a step back. To flee screaming. *Screaming*. She closed her eyes and got hold of herself. When she opened them he was still watching her, his face expressionless. 'What do you want?'

'My dad said you needed some help opening crates. I couldn't find the crowbar you were using yesterday, so I brought this.' He extended the ax. 'So which crates?'

She exhaled as quietly as she could. *Get a freakin' grip, Sophie.* She was seeing threats that didn't exist. 'Over here. I think these are from Ted the First's travels to southeast Asia. I'm thinking about an exhibit about the Cold War and communism and wanted to include his artifacts from the Korean peninsula and Vietnam.'

Theo Four came into the light, his dark eyes oddly amused. 'Ted the First?'

Sophie's cheeks heated. 'I'm sorry. That's how I think about all you Theodores.'

'I thought you were going to do an interactive exhibit. A dig.'

'I am, but this warehouse is big enough for three or four exhibits. I think this Cold War exhibit will touch people deeper. You know. Freedom isn't free.'

He said nothing more, but stripped the tops off the crates as if they were crepe paper instead of heavy wood. 'There. It's done.' He then left as silently as he'd come.

Sophie shivered. That boy was either deep or just plain off. How 'off' could he be? How much did she know about Theo or Ted, for that matter?

She laughed at herself. 'Get a grip, Sophie,' she said out loud. It was time to go anyway. Liz had said her ride would be at the museum at six. It was almost that now. She locked the warehouse door and stood inside the front door waiting, then laughed again when Jen McFain approached with a grin.

'Good night, Darla!' Sophie called, then pushed the door open. 'So you're my bodyguard?' she asked, looking way down at Jen.

Jen looked way up. 'That's right, Xena. You got something to say about it?'

Sophie zipped up her coat, chuckling. 'It seems silly. I should be protecting you.'

Jen pulled back the lapel of her jacket. 'A nine-mil adds a lot of inches, Xena.'

'Stop calling me that,' Sophie said as she got into Jen's car. She waited until Jen was in and buckled up. ' "Your majesty" will suffice.'

Jen laughed. 'Then let's go, Your Majesty. Your prince awaits.'

Sophie couldn't stop the smile that warmed her whole face. 'Vito's back?'

Jen's smile went grim. 'Yeah, they're back.'

'What's wrong?'

'The two guys they went looking for are missing, but they ID'd another one of the bodies from the graveyard. And . . .' Jen blew out a breath. 'They found someone who can ID the motherfucker who started all this.'

Thursday, January 18, 6:25 P.M.

'Tino.' Vito gripped his brother's arm in an abbreviated hug. 'Thanks again.'

'No problem. You get anywhere with the picture of the old man from the bar?'

Vito shook his head. 'I haven't even seen a picture of the old man yet. Nick and I just got back from New York fifteen minutes ago.'

'Here's another copy. I went home and did some more work, shadowing, hatching. It's a better representation than the quick sketch I did for your lieutenant this morning.'

Vito stared down at the man who'd met Greg Sanders on Tuesday afternoon. 'Man, he really is old. Hunched. It's hard to believe.'

'That's how the waitress saw him, but you know how accurate eyewitnesses *aren't*.'

'Yeah, but I really want her to be right. But I may have something better – I brought back a guy from New York who knew the artist that made the cut scenes in *Behind Enemy Lines*. He's waiting in the conference room. I was hoping you could . . .'

Tino grinned. 'Lead the way.'

Vito took him to the conference room where Nick waited with Tony England. 'Tony, this is my brother Tino. He's a sketch artist.'

'*I'm* a sketch artist,' Tony said with frustration, 'but I can't get any more from my mind than that.' He pointed to a paper on the table. 'My mind is frozen or something.'

It was a bare-bones sketch that could be almost anyone. Additionally, it had a cartoon quality that made Vito remember what Brent had said about Harrington's expertise – cartoons and dragons. Van Zandt had brought in someone more skilled than he at the game physics. Perhaps he'd chosen this Frasier Lewis because he was more skilled at faces than Harrington and England.

Tino opened his sketchpad. 'Sometimes it takes telling it to somebody else.'

Vito left them with Nick and went back to his desk. Jen and Sophie were back, he saw as he entered the bullpen. Jen had gone into Liz's office and Sophie stood at his desk, her back to him. His heart thumping like a teenager's, he quickened his pace, intending to surprise her with a kiss to the side of that long neck of hers. She liked that, he'd found. In two nights he'd found a lot of places she liked to be kissed. She jumped when he touched his lips to her skin, then settled back against him, like warm honey.

'You okay?' he murmured.

'Yeah. I've been good, stayed with my bodyguards. Even Thumbelina over there.'

Vito chuckled. 'Jen's little, but she's feisty.' He drew back reluctantly. 'Wait here. I need to go talk to Liz for a minute, but I'll be right back.' He'd gotten a few steps away when she called his name, her voice suddenly strange.

'Vito, who is this?' She was holding the sketch Tino had made of the old man.

Dread gripped his gut. 'Why?'

His dread became her fear. 'Because I've seen him. Who is this?'

Jen had been standing in Liz's doorway and turned at the panic that had crept into Sophie's voice. A moment later Liz was at Jen's side, watching with concern.

'We think that's the man who met Greg Sanders on Tuesday,' Liz said slowly.

Sophie sank into the chair at his desk. 'Oh, God,' she whispered.

Vito crouched down in front of her. 'Where did you see this man, Sophie?'

She raised her eyes to his, green and horrified and his blood ran cold. 'At my museum. He was at the Albright. He stopped me and asked for a private tour.' She pressed her lips together hard. 'Vito, he was as close to me as you are now.'

Breathe. Think. He took her hands in his. They were ice cold. 'When, Sophie?'

'Yesterday, after I'd finished the Viking tour.' She closed her eyes. 'I had a feeling, a creepy feeling about him. But I laughed it off. He was just an old man.' She opened her eyes. 'Vito, I'm scared. I was nervous before. Now I'm terrified.'

So was he. 'You don't leave my sight,' he said harshly. 'Not for a second.'

She nodded unsteadily. 'Okay.'

'Vito.'

Vito twisted to see Tino rushing into the bullpen. He was holding his sketchpad out so that Vito could see the picture he'd drawn. 'Vito, Frasier Lewis is the old man. The eyes are the same as the old man the waitress saw with Greg Sanders.'

Vito nodded. It felt like every breath had been sucked from his lungs. 'I know.' He stepped aside, revealing Sophie who still sat behind him. 'This is Sophie. The old man visited her at her museum yesterday.'

Tino let out a breath. 'Shit, Vito.'

'Yeah,' Vito muttered. He looked over at Liz. 'Encore?'

Liz shook her head, grim. 'I don't think my heart could take another curtain call.'

'Where's Tony England?' Vito asked his brother.

'On his way downstairs with Nick. Nick's gonna get him a cab to the train station.'

Liz perched on the side of Nick's desk. 'Let's call the troops together, Vito. We have some debriefing to do. But first, everybody take a deep breath. Sophie's safe and we now know the face of our killer. That's a hell of a lot more than we had this morning.'

For a full minute everyone did as she asked, breathing and focusing. Then once again the peace was shattered. 'Excuse me. I'm looking for Lieutenant Liz Sawyer.'

A couple stood in the doorway. She was five-three and dark. He was six-four and blond. The man had spoken.

Liz lifted her hand. 'I'm Sawyer.'

'I'm Special Agent Daniel Vartanian with the Georgia Bureau of Investigation. This is my sister, Susannah Vartanian with the New York City DA's office. We understand you have our parents. We believe we know who killed them.'

There was silence. Then Liz sighed. 'There's your encore.'

Thursday, January 18, 7:00 P.M.

Van Zandt was already seated when he arrived at the upscale seafood restaurant located inside his hotel. 'Frasier, please join me. Would you like some wine? Or perhaps some of this lobster Newburg. It's really quite wonderful.'

'No. I'm busy, VZ. I'm working on your new queen and I want to get back to it.'

Van Zandt's mouth turned up in a strange smile. 'Interesting. Tell me, Frasier, where *do* you get your inspiration?'

If he'd had hairs on the back of his neck, they would have lifted. 'Why?'

'Well, I was just thinking that you have such a realism to your art. I was wondering if you based your characters on anyone? Live models, maybe?'

He sat back and viewed Van Zandt through narrowed eyes. 'No. Why?'

'I was just thinking that if you did use live models, it would be patently foolish to choose local faces. That a truly wise man would go elsewhere. Bangkok or Amsterdam come to mind. Culturally diverse. Interesting clientele in Amsterdam's Red Light District. Seems an artist could find his pick of models from a population no one would miss.'

He drew a breath. 'Jager, if you have somethin' to say, then just spit it out.'

Van Zandt blinked. ' "Spit it out" ? Frasier, that sounds so . . . provincial. Very well.' He handed him a large envelope across the table. 'Copies,' he said. 'Of course.'

It was pictures. The first was Zachary Webber. 'Derek gave you this. He's insane.'

'Perhaps. Keep going.'

Gritting his teeth he flipped to the next picture in the stack and went still. Claire Reynolds's face stared up at him. *Van Zandt knew.*

Van Zandt sipped his wine. 'The resemblance is uncanny, wouldn't you agree?'

'What do you want?'

Van Zandt chuckled. 'Keep going.'

The next photo had his heart racing, but with rage. 'You sonofabitch.'

Van Zandt's smile was unpleasantly smug. 'I know. I really just wanted Derek watched. If he attempted to go to the police . . . about you . . . then my head of security would merely attempt to dissuade him. Imagine my surprise when I saw that.'

It was him, with Derek. He was the old man, but he stood upright. The photo didn't show it, but his gun had been pressed into Derek's back. Carefully he put the pictures back in the envelope. 'I repeat. What do you want?' *Before you die.*

'I didn't come alone, Frasier. My head of security is at one of those tables over there, ready to call the authorities.'

He drew a frustrated breath. 'What . . . do . . . you . . . want?'

Van Zandt's jaw tightened. 'I *want* more of what you've been giving me. But I *want* it untraceable.' He rolled his eyes. 'What kind of idiot kills people that can be identified?' He pulled a smaller envelope from his coat pocket. 'This is a cashier's check and a plane ticket to Amsterdam for tomorrow afternoon. Be on that plane. And when you get there, you change the faces of every character in the *Inquisitor* or our deal is off.' He shook his head, furious now. 'Are you that arrogant? Did you believe no one would find out? You have jeopardized everything I own with your stupidity. So fix it.' He drained his wine glass and slammed it to the table. '*That's . . . what . . . I . . . want.*'

He had to laugh, despite the fury boiling in his gut. 'You would have really liked my father, Jager.'

Van Zandt didn't smile. 'Then we have a deal?'

'Sure. Where do I sign?'

Thursday, January 18, 7:35 P.M.

'Please, sit down.' Vito Ciccotelli gestured to a large table in a conference room. Daniel did a quick count. Six people already sat around the table. Ciccotelli closed the door and pulled out a chair for Susannah, who was still shaking like a leaf.

Daniel had offered to do the ID of their parents himself, but Susannah had insisted she'd stand with him, and she had. The medical examiner had come back with them from the morgue and now sat at the end of the table, next to the tall blonde that Ciccotelli had introduced as their consultant, Dr Sophie Johannsen.

'Do you need more time?' This came from Ciccotelli's partner, Nick Lawrence.

'No,' Susannah murmured. 'Let's get this over with.'

'You've got our attention, Agent Vartanian,' Ciccotelli said. 'What do you know?'

'I hadn't seen my parents in many years. Our family is . . . was . . . estranged.'

'How many in your family?' Sawyer asked.

'Now, just Susannah and me. We hadn't talked in a while, not until this past week. The sheriff in our hometown called, said my parents had gone on a trip, but they hadn't returned. My mother's oncologist had called to check on our mother when she missed several appointments. It was the first either my sister or I had heard about her cancer.'

'Hell of a way to find out,' Nick murmured. He would be the good cop, Daniel thought.

'Yeah. Anyway, the sheriff and I searched the house. My parents had closed it up and taken all their suitcases. I found brochures in my father's desk for destinations out west. I thought it was my mother's last trip before she died.' He tried to block the picture of his mother on that metal table in the morgue. Susannah squeezed his hand.

'Do you need a minute?' Jen McFain asked kindly.

'No. The sheriff and I were ready to leave when I realized my father's computer was still running – in fact, it was being controlled remotely at that moment.' He'd been watching Ciccotelli and was rewarded with a flicker of interest in the man's dark eyes.

'Why didn't you report them missing then?' Sawyer asked.

'I almost did. But the sheriff thought my mother should be able to keep her privacy, and it looked like they really had gone on vacation.'

'The remote computer thing didn't concern you?' Nick Lawrence asked.

'Not so much at the time. My father was a computer person. He liked to play with networks and motherboards and such. So . . . I got a leave of absence. I wanted to find her, to make sure my mother was all right.' He swallowed. 'To see her again.'

He took them over his search, ending with the hotel safe and the mailbox store, but not mentioning the envelope his mother had left for him. He wasn't sure he could. 'I knew I had to report the blackmail. Susannah agreed. So here we are.'

'So the last time your father made a withdrawal was when?' Sawyer asked.

'November 16.'

Ciccotelli noted it. 'What did you do when you got to the mailbox store?'

'More than I should have, less than I wanted. I thought if I knew who was doing the blackmailing . . . I asked the kid behind the counter who rented the box. I wanted him to give me the contents of the box, but I knew I'd pushed too far as it was.'

Ciccotelli gestured impatiently. 'Drumroll, Agent Vartanian?'

'The name on the box was Claire Reynolds. She was blackmailing my parents and probably killed them. That's all I know.'

This time Ciccotelli's eyes did more than flicker. He blinked once, then sat back and looked at his partner, then his boss. Everyone at the table looked stunned.

'This sucks,' Nick Lawrence muttered.

For a moment Ciccotelli said nothing, then looked again at his boss. Sawyer lifted a shoulder. 'Your call, Vito,' she said. 'I checked them out while you were all at the morgue doing the ID. They're both legit. I'd bring them in.'

Daniel searched every face. 'What? What's going on here?'

Ciccotelli frowned. 'Claire Reynolds is an issue.'

Susannah stiffened. 'Why? She was blackmailing our parents and now they're dead. What's stopping you from finding her and bringing her in?'

'Finding her isn't the issue. It's arresting Claire Reynolds for your parents' murder that's problematic,' Ciccotelli said. 'She's dead. She's been dead for more than a year.'

Stunned, Daniel looked at Susannah, then shook his head. 'That's impossible. She's been blackmailing our father for the last year. The kid at the mailbox store said she'd paid her account on time just last month. In cash.'

Ciccotelli sighed. 'Well, whoever paid her bill wasn't Claire Reynolds. You don't know who else could have been blackmailing your father?'

Susannah shook her head. 'No. I don't know.'

'Do you know how or why?' Lawrence asked softly.

Daniel shook his head mutely. But it wasn't true. He knew. It was bad enough that it haunted him. So he held his counsel. Besides, he knew Ciccotelli wasn't telling him everything and until he did, and maybe even if he did, Daniel would not reveal what should have been his father's greatest shame.

And through him, mine.

Ciccotelli took a sketch from his folder and slid it across the table. 'Do you recognize this man?'

Daniel stared hard at the picture. The man had a hard face, rigid jaw, prominent cheekbones. His nose was razor sharp, his chin blunt. But his eyes made Daniel shiver. They were cold, and the sketch artist had imparted to them a cruelty that Daniel knew too well from years in law enforcement. Still, there was a familiarity about the man's eyes that gave him pause. The mailbox had dredged up all the old ghosts. But they were ghosts. This man was real and had murdered his parents and left them to rot in an unmarked grave. 'No,' he finally said. 'I don't. I'm sorry. Suze?'

'No,' she echoed. 'I was hoping I would, but I don't.'

'They should listen to the tape,' Nick said. 'Maybe they'll recognize the voice.'

'All right, but just the first part, Jen,' Ciccotelli said.

McFain opened her laptop. 'This part isn't very loud, so you'll need to listen.'

'Scream all you want.'

Daniel's blood ran cold. His heart froze and he stared at the sketch again. At the man's eyes. And he knew. But it was impossible.

Susannah's hand went lax, but he could hear her panting and knew she knew, too.

'No one can hear you. No one will save you. I've killed them all.'

He closed his eyes, clawing at denial. 'Not possible,' he murmured. *Because he was dead.* They'd buried him, for God's sake.

'They all thought they suffered, but their suffering was nothing compared to what I'm going to do to you.'

But it was him. *Dear God.* Bile rose in his throat.

'*Stop it,*' Susannah snapped. 'Stop the tape.'

Jennifer McFain did so instantly and Daniel felt every eye watching them. The room was suddenly too warm, his tie too tight. 'We didn't lie,' Daniel said hoarsely. 'It is just the two of us now. But we had a brother. He died. We buried him in the family plot in the church cemetery.'

'His name was Simon,' Susannah whispered, horror making her voice shake.

'He's been dead for twelve years. But that was his voice. And those are his eyes.' Daniel met Ciccotelli's dark eyes and choked out the words past the dread that closed his throat. 'If that's truly Simon on that tape, you have a monster on your hands. He's capable of just about anything.'

'We know,' Ciccotelli said. 'We know.'

Thursday, January 18, 8:05 P.M.

Vito dragged his palms down his face, his stubble scratching his skin. Daniel Vartanian told them about his brother's death in a fiery car crash and the subsequent burial. That their brother had been a cruel person who'd taken pleasure in tormenting animals, but who'd also been a gifted student with a broad base of talent. Everything from art, literature, and history to science, math, and computers.

Simon Vartanian was a twenty-first-century Renaissance man of sorts. But knowing all that brought them no closer to putting the monster in custody.

'I think we've got more new questions than answers,' Vito muttered.

'But now we have his real name,' Nick said. 'And his face.'

'It's not the way he looked before,' Daniel said.

'But his eyes are the same,' his sister said, still staring at Tino's sketch, her expression a mixture of pain and horror and grief.

Vito put the sketch back in his folder. 'We'll need to exhume the casket that's buried in your family's plot.'

Daniel nodded. 'I know. Part of me doesn't want to know what's inside. My father took care of everything when Simon "died." He identified the body, bought the casket, had Simon prepared, and brought him home to be buried.'

'It was a closed-casket funeral,' Susannah Vartanian added. She was dangerously pale but sat straight in her chair, her chin lifted as if she expected the next blow to be personal, and Vito wondered what these two knew that they weren't telling him.

'That's normal when the body is badly disfigured,' Katherine said. 'This body was in a car accident and burned badly. If you had seen the body, there's nothing to say you wouldn't have thought he was your brother, too.'

Daniel's mouth lifted, just barely. 'Thank you. But I'm not worried about the body we'll find inside, per se.'

Nick's eyes widened. 'You're worried the casket will be empty, that your father knew your brother wasn't really dead.'

Daniel just lifted his brows. Beside him, his sister stiffened a little more. This was the blow she'd been expecting, Vito thought.

'Why would your father fake an entire funeral and burial?' Jen said.

Daniel smiled bitterly. 'My father was in the habit of fixing Simon's messes.'

Vito had opened his mouth to probe when Thomas Scarborough cleared his throat.

'You said your family was estranged,' Thomas said. 'Why?'

Daniel looked at his sister, for support, for guidance. For permission even, Vito thought.

Susannah's small nod was almost indiscernible. 'Tell them,' she murmured. 'For God's sake, tell them all of it. We've lived in Simon's shadow long enough.'

DIE FOR ME

Thursday, January 18, 8:15 P.M.

Van Zandt thought he was smooth, instructing his hired gun to follow him from the restaurant. Of course that would never do, allowing VZ to know his true address. It would just give the Dutchman one more thing to hold over his head.

Taking pictures of me . . . Van Zandt had one hell of a lot of nerve. Although it was, in its own way, damn ironic, he supposed.

Van Zandt's security man had parked in an alley, his eyes fixed on the door of the Chinese restaurant across the street through which he'd had entered, waiting for him to return to his vehicle the same way. Instead, he approached from behind and tapped on the driver's side window. Startled, VZ's man swung around to look at him, then relaxed. He rolled down the window. 'What do you want, buddy?'

The man's tone was belligerent, but he only smiled. 'I'm sorry to bother you, sir, but my organization is selling calendars to—'

'No. Not interested.' He started to roll up his window, but the man was a second too late. His knife had found its target, and now Jager's head of security was bleeding like a stuck pig. The man's eyes widened, flickered, then went dead, treating him to yet another moment of death.

'That's okay,' he murmured. 'It was last year's calendar anyway.' Leaving his knife behind, he exited the alley and headed for his vehicle, parked conveniently right outside the Chinese restaurant's front door. He navigated the street with ease, passing all the poor motorists who'd been forced to find parking blocks away. Just another side benefit to his current mode of . . . personal transportation.

He was well below the line of sight of anyone who might later be asked if they'd seen anything related to the murder of the man they'd found dead in the alley. *If anyone can describe me, it would be in only the most general of terms.*

Not that he had to worry. It was a rare person who met his

eyes when he traveled this way. There was something about imperfection that made people look away. Leaving him free to move as freely as he chose.

Thursday, January 18, 8:30 P.M.

Daniel stared at his hands for a long moment before he spoke. 'Simon was always a cruel bastard. Once I stopped him from drowning a cat and he was furious. I tried to whale the tar out of him, but he beat me to a bloody pulp. He was ten.'

Katherine frowned. 'At ten Simon could overpower you? You're not a small man, Agent Vartanian.'

'Simon is bigger,' Susannah said, far too quietly.

Daniel looked at down at her, a combination of tightly bound fury and pain in his eyes. But he went on. 'Time passed, Simon got worse. My father became a judge. Simon's activities were embarrassing to his career, so Dad pulled strings to smooth feathers. You'd be surprised what people are willing to overlook for a buck. When he was eighteen, Simon ran away. Then we heard about the car accident.'

'And we buried him,' Susannah said.

'And we buried him,' Daniel repeated with a sigh. 'I moved to Atlanta and became a cop, but I was still coming home then. That last time I saw my parents, I'd come home for Christmas.' He paused for a long moment, then his shoulders sagged. 'When I walked into the house I found my mother crying. She didn't cry often. The last time had been at Simon's funeral. But she'd found some pictures. Drawings Simon had made.'

'Of animals he'd tortured?' Scarborough asked.

'Some. But mostly people. He cut out pictures from really hard-core, violent magazines. He'd made drawings from the pictures. Simon was a gifted artist, but he always had a dark side. He kept posters of dark paintings on the wall of his bedroom.'

'Like?' Vito asked.

Daniel frowned. 'I don't remember.' He looked down at Susannah. 'There was the *Scream* painting.'

'Munch,' she said. 'And he liked Hieronymus Bosch. He also had a poster of a Goya depicting a massacre. Another of a suicide. Dorothy somebody.'

Daniel was nodding. 'And there was the Warhol print. 'Art is what you can get away with.' That pretty much summed Simon up.'

'What summed him up,' Susannah murmured, 'was what he kept under his bed.'

Daniel's eyes widened. 'You saw the pictures?'

She shook her head. 'Not the pictures. I have no idea where he hid *them*.'

'What, Miss Vartanian?' Vito asked sharply. 'What was under the bed?'

'His copies of serial killer art. John Wayne Gacy's clown paintings. And others.'

Simon Vartanian had copied other people's pictures, revered dark artists. Now he created his own art. And his own victims. There was a tension around the table, and Vito knew the others understood it, too. For a moment he worried someone would blurt it out. But no one did and Vito was relieved. There were still things the Vartanians hadn't told them. Until they did, the flow of information couldn't be complete.

'Why didn't you tell anyone, Miss Vartanian?' Thomas Scarborough asked gently.

Again her chin came up, but in her eyes was shame. 'Daniel was gone, and I had to sleep sometime. Then Simon was dead and the paintings disappeared. I didn't know about the pictures from the magazines or his drawings of them. Until tonight.'

'Agent Vartanian, your mother had found these drawings and magazine clippings. So why did you fight with your father?' Vito asked.

Daniel looked at his sister. 'Tell him, Daniel,' she said tightly.

'There were other pictures – snapshots. The magazine

pictures were staged, but the snapshots looked real. Women, being raped . . . Simon had done drawings of these, too.'

There were a few beats of silence, then Jen cleared her throat. 'I'm surprised Simon didn't take the pictures with him,' Jen said. 'Where did your mother find them?'

'In one of my father's safes. He had several hidden through the house.'

'So your father knew about Simon's secret stash?' Jen asked.

'Yes. My mother confronted him, and he admitted he'd found them in Simon's room after he'd run away. Now I wonder if they weren't the cause of Simon's leaving. Maybe my father had finally had enough. I'll never know. Once I saw the pictures, I said we had to report it. That the people in the snapshots had been victimized by someone. My father was outraged. Why should we dredge it all up now? he said. Simon couldn't be punished. He was dead. It would only bring the family shame.'

His sister covered his hand with hers, her face grimly accepting of what was to come, but Daniel's was distant as he remembered.

'I was so angry. It was like years of watching my father clean up after Simon came to a head and something in me snapped. My father and I almost came to blows so I left the house and took a walk. When I came back I'd decided to take the pictures and report it myself, but I was too late. I found the ashes in the fireplace.'

Nick shook his head, disbelieving. 'Your father – a *judge* – destroyed evidence?'

Daniel looked up, his lips bent in bitter scorn. 'Yes. I was furious, and I did hit him then. And he hit me back. We did some damage to each other that day. I walked away and promised them I would never come back. And I didn't until last Sunday.'

'What did you do about the pictures?' Liz asked.

He shrugged. 'What could I do? I obsessed over it for days. In the end I didn't do anything. I had no evidence. I'd only gotten a glimpse of the pictures. I wasn't even sure a crime had been committed or if the pictures were staged or real. And at the end of the day, it was my word against his.'

'But your mother saw them, too,' Jen said carefully.

'She wouldn't have crossed my father,' Susannah said. 'It simply wasn't done.'

'Did you think these pictures were what Claire Reynolds was using to blackmail your father?' Vito asked.

'It crossed my mind at the beginning, but I didn't know how she'd know about them, and I wondered if there weren't other things that even I didn't know about. I needed to know what the blackmail was. My sister's career could be damaged.'

Susannah's chin lifted again. 'My career will stand on its own merits. So will yours.'

'I know,' he said. 'When I got to the mailbox store, I found my mother had opened a box for me. She left these.' He pulled a thick envelope from his laptop case.

Vito knew what he'd find inside. Still he cringed when he saw the pictures and the drawings a younger Simon Vartanian had created. 'Your father didn't destroy them.'

Daniel cocked his jaw. 'Apparently not. And I don't know why he kept them.'

Vito passed the photos to Liz and rubbed the back of his neck. 'Let's connect some dots, shall we? First, Claire Reynolds. How did she know your parents?'

'I don't know,' Daniel said. 'Neither of us remembers that name from Dutton.'

'She wasn't from Dutton,' Katherine said. 'She was from Atlanta.'

'Our father went to Atlanta from time to time,' Susannah said. 'He was a judge.'

Jen frowned. 'But that doesn't explain how Simon got involved. Did he know her?'

'The only time Simon ever went to Atlanta was when he had to be fitted,' Daniel said. 'He was an amputee, and his orthopedist was in Atlanta.'

'Yes,' Jen hissed. 'Claire was an amputee.'

'Why didn't you tell us that before?' Liz asked.

Daniel's jaw tightened. 'I didn't even suspect he was even alive until an hour ago.'

'I'm sorry,' Liz murmured. 'This has been a shock for you.'

Daniel's eyes flashed again, angrily. 'You think so?' he said sarcastically.

Susannah squeezed his hand. 'Daniel, please. So Claire knew Simon from the orthopedist. But how would she know about my father? And these pictures?'

'Plus there is the issue of Claire's continuing the blackmail a year after she was dead,' Vito pointed out.

Nick grimaced. 'Small problem, that. Maybe Simon picked up where she left off when he killed her. Maybe he wanted the money from your folks.'

'But the guy at the mailbox store said a woman had paid the bill,' Daniel said. 'And we can't check the store's security tapes. They only keep them for thirty days.'

'Accomplice?' Jen asked.

Thomas shook his head. 'Doesn't fit the profile. I'd be shocked if Simon would trust anyone enough to be an accomplice. A pawn, maybe. But not an accomplice.'

'So we need to find out who this other woman is,' Liz said.

A piece of the puzzle clicked in Vito's mind. 'Claire had a girlfriend. Dr Pfeiffer and Barbara at the library said Claire was gay.'

Liz's brows furrowed. 'And of course the library ladies didn't have a name.'

Vito felt a small surge of energy. It was second-wind time. 'No, but there was a newspaper photo – Claire kissing another woman. If we could find that picture . . .'

'You don't know which newspaper, do you?' Jen asked.

'No, but it was taken during a march. Claire only moved here four years ago and she's been dead a year. How many marches could there have been in three years?'

'So Claire just happened to end up at the same orthopedist

here in Philadelphia?' Susannah asked. 'The chances seem possible, but remote.'

'Pfeiffer was recruiting patients for a study to upgrade the microprocessor in the artificial knee,' Vito said. 'Maybe that's what brought both of them together.'

Daniel nodded. 'If Claire knew Simon from the Atlanta doctor, she'd have known he was supposed to be dead. Several of the amputee patients came to his funeral.'

'She must have blackmailed Simon, too,' Katherine said. 'That's why he killed her.'

'And the other woman took up where Claire left off.' Nick shook his head. 'Cold.'

'Why now?' Thomas Scarborough asked. 'Whoever this second blackmailer is, she continued for a year after Claire died. Why did your father wait a year to come here?'

'He was running for public office,' Daniel answered, in a way that made Vito believe he'd answered this question himself days before. 'He hadn't made the announcement yet. In fact, his e-mails kept putting off the man who wanted him to run. I guess he figured as soon as he threw his hat in the ring the blackmail price would go up.'

'So who was controlling your dad's computer last Sunday?' Jen asked. 'Simon or this blackmailer number two? We should look at your father's computer to find out.'

Daniel nodded. 'I'll have it priority shipped. How else can we help you, Detective?'

Vito stepped through the events in his mind. Several things weren't adding up. 'Your father came to Philly to find the blackmailer. But why did your mother come, too?'

Katherine nodded. 'Good question. Your mother was very sick. No doctor should have permitted her to travel.'

'I don't know,' Daniel said. 'I've wondered that myself.'

'She would have come to see Simon,' Susannah said flatly. 'It was always all about Simon.' Her words were tinged with brittle cynicism. 'Poor, poor Simon.'

'How did Simon lose his leg?' Katherine asked.

Daniel shook his head. 'My parents liked to tell everyone it was an accident.'

'But we knew better,' Susannah said. 'We lived far out, past town. There was this old man who had a small place about a mile in back of ours. He had a collection of antique traps. One day a bear trap turned up missing. Everyone knew Simon had stolen it, but he had a silver tongue and convinced everyone he had no idea who'd taken it.'

'He got trapped in it,' Vito said. 'Who found him?'

Daniel looked away. 'I did. He'd been missing for a day, and we'd all split up to find him. I found him, bleeding, in terrible agony. Simon had no voice left. He'd screamed for hours, but there wasn't anyone around to hear him.'

Vito felt a chill go down his back. There was the connection.

'And he blamed me,' Daniel continued heavily. 'Until the day he left, he believed I'd known where he was and left him to suffer. I didn't. But no one could make him see the truth. Simon was mean before he lost his leg, but after . . .'

Susannah closed her eyes. 'After, Simon became a monster. He ruled our house. My mother became devoted to him, which I've never fully understood. But I'm certain if she thought he was still alive, she'd beg to be taken to him, no matter how ill she was.'

'Which means your parents either knew all along Simon wasn't really dead or they found out and then made the trip.' Vito watched the Vartanians' faces. 'But you think at least your father knew all along Simon was alive, or you wouldn't be worried about what you'd find in the casket once we dig it up.'

'Yes,' Daniel acknowledged evenly. 'Now, we're tired. If there's nothing else—'

'I have two questions.'

Vito leaned forward to look at Sophie at the end of the table. She'd said not a single word the entire time. 'What is it, Sophie?'

'Agent Vartanian believes his father came looking for the blackmailer. Miss Vartanian believes her mother came looking for Simon.'

Daniel was watching her with deliberation. 'Yes.'

Susannah had narrowed her eyes, as if she'd just realized Sophie was there. 'What is your connection to this investigation, Dr Johannsen?'

'I located your parents' bodies, and I assisted the police in discerning their identity.'

Daniel's jaw cocked. 'All right. So what are your questions?'

'You said you found your parents registered in the hotel under your mother's name.'

'Our parents must not have wanted anyone to know they were searching for Claire Reynolds,' Susannah said stiffly.

'I'd be inclined to agree, except for a few things. First, you said the hotel staff remembered your mother spending a lot of time alone in the hotel room.'

'She was sick,' Daniel said, exasperated. 'She stayed and he searched for Claire.'

'She didn't stay behind the time your parents visited the library where Claire once worked. And there, your father gave his real name when he asked about Claire. Except, he didn't ask the librarian or anyone else that could have helped him. Your father chose an old man who spoke no English. My first question is why did your father choose an old Russian man to ask about Claire Reynolds and have that Russian man be the only one to whom he revealed his real name?'

Vito wanted to kiss her. Instead he calmly asked, 'And your second question?'

'Why did he bring the pictures to Philadelphia? I mean, if he was being blackmailed with the pictures, then why bring them and chance being caught with them? Why not leave them at home in his safe? For that matter, why did he keep them at all?'

Dark spots of color stained Susannah Vartanian's cheeks. 'Are you suggesting that our parents killed Claire Reynolds?'

Don't mention the game, Sophie, Vito thought. *Don't mention Clothilde.*

'Not at all, Miss Vartanian. I'm suggesting your father didn't want anyone to know he was searching for Claire, so he hid his identity. And I'm suggesting that he wanted your mother to believe he was looking openly.'

Understanding filled Susannah's eyes. 'Mother didn't know about the blackmail,' she said woodenly. 'She just thought they'd gone to search for Simon.'

'But your father never intended for her to see him,' Vito murmured.

'Because he knew Simon had been alive all this time and didn't want Simon to tell our mother,' Daniel finished grimly. 'And it has something to do with those pictures.'

'But she did see Simon,' Susannah whispered. 'Because he killed her. My God.'

Vito looked at Liz, his brows lifted in silent question. She nodded, so he cleared his throat. 'Uh . . . there's one more thing you need to know. When we found your parents, we also found beside them two empty graves. We weren't sure why then. Now . . .'

Susannah paled. 'Daniel.'

Daniel put his arm around her shoulders. 'It's okay, Suze. Now we know. We can be watching.' He lifted his eyes to Vito's. 'Can we see that sketch again, please?'

Vito put the sketches of the old man and Frasier Lewis side by side on the table in front of the Vartanians. 'I'll make you copies.'

'Thanks,' Daniel said. 'We appreciate—' But Susannah cut him off with a gasp.

With shaking hands she picked up the sketch of the old man. 'I know him.' She looked up, her face now deathly white. 'Daniel, I walk my dog every morning and night on a path in the park across the street from my apartment. This man . . .' She pointed to the sketch. 'He sits on a bench sometimes.' Her voice shook. 'We chat. He pets my dog. Daniel, he was as close to me as you are right now.'

Vito looked at Sophie. Her expression was one of pained understanding. He looked back to Susannah Vartanian. 'For how long? How long have you known him?'

She closed her eyes. 'At least a year. He's been watching me for a year.'

'We can give you protection,' Liz said. 'The one thing we can hope for is that he doesn't know you know he's alive. Come with me. I'll get you both settled for the night.'

Thursday, January 18, 9:15 P.M.

'Vito, wait.'

Vito stopped outside the precinct's front door. Katherine stood there, shivering, and his defenses went up. He'd managed to avoid her since the night before, but their avoidance dance was apparently over. 'How long have you been waiting here?'

'Since the debriefing ended. I figured you'd come down sooner or later.'

Vito looked over his shoulder to where Sophie stood in the lobby with Nick and Jen.

Katherine followed his gaze. 'You're not letting her out of your sight.'

'No. Every time I think about him coming to her museum and touching her . . .'

'Vito, I'm sorry. I was out of line last night.'

'No, you weren't. You were scared. And you were right.'

'I wasn't right, and being scared doesn't make it okay. I said I'm sorry. I would appreciate if you'd forgive me.'

Vito looked away. 'Katherine, I haven't even forgiven myself.'

'I know, and that needs to change. You didn't do anything wrong. What happened to Andrea was tragic, but not your fault and not anything you could have prevented.'

He stared down at his shoe. 'How did you know?'

'I was there when you saw the results of the ballistics report. I saw the look in your eyes when you realized one of yours had hit her. I saw the way you looked at her when she was first brought to the morgue. Vito, you loved her and she died.' Katherine sighed. 'But that's between you and your soul. I had no right to use that against you.'

'You were scared,' he said again. 'Sophie's your little girl.'

Katherine's lips trembled. 'I have known that girl since she was five years old.'

'How did you meet her? Why are you the mother she never knew?'

Katherine's eyes filled. 'She said that?'

'Yes, she did. So why?'

'She was my daughter Trisha's best friend in kindergarten. One day Trisha came home in tears. There was going to be this big mother–daughter tea and Sophie wasn't coming. She didn't have a mom to bring her.'

Vito's heart squeezed. 'What about her grandmother or her aunt?'

'Anna was on tour. Freya had something to do that night with one of her own girls, which was Freya's norm. Harry was going to bring her, but that kind of negated the whole mother–daughter tea idea, so I offered to pinch hit. I sat there with Trisha on one knee and Sophie on the other. Sophie's been mine ever since.'

'What about her grandmother?'

'Anna cut way back on her touring schedule and bought a house in Philly so that Sophie could be close to Harry. But it was still years before Anna completely gave up her career, so Sophie spent a lot of time with me.'

'What made Anna finally stop touring completely?'

'She'd missed so much of her own daughters' lives. I think she finally realized she'd been given another chance with Sophie and Elle.'

'Elle?'

Katherine's eyes flared in alarm. Then she shook her head. 'She'll have to tell you about Elle. Vito, I've seen that girl through every major up and down of her life. I'd do anything to keep her safe. And happy.'

He looked back at Sophie again. 'She's safe now. I'd like to think she's happy.'

'You're a good man, Vito. I've watched you go through lots of ups and downs, too. We're friends. I hope that one stupid comment on my part won't erase the good years.'

'It doesn't. It won't. I'd take the bullet myself before I let anything happen to her.'

'Don't say that,' she whispered. 'It's not funny.'

'It wasn't meant to be. What happened with the body bag, Katherine?'

'That one she'll also need to tell you herself.' She lifted on her toes, kissed his cheek. 'Thank you for forgiving me. I won't be so foolish as to risk our friendship again.'

'German chocolate cake would seal the deal,' he said and she laughed.

'When all this is over, I'll make you two cakes. Now I'm beat. I'm going home.'

'I'll walk you to your car,' Vito said. 'You need to be careful, too.'

Katherine frowned. 'I don't suppose that was meant to be funny either.'

'No. Come on.'

Chapter Twenty

'Wow.' Sophie blinked at the cars in Vito's driveway. 'What's going on here?'

'I called a mini-family meeting,' Vito said and helped her out of the truck.

'This is a *mini*-family meeting? Why?'

'Several agenda items.' He looked up and down the street, his eyes narrowed, and Sophie shivered. He'd been doing that all the way from the precinct, not once relaxing his guard. But she'd watched him talking to Katherine. They'd made their peace.

Katherine had told him something, though. It was impossible to miss the questions in his dark eyes every time he looked at her. But Sophie had questions of her own, and he'd had not a spare minute to talk to her since waking that morning at four a.m. Even on the ride back to his house tonight, he'd been on his cell to Liz and Nick.

The state's transportation unit had been busy over the last few hours, tracing oRo president Jager Van Zandt's path down I-95 via tollbooth cameras and operators. Van Zandt had come to Philadelphia. Vito had found that very interesting and, on a purely intellectual level, so did Sophie. It was only clinging to that intellectual level that kept her from descending into abject fear. And fear wasn't going to help anyone.

'What agenda items?' she asked and he turned her toward the driveway.

'The minivan belongs to my brother Dino, who's here to see
his five sons who have been staying at my house since Sunday.
How long they'll stay is one agenda item.'

'Five sons?'

Vito nodded. 'Yeah. Five. It's been interesting.'

She lifted a brow. 'So now your wanting to sleep over at my
house makes a lot more sense. You just wanted a good night's
sleep.'

'Like either of us have gotten one of those. Dino's wife's been
in the hospital, so another agenda item is an update on when
she'll get out. The old VW is Tino's. The Chevy is Tess's rental
car. The Buick is my father's, and he's here to meet you.'

Sophie's eyes widened. 'Your father is here? I'm meeting
your father? I look awful.'

'You're beautiful. Please. My dad's a nice man and wants to
meet you.'

Still Sophie held back. 'So . . . where's your bike?'

His brows lifted. 'In the garage with my Mustang. If you're a
good girl I'll let you see them later.' He hesitated. 'Sophie, if this
killer is watching you, he's seen me. I need to make sure my
family's safe. That's the last agenda item.'

'I hadn't thought about that,' she murmured. 'You're right.'

'Of course I am. Now, my ass is freezing off out here, so let's
go in.'

Sophie was swept inside a house filled with people. In the
kitchen a woman with long, dark curls stood at the stove while
a tall man with a little gray at his temples rocked a toddler on
his shoulder. At the table a teenaged boy sat with open books,
studying. On the sofa a brawny man with silver hair and a child
on one knee sat watching a blaring TV. A second kid lay
sprawled on his stomach on the living-room floor, his eyes
fastened to the screen, and a third sat by himself, obviously
sulking.

The only person Sophie recognized was Tino, who looked
like Sophie had always imagined the Renaissance artists looked
with his long flowing hair and sensitive eyes.

Vito closed the door and all activity ceased. It was like she'd walked into a spotlight.

'Well, well.' The woman came to the kitchen doorway, a spoon in her hand and a smile on her face. 'So this is the infamous Sophie. I'm Vito's sister, Tess.'

Sophie had to smile back. 'Deliverer of packages. Thank you.'

'Someday you'll tell me what the significance of that toy is and what the *heck* is wrong with your receptionist. For now, welcome.' Tess drew her into the living room and introduced everyone rapidly. There were Dino and Dominic. The little boy was Pierce, the bigger boy was Connor, the sulking one was Dante.

Then the big man got up from the sofa and the room seemed suddenly smaller. 'I'm Michael, Vito's father. Tino's sketch didn't do you justice.'

Sophie blinked. 'What sketch?'

'He wouldn't stop until I drew your picture,' Tino said and took her hand. 'How are you, Sophie? You had a bad shock.'

'Much better now, thanks.' She turned back to Vito's father. 'Your sons are talented and kind men. You should be proud.'

'I am. I'm also happy to finally see Vito with a woman. I was starting to worry that—'

'Pop,' Vito warned, and Sophie cleared her throat.

'Talented, kind, and *manly* men,' she revised and heard Tess snicker behind her.

Michael smiled and Sophie knew where Vito had gotten his movie-star looks. 'Sit down and tell me about your family.'

Tess leaned against Vito's arm as their father escorted Sophie to the sofa as regally as if it had been a throne. 'You are so busted. He's going to worm every last detail from her by the time you leave. Then I'll worm the details from him.'

Vito found he didn't really care. 'Sophie can hold her own. We need to talk, Tess.'

The smile in her eyes faded. 'I know. Tino told me the killer you're chasing came to see Sophie yesterday. She's got to be unnerved.' They sat down at the table with Tino, Dino, and Dominic. 'So talk, Vito.'

'You've all seen the news. We've found a field with a lot of bodies. The man who put them there has been watching Sophie. I'm not letting her out of my sight.'

Dino nodded, his face grim. 'And my boys? Are they in any danger?'

'There's no indication the killer is paying attention to us cops. But he's smart and knows we're after him, so I can't tell you no. I'll stay away from here until this is over.'

Dino looked torn. 'We can't go back in the house until every square inch of carpet's been replaced. I can look for a rental place between now and then, but it'll take me a few more days. Nobody else in the family has a house big enough for all of us.'

'I know Mom and Pop had to sell their place, but I wish they'd done it a little later,' Tino grumbled. 'We could have fit ten kids in there.'

But the old house where they'd grown up had stairs, and his parents' condo was all on one floor, enabling Michael to conserve his energy. Hopefully, every bit would extend his father's life a little longer, and Vito found himself wishing his father would live to see his own children, who in Vito's mind had blond hair and bright green eyes.

'We could get a hotel,' Dino said doubtfully.

'No. I think you're fine here, Dino, really. And when Molly gets out of the hospital you can use the top half of this house. I'll move downstairs with Tino.'

'He's right,' Tino said. 'Tess and Dom and I will watch the boys, and soon Vito will save the day and we can all go back to normal craziness.'

'And I'll stick around until Molly's a hundred percent,' Tess said. 'So don't worry.'

'Your psychiatric practice,' Dino protested. 'Your patients.'

'I have my patients covered. I don't even have that many anymore. I'd cut back.'

Because she'd been trying for babies of her own, Vito

realized with regret. Tess would make a great mother. If there was any justice, she'd have the family she wanted.

And so would Sophie. Vito stood up. 'I'm going to pack a bag. Dino, plan on moving in whenever you want.'

Tino's smile was sly. 'Maybe big brother is so quick to offer his roof because he knows he'll soon have another.'

'She's a looker, Vito,' Dino added with a grin. He nudged Dom. 'Don't you think?'

Dominic blushed. 'Stop,' he mumbled.

'He's got his eye on a girl at school,' Dino said, and Dominic glared at his father.

Tess patted Dominic's arm. 'Relax, Dom, and get used to it. Just hope your grandfather doesn't get wind of it or you'll really get the third degree.'

'Third degree about what?' Michael asked, strolling into the kitchen. Without waiting for an answer he began pawing through drawers, messing everything up.

'What are you looking for, Dad?' Vito asked.

'Long-handled wooden spoons and those pointy things for holding corn. Sophie's showing the boys how to make a trebuchet.'

'Like they needed another way to hurl things at each other,' Dino grumbled, but he got up to help his father look. 'A trebuchet, huh? That's actually pretty cool.'

Tino lifted a brow. 'She's got a fast bike, can make medieval siege weapons out of household items, and has nice . . . sweaters.'

Dino laughed. 'She sounds like a keeper to me, Vito.'

'That's my cue to exit. Tino, I'd appreciate a hand.' Vito had a granny-cam-related request and didn't want to ask in front of Tess, who had an understandable aversion to hidden cameras, having been an unwilling victim a few years before.

When Vito returned, his father was on the sofa whittling something from a block of wood. Sophie was on the floor helping the boys build a fort from the books that had once been stacked neatly on his shelves. Pierce looked up, his little face flushed with excitement. 'We're building a castle, Uncle Vito, with a moat and everything.'

'I never said a moat, Pierce,' Sophie said. 'Your uncle wouldn't like having his living room flooded, so we're not even going there.' Vito winced when Connor dumped another stack of books next to Sophie, but she just smiled sweetly up at the boy. 'Thank you, Connor. How are we doing on that counterweight for the trebuchet, Michael?'

His father looked affronted. 'Quality takes time, Sophie.'

'Edward the First only needed a few months to build the biggest trebuchet of all time, Michael,' she said dryly. 'It could hurl three-hundred-pound weights. We're only launching popcorn kernels, so hurry up.'

'We need to be going,' Vito said. 'It's the boys' bedtime.' *And mine*, he hoped.

'Oh, Uncle Vitooooo,' Pierce whined. 'Just a few more minutes.'

'Yeah, Uncle Vitoooo,' Sophie echoed, her whine even better than Pierce's, and the two co-conspirators snorted with giggles. 'Just let us finish the wall around the outer bailey.' She angled him an amused look. 'It would go faster if you would help.'

She looked so happy, Vito couldn't refuse. Folding himself into position on the floor, he looked around. 'Where is Dante? He should be helping.'

'He didn't wanna,' Pierce said. 'He said he wasn't feeling well.'

'He's sick? Should he go back to the doctor? Maybe he was exposed to more of that mercury than you thought.' Vito started to get up, but his father shook his head.

'Dante's physically fine. He's just dealing with some issues right now.'

'Dante broke the gas meter,' Pierce said matter-of-factly.

Vito remembered the stark despair on the boy's face when he'd found him crying on the back porch a few nights before. 'I thought as much. How did it happen?'

'Neighborhood snowball fight with ice balls in the center for ballast,' Michael said. 'One of the neighborhood boys told his mom and Dante had to come clean. On the bad side, he lied at first. Said he didn't know how it happened. On the good side, Molly's going to be okay and Dante has a future with the Phillies. The boy has a helluva arm.'

'He's got two arms, Granpop,' Pierce said. 'And you said the "H" word.'

'Good strong arms they are, too,' Michael agreed. 'And you're right, I did use the "H" word. I'm sorry, Pierce. I won't do it again. Here's your counterweight, Sophie.'

She'd been watching them with curiosity. 'You'll fill me in?' she asked Vito.

He let out a breath. 'On a lot of things.'

Thursday, January 18, 11:35 P.M.

'It was nice of Tess to send dinner home with us,' Sophie said, scraping her plate clean. She sat naked on her bed while Vito lounged against the pillows watching her, simply because he could. She licked her fork. 'It's even good cold.'

'It wouldn't have *been* cold if you'd have let us eat it when we first got back,' Vito teased. 'But no, you're a sex-starved fiend, dragging me up the stairs by my hair.'

She grinned and pointed her fork at him. 'You're gonna get it.'

He leered at her. 'Promises, promises. Come here and pay up.'

Sophie's grin faded. She carefully set their plates aside and Vito knew the moment of reckoning had arrived. 'Speaking of paying up, it's time to come clean, Ciccotelli. I want to know about the roses. I think I've waited long enough.'

'I know.' He sighed. 'Her name was Andrea.'

Sophie's cheeks grew dark. 'And you'll love her always.'

To deny it would be wrong. 'Yes.'

Sophie swallowed. 'How did she die?'

He hesitated, then let it out. 'I killed her.'

Sophie's eyes registered initial shock, then she shook her head. 'Tell me the whole story, Vito. Start at the beginning.'

'I met Andrea through a case, the murder of a teenager. Andrea's little brother.'

'Oh.' Her eyes grew sad. 'It's hard to lose family like that.'

Vito thought of Elle, the name Katherine had let slip, and wondered who she was. But it was his turn to come clean, and he was no welsher. 'Nick and I were working the case, and I was attracted to Andrea. She was attracted, too, but she fought it at first.'

'Why?'

'Part of it was that she was still grieving. She was afraid she'd turned to me on a kind of emotional rebound. But there were other complications. Not only was she part of an active case, she was a cop, and I outranked her. But I pushed and pursued.'

One side of Sophie's mouth lifted wryly. 'I think I've witnessed that myself.'

'And I thought long and hard before I sent you that present. I didn't want to push you if you really didn't want to be pushed. But you fascinated me, Sophie.'

'You did it just right. You left it all up to me. But this isn't about me, so continue.'

'Eventually I pushed enough that Andrea caved, but she was afraid her boss would find out. We decided to keep quiet until we figured out how far our relationship was going to go. Then we'd need to make some career decisions. Didn't seem worth rocking the boat until we knew if we had something permanent.'

'But you thought you did.'

'Yes. After a few months, we decided we'd come clean with our bosses. Liz was mine, and I trusted her to help us find the best solution. Andrea's boss wasn't so magnanimous, and Andrea expected trouble. All through this, Nick and I had been working her little brother's murder. Turns out her big brother did it. Andrea was devastated.'

'Why would one brother kill another?'

'Drugs. Big brother was a major meth user, little brother got in the way. The night she died, I'd just gotten home from her place when I got a call from Dispatch. A neighbor had seen Andrea's older brother come back and called 911.' He sighed. 'Later we found Andrea had given him money.'

Sophie winced. 'She was helping him escape.'

'Yeah, but Nick and I didn't know that. I never would have dreamed it even possible. We got to her place, had backup covering the exits. Andrea wasn't even supposed to be there. She'd left her apartment when I did. She was on duty.'

'But she was there.'

Vito closed his eyes, remembering it all too clearly. 'Yeah. She was there. Andrea's brother heard us announce ourselves. We think Andrea tried to get him to surrender and when he wouldn't she pulled her gun on him. But he hit her in the head with a chair. We found the chair with her hair and blood on it. Again, later. We evacuated the residents and stormed the apartment. Her brother started shooting.'

'He'd taken her gun.'

'Yeah. It was night by then and we trapped him in a stairwell. He shot out the light and it was . . . really dark. Nick turned on his flashlight and the punk bastard shot at him. Grazed Nick's shoulder and Nick shut the light off. The brother kept firing. When our eyes got used to the dark we could see his outline, so we returned fire. After a minute he stopped firing and we turned our maglights back on. He was dead. So was she.'

She rubbed his arm. 'Oh, Vito. He'd used his own sister as a shield?'

'We didn't know. We didn't even know she was in the building. He'd knocked her unconscious and was dragging her down the stairs. I guess he figured he'd have a hostage. If I'd allowed him to get outside, we would have seen her.'

'If you'd allowed him to get outside, he would have had a whole lot more targets, Vito. Every evacuated resident and every curious passerby. You contained him. I can't imagine you were found at fault.'

'I wasn't. There was an investigation, just like every time you fire your weapon. This one was deeper, because people died. A cop died.'

'Nobody found out about you and Andrea?'

'No. We'd done a really good job of being discreet. Only Nick knew, because I said something when I saw her lying on the stairs.' Covered in blood. 'Tino knew, because I told him last year on the one-year anniversary. I was ploughed.'

'I can understand that.'

'Liz suspected. I didn't know Katherine knew until last night.'

Sophie sighed. 'For what it's worth, she never would have mentioned it if she hadn't been terrified for me. She's a good keeper of secrets. Veritable cone of silence.'

Vito lifted a brow. 'Not that veritable. She mentioned Elle.'

Sophie's eyes rolled. 'I guess the cone of silence has a crack.'

'Elle died,' Vito said. 'She was your . . . what, sister?'

'How did you guess?'

'Katherine said that Anna finally gave up her touring when she realized "she'd been given another chance with Sophie and Elle."' He shrugged. 'Plus, I *am* a detective.'

'Not a good builder of trebuchets, though, but I'll let that pass.'

He ran his fingertips along the fine line of her jaw. 'Who was Elle, Sophie?'

'My half sister. She was born when I was twelve. I'd been in France for the summer and came home to find everyone in an uproar. Gran had been on tour when Lena dropped another bundle of joy into Harry's arms. Elle wasn't even a week old.'

'Your mother has the maternal instincts of a crocodile.'

'Crocodiles take much better care of their young. That was when Anna completely retired. She canceled all her engagements except for *Orfeo*, because it was in Philly.'

'So I really was lucky to have heard her when I did.'

'Yes, you were.'

'So Anna raised Elle.'

'Anna and I. Mostly me. Anna was never the maternal type. 'Do something with this baby,' she'd thunder when I got home from school, but I didn't mind. Elle was mine.'

'The first time you truly had someone of your own?'

She smiled, very sadly. 'Once again, I'm not that hard to figure out. Elle had some health problems, including a really serious food allergy, so I watched her like a hawk. Especially the times Lena would breeze back in. She was never careful with Elle.'

'Lena came back?'

'From time to time. She'd feel a little guilty, come back, hold Elle, then leave a day or two later. At the beginning I hoped Elle would be enough to make Lena finally settle down, even if she hadn't for me. But she didn't. Time passed, Elle got bigger.' Sophie's mouth curved. 'She was a beautiful child. Looked like a Botticelli angel with ringlets and these big blue eyes. My hair was straight as a board and I was tall and gawky, but Elle was truly stunning. People would stop and stare. And give her things.'

'Things? Like?'

'Usually harmless things like stickers or a doll. Sometimes they'd give her treats, which would scare me because she was so allergic. We had to read every label.'

Vito thought he could figure out where the story was going. 'So one day Lena came back when you weren't around and fed her the wrong thing.'

'The night of my senior prom. I'd never had many dates. I was always too busy with Elle. I'd even stopped going to France during the summers. But it was my prom. And my date was Mickey DeGrace.'

'He was something special, I take it,' Vito said dryly.

'I'd drooled over Mickey DeGrace all through high school. He'd never paid attention to me, but Trisha, Katherine's daughter, got it in her mind that I needed a makeover. It worked, and for the first time in my life, Mickey was drooling over me. Prom night came, and we'd . . . well, we'd stepped away from the dancing. Mickey knew all the best make-out places in the school. I was just so thrilled to have him interested, I went with him.'

This was definitely not good, Vito thought. Dead sister guilt layered with the guilt of sexual experimentation. 'What happened, Sophie?'

'We were . . . you know. Then I get this tap on the shoulder and I thought, 'I'm gonna get expelled.' I could see my college hopes dashed with my first and only indiscretion.'

'You were a virgin,' he said and she nodded.

'I think that was the draw for Mickey. He'd had all the other girls. I was fresh meat. Anyway, I was thinking of how I was going to explain . . . that . . . away, then I saw the teacher's face and . . . I knew. She never even noticed Mickey pulling up his pants.'

'It was Elle. Lena had come.'

'Lena had come and taken Elle out for ice cream. The teacher rushed me to the ice cream parlor, but it was too late. Katherine was there, crying.' Sophie exhaled heavily. 'She was zipping up the bag when I ran up, still in my prom dress. She looked up and saw me and . . .' Sophie shuddered.

'Just like on Sunday,' Vito said, and she nodded.

'Just like. Next thing I remember I was waking up right here. Uncle Harry was asleep, there.' She pointed to a chair. 'Elle was dead. Lena had gotten her a sundae with extra nuts. Her throat swelled and she suffocated. Lena killed her.' She looked up, bitter anger in her eyes. 'I'd say that's a damn good reason to hate my mother, Vito.'

'Did Lena know she had an allergy?'

Sophie's eyes flashed. 'She might have had she stuck around long enough. I don't know what Lena knew, but Elle wasn't her child to just take. She was *mine*.'

Vito remembered Katherine's words at the crime scene the Sunday before. 'It was an accident,' she'd said. Vito wisely decided that although he agreed, he would not make the same mistake of telling Sophie so. 'I'm sorry, honey.'

She drew a deep breath and let it out. 'Thank you. It actually helps, telling it. After she died I was so depressed. I couldn't stand being in this house. Everything reminded me of Elle. So Harry sent me to my father. Alex convinced me to stay in France, go to the university in Paris. That's where I met Etienne Moraux. Alex had connections and cash to pay for my schooling. I had good grades, fluent French, and dual citizenship. I made a good assistant to Etienne, who was one of the leading archeologists in France.'

'So how did Brewster fit in the picture?'

'Anna wanted me to come home, so I applied at Shelton College for grad school. Alan Brewster was already a legend, and getting my grad degree under him would have been very, very prestigious.' She winced. 'I didn't mean that as a joke. Under him.'

'I didn't think you did,' Vito said. 'So you studied with Brewster and . . .?'

'Fell madly in love. Every time I'd try to date a guy my own age I'd think of Mickey DeGrace, and then Elle, so I didn't date. Until Alan. He was the first man who didn't remind me of Mickey. I thought he loved me. We were on a dig in France and Alan paid me attention. Pretty soon we were burning up the sheets in his tent. Then I found out Alan was married, that he slept with all his assistants and . . . that he talked about it. Freely. But he did give me an A,' she ended bitterly. 'I was a "most able assistant." '

He remembered the words coming from Brewster's mouth and wished he'd hit the snake when he had the chance. Now Brewster was missing. Vito should probably have cared a little more. 'Like I said. He's an asshole. Move on.'

'I did, kind of. I ran back to Etienne, who found a place for me in his graduate program. I graduated and Anna wanted me to come home. I got a position with a college here in Philly, but between Amanda and Alan, I found myself either shunned or ridiculed. So I went back to France where it wasn't an issue. I'd been working for months to be assigned the dig at Mont Vert castle, and then Harry called to tell me that Anna had a stroke. I dropped everything and finally came home.' She lifted her brows. 'I found jobs with Ted and teaching at Whitman. And I met you.'

'But your father was rich. Why do you need the money so badly?'

'Alex left me an inheritance, but I've used most of it on nursing homes. That's it.'

'Thank you for telling me.' He held out his arm and she snuggled against him.

'Thank you, too. Whatever happens with us, Vito, I won't tell anyone about Andrea, although you have nothing to be ashamed of. She made her choice. You did your job.'

He frowned. He'd already decided what he wanted to happen. He'd wanted her the moment he'd met her, but he knew he wanted her permanently as he'd watched her make his nephews smile by launching popcorn kernels from a trebuchet made from a wooden spoon, a corn holder, and the counterweight his father had carved.

That she was uncertain troubled him. But there would be time to worry about that later. He pressed a kiss to her temple and turned off the light. 'Let's go to sleep.'

'Oh, Uncle Vitooooo,' she whined in the dark. 'Do we have to?'

He chuckled. 'Five more minutes.' Then sucked in a breath as her hand slid down his body and wrapped around him. 'Or ten.' Her head disappeared under the covers and he closed his eyes in anticipation. 'Or you could just take your time.'

Friday, January 19, 7:15 A.M.

'Hello?' Sophie called, letting herself into the Albright. 'Anybody home?'

'It's spooky in here when it's dark,' Vito whispered. 'All those swords and suits of armor. I'm expecting Fred and Velma and Scooby-Doo to pop out any minute.'

She shoved an elbow in his ribs and was gratified to hear him grunt. 'Hush.'

Darla came out of the office, her eyes widening as she saw Vito. 'Who's this?'

Sophie unzipped her coat and turned on the lights. 'Darla, Detective Ciccotelli. Vito, Darla Albright, Ted's wife. Please tell Darla that I am not in trouble with the law.'

Vito shook hands with Darla. 'It's nice to meet you, Mrs Albright.' He dipped his head a little lower. 'Sophie's not in any trouble. She just is trouble.'

Darla chuckled. 'Don't I know it. Sophie, why are people driving you around?'

'Car trouble,' Sophie said, and Darla looked as unconvinced as Ted had.

'Uh-huh. It was nice to meet you, Detective. Sophie, you got a package. It was sitting out front when I came in.' She pointed to the counter, then returned to her office.

Sophie looked at the small brown box, then at Vito. 'I've had one good and one bad package this week. Should I take the box or see what's behind curtain number two?'

'I'll open it,' Vito said, pulling on a pair of thin gloves. He opened the card and blinked. 'This is either spy code or Russian.'

Sophie smiled as she read the note. 'It's Cyrillic. This is from Yuri Petrovich. 'For your exhibit.' Open it, please.' Vito did and Sophie gasped in shocked delight. 'Vito.'

'It's a doll,' he said.

'It's a *matryoshka*. A nested doll.'

'Is it valuable?'

'Monetarily, no.' She lifted the first layer and found another note which made her throat close. 'Sentimentally, it's priceless. This belonged to his mother. It's one of the few things he brought with him from Georgia. He wants to loan it to me for

382

my Cold War exhibit. He was here yesterday, thanking me. I never dreamed he'd give me this.'

'Why was he thanking you?'

'I sent him a bottle of very good vodka through Barbara at the library. It was sitting on Gran's bar, never been opened. I thought he'd appreciate it more than she could.'

'You've obviously made an impression on him, Sophie Alexandrovna,' Vito teased, then kissed her gently. 'You made an impression on me, too.'

She smiled as she put the doll back in the box. 'You want a tour?'

'Don't have time. But,' he sobered, 'I want you to show me where you saw Simon.'

Sophie led him to the wall with photos of Ted the First's expeditions. 'He was here.'

Vito nodded. 'And he said exactly what?'

She told him. Then shook her head, staring at the place Simon had stood.

'What?' he asked. 'Did you remember something else?'

'Yes, but not about Simon.'

'Then what, Sophie?' he asked softly. 'Talk to me.'

'There's a story about Annie Oakley, the sharpshooter. She was doing exhibitions for the crowned heads of Europe. One day Annie chose a volunteer from the audience and clipped the ash right off the end of the cigar he held between his teeth. Turned out it was the man who later became Kaiser Wilhelm. That part's fact. The story goes on to say that Annie wished she'd missed, that she might have averted World War I.'

'It wouldn't have,' Vito said. 'One man didn't start that war.'

'No, that's true. But I think I understand a little about how Annie must have felt. When I saw Simon, I'd just finished the Viking tour,' she said softly. 'I had a battle-ax on my shoulder and when he looked at me, I actually tightened my grip on the handle. He creeped me out. I controlled myself of course. Now, I wish I hadn't.'

Vito gripped her shoulders and turned her to him. 'Sophie,

he's killed so many. You couldn't have stopped that. And I wouldn't want you to live with the image of your ax in his head. Let us catch him. Then you can stare at him through prison bars, okay?'

'Okay,' she murmured, but thought the image of the head of her ax in the head of the man who'd killed so many was a damn appealing one.

Friday, January 19, 8:00 A.M.

Vito tossed the box of doughnuts on the table. 'I hope you're satisfied.'

Jen peered inside the box. 'These aren't from the bakery in your neighborhood.'

Vito narrowed his eyes at her. 'Don't make me hurt you, Jen.'

She grinned at him. 'I never thought you'd actually bring more doughnuts. I was just being a squeaky wheel.'

'And speaking of squeaky wheels,' Nick said, dropping into one of the chairs, 'the boys in electronics think that one sound on the tape – the one that sounds like a spooky, echo-y squeaky wheel? They think it's a pulley in an elevator shaft.'

'So we're looking for a building that might be a church that might have an elevator.' Jen took out a frosted doughnut. 'That could actually narrow it down a little bit.'

The rest of the team filed in and took their places around the table, Liz, Nick, and Jen on one side, Katherine and Thomas Scarborough on the other. Vito walked to the whiteboard and wrote 'Zachary Webber' in the third square on the first row before taking his seat at the head of the table. 'That leaves two victims we need to identify.'

'Not bad, Vito,' Liz said. 'I never thought you'd have identified seven of the nine in less than a week. Since you've got nearly all the victims ID'd, I reassigned Bev and Tim. I had other caseloads building.'

'They were a big help,' Nick said. 'And we will miss them,'

he added mournfully, then perked up. 'But since they're not here, it's more doughnuts for us.'

'A man after my own heart.' Jen grinned. Licking her fingers, she slid a sheet of paper toward Vito. 'According to the geologists at the USDA, those are the areas in a one – hundred-mile radius where the soil we found in the graves commonly occurs.'

Vito shook his head at the map. 'This doesn't help. This is hundreds of acres.'

'Thousands,' Jen said. 'Sorry, Vito, it's the best we can get at this point.'

'What about the silicone lubricant?' Vito asked, and Jen shrugged.

'I sent copies of the formula to every mom-'n'-pop shop in the back of that magazine you got from Dr Pfeiffer. I haven't heard back from any of them yet. I'll follow up today.'

'Katherine?'

'I sent a request to the Dutton ME for the death certificate on Simon Vartanian. And I've started the procedure for exhumation of whoever's buried in Simon's tomb.'

'When will they start digging?' Liz asked.

'Hopefully sometime this afternoon. Agent Vartanian smoothed the way with a few phone calls last night after they left.'

Vito looked around the table. 'Daniel and Susannah Vartanian. Opinions?'

'They were genuinely shocked to learn that Simon was still alive,' Thomas said. 'But it was curious that they didn't ask questions about how we'd found their parents.'

'Maybe they thought we wouldn't tell them,' Jen said.

Nick shook his head. 'I would have asked. Especially with the news coverage we've gotten on this case. It's no secret that we found a shitload of bodies up there. Even covering the area with a tarp, we've had flyovers and aerial shots on the news and Daniel has been in Philly for a few days now. If it'd been me, I would've wanted to know if my folks were part of that big graveyard. But the Vartanians didn't even ask.'

'I might have asked,' Jen said. 'Then again, maybe I wouldn't want to know.'

One corner of Liz's mouth lifted. 'We did get some good news. Greg Sanders's ex-girlfriend showed up last night for his memorial service. She'd been hiding from his creditors. All that damage to her apartment was done by people to whom Greg owed a lot of gambling debts. Mr Sanders said he'd pay his son's debts to keep Jill safe.'

'Cleaning up after Greg even after death,' Vito murmured. 'I wonder how much Simon's father was cleaning up after him versus covering his own ass. What else?'

'Analysis on the Claire Reynolds letters,' Jen said. 'The handwriting expert I talked to said he was "reasonably sure" the same person had signed both letters.'

'Oh,' Vito remembered. 'We got handwriting samples from oRo – Van Zandt's and his secretary's. You can get the expert to compare them to the signatures, too.'

'Will do. Now, regarding that letter requesting Claire's records, from a Dr Gaspar in Texas? There is no such person. The address itself was a veterinarian.'

Liz tilted her head, puzzled. 'Did they receive Claire's records?'

'Don't know, I'll call today. The lab ran a check on the ink. Same ink on both letters. Of course it's the same ink that you'd find on a million other pieces of paper across the city, but it is the same brand name, same printer model. It's something.'

'Prints?' Vito asked.

Jen scoffed. 'On the resignation letter? Tons. You'll probably never sort them out. But on the doctor's letter, only a few sets. Who would have touched it?'

'Pfeiffer and his receptionist. We'll get them printed and eliminate their prints.'

'I'll run them through as soon as they come in,' Jen said.

'Did you get Sophie to look at that brand on the Sanders kid's face?' Nick asked.

Vito frowned. He'd dropped that ball. 'No, things got too

crazy that night with her hearing the tape. I'll ask her today.'

'Did you run a check on that student who asked her about branding?' Nick asked.

'What student?' Liz wanted to know.

Vito's frowned deepened. 'No. With all the oRo commotion yesterday, I didn't. Sophie said one of her students mentioned branding a few days ago, but she also said he was a paraplegic in a wheelchair.'

'Give me the guy's info,' Liz said. 'I'll run a check. You track down Simon.'

'Thanks, Liz.' Vito focused on organizing his thoughts. 'The only people who we know have actually seen Simon other than his victims are oRo employees, specifically Derek Harrington and Jager Van Zandt, and they're both gone.'

'And Dr Pfeiffer,' Katherine said. 'If Claire crossed Simon's path through the orthopedist, then Pfeiffer's seen him, too.'

Vito's smile was sharp. 'You're right. We'll need a court order for Simon's medical records. Names we should request? I doubt he signed in as Simon Vartanian.'

'Frasier Lewis,' Nick counted on his fingers. 'Bosch, Munch.'

'Warhol, Goya, Gacy . . .' Jen shrugged. 'All the paintings the Vartanians said Simon had on his walls and under his bed as a kid.'

Nick was writing the names down on his notepad. 'We also need to find that second blackmailer. If she was involved with Claire, she might know if Claire knew where Simon lived. Maybe Claire followed him home from the doctor's office one day.'

'So we look for that newspaper photo,' Vito said.

There was a knock on the door and Brent Yelton stuck his head in. 'Can I come in?'

Vito waved him in. 'Please. What do you have?'

Brent sat down and set his laptop on the table. 'I've gone through Kay Crawford's computer with a fine-tooth comb. She's the model that Simon didn't get his hands on. I found the virus he'd planted. It's what I thought – a time-delayed Trojan that's activated by an e-mail reply. The drive I was using when I replied to her original e-mail from 'Bosch' was wiped this morning, so it's about a day delay.'

'Any response to our acceptance of his job offer?' Liz asked.

'Nope. Nor has there been any activity on her résumé on UCanModel's site. He seems to have lost interest in her, which is good for her and bad for us.'

'She's alive,' Vito said. 'That's more than we can say for the others.'

'Speaking of the others,' Brent said, 'I have something to show you. I got a call from the computer forensics guy that works with those two NYPD detectives.'

'Carlos and Charles,' Nick said.

'Carlos and Charles?' Liz laughed. 'That's almost as good as—'

'Yeah, yeah, Nick and Chick.' Vito rolled his eyes. 'We thought of that already. So what did the computer guy tell you?'

'Not what he *told* me as much as what he *gave* me.' Brent turned his laptop around so Vito and the others could see. 'Cut scenes they found on CDs in Van Zandt's desk.'

Horrified, they watched. 'It's Brittany Bellamy,' Vito murmured as the girl in the scene was dragged to an inquisitional chair. They watched in silence, listened to the girl's screams until Brent reached forward to cut it off. 'It gets a lot worse,' he said, his jaw tight. 'Warren Keyes is on the second CD, getting stretched on a rack and then . . .'

'Disemboweled,' Katherine said grimly.

Brent swallowed. 'Yes. Bill Melville is on the third CD, but his isn't a cut scene. It's game play. The player is the inquisitor and fights Bill, who's a knight. The action is incredible. The game physics are some of the best I've ever seen.'

'Would the guy who did the game physics,' Vito said, 'the one Van Zandt lured away from another company – would he have worked with Simon to produce this?'

'Not necessarily. The beauty of a game engine is that it's like this repository of movement. Running, jumping, jabbing – it's all programmed in, like a framework. The artist decides the character's attributes, height, weight, and the game engine takes all the movements in its brain and creates the action figure that moves the right way. A light person moves spryly, while a heavier person clomps. The artist will then create a face in another program and import it to the action figure's form. It's like building a moving person from the skeleton out. Once the game physics guy designed the engine Simon could have worked independently, especially with his knowledge of computers.'

'That's amazing,' Jen murmured, then blinked, embarrassed. 'Sorry. I get sidetracked by the techie stuff. So is Bill killed with a flail?'

'Yes and . . . yes. In the main version he's hit and buckles at his knees. Boring. But if you use this . . .' Brent held up a sheet of paper. It was a copy of a smaller sheet with numbers written on it. 'It unlocks an Easter egg. A "gift" from the programmer to the gamer. This Easter egg shows Bill Melville getting the top of his head knocked off.'

'Just like he was really killed,' Katherine murmured.

'Let me see that paper,' Nick said and frowned down at it. 'This wasn't written by Van Zandt. If you compare it to the note he left us, the writing is different.' He looked over at Vito. 'We could be looking at a genuine copy of a Simon Vartanian original.'

Vito chuckled. 'Jen, have your handwriting guy compare that writing to the signature on the letter, too. It's numbers versus letters, but maybe he can match something. Good job, Brent. What else?'

'The church. You know how Simon mentioned a church on the tape? Well, after the fight scene where Bill Melville dies, it goes to a cut scene. You go into a crypt and see two tomb effigies. Woman's hands folded in prayer, the man holding a sword.'

'Warren and Brittany,' Vito said. 'What then?'

'Well, you're in a crypt, which is attached to a church. And from the church you descend to the dungeon.'

Vito sat up. 'You mean he shows the church?'

Brent winced. 'Yes, but no. The church itself is a model of a French abbey, a famous one. Simon doesn't create, but he does one hell of a copy job.'

'So is he killing in a church, or were his references on the tape just symbolic?' Vito asked. 'Thomas?'

'I'm betting they're symbolic,' Thomas said. 'Most churches around here wouldn't have the look he wanted anyway, he's so stuck on authenticity. And anything that big is going to be in a neighborhood or close to people. People would hear, and he said "no one can hear you." But, on the off chance I'm wrong, we could check churches that are built in areas on Jen's USDA soil map.'

'Okay.' Vito considered. 'We have our next steps. Exhume whoever's buried in Simon's tomb, just to be sure it's not him. Get Simon's records from Dr Pfeiffer. Find that second blackmailer. Check out Sophie's student and the churches on Jen's map. And find Van Zandt. He was on the turnpike in Pennsylvania yesterday, and according to Charles and Carlos, he hasn't come back to his place in Manhattan yet. They put an APB on him, including all the airports, in case he tries to skip the country.' Vito looked around the table. 'Anything else?'

'Just that Kay Crawford sends her thanks,' Brent said. 'She doesn't know much about the investigation, but she knows enough to understand she barely escaped from something very bad. She wanted me to tell you all thank you.'

'And did she thank you?' Liz asked him, mild amusement in her eyes.

Brent tried to bite back his smile but wasn't successful. 'Not yet. She asked me to dinner and I told her I'd go when this was all over. Hey,' he protested when Nick snickered, 'how else would a guy like me get to go out with a hot six-foot-tall blonde?'

Vito's smile disappeared. 'What?'

Brent looked around. Everyone was frowning. 'She's a tall blonde. What did I say?'

'Do you have a picture of her?' Nick asked.

'Just the one on the UCanModel site.' Brent pulled it up and Vito's heart stopped.

'Oh my God,' he whispered.

'What?' Brent demanded.

Nick's face was grim. 'She looks like Sophie Johannsen.'

Jen looked ill. 'Now we know why Simon's lost interest in this model.'

'Because he's picked Sophie instead.' Katherine's voice trembled. 'Vito.'

'I know.' Vito swallowed back his fear. 'Liz, we—'

'I'll send a uniform to the museum,' Liz said. 'Sophie will have 24/7 protection until we have Simon in custody. He won't touch her, Vito.'

Shakily, Vito nodded. 'Thanks. Let's go. Stay safe. And let's find him. Please.'

Chapter Twenty-One

Friday, January 19, 9:30 A.M.

'Sophie.'

Sophie looked up from her computer to find an irate Ted the Third standing in her office doorway. 'Ted.'

'Don't you "Ted" me. What's this all about?' Ted demanded. 'Cops dropping you off at work is one thing, but now cops are in my museum. What the hell is going on?'

Sophie sighed. 'I'm sorry, Ted. I didn't know about this until a half hour ago myself. I'm helping the police with a case.'

'By answering their history questions. Yes, I remember.'

'Well, somebody didn't like me helping them. They think I might be in some danger. So they sent someone to watch over me. It's only temporary.'

Ted expression swung from ire to concern. 'My God. That's why they've been driving you around all week. Your car and bike are fine.'

'Well, my bike's not. Somebody dumped sugar in my tank.' But Amanda Brewster had been smart enough to wear gloves. The police hadn't found a single print.

'Sophie, don't try to distract me. What does this person look like?'

'I don't know.'

'Sophie.' Ted's brows snapped together. 'If someone's threatening you, that puts this whole museum at risk. Tell me.'

Sophie shook her head. 'I would if I could. But I honestly

don't know.' He could be young, old. *He could be any face in any crowd*. He'd stalked his own sister for a year and she hadn't recognized him. A chill ran down Sophie's back. She could be looking right at him and not have a clue. 'If you want me to leave, I will.'

Ted blew out a breath. 'No, I don't want you to leave. We've got four tours scheduled today.' He looked at her with wry affection. 'This isn't an elaborate ploy to get out of being Joan, is it?'

She laughed. 'I wish I'd thought of it, but no.'

Ted sobered. 'If you're in danger, scream for us.'

Another chill ran down her back, harder this time, and she felt her smile slide right off her face. 'Okay. I will.'

Ted glanced at his watch. 'Unfortunately, the show must go on. You're the Viking queen at ten. Better get into make-up.'

Atlanta, Georgia, Friday, January 19, 10:30 A.M.

Frank Loomis met them at the airport. 'I'm so sorry to hear about your parents.'

'Thanks, Frank,' Daniel said. Susannah said very little. She looked fragile. After finding out Simon had been stalking her for the past year, both of them were on edge.

'I have to tell you, Daniel, it didn't take much for word to spread through town that we're diggin' up Simon's grave. Y'all need to prepare to face some reporters.'

Daniel helped Susannah into Frank's car. 'When will they start digging?'

'Sometime after two, most likely.'

Daniel got in the front passenger seat and turned to check on Susannah, only to find her lifting the top off a copy-paper box. 'What is it?'

'Your parents' mail,' Frank answered. 'I went by the post office and picked it all up this morning. There are another three boxes in the trunk. I had Wanda do some sorting, so most of the non–junk mail is in that box you have there, Suzie.'

'Thank you.' Susannah swallowed hard. 'Welcome home to us.'

Philadelphia, Friday, January 19, 10:45 A.M.

Vito leaned into the sign-in counter. 'Miss Savard.'

'Detective.' Pfeiffer's receptionist looked at Nick with interest. 'And this would be?'

'Detective Lawrence,' Nick answered. 'Can we talk to Dr Pfeiffer?'

'He's with a patient right now, but I'll tell him you're here.'

Pfeiffer himself came to the waiting-room door. 'Detectives.' He led them back to his office and shut the door. 'Did you find the person who killed Claire Reynolds?'

'Not yet,' Vito said, 'but another one of your patients has come up in the course of our investigation.' They all sat down, Pfeiffer with a sigh.

'I can't discuss my live patients, Detective. As much as I'd like to help you.'

'We knew that,' Nick said. 'We came with a court order so that you could help us.'

Pfeiffer's brows went up. He held out his hand. 'Well, let's have it.'

Vito felt a strange reluctance to hand it over. 'We're depending on your discretion.'

Pfeiffer just nodded. 'I understand the rules of the game, Detective.'

Vito sensed Nick stiffen next to him and knew his instinct was shared. Nevertheless, he had to get the records, so he handed the court order over the desk.

Pfeiffer stared at the names on the court order for a long moment, his expression unreadable. Then he nodded. 'I'll be right back.'

When he was gone, Nick folded his arms over his chest. 'Rules of the game?'

'I know,' Vito said. 'When we get back, let's check him out.'

A minute later Pfeiffer was back. 'Here is Mr Lewis's file. We took a picture of each patient for the study. I included the photo, as well.'

Vito took the file and flipped it opened and found himself looking at yet a different view of Simon Vartanian. It was a candid photo, taken as simon sat in Pfeiffer's waiting room. His jaw was softer, his nose less sharp than in the picture Tino had drawn of Frasier Lewis. He passed the file to Nick.

'You didn't seem surprised, Doctor,' Vito commented blandly.

'You know how somebody shoots up his family and all the neighbors say, 'He was so nice. We're so shocked.' Well, Frasier wasn't nice. He had a coldness that made me nervous. Kind of like I'd walked into a cage with a cobra. And that hair is a wig.'

Vito blinked. 'Really?'

'Yes. I came back after an exam and his wig had gone askew. I closed the door, then knocked and waited for him to tell me to come in. He'd fixed the wig by then.'

'What color was his hair underneath?' Nick asked.

'He'd shaved his head bald. In fact, Frasier Lewis had no body hair at all.'

'You didn't think that was odd?' Vito asked.

'Not especially. Frasier was an athlete. Lots of athletes wax their body hair.'

Nick closed the file. 'Thank you, Dr Pfeiffer. We'll see ourselves out.'

They were in Nick's car when Vito's cell began to ring. It was Liz.

'Get back here,' Liz said, excited. 'Christmas just came all over again.'

Friday, January 19, 1:35 P.M.

They'd found Van Zandt through an 'anonymous' tip. Vito and Nick took some time to get their evidence ducks in a row with Jen before meeting Liz in the interrogation room. They found her studying Van Zandt through the one-way glass.

Vito's smile had claws as he looked at Van Zandt through the glass. Van Zandt looked annoyed but crisp in his three-piece suit. His attorney was a thin man, who looked just as annoyed, but not nearly as crisp. 'I'm looking forward to this.'

One side of Liz's mouth lifted. 'Me, too. The tip was called in to 911 from an untraceable cell. The caller told us we could find Van Zandt at his hotel, gave us the room number, then called back when we'd brought him in, this time to my private line.'

'He was watching to be sure we picked him up,' Nick said. 'Simon's still in Philly.'

'Yep. He sounded just like the voice on the tape. Gave me a damn shiver.'

'What did you say to him?' Vito asked.

'I asked him who he was and he just laughed. Van Zandt's car was missing from the hotel parking lot when they picked him up. Van Zandt claimed it wasn't where he'd parked when he went to leave this morning.' She held out a piece of paper. 'When Simon called me, he told us where to find Van Zandt's car, then suggested we look in the trunk and asked me to pass on that message to "VZ."' She punctuated the air. 'Normally I wouldn't play messenger for a killer, but under the circumstances . . .'

Vito already knew what Jen's CSU team had found in Van Zandt's trunk, and he and Nick had come heavily armed, so to speak. Vito took the paper Liz offered and laughed grimly. 'Van Zandt didn't know who he was dealing with.'

'Neither does Simon Vartanian,' Liz said, just as grimly. 'Get in there and let that arrogant bastard know he's fucked.'

Van Zandt looked up when Vito and Nick entered the

interrogation room. His eyes were cold, his mouth a thin line. He stayed seated and said nothing.

His attorney came to his feet. 'I'm Doug Musgrove. You have nothing with which to hold my client. Let him go or I'm filing formal charges against the Philadelphia PD.'

'You do that,' Vito said. 'Jager, if this suit is your contracts attorney, you might want to get out the old phone book and hire a criminal defense attorney.'

Van Zandt just glared.

Musgrove bristled. 'Arrest him, or let him go,' he said, and Vito shrugged.

'Okay. Jager Van Zandt, you're under arrest for the murder of Derek Harrington.'

Van Zandt surged to his feet, unholy rage on face. '*What*?' He looked at his attorney. 'What the *fuck* is this?'

'Oh, let me finish,' Vito said. 'It's not official if I don't finish.' He quoted the rest of Miranda, then sat down and stretched out his legs. 'I'm done. Your turn to play.'

'I did not kill anybody,' Van Zandt gritted. 'Musgrove, get me out of here.'

Musgrove sat down. 'They've arrested you, Jager. We'll get you out on bail.'

Jager sneered. 'I didn't kill Derek. You have nothing.'

'We have your car,' Nick said and Van Zandt blinked.

'It was stolen,' he said stiffly. 'That was why I was still at my hotel.'

Vito scratched his chin. 'Uh-huh. Did you report it stolen?'

'No.'

'Three-month-old Porsche. I'd have reported it the second it was stolen.'

'Well, you know what they say about rich boys and their toys,' Nick drawled.

Van Zandt pounded the table. 'I did not kill Derek. I don't even know where he is.'

'That's okay. We do,' Vito said. 'He's in the trunk of your Porsche. At least he was. Now he's in the morgue.'

Van Zandt's eyes flickered. 'He's dead? He's really dead?'

'A bullet from a 1943 German Luger between the eyes tends to have that effect.' Nick's voice was harsh. 'The same gun we found hidden with your tire-changing kit. The same gun that killed Zachary Webber.'

'Oh,' Vito added, 'and Kyle Lombard and Clint Shafer. Mustn't forget about them.'

They had the pleasure of seeing Van Zandt pale. 'The gun was planted,' he hissed furiously. 'And I've never even heard of those other two men.'

'Jager, be quiet,' Musgrove said.

Van Zandt shot him a contemptuous glare. 'Go get me a criminal attorney. I did not kill Derek or anyone else. I didn't even know Derek was missing.'

'Of course you could tell the jury you shot him to put him out of his misery,' Nick said, stone-faced. 'He'd suffered enough, what with having his feet burned and his intestines ripped out.'

Van Zandt stiffened. 'What?'

'And his hands broken and his tongue cut out.' Nick sat down. 'Then again, I can't imagine any jury seeing you as merciful, Mr Van Zandt.'

Van Zandt's swallow was the only indication he was affected by the torture of the man he'd once called his friend. 'I didn't do any of those things.'

'The gun was with these,' Vito said. He laid a picture on the table and had the further pleasure of seeing Van Zandt flinch. 'That's Derek Harrington's car and your chief of security peeking in the window. And that's your reflection in the window. You were standing behind him.' Vito leaned back in his chair. 'You knew Derek was missing yesterday when you gave us his home address.'

'I did not.' Van Zandt spat the words from behind tightly clenched teeth.

'Derek confronted you with pictures of Zachary Webber,' Nick continued, 'the boy in your *game* who got shot with a German Luger. You had Derek followed. Then you took him and you killed him and you stuck him in your trunk and left it at a rest stop.'

'You can't know when that photo was taken,' Musgrove scoffed.

'Ah, but we do. The photographer was quite clever,' Nick said.

Vito slid another photo across the table. 'An enlargement of the detail of that bank sign behind Harrington's car. It gives the temperature, and the time and the date.'

Van Zandt drew his body ramrod straight, but his face was still ashen. 'Any ten-year-old with Photoshop could have doctored those photos. They mean nothing.'

Jen thought they'd been doctored, but they weren't telling Van Zandt.

'Perhaps that's true, but your secretary already gave you up,' Nick said.

Vito nodded. 'Yeah, it's true. NYPD just got done taking her statement this morning. Faced with charges of obstruction, she admitted you and Harrington quarreled three days ago and that he quit. Then you immediately called in your security guy.'

'Circumstantial,' Musgrove said, but there was doubt in his tone.

Vito lifted a shoulder. 'Perhaps. But there's more. With the gun we also found bank records showing you'd paid money to Zachary Webber and Brittany Bellamy and Warren Keyes.' Vito put pictures of the victims on the table. 'You recognize them, don't you?'

'We found your CDs,' Nick said, mildly now. 'You're a gruesome sonofabitch, Van Zandt, thinkin' up shit like that.'

Van Zandt's jaw cocked. 'This is a setup.'

'We found you on an anonymous tip . . . VZ,' Nick said, and Van Zandt's eyes flashed. 'The tipper asked us to pass on a message. What was it again, Chick?'

' "Checkmate," ' Vito said, and the look on Van Zandt's face was priceless.

'You played with fire, Jager,' Nick said. 'And you got burned. Now you're going down for murder.'

Van Zandt stared at the table, a muscle in his jaw twitching erratically. When he looked up, Vito knew they'd won. 'What do you want?' Van Zandt said.

'Jager,' Musgrove started and Van Zandt turned on him with a snarl.

'Just shut up and go get me a real attorney. Now, detectives, *what do you want?*'

'Frasier Lewis,' Vito said. 'We want the man you called Frasier Lewis.'

Dutton, Georgia, Friday, January 19, 2:45 P.M.

If she hadn't been nearly breaking his hand, Daniel would have thought Susannah's poise was complete. Her expression was flat, her features composed, just like he'd expect to see her in a courtroom. But this was no courtroom. There was a wall of flashing cameras behind them and it seemed most of the county had turned out to see who was buried in Simon's tomb. Daniel knew it wouldn't be Simon.

'Daniel,' Susannah murmured, 'I've been thinking about what that archeologist said. About Dad not wanting Mother to know that he'd found Simon.'

'Me, too. Dad had to have known Simon was alive. He wouldn't have wanted Mom to know what he did. I've been wondering why he took the pictures to Philadelphia.'

Susannah's chuckle was mirthless. 'He was blackmailing Simon. Think about it. If he knew Simon was alive, why all this?' She nodded at the crane moving into position. 'And if he faked all of this, how could he be sure that Simon wouldn't come back?'

'He kept the pictures as insurance,' Daniel said wearily. 'But why do any of this at all? Suze, if you know something, please tell me. *Please.*'

Susannah was quiet for so long that Daniel thought she wouldn't answer. But then she sighed. 'Things were bad when you lived at home, Daniel, but after you went away to college things got a whole lot worse. Dad and Simon fought all the time. Mother would always intervene. It was ugly.'

'And you?' Daniel kept his voice gentle. 'What did you do when they fought?'

She swallowed hard. 'I got involved in every after-school activity I could find, then when I got home, I hid in my room. It was the easiest way. Then, one day right after Simon graduated from high school it all came to a head. It was Wednesday and Mother was at her hair appointment in town. I was in my room and I heard Dad bust open Simon's door and they had this huge fight.'

She closed her eyes. 'They were yelling about pictures. At the time I thought they were talking about the paintings under his bed, but now I know the pictures were probably the ones you found. Dad was up for judge reelection and he said Simon's fuckups were killing his career, but that this one took the cake, that he'd fucked up one time too many. And then everything got real quiet.'

'And then?'

She opened her eyes and stared at the crane. 'They were still arguing, but too low for me to hear. Then Simon yelled, "I'll see you in hell before I let you send me to jail, old man," and Dad said, "Hell's the best place for you." Simon said, "You ought to know. We're birds of a feather."' She swallowed hard. 'Then Simon said, "And someday my gun will be a lot bigger than yours."'

Daniel let out the breath he'd been holding. 'Dear God.'

She nodded. 'The front door slammed and . . . I'm not sure why, but something told me to hide, so I did, in my closet. A minute later, my door opened, then shut. I think Dad was looking to see if I'd overheard.'

He shook his head, but it didn't clear his bewilderment. 'Suze. My God.'

'I've never been sure what he would have done if he'd found me. That night Simon didn't show up for supper. Mother was distraught. Dad said Simon had probably gone off with some friends, that she shouldn't worry. A few days later, Dad told us he'd gotten a call that Simon was dead.' She looked up at him, pain in her eyes. 'All these years I thought Dad had killed him.'

'Why didn't you say anything?'

'Same reason you didn't when you thought Dad had burned the pictures. My word against his. I was only sixteen. He was a respected judge. And like I said, I had to sleep sometime.'

Daniel was sick to his stomach. 'And I left you there. God, Suze. I'm sorry. If I'd known you were in danger . . . even that you were afraid, I would have taken you with me. Please believe that.'

She returned her gaze to the crane. 'What's done is done. Last night I realized Dad probably found those pictures and knew his career wouldn't survive if anyone saw them. He probably told Simon to leave and never come back and threatened him with prison if he didn't. He knew Mother would never stop looking for Simon as long as there was any hope that he was alive. So . . .'

'So he fixed it so she'd believe Simon was dead.'

'It's the only way it makes sense to me.' She bit at her lip. 'I thought about them both all night. He tortured Dad, Daniel.'

'I know.' It had kept him awake all night as well.

'Do you think Simon tortured him so that he'd tell where Mother was?'

'I considered it,' Daniel admitted. 'I think Simon's capable.'

'Oh, I know he's capable.'

'Suze . . . What happened? What did he do to you?'

She shook her head. 'Not now. Someday. But not today.'

'When you're ready, you'll call me.'

She squeezed his hand tighter. 'I will.'

'I want to think Dad would have died before letting Simon get to Mother,' he said.

'I'd like to think it,' she said flatly, which said a great deal.

'You know Simon's not in there,' Daniel said as the crane brought up the casket.

'I know.'

Philadelphia, Friday, January 19, 4:20 P.M.

'Sophie.'

Sophie's stomach dropped to her toes as Harry hurried across the lobby, passing Officer Lyons without a glance. 'Harry? What's wrong with Gran?'

He cast a wary glance at the ax on her shoulder. 'Nothing, Anna's fine. Can you put that down? It makes me nervous.'

Relieved, she set the ax head on the floor. 'I've got a tour in a few minutes, Harry.'

'I needed to tell you something. In person. And it's not good. Freya told me you'd called asking if we'd put Anna's record collection away for safekeeping. We didn't. I did some checking and . . . um . . . it's been taken.'

Her eyes narrowed. 'By whom?' But she already knew.

'Lena. She showed up after Anna's stroke, but I sent her away. Instead she went to Anna's house and took the records and other valuables. I found some of them on eBay. The seller on eBay believed he'd bought them legitimately from Lena. I'm sorry.'

Sophie let out a slow breath, her heart pounding in her head. 'Is there more?'

'Yes. When I found out about the missing records, I talked to Anna's lawyer. She had a lot of money tied up in bonds that I knew nothing about. If she'd died, her lawyer would have told us. As it was . . .' He took a breath. 'The lawyer checked the serial numbers on the bonds. They've been cashed. I'm so sorry, Sophie. A good part of what would have been your inheritance – yours and Freya's – is gone.'

Sophie nodded, numb. 'Thanks for telling me in person. I have to work now.'

Harry frowned. 'We have to call the police and press charges.'

She swung the ax on her shoulder with too much force. 'You do it. If I press charges, I might have to see her. I'd really rather never see her again.'

'Sophie, wait.' Harry had noticed Officer Lyons. 'Why is there a cop in your lobby?'

'He's here for security.' It was a half-truth more than a half-lie. 'Harry, I have a tour group waiting for me in the Hall. I have to go. Do what you want with Lena. I don't care.'

Friday, January 19, 5:00 P.M.

Vito dropped into his chair at the conference room table and rubbed the back of his neck, tired and frustrated. 'Fuck.' Three hours of interviewing Jager Van Zandt had at times brought new insights but ultimately hadn't yielded the real information they sought.

Liz sat down next to him. 'Van Zandt really might not know where Simon is, Vito.'

'You could try torturing it out of him,' Jen muttered, then shrugged when Liz raised her brows. 'It was just a thought.'

'Damn good thought,' Katherine said, and by the looks on the faces around the table, a thought everyone else shared.

Gathered for the evening debrief, Nick and Jen, Katherine and Thomas, and Liz and Brent all wore grim expressions. They'd been joined by a new face – ADA Magdalena Lopez who, along with Thomas and Liz, had observed the interrogation of Van Zandt. Maggy was a delicate woman with dark brown eyes that now narrowed as she spoke.

'He might know and he might not. But I'm not prepared to give him anything more than I have, particularly not full immunity.'

Maggy had offered to reduce his murder charge to man-slaughter if he told them where to find Frasier Lewis, aka Simon, but Van Zandt had demanded full immunity, the arrogant little bastard. 'We don't want you to give him immunity, Maggy,' Vito said. 'He might not have killed anyone, but he was sure as hell prepared to profit from it.'

'Besides,' Nick said, 'if Simon had believed Van Zandt really knew anything useful, he wouldn't have handed him over to us. You did okay, Maggy.' The last was added with a grudging admiration, probably, Vito thought, because of the guilty verdict Maggy had gotten on Nick's Siever case. Now Nick could finally feel like he deserved the Christmas cards the Siever girl's parents sent every year.

'He did give us Simon's cell phone number,' Vito said.

'Same number he used to call me,' Liz said. 'No GPS. Untraceable.'

'I found Van Zandt's reaction to knowing real people died to make his game to be the most telling,' Thomas mused. '"You must prune dead wood to save the tree,"' he mimicked in Van Zandt's thick accent. '"Sometimes you cut living wood."'

'Ultimate break-the-eggs-to-make-the-omelet approach,' Nick agreed. 'Slimy SOB.'

'Sophie told us that the big R in oRo was Dutch for wealth,' Vito said. 'I guess Van Zandt's never made a secret that he's in it for the money.'

Thomas shook his head. 'Van Zandt could be an even worse sociopath than Simon Vartanian. At least Simon's doing this for art.'

'Van Zandt claimed he hadn't paid Simon yet,' Vito told Katherine, Brent, and Jen. 'Simon's pay was based on royalties, which wouldn't be paid for another three months.'

'And the royalties are piddly shit,' Nick added. 'Simon didn't do this for money.'

'How did Simon hook up with Van Zandt?' Jen asked.

'Van Zandt was in a bar near his apartment in SoHo,' Vito

answered. He shook his head. 'The bar is right down the street from the park where Susannah Vartanian walks her dog. We think Simon met up with Van Zandt one of the times he was stalking Susannah. Anyway, Simon approached Van Zandt in the bar a year ago, bought him a few drinks, and showed him a demo disk.'

'It was the Clothilde strangulation scene,' Nick said. 'But it was done in a modern-day setting. Van Zandt saw "promise" and told Simon if he converted it to a World War II theme, he'd get it in his next game. Simon did and Van Zandt asked for more. Simon did the scenes with the Luger and the grenade. It's all Van Zandt had time to put in *Behind Enemy Lines* because he was up against the delivery deadline.'

'Derek protested,' Thomas said and frowned. ' "Because he was weak." '

Maggy Lopez sighed. 'Van Zandt's quite a guy.'

'And I hope he rots in hell,' Nick said. 'But bottom line, Van Zandt says he doesn't know where Lewis came from or where he lived, or who the boy with the grenade was.'

'Well, I got some info on Frasier Lewis,' Katherine said. 'The real Frasier Lewis.'

Vito blinked, surprised. 'He really exists?'

'Oh, yes. He's a forty-year-old farmer in Iowa. Simon's been using his medical insurance for some time. The real Frasier's medical insurance has a lifetime cap of a million dollars. If he ever got really sick, he'd be in trouble, because a lot of that money is gone. I wondered how Simon afforded the fancy prosthetics Dr Pfeiffer's file said he used. He paid for his own medical care through medical insurance fraud.'

'Does the real Frasier Lewis have two legs?' Nick asked.

'Yes,' Katherine said.

Nick was frowning. 'Wouldn't Pfeiffer have seen that there was no amputation?'

'Not necessarily,' Brent said thoughtfully. 'Simon is good with computers. We already thought he could get into people's financials. What if he could get into a medical-records database, too? What if that's why he picked Lewis's medical identity to steal? Because he had access to Lewis's medical history to change it? It's just a thought.'

'It's a good thought. Run with it,' Vito said. 'See what you come up with.'

'I'm glad I could offer something, because I didn't get anything off Daniel's father's PC. At least nothing to lead you to Simon directly. There was a utility downloaded – it allowed whoever put it on there to access the father's computer remotely, but it was nothing fancy. Just a common UNIX utility that anyone could have downloaded.'

'You sound disappointed,' Nick said and Brent chuckled.

'Maybe a little. I was expecting something huge based on the Trojan 'bots with timers he used on the models' computers. But this was simple and elegant. And untraceable. Maybe I'll have more luck with the medical databases. They tend not to be so elegant. Oh.' Brent handed Vito a framed photo. 'The Dutton sheriff that sent the computer sent this. He said Daniel and Susannah had asked him to give it to us.'

'It's Simon,' Vito said. 'Younger. This is the same face as the one in Pfeiffer's picture. I guess even Simon found it difficult to disguise himself in anything more than a wig at a doctor's exam. It's one more piece of the puzzle.'

Nick was frowning. 'That remote control download. Can you tell when it was done?'

'Sure,' Brent said. 'A few days after Thanksgiving.'

'Would Simon have to have been in the house to do the download?' Nick asked.

'I don't know of any other way he could have independently done it.'

Troubled, Liz followed the thought. 'Mr and Mrs Vartanian come here looking for their blackmailer and, presumably, Simon. At some point they find Simon, or he finds them, because they're dead and buried in Simon's graveyard. So then Simon goes back to Georgia and fixes his father's PC for remote access, plants the travel brochures, and makes it look like they've gone on vacation. He even keeps paying their bills. Why?'

'He didn't want anyone to know his parents were dead,' Jen said. 'Arthur was a retired judge – somebody would have investigated.'

'And Daniel and Susannah would have gotten involved, which they did.' Nick looked at Vito. 'He wanted to keep them away, because he wasn't ready for them yet.'

'At least they know to be on alert,' Vito said. 'Where are they now?'

'Back in Dutton,' Katherine said. 'They went back for the exhumation.'

'So did you get the results?' Vito asked.

'Only that the body isn't Simon's. The bones are those of a five-foot-ten-inch man.'

'Wasn't an autopsy done?' Liz asked and Katherine rolled her eyes.

'Mexican autopsy,' Katherine said. 'That supposed car crash was in Tijuana. Vartanian's father went down and got the death certificate, bought the casket, and brought it back through customs. Either he greased some palms or whoever peeked inside saw a horribly charred corpse and shut the coffin back up quick.'

'So he still might not have known whether Simon was really dead,' Jen said.

Katherine shrugged. 'I don't know. I imagine Daniel and Susannah want to know, but at this point, I'm not sure how that helps us find Simon.'

'Did Pfeiffer or his receptionist come in to be printed?' Nick asked.

Jen shook her head. 'Not yet.'

'Let us know when they do,' Vito said. 'What else? What about churches in the quarry areas, Jen? Or the silicone lubricant manufacturer?'

'I've got a tech calling lube manufacturers and two techs mapping churches. Nothing yet. I was personally working Van

Zandt's car all day. Sorry, Vito. We're doing our best.'

Vito sighed. 'I know.' He thought of Sophie. 'But we have to try harder.'

'Now that Van Zandt's in jail,' Nick mused, 'what if Simon decides to leave town? oRo's going to fold. Simon doesn't have a job anymore.'

'We need a way to make him stay,' Vito said. 'To draw him out into the open.'

'He thinks he's got Van Zandt fucked over a barrel.' Nick looked at Maggy Lopez. 'What if Van Zandt were to get released?'

Maggy shook her head. 'I can't let just let him go. We charged him. He hasn't agreed to the plea, and I'm not giving him immunity. He's got to go through the system. Nick, I can't believe you of all people want me to deal him down.'

'I don't want to deal him down,' Nick said. 'But I want him on the street, so we can follow him. You don't have to let him go, exactly. His bond hearing is tomorrow morning, right?'

'So? Two hours ago you wanted to push the plunger on the lethal injection syringe yourself. Now you want me to put him on the streets. You want me to make him *bait*.'

'I don't see a problem with it,' Nick said. 'We keep close to him. Simon won't be able to resist. It'll be like we painted a big bull's-eye on Jager's ass.'

'More like an R,' Brent said dryly. 'For riches.'

'And don't forget the dead wood comment,' Vito added. 'Van Zandt deserves whatever he gets, Maggy. But we won't let Simon get him, because we want to see Van Zandt behind bars, too. If he knew about these murders and let it go on, he's complicit.'

Maggy sighed. 'If we lose him . . .'

'We won't,' Nick promised. 'All you have to do is ask for a teensy bail.'

'All right,' Maggy said. 'Don't make me regret this.'

'We won't,' Vito promised, feeling a surge of energy. 'Liz, can we get Bev and Tim back for a few more days? Maybe even just tomorrow? We need surveillance eyes.'

'I'll arrange it,' Liz said. 'But only for one day. We'll have to reevaluate if this drags.'

'Fair enough.' Vito stood up. 'Let's meet early tomorrow and coordinate.'

Chapter Twenty-Two

Friday, January 19, 7:00 P.M.

Sophie sank into the front seat of Vito's truck. She'd pushed the fury aside, but with the day done, it started to churn anew. What more could Lena possibly take?

Vito started the engine and sat quietly as the heater began to warm the cab. He was waiting for her to say something, she knew. She also knew he'd had a bad day himself. His problems were a lot bigger than hers. He had a killer to catch.

Getting angry about a few missing vinyl records had kept her own mind off the fact that that same killer had been watching her, so maybe indirectly Lena had finally done something good. She rolled her head to look at him. 'I'm sorry I kept you waiting, but what did you think of my Viking tour?'

His eyes shifted, heated, and his lips curved, making her pulse quicken. 'I thought you made the sexiest Viking warrior I ever saw. I wanted to jump you right there.'

She laughed, as he'd meant her to. 'In front of all those children? Shame on you.'

He brought her hand to his lips. 'What's wrong, Sophie?'

His tone was so gentle, her eyes stung. 'Harry came by today.' She told him about the visit and watched his eyes harden.

'You should press charges.'

'You sound like Harry. I didn't press charges when Lena killed my sister. Why would I press charges over her stealing a few old phonograph records?'

411

Vito shook his head. 'Elle's death was an accident. This theft wasn't.'

Sophie's chin came up. 'Now you sound like Katherine.'

'Because Katherine was right. Sophie, Lena's a terrible mother, but she didn't mean to kill Elle. But this theft, this she meant to do. She planned it and she profited from it. If you're going to hate her, hate her for the things she's really done. Hating her for feeding nuts to a kid who she didn't know was allergic is pointless.'

Sophie gaped at him. '*Pointless*?'

'And childish,' he added quietly. 'Last night you said that Andrea made her choices, and you were right. Lena's made her choices, too. Hold her accountable for those, for abandoning you and for stealing from your grandmother, Sophie, but not for killing Elle. That kind of hate is just wasted energy.'

Sophie felt angry tears building. 'I can hate her for anything I want to hate her for, Vito, and it really isn't any of your business, so just butt out.'

He flinched at that and looked away. 'Okay.' He pulled his truck into the stream of traffic. 'I guess that tells me where I stand.'

Guilt speared. 'I'm sorry, Vito. I shouldn't have said that. I'm just disappointed that I don't have any music to play for Gran, and I really wanted to see her happy again.'

'Just seeing your face makes her happy.' But he wouldn't look at her, even though he'd stopped at a red light, and that made her panic.

'Vito, I'm sorry. I shouldn't have told you to butt out. I'm not used to worrying about what somebody else thinks about me. Someone whose opinion matters anyway.'

'It's all right, Sophie.' But it wasn't. She could see that. She wasn't sure how to make it right, so she mentally backed away and approached from another direction.

'Vito, you didn't find him, did you? Simon Vartanian.'

His jaw tightened. 'No. But we found both the game guys.'

'Alive?'

'One's alive.'

She drew in a breath. 'Simon's snipping off all his loose ends, isn't he?'

A muscle twitched in his cheek. 'It looks that way.'

'I'm being careful, Vito. You don't need to distract yourself worrying about me.'

He looked over at her then, his eyes intense, and relief pushed away her panic. 'Good. Because I'm getting attached to you, Sophie. I want you to care about what I think, and I want it to be my business to care about how you feel.'

She was unsure of how to respond. 'That's a big step, Vito. Especially for me.'

'I know. That's why I'm prepared to be patient.' He patted her thigh, then took her hand. 'Don't worry, Sophie. My caring about you isn't meant to cause you stress.'

She stared at his hand, strong and dark against her skin. 'It's just that I fuck things up sometimes. I really don't want to fuck this up. Whatever it is that we have.'

'You won't. For now, just sit back and enjoy the ride.' His lips quirked. 'Over the river and through the woods. To Gran's we go.'

She narrowed her eyes at him. 'Why do I get the feeling you're the big bad wolf?'

He grinned lightly. 'Better to eat you with, my dear?'

She smacked him even as she laughed. 'Just drive, Vito.'

For the rest of the drive they kept the conversation light, away from Lena, Simon, and any talk of serious relationships. When they got to the nursing home, Vito helped her out of the truck, then reached into the back and pulled out a big shopping bag.

'What's that?'

He hid the bag behind his back. 'It's my basket of goodies for Grandma.'

Her lips twitched as they walked. 'So now *I'm* the big bad wolf?'

He kept his eyes forward. 'You can blow my house down any time.'

She snickered. 'You're bad, Vito Ciccotelli, just bad to the bone.'

He dropped a quick kiss on her mouth as they stood at Anna's door. 'So I'm told.'

Her grandmother was watching them with eagle eyes from her bed, and Sophie suspected that was the reason Vito had chosen the doorway to kiss her. Anna looked good, Sophie decided as she kissed both her cheeks. 'Hi, Gran.'

'Sophie.' Anna reached up a feeble hand to touch her cheek. Still, the movement was more than she'd done in a long time. 'You brought back your young man.'

Vito sat down next to her bed. 'Hello, Anna.' He kissed her cheek. 'You're looking better today. Your cheeks are downright rosy.'

Anna smiled up at him. 'You're a flatterer. I like that.'

He smiled back at her. 'I thought you might.' He reached into the bag, pulled out a long-stemmed rose and handed it to her gallantly. 'I thought you might like flowers, too.'

Anna's eyes went shiny and Sophie felt her own eyes sting. 'Vito,' she murmured.

Vito glanced over at her. 'You could have had some too, but no. It was "Stop, Vito" and "You're so bad, Vito."' He closed Anna's hand over the stem. 'I had them strip off the thorns. Can you smell it?'

Anna nodded. 'I can. It's been a long time since I've smelled roses.'

Sophie kicked herself for not thinking of it herself, but it didn't appear that Vito was finished. He brought out an entire bouquet of roses just ready to bloom and then a black porcelain vase, which he set carefully on the nightstand next to her bed. Embedded in the porcelain were crystals that shimmered like the stars in the night sky. He arranged the roses and again adjusted the vase on the nightstand.

'Now you can smell them even better,' he said and handed

Sophie the plastic pitcher from the nightstand. 'Can you get us some water for these flowers, Sophie?'

'Of course.' But she lingered in the doorway, the pitcher in her hands. Vito still wasn't finished. He took out a small cassette player.

'My grandfather had a record collection,' he said and Anna's eye widened.

'You brought music?' she whispered and Sophie damned Lena to hell. Then she damned herself for not having thought of music in general before now.

'Not just any music,' Vito said with a smile that made Sophie's breath catch.

Anna's mouth opened, then her lips pressed tight. 'You have . . . *Orfeo*?' she asked, then held her breath like a child who is afraid she'll be told no.

'I do.' He started the tape, and Sophie instantly recognized the opening strains of *Che faro*, the aria that had brought Anna fame a lifetime ago. Then Anna's pure mezzo-soprano soared from the small speaker and Anna released the breath she held, closed her eyes and settled, as if she'd been waiting for just this. Sophie's throat closed and her chest hurt as she watched her grandmother's lips begin to move with the words.

Vito hadn't taken his eyes from her grandmother's face, and that made Sophie's chest hurt even more. He hadn't done this thing to impress her. He'd done this beautiful thing to make an old woman smile.

But Anna wasn't smiling. Tears were rolling down her cheeks as she tried to draw the breath to sing. But her lungs were fragile and nothing emerged but a pitiful croak.

Sophie took a step back, unable to watch Anna's futile attempts or the misery that filled her grandmother's eyes as she gave up. Clutching the plastic pitcher to her chest, Sophie turned away and started walking.

'Sophie?' one of the nurses tried to stop her. 'What is it? Does Anna need help?'

Sophie shook her head. 'No, just water. I'm getting it.' She made it to the little kitchenette at the end of the hall and, her hands shaking, turned on the water. She filled the pitcher, reining in her emotion as she turned off the water.

And went still. Another voice now soared. But it wasn't Anna's smooth mezzo. It was a rich baritone. And it drew her like a lodestone.

Heart pounding, she walked back to Anna's door, where six nurses stood stock still, hardly breathing. Squeezing through, Sophie stumbled to a halt and could only stare.

It was, she would reflect later, an odd moment to fall in love.

She'd been wrong. Aunt Freya hadn't gotten the last good man. One sat at her grandmother's side, singing the words Anna could not with a voice that was both powerful and pure. On his face was gentle tenderness as Anna's eyes watched every movement of his mouth, drinking in each note with a joy that was almost painful to behold.

But behold Sophie did, and when Vito had sung the last note she stood, her cheeks wet, but her mouth smiling. Behind her went up a collective sigh from the nurses, then they went back to their duties, sniffling.

Vito looked over at her, his brows lifting. 'If you filled that pitcher with tears, it'll kill the roses, Sophie,' he teased. He dipped his head close to Anna's. 'We made her cry.'

'Sophie's always been a crier. Cried at the cartoons even.' But the words were uttered with unmistakable affection.

'I didn't know you watched when I cried at cartoons, Gran.'

'I watched you all the time, Sophie.' She patted Sophie's hand awkwardly. 'You were such a pleasure to watch grow up. I like your young man. You should keep him.' One of her brows went up. 'Do you understand my meaning?'

Sophie met Vito's as she answered. 'Yes, ma'am. I certainly do.'

Friday, January 19, 8:00 P.M.

Something was different, Vito thought. A closeness. The way Sophie leaned against him as they walked to his truck. And she was smiling at him, which was always a plus.

'If I'd known the singing would trip your trigger I would have sung to you Sunday night. In fact, if it'll get me lucky, I can sing anything you want.' He opened her door, but she turned in his arms instead of getting in. Her kiss was warm and fluid and left him wishing they weren't in an icy parking lot.

'It wasn't the singing. It was everything, the way you held her hand and the way she watched you. You're a very nice man, Vito Ciccotelli.'

'You said I was bad to the bone.'

She nipped at his lip, sending lust surging along every nerve. 'The two don't have to be mutually exclusive.' She got up into the truck and faced him. 'I think I'll call the local opera society. Maybe they can send some visitors to Gran. I should have thought of the music, Vito. It was her whole life. I can't believe I didn't see it.'

'You've been concentrating on getting her well.' Vito climbed behind the wheel and pulled his door closed with a slam. 'Don't beat yourself up.' He pulled into traffic, toward Anna's house. 'Besides, Tino made the recording for me.'

'But you thought of it. And the flowers. I should have thought of that, too.'

'I have to admit to an ulterior motive for the roses. The vase is your granny-cam.'

Sophie blinked at him. 'What?'

'All those crystals? One is a camera. Now you'll know if Nurse Marco is really mean.'

Sophie looked at him. 'You're amazing.'

'No, not really. Tino picked it out after my brother-in-law Aidan gave us a few ideas while you were building the castle last night. I'd appreciate it if you wouldn't mention the camera

417

to Tess. She gets a little uptight about people being filmed against their will.'

'My lips are sealed.'

'Good. Now we're going back to your place where I'm going to sing to you again. Just keep remembering that I'm amazing.'

She laughed. 'Later. I promised the boys I'd help them finish the castle. So first, your house. Then we can go back to Gran's and . . . make love. Amazingly.'

Vito drew a pained breath. 'I was thinking about fucking like minks on the stairs.'

Her chuckle was evil. 'First I build a castle. Then you can lay siege.'

He watched them drive away. He'd been lucky, he thought, removing the earpiece before the slamming truck door burst his eardrums. If the cop had closed his door a minute sooner he would have missed the magic words.

But he didn't believe in luck. Just intellect, skill, and fate. Only fools believed in luck, and he was no fool. He'd survived on his own wits. And he'd continue to. He thought of Van Zandt, sitting in a jail cell in his expensive suit, and felt intense satisfaction. But there was a little regret, too. It was a shame to waste a business mind like Van Zandt's. But there were lots of good business minds out there.

He already had one lined up. Van Zandt's most eager and vicious competitor, still on his way up the ladder. Simon had contacted him with the work he'd done so far and it had taken less than fifteen minutes to agree to terms. *The Inquisitor* would still be released and the furor around Derek's murder and Van Zandt's incarceration, not to mention all the murdered victims, would send sales soaring to the moon.

And in the end, he'd still get what he wanted. Exposure. A platform to launch his own career. Notoriety to sell his paintings. He wouldn't be able to use the name Frasier Lewis anymore, but that was all right. It didn't matter what name went on his work. *As long as people know it's mine.*

Just one more series of paintings needed to be completed. Van Zandt had been right about the queen. As soon as Simon had seen Sophie Johannsen in full glory he'd known she was exactly what he needed, what he wanted. And he knew himself well enough to know he wouldn't be able to able to walk away from the game until every piece was perfect. He needed to see Sophie Johannsen die.

Except the woman had proven herself smart and careful. Every moment she was with a cop. But now he knew how to separate her from the herd.

Friday, January 19, 11:30 P.M.

'It's a nice keep.' Beaming, Sophie nodded at Michael. 'These are beautiful blocks.' She and Pierce sat behind a semicircle about four feet in diameter and three feet high constructed of smooth wooden blocks. They'd even included the skinny windows Sophie had informed them were arrow slits for defense against their attackers.

Which had then required a run to the local toy store for a Nerf archery set. At least the books they'd been using the night before were neatly back on Vito's shelves, so he wouldn't complain too much that his living room was now a Norman castle.

Sophie rubbed her fingers over one of the blocks and Vito knew she wouldn't find a single splinter. 'They must have cost the Earth.'

Vito's father pretended nonchalance. 'Just some old blocks I had in storage. Dom and Tess got them after school today.' But Vito could see he was beaming, too.

'Dad handmade the blocks for us when we were kids,' Vito said from his recliner, which had been turned into the drawbridge. The rest of the furniture had either been removed or turned over and converted to battlements. 'Dad is a master carpenter.'

Sophie's eyes widened. 'Really? Well, then the trebuchet makes sense. Cool.'

'I'm ready,' Connor said, guiding the model into place. Gone was the makeshift wooden-spoon trebuchet they'd fashioned last night, replaced with a scale model that could probably hurl a Thanksgiving turkey. Connor had wanted to try a frozen chicken, but thankfully Sophie had put her foot down on that one.

Vito suspected his father had been working on the model all day, carving it with the whittling knife he was never without. In the old days Michael could have cranked out a model like that in an hour with his woodworking tools, but those had been sold when Michael had been forced to give up his cabinet-making business because of his heart.

'No, you're not ready,' Sophie told Connor. 'You don't have anything to hurl yet.'

'You need to get this battle on the road,' Vito said dryly. 'It's almost midnight and Pierce and Connor have to go to bed.' Which is where he'd wanted to be all evening.

'Uncle Vito,' Pierce whined. 'Tomorrow's Saturday.' He looked to Sophie hopefully.

'Sorry, kid,' Sophie said. 'I have to work tomorrow, too. Tess, Dominic?'

'We're coming,' Tess called, and she and Dom emerged from the kitchen with Ziploc bags filled with cooked pasta. 'I've never cooked for a siege before, but here it is.'

A fierce military campaign ensued, each of the boys taking turns manning the trebuchet while Sophie and Michael rebuilt the battlements as needed.

Tess took cover behind Vito's chair. 'Dad hasn't had so much fun in years.'

'Mom won't let him,' Vito murmured. 'She worries about every breath he takes.'

'Well, Mom's not here. I sent her and Tino to the all-night Wal-Mart with a long grocery list. You guys don't exactly keep a well-stocked kitchen, and I'm going to be cooking lots of meals to put in the freezer for when Molly comes home from the hospital.' She shrugged. 'Mom needed to feel useful, so she's happy. Dad's happy. The kids are ecstatic. You look happy, too, Vito.'

Vito looked up at her. 'I am.'

Tess sat on the arm of his chair. 'I'm glad. I like your Sophie, Vito.'

His Sophie was currently ducking a bag of cooked pasta. 'So do I.' He realized both he and Sophie had achieved something for the other's family tonight. It was a solid beginning to a relationship Vito intended to nurture for a long, long time.

'This is a good start,' Tess murmured, 'to a nice life. You deserve that.' Then Tess squealed along with Sophie when one of the bags hurled from the trebuchet slammed into the ceiling and broke on impact, sending sticky pasta flying everywhere.

Vito grimaced. 'This is never gonna come off my walls and ceiling, is it?'

Tess chuckled. 'I see a lot of pasta-covered walls in your future, Vito.'

Sophie and Michael were laughing like loons and Vito had to laugh, too. Finally Sophie stood, picking pasta from her hair. 'On that note, it's bedtime. No,' she said when Pierce whined. 'Generals don't whine, they march. Now go downstairs, quietly. Don't wake Gus.' When the boys were gone, Sophie looked at Vito. 'Bucket and rags?'

'Back porch,' he said and got up from the chair. 'Sit down, Pop. You look tired.'

Michael did, which showed he was worn out. But he still laughed. 'That was fun. We should do this every Friday night. You've set a precedent, Vito.'

Vito sighed. 'Pasta on my walls and doughnuts for my team. Dom, Tess, help me pick up these blocks.' They'd stacked them along the wall when Vito realized Sophie wasn't back with the bucket. His pulse started to race. He'd let her out of his sight.

Just to his back porch, but out of his sight. 'I'll be back,' he said tightly.

Then breathed again when he got out to the back porch where Sophie was standing next to Dante, who sat on the overturned bucket, looking sullen.

'Seems to me you just hurt yourself,' she was saying. 'You missed all the fun.'

'Nobody wants me in there,' he muttered. 'So why should I give you the bucket?'

'One, because I'm an adult and it's respectful. Two, because your uncle is probably getting antsy right now, seeing the pasta congealing on his walls. Three, because I'm getting ready to push you off the bucket and take it, and I don't want to do that.'

Dante narrowed his eyes. 'You wouldn't.'

'You watch me,' she said. 'You're being a real brat, Dante, sulking out here.'

Dante lurched to his feet and kicked at the bucket. 'Stupid old bucket and stupid game and stupid family. Everybody hates me anyway. I don't need them.'

Sophie grabbed the bucket and started to leave, then sighed. 'Your family isn't stupid, they're pretty special. And everybody needs a family. And nobody hates you.'

'Everybody looks at me like I'm scum or something. Just 'cause I broke the meter.'

'Well, I'm just an outsider looking in, but it seems to me that nobody's mad because you broke the meter. I mean, you didn't mean to any more than you meant to hurt your mother. You . . . didn't mean to hurt your mother, did you, Dante?'

Dante shook his head, still sullenly. Then his shoulders sagged and Vito heard him sniffle. 'No. But my mom's going to hate me.' He started to cry in earnest, and Sophie put her arm around his shoulders. 'I almost killed her and she's going to hate me.'

'No, she won't,' Sophie murmured. 'Dante, you know what I think? I think they're all disappointed because when they asked if you did it, you lied. Maybe it's time you started making up for the bad thing you really meant to do and let go of the thing that you didn't.' Vito watched her shoulders stiffen, then heard her chuckle softly. 'Touché to me. You planning to stay out here all night, Dante?'

Dante scrubbed his face. 'Maybe.'

'Well, then I recommend you get a blanket, 'cause it's gonna be a cold night.' She turned and started when she saw Vito watching. She lifted the bucket. 'I'm going to clean.'

'Thank God.'

She lifted her brows. 'And I'm going to press charges against Lena.'

'Thank God.'

She walked past him and murmured, 'Then . . . minks.'

He grinned at her back. 'Thank God.'

Saturday, January 20, 7:45 A.M.

'You're here early.'

Sophie spun around in the warehouse, her breath in her throat and her hand over her mouth. For a moment she stared at Theo Four, her heart pounding in her chest.

'You've suddenly become extremely interested in our little museum, Sophie. Why?'

Sophie got control of her breathing and took a step back. Vito had walked her into the Albright a half hour before. Officer Lyons had already been waiting inside, let in by Ted the Third and Patty Ann, who'd been polishing glass cases. Sophie hadn't realized Theo was in the museum as well. 'What do you mean?'

'A few days ago you hated doing the tours and you treated my father like he was an idiot. Now you're here early and you stay late. You've been unpacking crates and developing new tours that make my father happy and have my mother counting the money that's going to be coming in. I want to know what changed.'

Sophie's heart was still knocking in her chest. Simon Vartanian was still out there, and she really didn't know anything about Theo Albright. Except that he was a big guy, over six-two. She took another step back, grateful that Lyons was only a scream away.

'Maybe I decided to start earning my paycheck, although I'd ask you the same question. A few days ago, you were making yourself scarce. Now you're here, every time I turn around. Why?'

Theo's expression darkened. 'Because I'm watching you.'

Sophie blinked. 'Watching *me*? Why?'

'Because unlike my father, I'm not an idiot who trusts for no reason.' He turned on his heel and walked away, leaving Sophie staring at his back, her mouth open.

She shook her head. She was being ridiculous, being scared of Theo. But what did she really know about the Albrights? *Sophie, come on.* Simon was thirty years old and his father had been a judge. Theo was barely eighteen and his father was the grandson of an archeologist. She was truly being ridiculous. Theo was just a weird kid. Still . . .

She found the ax Theo had used to open crates for her before and set it where she could reach it quickly. Even with Officer Lyons on guard, it wouldn't hurt to be prepared.

Atlanta, Georgia, Saturday, January 20, 8:45 A.M.

'Daniel. Look. It's from Mom.'

Daniel looked up from the mail he was sorting to find Susannah focused on a piece of paper that he instantly recognized as stationery from the hotel where his parents had stayed. 'She wrote us? And sent it to herself? Why?'

Susannah nodded. 'She says that she also sent you a letter.' She sorted through her stack and found it, handing it over to him. She held hers to her nose as Daniel opened his. 'It smells like her perfume.'

Daniel swallowed. 'I always liked that perfume.' He scanned the letter and his heart sank even as he appreciated the missing pieces his mother had settled into place. 'She knew Dad was lying about finding Simon for her but didn't have the strength to follow him everywhere.'

'Are they the same letter?' Susannah asked.

They put them side by side. 'Appears so. I guess she was taking no chances.'

'She sat in that hotel for two days, Daniel, while she waited for Dad to come back.'

'I guess he'd gone to see Simon,' Daniel murmured.

'But I was only two hours away.' There was hurt in Susannah's voice. 'She sat there in pain and alone for two days and never called me.'

'Simon was her favorite, from the time we were little. I don't know why it still hurts that she saw it as a black-and-white thing. Love us or love Simon.'

'Up to the end she hoped he would be good.' Susannah put the letter down hard on the table. 'And she trusted him.' Tears sprang to her eyes. 'She knew Dad was missing and still went to meet Simon.'

Daniel blew out a breath. 'And he killed her.' *If you're reading this, then I'm probably dead. If you're reading this, you can be satisfied that you were right about your brother.* 'She met him and he broke her neck and threw her in an unmarked field.' He looked at Susannah, unable to control the bitterness. 'And part of me thinks she got what she deserved.'

Susannah looked down. 'I thought it, too. That's why she sent these letters to herself. If her time with Simon was just an innocent visit, she would have exposed her true fears about her golden child's character for nothing. If she sent it to us, we'd know. If she sent it to herself, she could scoop them back up before anyone was the wiser.'

'And she was going to die anyway.' Daniel tossed the letter to the table. 'What did she have to lose? Except time with us.'

'He's still out there.'

425

Daniel hesitated. He'd tried to find a way to tell her all morning. *Just spit it out and get it over with.* 'There's more, Suze. I didn't want to think about it, but all night I couldn't think about anything but when Ciccotelli told us they'd found Claire Reynolds, our parents, and two empty graves. What they didn't tell us is that they found them with six other bodies.'

Susannah's eyes widened. 'You mean the graveyard they found . . . I saw it on the news. I didn't put it together. I should have.'

'I should have, too. I guess I was too shocked finding out Simon wasn't dead.' Daniel stopped himself. 'No, that's not true. I didn't want to think about it. But it was nagging at me, so I called Vito Ciccotelli this morning and asked. He confirmed that Simon was wanted for ten murders. Maybe more.'

Susannah shut her eyes wearily. 'I keep thinking it can't get worse.'

'I know. For years I would lie awake and worry about the people in the pictures, if they were real. That Simon had a hand in their deaths. That I couldn't help them. Now there are more victims and this time I can't look away. I need to go back to Philadelphia, to help Ciccotelli and Lawrence now.'

'We go together. This week we stood together over our parents. When this is over, I hope Simon will finally be dead and we can stand over his body together, too.'

Saturday, January 20, 9:15 A.M.

'We ready?' Nick asked, handing Vito a cup of coffee as he slid behind the wheel.

'Yep.' Vito peeled back the plastic lid. 'Bev and Tim are in position around the block. Maggy Lopez just called to say Van Zandt's next up in the docket. If the judge allows him bail, he should be out in an hour.'

'I hope this works,' Nick murmured. 'I'd hate to see Van Zandt get away.'

'Me, too.' The words came out a lot shakier than he'd intended.

Nick looked over at Vito. 'You're scared.'

Vito didn't say anything for a long minute, then cleared his throat gruffly. 'Yeah. I'm scared to death. Every time my phone rings I wonder if it's a call saying he's gotten to her. That I didn't keep her safe enough.'

'This is different from Andrea, Chick. This time you're not in this alone.'

Vito nodded, wishing he was reassured. But he knew he wouldn't breathe easily until Simon Vartanian was behind bars. Still, his friends cared. 'Thanks.' Then his cell phone rang, making him jump. But it was Jen. 'What's up?'

Jen yawned. 'I've been up all night, Vito.'

'So was I,' he said, then winced. 'Um . . . never mind.'

Jen growled. 'I'm ready to hate you, Ciccotelli. I worked all night while you were having hot sex. No, I think I hate you already.'

'I'll buy you crullers every day next week. From the place in my neighborhood.'

'Not good enough, but it's a start. We've charted churches in a fifty-mile radius on the soil map. Nothing that remotely resembles the church in the game.'

'Well, it was a long shot. Thanks for trying.'

'Don't you dare hang up on me, Chick. I found your picture.'

'Which picture?'

'The newspaper photo of Claire Reynolds and her lover. It was taken at a march three years ago. The woman is about thirty with light hair. She's thin. Not really any physical attributes to set her apart. I've never seen her before.'

'Damn,' Vito muttered. 'I was hoping. I wish I could come in and see it, but we need to stay here. Van Zandt could be coming out any time.'

'Can your phone receive pictures?'

'No, but Nick's can. Can you send it?'

'It's on its way.'

'Give me your phone,' Vito said to Nick, then squinted at the screen when the picture downloaded. Every muscle in his body went taut. 'Fuck.'

'Who is it?' Nick asked. He took the phone, then whistled. 'What a cold bitch.'

Jen's voice perked up. 'You recognize her, Vito?'

'It's Stacy Savard,' Vito said. 'Pfeiffer's receptionist is blackmailer number two.'

'I'll get her address and send a cruiser out right now,' Jen said.

Vito took Nick's phone and stared again at the grainy photo. 'She knew Claire was dead and she looked us in the eye and never blinked.'

'What you want to do, Vito? Go work over Savard or wait for Van Zandt?'

'Let's let the cruiser pick up Savard. I'll request a warrant for her house. If this thing with Van Zandt doesn't pan out, then blackmailer number two becomes plan B.'

Saturday, January 20, 12:45 P.M.

It was probably inadvisable, but Simon couldn't resist. If he was going to have to leave his Frasier Lewis identity behind, he might as well do it with style. Of course, if the DA's office had managed to keep Van Zandt in jail instead of allowing him out on bail, this whole opportunity would never have arisen.

It was, overall, a delicious irony. Simon had wanted the second German killed in *Behind Enemy Lines* to be skewered with a bayonet. There had been something more up-close and personal about using a bayonet. But Van Zandt had insisted on a big bang.

Simon had been worried about the sensitivity of the detonator on a sixty-year-old grenade. What if he'd set up the scene, only to find he'd purchased a dud? So, being a thorough man, he'd planned for that scenario. Simon smiled. Kyle

Lombard, being a greedy man, had offered him a volume discount.

Saturday, January 20, 12:55 P.M.

'What do you mean, *she's gone*?' Vito barked into his cell.

'I mean she's not at her apartment,' Jen said, annoyed. 'Her car is gone. A neighbor saw her leaving with a suitcase this morning. We have an APB out.'

'We tipped our hand when we asked for Lewis's file.' Vito rubbed his temples. 'Call the airports and bus stations. And can you send a cruiser out to Pfeiffer's residence?'

'We arresting him, too?'

'We just want to talk to him. Ask him to come in for questioning. We'll be in soon.'

'Van Zandt hasn't come out yet?' Jen asked.

Vito glared at the courthouse. 'He must be paying his bail with pennies.'

Jen's chuckle was brief. 'Well, we did get one hit. Stacy Savard has the same printer model in her apartment that printed Claire's letters.'

'Chick,' Nick hissed. 'Look, it's Van Zandt.'

'Gotta go, Jen. It's showtime.' Vito dropped his phone in his pocket as Van Zandt exited the courthouse, his expression cold and hard and his attorney a good twenty feet behind him. He rushed to the curb with huge ground-eating strides, his arm out to hail a cab, pushing an old man who'd stumbled into his way.

The hairs raised on the back of Vito's neck. There was something . . .

'*Nick,*' Vito said. 'That old man.'

'Fuck,' Nick said, and they jumped from the car at the same time.

'Stop! Police!' Vito shouted it and the old man looked up. For a split second, Vito found himself staring into Simon Vartanian's cold eyes.

Vartanian began to run. Really fast. Vito and Nick were in pursuit.

Then all hell broke loose when, before their eyes, Jager Van Zandt blew up.

Chapter Twenty-Three

He'd almost been caught. Simon sat in front in his vehicle, still furious. A single misstep and he'd be in the hands of the authorities right now.

And wouldn't they like to get their hands on me?

That cop Ciccotelli was smarter than Simon had thought. And more ruthless. The cops had used Van Zandt as a pawn . . . *to try to draw me out.* Had it not been so close, Simon would have found that brazen ruthlessness an admirable quality.

It had been too close. But in the grand scheme, a mere skirmish. The cops only knew of Frasier Lewis. The only people who knew he wasn't really dead, were dead.

Except the blackmailer whose amateurish tactics had drawn his parents to him. He needed to find that blackmailer and make that person pay, whoever he or she was. Then on to Susannah and Daniel. Miss and Mister Goody Two-Shoes.

That each of his siblings had two shoes was reason enough to hate them both. That they'd both become vanguards of justice made them dangerous foes.

It would soon become impossible to continue the charade that Arthur and Carol Vartanian were only on vacation, that they were indeed missing. Daniel and Susannah would never let it go. They'd dig until they found where their parents had gone. They were certainly smart enough to make the connections. And if they dug deep enough, they just might find that someone else lay under Simon's tombstone.

Simon had often wondered who inhabited that plot, who his father had found to take his place, so to speak. He'd been tempted to check for himself when he'd gone back to Dutton for the first time in twelve years, to set up his parents' little vacation and to fix their computer so that he would have ultimate access.

His father had come to him, but he'd have to go get Daniel and Susannah. He knew exactly where to find them. Daniel had a little house in Atlanta, while Susannah had an apartment in SoHo. Daniel was the 'Law,' and little Susannah was the 'Order.'

Artie should have been proud. But he hadn't been. *Because underneath that judge's robe, Arthur Vartanian was as rotten as me.* Daniel and Susannah would have to go. But first there was a little matter of payback. Because as he'd fled from the police like a common street criminal, it had registered that they'd recognized him – not as Frasier Lewis, but as the *old man*. And the only person who'd seen him as the old man and lived was . . . Dr Sophie Johannsen. His eyes narrowed. Everywhere he turned, he ran into that woman's interference.

Everything had been progressing according to plan until Sophie Johannsen began asking questions about black market artifacts. It had all unraveled from there. She knew far too much, and he wouldn't rest until she was silenced.

He cocked his jaw. Besides, she had a great face, such expression. She should have been an actress or model herself. Soon, she would be.

That he would hurt that cop Ciccotelli in the process was . . . He smiled. Bonus points.

I might even earn an extra life. Simon chuckled. His internal balance restored, he got out of his vehicle and walked into the nursing home.

Saturday, January 20, 4:15 P.M.

Liz winced when Vito and Nick came into the bullpen. 'Oh . . . guys.'

'Just some minor burns,' Vito said. 'We were lucky. The only people hurt were Van Zandt's lawyer, two pedestrians, and us. The pedestrians were treated and released.'

'The lawyer?' Liz asked.

'He'll be okay,' Nick said. 'He was twenty feet behind Van Zandt when he blew.'

Vito sat down at his desk. 'We just got grazed by a few pieces of flying shrapnel.'

'I've got Bev and Tim and a half-dozen others beating the bushes,' Liz said, 'but . . .'

Nick shook his head. 'That sucker could run on that prosthetic leg, Liz. Surprised the hell outta me. Then Van Zandt blew. That surprised me a little more.'

'What the hell happened? You were supposed to be *watching* him.' ADA Maggy Lopez rushed in and stopped short when she saw them. 'Good God.'

'Simon was waiting for Van Zandt.' Vito massaged the back of his neck. 'He dropped a grenade in the pocket of Van Zandt's overcoat. CSU's got the fragments. We're betting it matches the shrapnel we took from the kid we haven't yet identified.'

Nick sank into his chair and closed his eyes. 'I'm sorry, Maggy.'

Lopez gave both of them a once-over. 'Nothing to feel sorry about. Van Zandt probably would've gotten bail regardless of our plan. We didn't have enough to get remand. Not with all the other factors. So now what?'

Nick looked at Vito. 'Plan B? Stacy Savard.'

Vito scoffed. 'Shit. We don't even know where Savard is.'

Liz smiled. 'Yes, we do. You were at the hospital when we brought her in.'

Vito straightened in his chair. 'We have Stacy Savard? Here?'

'Yep. We found her parking her car at the airport. Apparently she was going to take whichever flight left the country first. When you're up to it, she's all yours.'

Vito smiled grimly. 'Oh, we're up to it. I can't wait to talk to that cold bitch.'

Saturday, January 20, 4:50 P.M.

Taking out Van Zandt had been harder than he'd planned, but now that he knew his adversary, taking Johannsen would be easier. He'd planned for every contingency, from a uniformed police escort to the detectives who'd stuck to her like glue. He was ready.

Simon's mouth curved. Soon a nurse would be changing Grandma's IV. Bells would ring, alarms would clang. Sweet Sophie would get a frantic phone call. A frantic *authentic* phone call. One thing he'd always admired about Johannsen was her passion for authenticity. There was a certain . . . symmetry in Sophie's fate.

Grandma was dying, so she'd come home. Because she was home, he'd met her. Because he'd met her, studied under her, he'd gained superior knowledge of the medieval world, and because of that knowledge, he'd created one hell of an authentic game. But because of the game and because of Johannsen's involvement, the police were entirely too close. He'd always planned to eliminate her when the time was right, but the proximity of the police had forced him to play his hand sooner than he'd planned, and because of *that* . . . He checked his watch. It was time. Because of *that*, Grandma was dying. Authentically.

It was one big, beautiful circle. It was fate.

He straightened abruptly. There she was, coming into the lobby from the Great Hall, dressed in a suit of armor. He hoped she'd take it off before making what would certainly be a mad dash. She was a tall woman. It would take a great deal of strength to move her in regular clothes. The armor would be an

434

unwelcome impediment, but he would deal with it if he must. He moved a little closer to the window. Soon there would be no glass between them to denigrate his entertainment experience. Soon, he'd have her in his possession, in his dungeon, where there were cameras and lights. *The better to see you die, my dear.*

Saturday, January 20, 5:00 P.M.

Stacy Savard sat at the interrogation table, her arms crossed tightly over her chest. She stared ahead sullenly until Vito and Nick came in, then looked at them with eyes dripping with pathetic despair. 'What's happened? Why have you brought me here?'

'Cut the drama, Stacy.' Vito took the chair next to hers. 'We know what you've done. We have your laptop and Claire's laptop. We know about Claire and Arthur Vartanian, and we found your fat little bank account.' He made his expression puzzled. 'What I don't get is how you could have betrayed Claire like that. You loved her.'

Stacy's face was impassive for a long moment, then she shrugged. 'I didn't love Claire. Nobody loved Claire except her parents, and that's only because they didn't know who she really was. Claire was mean . . . and a good lay. That's all.'

Nick's laugh was short and incredulous. 'That's all? So what happened, Stacy? Did you know she was blackmailing Frasier Lewis from the beginning?'

Stacy scoffed. 'Like Claire would share something like that. She was going to keep everything she got from the Vartanians for herself. She was a bitch.'

Vito shook his head, disbelieving. 'So when did you know Claire was dead?'

She narrowed her eyes. 'I want full immunity.'

Vito laughed hard, then sobered abruptly. 'No.'

Stacy sat back. 'Then you get nothing more from me.'

Anticipating just such a reaction, Nick slid a photo of the

mangled Van Zandt across the table and they watched Stacy pale.

'Who . . . who is that?'

'The last idiot who wanted immunity,' Vito said caustically.

'And the last idiot who tried to cross Frasier Lewis,' Nick said softly. 'We could let you go, you know. And tell Frasier where to find you.'

Her eyes darkened in fear. 'You wouldn't tell him. That would be murder.'

Vito sighed. 'She's got us there. But, if the story were to leak . . . It might not be until this comes to trial, but he will find out. It's too sensational to keep quiet.'

'And you'll be lookin' over your shoulder until he drops a grenade in your pocket.'

Stacy sucked in a cheek, stewing. Then she looked up. 'I was supposed to have dinner with Claire back in October, fifteen months ago. She never showed, so I went to her apartment. I had a key. I found her laptop and pictures she'd taken of 'Frasier Lewis' while they sat in the waiting room.' One side of her mouth lifted. 'One thing about Claire, she took good notes. She'd planned to write a book about it somewhere down the line. She recognized Lewis as Simon Vartanian, which she thought was odd.'

'Because he was supposed to be dead,' Vito said.

'Yeah. She researched Frasier Lewis, found out he was some guy in Iowa.'

Nick blinked at her. 'So you knew about the insurance fraud, too.'

Stacy's lips firmed stubbornly, and with a long-suffering sigh Vito put a photo of Derek Harrington with a hole in his forehead next to Van Zandt. 'You don't want to mess with Simon Vartanian, Stacy. Any more than you want to mess with us. Answer Detective Lawrence's question.'

'Yes,' she bit out. 'I knew about the insurance fraud. I found the e-mails on Claire's computer – the ones she'd sent to Simon and his father. The father's said "I know what your son did." '

'What did you think she meant?' Nick asked and she shrugged.

'That he was cheating the insurance company and that he'd faked his death. Her e-mail to Simon said 'I know who you are, Simon.' The father paid. Simon insisted she meet him, and like a stupid idiot, Claire did.'

'Where?' Vito asked tightly. 'Where did she meet him?'

'Simon mentioned meeting her outside the library where she worked. But she didn't show up for a few days, anywhere. So I made the logical assumption she was dead.'

'You sent the letters,' Nick said. 'To the library and to yourself.'

'Yes. I sent the letters.'

Vito kept thinking he'd seen his fill of sociopaths on this case, but they just kept coming. 'And you took up where she left off.'

'Only with the father, not with Simon.'

'Why not?' Nick asked and Stacy shot him an incredulous look.

'Because he was a killer. Duh. Claire was stupid. I'm not.'

'Here you are, so your intelligence isn't necessarily a fact in evidence,' Nick said mildly. But a muscle in his cheek twitched and Vito knew the calm was a thin facade.

'Because he was a killer.' Vito shook his head. 'You looked at him every time he came into your office for a checkup. You knew he wasn't Frasier Lewis. You knew he'd killed Claire Reynolds and *you never said a word*?'

Again she shrugged. 'What was the point? Claire was dead. Nothing I could do would bring her back, and obviously Arthur Vartanian could spare the money.'

Nick huffed out a chuckle. 'God, this case just keeps getting better and better. So, Stacy, tell us. What made Arthur Vartanian come to find you?'

Stacy blinked. 'He never came to find me. He just kept paying.'

'Oh, he came to find you all right. Now he's dead. We found

him and his wife buried near Claire.' Nick raised a brow. 'You wanna see the pictures?'

Stacy shook her head. 'He wanted proof that I knew his son, but he kept paying.'

Vito flicked a glance at Nick. 'How did you prove it to him, Stacy?' Vito asked.

'I sent him a picture of Simon. The one I took for Pfeiffer.'

'It was a candid photo,' Vito remembered. 'He didn't pose for it.'

'Of course not. He wouldn't let me take his picture, so I snapped one when he wasn't looking. I thought I might need it someday.'

'Okay,' Nick said quietly, 'now we're going to want your help.'

Saturday, January 20, 5:00 P.M.

'You see the skinny bald guy?' Ted the Third whispered as he and Sophie stood waving good-bye to the final tour group of the day. 'He's runs a philanthropy group.'

Sophie smiled and waved. 'I know. He told me. Three times.'

'He is a bit of a blowhard,' Ted admitted. 'But he represents lots of rich people who want to use their money to further "education and the arts." He liked you. A lot.'

'I know. It was the only time I was glad to be in this armor. He tried to pinch my ass, Ted.' She scowled, but Ted just grinned.

'You had a sword, Sophie. Look at the bright side. Next time you might have the battle-ax.' He loosened his tie. 'I think I'm going to splurge and take Darla out tonight.'

'Moshulu's or the Charthouse?' she asked, and Ted choked on a shocked laugh.

'Our idea of a splurge is Chinese takeout.' He walked away, shaking his head.

'They never go out. They don't have the money.'

Once again Sophie spun, the armor making her movement awkward. She glared up, more angry than startled this time. '*Theo.*'

'I can't remember the last time we had an evening out.' Theo tilted his head. 'Oh, wait. Yes, I can. It was just before Dad hired you.'

'Theo, if you have something to say, then for God's sake, just say it.'

'Fine. Your salary is more than what my parents bring home together.'

Stunned, Sophie stared for a moment. 'What?'

'They were so excited to hire you,' Theo said coldly. 'My mom gave up her salary. They figured a "real historian" would help them increase revenue. "Short-term sacrifice."'

He turned on his heel to walk away, but Sophie grabbed his arm. 'Theo. Wait.'

He stopped, but didn't look at her.

'I had no idea my salary was a hardship for them.' And in turn, for him. She wondered what the financial hardship meant for Theo, for his future.

'Well, now you do.'

'You graduated from high school last year. What about college?'

He stiffened. 'No money.'

Guilt swelled up within her and she pushed it back. Ted the Third had made sacrifices to keep this place going. But ultimately sacrifices were choices. 'Theo, believe it or not, what your parents pay me is less than I'd make managing a McDonald's. I could tell you I'd give the money back, but every penny I make pays for my gran's nursing home.'

He turned and she saw she'd scored a small point. 'McDonald's? Really?'

'Really. You know, rather than being angry, why don't we try to find some ways to bring more business in? More tours, new exhibits.'

His jaw tightened. 'I hate the tours. They're so . . .

embarrassing. I mean, Patty Ann's into all that theater stuff, but . . .'

'I thought it was embarrassing, too. But it reaches people, Theo. The other day when we talked, you seemed interested in building the interactive exhibit. Are you still?'

He nodded again. 'I'm good with my hands.'

'I know. You did an awesome job on the paneling in the Great Hall.' Sophie thought of Michael and his blocks and the trebuchet he'd made. 'Give me some time to think of a way for you to use your hands and help your—'

Her cell, which she'd tucked inside her bra, vibrated, making her jump. Quickly she loosened the strips that held on the breastplate. 'Help me get this off, Theo.'

One look at the caller ID drove every thought from her mind. 'It's my Gran's nursing home.' She answered, her heart thumping. 'Hello?'

'It's Fran.' Fran was the head nurse and her tone was urgent.

Sophie's thumping heart stopped. 'What's wrong?'

'Anna went into cardiac arrest and we've called an ambulance. Sophie, you need to hurry. It's bad, honey.'

Sophie's knees buckled and were it not for Theo's steadying hand she might have fallen. 'I'm on my way.' Sophie closed her phone, her hands shaking. *Think.*

Simon. Maybe it was a lie. *A trap.* Conscious of Theo's watchful eye, she dialed the nursing home, calling the main switchboard. 'Hello, it's Sophie Johannsen. I just got a call and wanted to confirm my grandmother was—'

'Sophie? This is Linda.' Another nurse. Sophie doubted even Simon Vartanian could get two nurses to lie. 'Didn't Fran call you? Get to the hospital. Now.'

'Thank you.' Sophie hung up, feeling sick. 'I have to go to the hospital.'

'I'll drive you,' Theo said.

'No. That's okay. I'll go with Officer Lyons.' She looked around, panic mounting with every wild beat of her heart. 'Where is he?'

'Sophie, why are cops following you around?' Theo asked, following her as she moved toward the lobby door as fast as her armored legs would allow.

'Later. Where is Lyons? Dammit.' She stopped at the door and looked out. It was dark outside. The minutes were ticking and Anna was dying. She'd been too late for Elle. She wouldn't allow Anna to die alone. She ripped at the Velcro that held her greaves on her shins. 'Help me get these things off. Please.'

Theo dropped to a crouch and removed the greaves. He grabbed her foot. 'Lift.'

She obeyed, balancing one hand on the cold window as he removed her boot. She squinted out the window and saw a cop, his face half turned from view. The red glow of a cigarette hovered a few inches from his mouth. Not Lyons. She looked at her watch. It was after five. *Shift change.* Theo pulled off the other boot and she raced out the door, waving behind her. 'Thanks, Theo. I'll call later.'

'Sophie, wait. You don't have any shoes on.'

'I can't go back for them. No time.'

'I'll get your shoes,' Theo said. 'It'll just take a second. Wait here.'

But there was no time. She ran toward the new officer, ignoring the shock of the cold sidewalk on her feet. It was only until she got to his cruiser. She'd get slippers at the hospital. 'Officer, I need to go to the hospital. *Now.*' She headed for the curb where his cruiser was parked, hearing his footsteps behind her.

'Dr Johannsen, *stop.* I'm under orders to wait with you until one of the detectives arrives.'

'I don't have time to wait. I have to get to the hospital.'

'Fine.' He caught up to her, took her arm. 'Slow down or you'll slip on the ice. You're no good to your grandmother if you're knocked unconscious.'

She opened her mouth to tell him to hurry, then froze. She hadn't mentioned Anna. *Simon.* She jerked her arm away. 'No.' She'd taken two steps when his arm came around her throat and he covered her mouth with a cloth. She fought like an animal, but he was big, strong, and she heard Susannah Vartanian's voice, hauntingly quiet. *Simon was bigger.* 'No.' But the word was muffled by the cloth and her vision began to blur.

Fight. Scream. But her body was no longer obeying her command. Her scream was shrill and loud and totally inside her own head. No one could hear her.

He was dragging her. She fought to turn her head. To see where he was taking her, but she couldn't. She heard a door sliding open and suddenly pain was radiating up her spine. She could feel, but she could move nothing more than her eyes as she lay on her back looking out the side door of a van.

She strained past the blurred double images to see Theo come up behind him. *Her shoes.* Theo was holding her shoes. The darting of her eyes must have alerted Simon because Theo Albright was leveled with a single blow of Simon's fist to his head.

Then they were moving. The van thumped as it ran over something big, then sped from the lot with a squeal of tires. *Vito,* she thought, fighting the pull of whatever had been on that rag. *I'm sorry.* Then there was nothing but darkness.

Chapter Twenty-Four

Saturday, January 20, 5:30 P.M.

Stacy Savard stared at them defiantly. 'I'm not talking to him. You can't make me. I'll end up like that.' She shoved the photos. 'No fucking way. You've got to be crazy.'

Vito swallowed back his anger and disgust. 'You could have reported Simon Vartanian at any time and avoided the deaths of more than ten people. They're on your head. So you will help us. We want you to draw Simon out into the open.'

'Through the telephone,' Nick added calmly. 'You don't have to talk to him in person. And if you don't choose to help . . . Well, we can't always control the press.'

Savard cocked her jaw. 'I don't seem to have much choice. What do I say to him?'

Nick's smile wasn't pleasant. 'You always have a choice, Miss Savard. This might be your first good one. You noted in his file that Simon ordered more silicone lubricant.'

'Two days ago. He normally gets it from one of those specialty places, but he was almost out, so he ordered some through us because we can get it faster. So?'

'So,' Nick said, 'you're going with us to Pfeiffer's office, where you'll call him from the office phone and tell him his order is ready.'

'But the office is closed today,' she said, her voice starting to shake.

'Dr Pfeiffer will open it up,' Vito told her. 'He's very eager to help us. Setting a trap with the lubricant was his idea, actually.'

He enjoyed seeing her jaw drop. 'How do you think we found you so quickly, Stacy? We had the airports looking for you, but you didn't have a reservation and you never even made it to the check-in counter. Pfeiffer had been thinking through things and came to the conclusion you were likely involved. So he followed you this morning and when you got to the airport, he called us.'

The door opened and Liz looked in, her expression unreadable. 'Detectives?'

Vito and Nick stood, and Nick fired the parting shot. 'Practice your best receptionist voice, Stacy,' he said mildly. 'Because Vartanian's no fool. He'll spot a nervous twitch a mile away.' Nick shut the door when they were on the other side of the glass.

'Do you hear all that?' Vito asked.

Nick shook his head. 'What a piece of work. Prison's just going to hone her edge.'

'Vito,' Jen whispered harshly.

Vito turned from the window and his blood went cold. Jen was white as a sheet and Liz's expression was no longer unreadable but stark with controlled fear.

'It's Sophie,' Liz said. 'Her grandmother was rushed to the hospital. She had a heart attack.'

Vito forced himself to stay calm. 'I'll go to the museum and drive her to the hospital.'

Liz caught his arm and held tight when he tried to move past her. 'No, Vito. Listen to me. Emergency personnel got a call to the Albright Museum. They found the Albright boy unconscious on the street in front of the museum.' She visibly steeled herself. 'And they found Officer Lyons dead in the back seat of his cruiser.'

Vito opened his mouth but nothing came out.

'And Sophie?' Nick asked hoarsely.

Liz was trembling. 'Witnesses saw her being forced into a white van before it backed up over the Albright boy and drove away. Sophie's gone.'

Vito could only hear the rush of his own blood as his heart went from a dead stop to clubbing out of his chest. 'He's got her, then,' he whispered.

'Yes,' Liz whispered back. 'I'm sorry, Vito.'

Numbly he looked back through the glass and had to restrain the unholy need to put his hands on Savard and choke her dead. 'She knew he was a killer and she said nothing.' He was breathing hard, every word ripped from his throat. 'Now it's too late. We can't even use her to draw him. He's got what he wants. He's got Sophie.'

Nick grabbed his other arm and squeezed until Vito turned to him. 'Vito, calm down and think. Simon still needs that lubricant. It could still work. We have to try.'

Vito nodded, still numb. But in his heart he knew better. He'd seen Simon's eyes, right before Van Zandt died. They'd been cold, calculating. *Like walking into a cage with a cobra*, Pfeiffer had said. And now Sophie was in that cage.

Saturday, January 20, 6:20 P.M.

Simon's cell phone rang. Frowning at the caller ID, he cautiously answered. 'Hello?'

'Mr Lewis, this is Stacy Savard, from Dr Pfeiffer's office.'

Simon sucked in his cheeks. The office wasn't open on the weekends. 'Yes?'

'Dr Pfeiffer's had a family emergency and the office is going to be closed for about a week. He and I are here, taking care of last-minute details. I wanted to tell you your silicone lubricant came in.'

Simon almost laughed. 'I'm a bit busy right now. I'll come in on Monday.'

'But we'll be closed on Monday. We'll be closed all week. If you want the lubricant, you have to come in tonight. I'd hate for you to run out.'

She was good, Simon had to admit, but there was the

slightest quaver in her voice. 'I'll find another source. I may be moving soon anyway.' He hung up before she could say another word, chuckling out loud now. Savard was cooperating with the cops, any idiot could figure that out.

'Your boyfriend is really smart,' Simon called behind him. 'But I'm smarter.' There was no response. If she wasn't awake already, she'd be waking up soon, he knew, but he'd have no further trouble from her. He'd pulled over to change his license plates and tie her wrists and ankles once he got away from the main roads.

Stacy Savard hung up the phone, her hands shaking. 'I did my best.'

'Your best wasn't good enough,' Nick snapped. 'He knew.'

Vito dragged his hands down his face as two uniformed cops took Stacy Savard back to the station in handcuffs. 'I didn't think it would work.'

Pfeiffer stood, wringing his hands. 'I'm sorry. I was hoping it would.'

'You've been a big help, Doctor,' Nick said kindly. 'We do appreciate it.'

Pfeiffer nodded, looking at Savard as she was taken through the door. 'I can't believe I shared this office with her for so long and never knew her. I kept hoping I'd been mistaken. That's why I didn't say anything when you were here yesterday. I would've hated to point the finger and have been wrong.'

Vito wished Pfeiffer had just pointed the finger, but he said nothing.

'So what next?' Nick asked when they were back in his car.

'We go back to the beginning,' Vito said grimly. 'There's *something* we've missed.' He stared out the window. 'And we pray Sophie can hold on until we find her.'

Saturday, January 20, 8:15 P.M.

'We got him on tape,' Brent said, coming into the conference room with a CD in his hand. He handed it to Jen. 'Sonofabitch tampered with the old lady's IV.'

Vito had remembered the camera he'd left at Anna's bedside as he and Nick had been driving back from Pfeiffer's office. Now he stood behind Jen's chair as she inserted the CD containing the camera's footage into her laptop. Nick and Liz stood to his right, Brent came to stand on his left. Katherine stayed seated, pale and numb.

Vito hadn't been able to meet her eyes. He'd promised her he'd take care of Sophie. And he hadn't. He should have kept Sophie under lock and key until Simon was caught. He should have done a lot of things. But he hadn't and Sophie was gone. Simon Vartanian had her and they all knew what Simon Vartanian could do.

He had to stop thinking like that. He'd go quietly insane. *So focus, Chick. And find the thing you missed.*

Brent slanted him a look. 'Simon shows up five hours into the tape. The camera is motion activated. The first two hours are you and Sophie with the grandmother last night. I fast-forwarded through that visit and through the nurses' visits, blood pressure checks, medicine, meals. There's a card game in there, too.'

Vito looked at him. 'A card game?'

'Some nurse came in with a deck about ten a.m. this morning. Said it was time for their daily game. Sophie's grandmother lost and called the nurse mean.'

'Was the nurse's name Marco?'

'Yeah. She was also the one that saved the old lady's life.'

'Well, at least her grandmother wasn't being abused by the nurses.' Vito shook his head. 'Anna just didn't like losing at cards.'

'I've got it cued,' Jen said. They watched Simon Vartanian come into Anna's room and sit at her bed. He was dressed as the old man.

'He must have come straight from blowing up Van Zandt,' Nick murmured.

'Busy day,' Jen said flatly. 'Dammit.'

Brent leaned over Jen and fast-forwarded the tape. 'He tells her he's from the opera society. That Sophie sent him. He calls her by name. They chat for twenty minutes, until the grandmother falls asleep. Here's where he tampers with the IV.'

On the tape, Simon pulled a syringe from his pocket and injected it into the IV the nurse had left prepped next to her bed. He pocketed the syringe, checked the IV that currently dripped, then checked his watch.

'A very simple and effective time delay,' Jen said dully. 'It gives him time to get away from the nursing home and lie in wait for Sophie at the hospital.'

Once again, Simon had thought of everything.

Which once again made Vito's blood run cold.

Brent cleared his throat. 'The nurse comes in to change the IV.' Jen fast-forwarded and again they watched. It was Marco again, and she recorded Anna's vitals on her chart after changing the IV. The screen went dark, then a second later was full of activity as Marco ran back in. The cardiac monitor was beeping and Anna was jerking in pain. Marco leaned close to Anna's mouth.

'The nurse said that Anna was saying that it burned,' Liz said. 'The nurse is good. She took one look at the cardiac monitor and recognized the signs of potassium chloride overdose. She gave her an injection of bicarb. Stopped the heart attack.'

'And saved Anna's life,' Vito murmured, swallowing hard.

'Marco thought she'd made a mistake on the IV,' Liz said. 'She was prepared to face disciplinary actions, even dismissal. But she said she couldn't lie, that if she'd harmed a patient, she'd accept accountability.'

Vito sighed. 'Does she know about the camera?'

'No,' Liz said. 'Telling her will ease her mind about her own culpability.'

DIE FOR ME

'And will let her know Sophie didn't trust her,' Vito finished. 'But she should know anyway. So should Sophie's family. I'll go by the hospital in a little while.' He sat down in his chair at the head of the table. At the beginning of this case he'd welcomed the responsibility for leading an investigation of this magnitude. Now the responsibility hung around his neck like a lead weight. The investigation was his. Where it went from here would be on him. That meant what happened to Sophie was on him as well.

'So what are we missing?' Vito demanded. 'We need details.'

'Isolated buildings with elevators built on quarry soil,' Jen said.

'Identities of the old woman and the man at the end of the first row,' Nick added.

Liz pursed her lips. 'That damn field,' she said and Vito narrowed his eyes.

'You mean why *that* field?' he asked and Liz nodded.

'We never answered that question, Vito. Why that field? How did he pick it?'

'Winchester, the old postal worker who owns that land, said it had been owned by his aunt.' Vito swiveled in his chair to look at the whiteboard. 'The old woman buried next to Claire Reynolds can't be Winchester's aunt.'

'Because Winchester's aunt didn't die until October of this year,' Nick continued. 'This old lady died a year earlier.'

'She was from Europe,' Katherine said. They were the first words she'd uttered since entering the room. 'I had her dental work analyzed and the report came back late yesterday. Her fillings are an amalgam that was never used in this country but was common in Germany in the fifties.' She shook her head. 'I can't see how that's going to help you. Thousands of people emigrated from that part of the world after the war.'

'It's a piece we didn't have before,' Vito said. 'Let's go out and see Harlan Winchester again. Let's find everything we can on his aunt. We need something to tie that land to Simon, and right now the only thing that ties to the land is the aunt.'

449

Liz put her hand on his shoulder. 'I have a better idea. Nick and I will go see Winchester. You go see Sophie's family.'

Vito's chin came up. 'Liz, I need to do this.'

Liz's smile was kind but firm. 'Don't make me take this case, Vito.'

Vito opened his mouth, then closed it. 'You're about to knock me off my bucket,' he said quietly, remembering Sophie and Dante.

'It's a strange word association, but yeah, I guess it works.' Liz lifted her brows. 'Your emotions are running high. Go home. Recharge. That's an order.'

Vito stood up. 'Okay. But only for tonight. Tomorrow morning I'm back here. If I don't do something to find her, I'll go crazy, Liz.'

'I know. Trust us, Vito. We'll leave no stone unturned.' She looked over at Jen. 'You were here all last night. You go home, too.'

'I'm not going to fight you,' Jen said, closing up her laptop. 'But I'm not sure I can even get home. I think I'll just crash in the crib for a while.' She gave Vito a hard hug on her way out. 'Don't lose hope.'

'Nick, you're with me,' Liz said. 'I'll get my coat.'

'I call shotgun,' Nick said, then paused next to Vito. 'Just sleep, Chick,' he muttered. 'Don't think. You think too damn much.' Then he and Liz were gone.

Brent hesitated, then gave Vito a CD in a plastic case. 'I thought you'd want a copy.' One side of his mouth lifted sadly. 'You have a hell of a set of pipes, Ciccotelli. There wasn't a dry eye on the IT floor when I was viewing that part of the tape.'

Vito's eyes burned. 'Thank you.' Then Brent was gone and it was just him and Katherine. Not caring if she saw, he swiped at his eyes with the heels of his hands. 'Katherine, I don't know what to say.'

'Neither do I, except that I'm sorry.'

He blinked at her. 'You're sorry?'

'I damaged our friendship this week more than I thought.

Because I hurt you before, you're thinking I blame you for this, and nothing could be further from the truth.'

Vito turned the CD over and over in his hands. 'You should. I blame myself.'

'And I blame myself for bringing her in in the first place.'

'All I can see in my mind are all his victims.'

'I know,' she whispered harshly.

He looked at her then. Her eyes were haunted. She'd done twelve autopsies this week, each one a victim of Simon Vartanian. 'You understand better than anyone.'

She nodded. 'I also know Sophie Johannsen. If there's a way to survive, she will. And you have to hold on to that, because right now it's all we have.'

Saturday, January 20, 9:15 P.M.

Sophie was waking up. She lifted her eyelids and swept her gaze from one edge of her peripheral vision to the other, without moving her head. Above her was waffleboard. It was, she knew from all those times she'd accompanied Anna to recording studios, used for soundproofing and controlling sound quality. The walls were covered with rock. Whether it was real or not was hard to tell. The torches in wall sconces appeared real enough, their flickering flames creating shadows on shadows.

She smelled death. And she remembered the screams. Greg Sanders had died here. As had so many others. *So will you.* She gritted her teeth. *Not if I have an ounce of strength left.* She had far too much to live for to give up.

It was a good thought, but pragmatically she was bound, hands and feet, and was lying on a wooden table. She had clothes, but they weren't the ones she'd been wearing. She wore a dress or robes. She heard footsteps and quickly closed her eyes.

'No need to pretend, Sophie. I know you're awake.' He had a soft, cultured drawl. 'Open your eyes now. Look at me.'

Still she kept her eyes closed. The longer she could put off a confrontation, the more time she'd give Vito to find her. Because he would find her. Of that she was sure. Where and what shape she'd be in were the only questions in her mind.

'Sophie,' he crooned. She could feel his breath wash over her face and fought not to flinch. She felt the breeze his body made when he straightened. 'You're very good.' Because she was anticipating it, she controlled the flinch when he pinched her arm. He chuckled. 'I'll give you a few more hours, but only because I need to recharge my circuits.' He'd said the last few words with an almost self-deprecating amusement.

'Once I'm all charged up, I'll be fit and ready to roll for another thirty hours. Just imagine all the *fun* we can have in thirty hours, Sophie.' He walked away chuckling, and Sophie prayed he didn't see the shiver she couldn't control.

Saturday, January 20, 9:30 P.M.

'Hi, Anna.' Vito sat in the chair next to her bed in the cardiac intensive care unit. Anna was barely lucid, but her good eye flickered. 'It's okay,' he said. 'I understand if you can't talk. I just came to see how you were.'

Her eye moved toward the door and her lips trembled, but no words came out. She was looking for Sophie, and Vito didn't have the heart to tell her the truth. 'She had a long day. She fell asleep.' It wasn't untrue. Witnesses said she'd been dragged to the white van in which she was taken, limp as if she'd been drugged. Vito hoped she had been and that she still slept. Every hour she slept gave them another hour to find her.

'Who are you?'

Vito turned to find a shorter, younger version of Anna in the open door. That, he guessed, would be Freya. He patted Anna's hand. 'I'll come back when I can, Anna.'

'I said, *who are you*?' Freya's voice was shrill, but under it Vito heard panic.

Panic he understood. 'I'm Vito Ciccotelli, a friend of Anna's. And Sophie's.'

A man with a thin ring of hair around the back of his head appeared behind Freya, fear and hope warring in his eyes. This would be Uncle Harry.

The man confirmed it. 'I'm Harry Smith, Sophie's uncle. You're her cop.'

Her cop. Vito's heart broke a little more. 'Let's find a place to talk.'

'Sophie?' Harry said when they'd sat down in a small family waiting room.

Vito looked at his hands, then back up. 'She's still missing.'

Harry shook his head. 'I don't understand. Why would anyone hurt our Sophie?'

Vito watched the corner of Freya's mouth tighten. A tiny movement, probably caused by stress. He wasn't sure. What he did know was that the man before him was the closest thing Sophie had ever had to a real father and he deserved to know the truth.

'Sophie was helping us with a case. It's gotten some press coverage.'

Harry's eyes narrowed. 'The graves the old man discovered with a metal detector?'

'That's the one. For the last week we've been tracking the man who killed all those people.' He drew a breath. 'We have reason to believe he abducted Sophie.'

Harry paled. 'My God. They found nine bodies up there.'

Now there were five more, perhaps six considering Alan Brewster had never been found. But Harry didn't need to know that. 'We're doing everything we can to find her.'

'My mother's heart attack,' Freya said slowly. 'It happened not an hour before Sophie was taken. The timing can't be coincidental.'

Vito thought of the look on Nurse Marco's face when he'd

told her about the tape and the tampering. She'd been, as he'd anticipated, both hurt and relieved. He wondered what Freya Smith's response would be. 'We know it wasn't. The killer tampered with your mother's IV, injected a high concentration of potassium chloride.' Probably a coarse grade, Jen had thought. The kind used to melt ice on roofs and streets, available at any hardware store this time of year.

Freya's mouth pressed to a hard line. 'He tried to kill my mother. To get to *Sophie*.'

Vito frowned, not at the words, but by the way in which she said them. Apparently Harry was as well. An expression of appalled shock crossed his face.

'Freya, Sophie didn't cause this.' When Freya said nothing, Harry rose unsteadily to his feet. 'Freya? Sophie's gone. A man who killed nine people has our Sophie.'

Freya began to cry. 'Your Sophie,' she spat. 'Always *your* Sophie.' She looked up at him. 'You have two daughters, Harry. What about them?'

'I love Paula and Nina,' he said, his shock becoming anger. 'How dare you insinuate otherwise? But Paula and Nina have always had us. Sophie had no one.'

Freya's face contorted. '*Sophie had Anna.*'

Harry paled further, then dark red stained his cheekbones as realization began to dawn. 'I always thought it was because of Lena. That you couldn't love Sophie because she was Lena's. But it was because of Anna. Because Anna took her in.'

Freya was sobbing now. 'She gave up everything for that girl. Her house, her career. She never stayed home for us. But for Sophie . . . Everything was for Sophie. And now my mother's lying in there, *dying*.' She choked on a sob. 'Because of *Sophie*.'

Vito let out a breath. Freya the Good wasn't so good.

'My God, Freya,' Harry said quietly. 'Who are you?'

She buried her face in her hands. 'Go away, Harry. Just go away.'

Shaking, Harry walked outside the little waiting room and slumped against the wall. With a look of bewildered contempt at the sobbing Freya, Vito joined him. Harry's eyes were closed, his face drawn. 'I never understood before tonight.'

'You were wrong about something,' Vito said softly.

Harry swallowed hard, but opened his eyes. 'What's that?'

'Sophie didn't have "no one." She had you. She told me you were her real father, that she didn't think she'd ever told you that before.'

Harry's throat worked. 'Thank you,' he said hoarsely.

Vito squared his shoulders. 'She had you and Anna. And now she has me. And I'm going to find her.' His own throat closed, but he forced the words out. 'And I'll love her, Harry, and give her the home she's always wanted. You have my word.'

Harry held his gaze, weighing both the promise Vito had made and his own response. 'I told her that there was someone out there for her. That she just needed to be patient and wait.'

Patient and wait. Patience wasn't something Vito had a whole lot of right now. He knew Liz had told him to go home, but he couldn't. He owed Sophie more than patience and waiting. 'I'll call you as soon as I know something,' Vito said. 'When I've found her.'

Vito walked a few steps, then thought again of the tape. 'Anna's nurse, Lucy Marco? Her quick thinking saved Anna's life.'

Harry closed his eyes. 'We yelled at her,' he murmured. 'She told us she'd made a mistake with Anna's IV and we yelled at her. I promise I'll make that right.'

Vito had expected no other reply. 'Good. You should also know that the young man whose father owns the museum risked his life to stop the man who took Sophie.'

Harry's eyes blinked open. 'You mean Theo Four? Sophie didn't think he liked her.'

Vito thought about the worry in the eyes of all the Al-brights, both for Theo, who'd sustained serious internal injuries when Simon had backed over him with his van, and for Sophie. 'They all like her, Harry. They're terrified for her.'

Harry nodded unsteadily. 'Theo. Will he be all right?'

'They hope so. It's touch and go.'

Again he nodded. 'Do they need . . . anything?'

Vito sighed. 'Insurance. They didn't have any. No money.' *Insurance*. Simon had stolen his. Vito sucked in a breath as it hit him like a sucker punch. In all the flash of this case he'd forgotten the most fundamental principle. *Follow the money*.

'What?' Harry grabbed his arm, panicked. 'What?'

Vito clasped the older man's shoulder. 'I had a thought. I have to go.' Then he took off for the elevator, dialing ADA Maggy Lopez as he ran.

Saturday, January 20, 9:50 P.M.

He'd plugged his leg into the wall just in time. He'd been so busy lately, he'd run the battery until it was almost dead. It would take hours to fully charge. He had other legs, but none provided the same range of motion or reliability of movement as the microprocessor he'd acquired from participation in Pfeiffer's study, and he had the feeling killing Sophie Johannsen would require that he have a physical edge.

He thought about her in full costume, swinging that battleax over her head. No fragile flower, she. Yes, he'd need every advantage Pfeiffer's unit could give him.

Sitting on the bed in his studio, he paused, considering the issue of Dr Pfeiffer. Pfeiffer and that nurse of his were helping the cops. It was the only explanation for the phone call he'd received. Come and get your lubricant. Ha. He'd honestly thought better of Ciccotelli than that. It was a damn good thing he hadn't allowed Pfeiffer's nurse to photograph him. Otherwise, Ciccotelli would also know his true face. That could present problems the next time he chose to surface with a new life.

With the death of Sophie Johannsen, all that would be left were the old man's spawn. He smiled, suddenly eager for a family reunion. Especially Daniel. He looked at the trap on the table next to his unfinished matrix. That his beautifully planned graveyard would go unfinished gnawed at him. He would have to make up for it by finishing what his brother had started so many years ago. He'd dreamed of his revenge so many times . . . Maybe he'd dream of Daniel snared like an animal tonight.

But he was too restless to sleep. Had his leg been charged, he'd go for a run. He'd need to work off this nervous energy another way, and he had just the right thing. Pulling on his old leg, he crossed to the doors set into the stairwell. Opening them, he smiled. Brewster lay curled in a fetal ball, bound hands and feet. But he breathed.

'Have you given up hope yet, Brewster?'

The bound man's eyelids flickered, but he made not the slightest noise. Not even a whimper. He could take Brewster standing one-legged in a hurricane. But he had other plans for Alan Brewster. 'You know, Alan, I've never properly thanked you. You were the hub that brought my support staff together. How fortuitous that your name was one of the first I found when I searched for experts in medieval warfare. And how fortuitous that you associate with such . . . helpful merchants.' He pulled Brewster so that he sat up, his back propped against the wall.

'Thank you, by the way, for telling me about Dr Johannsen, back from France and – how did you put it? A most able assistant. You were quite right. I found her expertise most helpful. Of course, our view on her specific expertise is quite different. I'm glad you were too busy reveling in the baser thoughts to fully utilize her academic assets.'

He stood looking Brewster over, framing the scene in his mind. Van Zandt had been right about needing a regal queen, and after much consideration, he'd agreed VZ was right about the flail scene too. He needed something more dramatic.

VZ had wanted to see someone explode. Simon smiled. And he'd given VZ his wish, up close and personal. This time, he'd capture it on tape.

Saturday, January 20, 9:55 P.M.

Vito caught up with Maggy Lopez as she was entering the precinct. 'Maggy. Thanks for coming.' He took her elbow and hastened her toward the elevator. 'We have to hurry. He's had Sophie for five hours now.' And he was using every ounce of concentration not to think about what Simon could have done to her in those five hours.

Maggy was jogging to keep up with him. 'I'm gonna break my ankle. Slow down.'

He slowed a little, chafing at every minute that slipped away. 'I need your help.'

'I figured that out.' She drew a breath when they stopped at the elevator. 'Exactly what do you need, Vito?'

The elevator doors opened and he ushered her in. 'I need access to Simon Vartanian's financial records.'

She nodded. 'Okay. I'll get a warrant started, using all the same aliases we used to get his medical records from Pfeiffer.' Her eyes narrowed. 'But you could have asked me to do that on the phone. What do you want, Vito?'

The elevator dinged and he tugged her into the hall outside the homicide bullpen. Maggie stopped and yanked her arm away. 'Stop it. What do you want, Vito?'

He drew a breath. 'We can't wait for a warrant, Maggy. There's no time. Simon bought things. He had to have a money source. I have to find that source.'

'So we subpoena bank records, canceled checks.' She frowned at him. 'Legally.'

'I don't have canceled checks. I don't have a single thing he bought. Dammit,' Vito hissed. 'He's had Sophie for *five hours*. If these aren't exigent circumstances, I don't know what the hell is. You know people who can get this information quickly. Please.'

She faltered. 'Vito . . . last time I helped you, a man died.'

Vito struggled for calm. 'You said Van Zandt would have made bail anyway. Besides, he deserved to die. *Sophie doesn't.*'

She closed her eyes. 'You don't get to decide who lives and who dies, Vito.'

Vito grabbed her shoulders and her eyes flew open. Ignoring the warning flare in her eyes, he tightened his grip. 'If I don't find her, he will torture and kill her. I'm begging you, Maggy. Please. Anything you can do. *Please.*'

'God, Vito.' He held his breath as indecision warred in her eyes, then she sighed. 'Fine. I'll make some calls.'

He exhaled slowly, able to breathe once more. 'Thank you.'

'Don't thank me yet,' she said darkly and pushed past him into the bullpen.

Brent Yelton was waiting for them at Vito's desk. 'I got here as fast as I could.'

Maggy shot Vito a glare. 'Your own hacker? Pretty sure of yourself, hotshot.'

Vito refused to feel guilty. 'You can use Nick's desk, Maggy.'

Maggy sat, muttering to herself as she dug her Palm Pilot from her purse.

Brent gave a satisfied nod. 'What do you need me to hack?'

He sounded so eager that Vito almost smiled. 'I don't know yet. I've been wracking my brain trying to remember something he bought.'

'He bought lubricant from the doctor,' Brent said, but Vito shook his head.

'He always paid Pfeiffer in cash. Co-pays and lubricants. I checked that on my way over. Can't we look up all the area banks? Maybe he had a checking account.'

Brent puffed out his cheeks. 'It would be easier if we knew where to start. Bank hacking is delicate work. It'll take time. It'd be easier to check the credit bureaus to see if he has a credit card.'

Maggy groaned. 'I don't want to hear any of this.' She got up and moved to another desk, out of earshot. But she had her cell in her hand and was making calls.

That was something, Vito supposed.

Brent opened his laptop. 'How did oRo pay him?'

'They hadn't yet. Van Zandt said he wouldn't get any royalties for three months.' Vito unlocked his desk drawer and found the Pfeiffer medical file. 'Here's the Social Security number he gave Pfeiffer. Search all his aliases.'

Brent looked up, sympathy on his face. 'Go away, Vito.'

Vito's shoulders sagged. 'I'm sorry. I'm telling you what you already know.'

'Get some coffee.' Brent's mouth quirked up. 'I take two sugars.'

Vito turned around – and ran straight into Jen. She bounced, landing on her heels. 'What are you doing here?' she demanded. Her hair was sticking out at all angles and she looked like she'd just woken up. Her eyes narrowed. 'What are you up to?'

'Following the money,' he said grimly, 'like I should have been doing all along. What are you doing here?'

Jen looked over her shoulder, and it was then Vito noticed the two young people who'd followed her in. 'Meet Marta and Spandan. They're Sophie's grad students.'

Marta was a petite young woman with dark hair and a tear-stained face. She gripped the arm of a young Indian man with scared eyes. 'We saw it on the news,' Marta said, trembling. 'The shooting outside the Albright. And Dr J . . . Somebody took her.'

'We came as soon as we heard,' Spandan said. 'My God. We can't believe it.'

'The desk sergeant called Liz and she called me.' Jen gestured to some chairs and the students sat down. 'This is Detective Ciccotelli. Tell him what you told me.'

'The reporter,' Spandan started unsteadily, 'said Dr J was helping the police with a case. Your case, Detective. She said it involved all those graves in the field and that Greg Sanders was the last victim.' He swallowed. 'She said his limbs had been amputated.'

Vito shot a frustrated look at Jen and she shrugged. 'We knew we couldn't keep the lid on it forever, Chick. We're lucky it took the press this long to connect the dots.' She gave Spandan a nod of encouragement. 'Keep going.'

'We work with Dr J on Sundays. At the museum.'

'We talked about amputation as a medieval punishment for theft,' Marta burst out. 'Hand and the opposite foot. Then she's kidnapped. We had to come and tell you.'

Vito opened his mouth but no sound came out and no breath went in. 'Oh my God,' he whispered. 'I never got a chance to ask her about the brand or the amputations or the church. If I'd asked her . . .'

'Don't go there, Vito,' Jen snapped. 'It doesn't help.'

'Brand?' Spandan asked, frowning. 'We didn't talk about branding.'

'One of her students did,' Vito said, making himself breathe. 'It wasn't you two?'

Both students shook their heads. 'There are four of us,' Marta said. 'We couldn't find Bruce or John, so we just came ourselves.'

'John was the name Sophie mentioned. John . . .' Vito closed his eyes. 'Trapper.'

Jen sighed. 'Hell.'

'Do you know where John lives?' Vito asked, but again they shook their heads. 'What does he drive?'

'A white van,' Spandan said immediately. 'He gave Dr J a ride Tuesday night.'

'Because her bike had been tampered with.' *Breathe. Think.* Then a piece of the puzzle fell into place. 'If he was a student, he'd have to pay tuition.' He turned to Brent.

Brent was typing. 'Already on it. It would help to know his student number.'

'We don't know each other's numbers,' Spandan said. 'But

461

the library would have it. He'd need it to check out books.'

'I'll call the library,' Brent said. 'But they're probably closed.'

Maggy rose from where she'd been sitting. 'Perhaps our guests would like a snack.'

Jen's brows lifted and understanding filled her eyes. 'I'll take them to the cafeteria.'

Marta shook her head violently. 'No, I couldn't eat a bite.'

'They want us to leave,' Spandan murmured. He looked at Vito. 'We'll go back to campus. Please call us as soon as you find her.'

Brent waited until they were gone. 'Library's closed. You want me to find a way in?'

Jen raised her hand. 'Wait. Liz had Beverly and Tim run a check on John Trapper. Bev called and told me he checked out, that his medical file listed him as confined to a wheelchair.'

'But we know Simon can change medical files,' Vito said. 'If Bev and Tim have seen his medical file, they'll have whatever Social he's been using. If he paid tuition or for anything at the university, we can track it to his bank.'

'I'll call them,' Jen said and sat down at an unoccupied desk as Maggy Lopez approached, her expression sober.

'I've got a name at the IRS. Vito, you need to be clear on what happens from here. This is an unauthorized search. Anything we find from this point is fruit from the poisoned tree. It won't be admissible in court. If you apprehend Simon Vartanian based on what we find next, he could walk on thirteen murders.'

Vito met her eyes. 'Let's just make sure it's not fourteen.'

Chapter Twenty-Five

Saturday, January 20, 10:30 P.M.

Sophie's body ached. Every one of her muscles was tensed beyond the ability of meditation to relax. There had been an explosion, so loud her ears still rang, so hard that some of the rock had fallen from the walls. She'd quelled the scream before it escaped her throat, but she hadn't been able to hide the reflexive tensing of her body. If Simon Vartanian came down now, he'd know she was awake.

So she had to relax. She thought of soothing music. She thought of Vito's *Che faro*. Remembering the way he'd looked as he sang to Anna . . . *Anna. Please be alive, Gran. Please be safe.*

She prayed for Anna. She prayed that Simon had died in whatever exploded.

The ceiling above her head creaked, loud and long, and her heart sank. Simon wasn't dead. He was walking around up there. So she prayed that he would stay where he was, at least until the tears that seeped from her closed eyes dried.

Saturday, January 20, 11:45 P.M.

Liz set a box down hard on Vito's desk. 'Vito, I thought I told you to go home.'

She frowned at Maggy who sat at Nick's desk and at Jen who'd pulled a chair up to Vito's desk and propped her feet on the edge, her laptop on her thighs. Brent had assumed a similar pose and power cords crisscrossed their legs.

'And you three,' Liz accused, 'encouraging him, against my orders.'

Jen shrugged. 'He got crullers.' She nudged the box with her toe. 'Have one.'

Nick came in with another big evidence box. 'Hey, crullers. I'm starved.'

Liz's sigh was exasperated, and had they not found what they'd been looking for, it would not have boded well at all. 'Okay, so what's going on here?'

Vito looked up from his computer screen. 'He's a network engineer.'

Liz shook her head as if to clear it. '*Who's* a *what?*'

'Simon Vartanian is a network engineer.' Vito pulled a sheet of paper from the printer. 'We got into his tax records.'

Liz frowned. 'How? Or don't I want to know?'

Jen shrugged. 'Brent had a friendly conversation with a fellow computer geek who happens to work for the IRS.'

'Who happened to be a friend of a friend of a friend,' Brent said with a smile at Maggy. 'We got the Social Security number Simon used when he enrolled at Sophie's college as John Trapper. He paid his college tuition by check and that checking account had a number of deposits over the last year. Trapper had his own business setting up computer networks.'

Vito handed Liz the paper. 'John Trapper was issued 1099 forms by twenty firms last year.' He shot Liz an ironic look. 'He was a frickin' consultant.'

Vito could see the wheels turning in Liz's mind. 'Who didn't work for free,' she said.

'No.' Vito smiled grimly. 'Not by a long shot.'

'Vito was wondering where Simon was getting all his money,' Jen said. 'He was getting his medical care by stealing Frasier Lewis's medical benefits. But Simon had to have a place to live, some pretty expensive computer equipment, and cash to buy his goodies from Kyle Lombard. Claire didn't have any money, so he didn't steal it from her and he didn't steal it from his parents. So what's he been living on?'

'Follow the money,' Nick mused with his mouth full of cruller. 'Smart.'

'Okay,' Liz said. 'I'm hooked. What does a network engineer do, exactly?'

'Well, he sets up networks,' Brent said. 'Connects computers in an office to each other and to other systems. All these computers are hooked into the PD's network. There are files on shared servers you can see if you have access. There are databases you can search, if you have access. The key here is access.'

Liz pulled a doughnut from the box. 'Keep talking, Brent. You haven't lost me yet.'

'Big companies like Philly PD have an internal IT department to set up the networks and make sure everybody can get to the information they need. E-mail accounts, et cetera. But you gotta make sure people have access on a need-to-know basis. Everybody can download medical insurance forms from HR, but a mail clerk shouldn't get access to AFIS. Jen gets access because she needs to run fingerprints.'

'Big companies have IT departments,' Vito said. 'Little companies that have ten employees still need a network, but they hire a consultant to set it up.'

'And Simon was one of these consultants.' Liz nodded. 'I'm guessing that Simon didn't limit his evil deed-doing to his art. He stole from these companies?'

Brent smiled. 'Not from the companies. From their clients. Every network has an administrator, the guy who sets up who gets access to what. We're guessing Simon left a back door open in some or all of these companies' networks, giving himself admin power. He could go back into their systems at any time to see anything on anybody.'

'Like financials,' Nick said. 'The models – Warren and Brittany, Bill Melville and Greg Sanders. That's how he knew they were desperate for cash. Sonofabitch.'

Vito tapped his printout. 'Twenty companies hired Frasier Lewis. Among them are six investment brokers, three realtors, and two medical insurance companies.'

'But now we're stuck,' Maggy said. 'We've been checking these companies for anything that links them to Vartanian or one of our victims, but so far, nothing has.'

'God.' Liz took the paper from Vito's hands. 'Simon really thought of everything.' Then she laughed, a smug yet joyful sound. 'Good thing we did, too.' She handed the paper to Nick. 'Look at the sixth company down, Nick.'

Nick's grin was sharp. 'Fuckin' bastard.' He slapped Vito on the back and put the list on the desk. 'Chick, that company handled all the finances for Winchester's aunt.' He thumbed over his shoulder at the evidence box. 'Five years of broker's statements.'

'Rock Solid Investments is a brokerage firm that has a huge client base of retirees,' Liz added. 'Lots of old people have their money there.'

'Maybe the old woman buried next to Claire did, too.' Vito drew a breath. They were close. He only prayed they wouldn't be too late. 'Okay. So we need to do what?'

'I'd say we need a warrant to search Rock Solid's client files,' Maggy said. 'I hope the judge on call is an insomniac. Who wants to go?'

Vito got up, but Liz and Nick each grabbed one of his shoulders and pushed him back down. 'Dammit, Liz,' Vito gritted. 'This isn't funny.'

Liz got serious fast. 'Maggy, take Nick. Brent, you go, too, in case they need someone to speak computerese with their network guy. Vito, you're staying with me. If you want to help Sophie, get some rest. You'll need it when you find Simon Vartanian.'

DIE FOR ME

Sunday, January 21, 3:10 A.M.

The phone on Vito's desk rang and he snatched it up. 'Ciccotelli.'

'It's Tess. I know you'd call if you'd heard anything. But we're all here, the whole family, sitting in your living room, worrying about you. We just wanted you to know.'

He could picture it, his family gathered to support him, and he yearned to go be with them, to take their comfort. 'Don't worry about me. Worry about Sophie.'

'We are. Don't worry. We have plenty of worry to go around,' Tess added wryly. 'Don't give up. I guarantee Sophie knows you're doing everything you can to find her.'

If anyone understood, it was Tess. 'Thank you. Tell them all thank you. I'll call you when I can.' He hung up, then sat back, arms crossed tight over his chest. It had been ten hours since Simon had taken Sophie, three since Maggy, Nick, and Brent had gone off in search of Rock Solid Investment's client list. 'Where the hell are they?'

Jen looked up from her laptop sympathetically. 'Try to relax, Vito. I know it's hard.'

Maggy Lopez had gotten the warrant easily enough. But finding someone at Rock Solid Investments who had access to the full client list was turning out to be harder than expected. The one broker who played network administrator in his spare time was on vacation and couldn't be reached. Nobody else seemed to know all the passwords and ironically, someone had actually suggested they call their network consultant.

Vito tried to relax, but it wasn't going to happen. His gaze settled on the CD Brent had made from the camera feed. He remembered Sophie watching that movie of her father's, because she 'needed to see him.' Now Vito needed to see her. He slid the CD in his computer, then saw himself sitting next to Anna's bed, and Sophie waiting at the doorway, that plastic pitcher in her hands.

He muted the sound, then fast-forwarded until he saw

467

Sophie again, the pitcher in her hand and tears on her face. He watched her expression soften and her eyes change. And saw what he hadn't seen Friday night because he'd been focused on Anna – Sophie looking at him with love in her eyes. Neither of them had said the words. She'd been so scared of messing things up, but now he'd seen for himself. Vito closed the file, then closed his eyes and did what he hadn't done in two years. He prayed.

Sunday, January 21, 4:15 A.M.

Nick came running in, clutching a stack of papers in his hand. 'We got the list.'

Vito was on his feet, grabbing it, but it was page after page of names that meant nothing. He looked up at Liz who'd rushed from her office at the sound of Nick's voice.

'What are we supposed to do with this?' he said, frustrated.

Brent was right behind Nick, laptop under his arm. 'We sort and filter. Katherine said she thought the old woman in the graveyard was between sixty and seventy, so I ran the search on female clients fifty-five to eighty, just to be sure. There are over three hundred names. When I just look at sixty to seventy, it's still over two hundred.'

Vito sank into his chair. 'Two hundred.' He'd hoped a single name would pop. But the others weren't discouraged. They were energized and Vito drew from their energy.

Jen was pacing. 'Okay, let's think. What did he steal from these people? Money?'

'Real estate,' Liz said. 'He took Winchester's aunt's field. Maybe he took another field from somebody else. A field near a quarry, far enough out that he could do what he wanted without raising suspicion.'

'Or anybody being able to hear,' Nick added.

Vito closed his eyes, despair threatening again. 'Of course

we've also assumed he took Sophie to the place he took everyone else.'

'Don't borrow trouble,' Nick ordered. 'Until we have a reason to think otherwise, there's no reason to believe Simon will do anything more than stick to his routine.'

Vito stood up with a hard nod. 'Okay, we're going to split these lists and figure out which of these people have property in the USDA soil areas that match the grave fill dirt. Then we find out which of those are homes with more than one story.'

'The elevator shaft,' Nick said. 'Don't forget about the old woman's dental fillings. Check for anyone who lived in Europe before 1960.'

'Daniel called me last night,' Liz said. 'He and his sister are back in town and want to help. I'll put them on call to give us information if we end up in a hostage negotiation.'

Vito made himself breathe. 'Then let's move. He's had Sophie eleven hours now.'

Sunday, January 21, 4:50 A.M.

Simon leaned away from his computer, stretching his shoulders. Alan Brewster had been a lot heavier than he looked. Carrying him out to the barn for the filming had been the right choice, though. The mess from Brewster's exploding head would have been bad enough, but percussion from the grenade had blown part of the barn wall away. Had he executed the film inside, he might have damaged his studio.

He'd planned to leave Brewster's body outside, but discovered the lighting in the barn hadn't been sufficient to achieve the level of detail he required while filming. The video was grainy and the camera lens had been dirtied by flying debris of the human variety. So he'd brought Brewster back inside to get a closer look at what remained. Of course, carrying Brewster back indoors had been a tad easier. He estimated

Brewster's head alone had weighed a good ten pounds.

With a click of his mouse Simon replayed the changes he'd made to Bill Melville's death by flail. As much as he hated to admit it, Van Zandt had been one hundred percent correct. Seeing the knight's head explode made playing *Inquisitor* a far more exciting experience. Not authentic, but damn exciting.

Simon rubbed his hands together in anticipation. Sophie would provide both authenticity and excitement and he couldn't wait. He checked his watch. Another few hours and his leg would be fully charged and ready to roll.

As would parts of Sophie.

Sunday, January 21, 5:30 A.M.

'Dammit.' Vito stared at the USDA soil map, pock-marked with nearly forty thumbtacks representing each old woman who lived in the identified soil area and held an account with Rock Solid Investments. And the clock continued to tick. Almost thirteen hours had passed through their fingers.

'There are still too many names,' Nick muttered. 'And not one of them German.'

'The old woman could have a German maiden name,' Jen said. 'We have to start making calls. It's the only way.'

'But if we find the right one, Simon will answer,' Brent protested. 'We'll tip our hand.'

Everyone looked at Vito expectantly. For a moment his brain spun uselessly, then it clicked. 'Next of kin?' he asked. 'Do we have next of kin contacts on these brokerage applications for Rock Solid?'

Brent nodded excitedly. 'It's all in the database.'

'Then we split it up.' Vito blinked at the list of names he held in his hand. 'Nick, you've got Dina Anderson to Selma Crane. Jen, you take Margaret Diamond up through Priscilla Henley.' He gave Liz, Maggy, and Brent their names, then took the remaining share. And prayed again.

DIE FOR ME

Sunday, January 21, 7:20 A.M.

'Sophie.' He sang it sweetly. 'I'm back.'

When Sophie didn't respond, he chuckled. 'You're quite an actress. But then, it's in your blood isn't it? Your father was an actor and your grandmother an opera diva. But then . . . I've always known. I was hoping you'd tell me yourself.'

No. It couldn't be. Sophie did her best not to tense. The words had been Ted's.

'It's nice to finally meet you, Sophie.'

But no. She knew what Simon looked like. Ted was big. Was he that big? She couldn't remember. She was so tired and the fear was backing up in her throat.

'I've been thinking about Marie Antoinette. With her head of course.' He ran his fingers across her throat and she flinched and he laughed. 'Open your eyes, Sophie.'

Slowly she did, praying it would not be Ted. A face was an inch from hers, broad boned, hard jawed. The smile gleamed, as did the bald head. He had no eyebrows.

'*Boo,*' he whispered and she flinched again. But it wasn't Ted. *Thank God.*

Her relief was amazingly short-lived. 'Your charade is over, Sophie. Aren't you the least bit curious as to your fate?'

She lifted her chin and looked around, horror congealing, clawing in her gut. She saw the chair, as it had looked in the museum. She saw a rack and a table with all the artifacts of torture this man had used to kill so many. She looked down at herself and saw she wore a gown, cream velvet, edged in purple. The thought of him touching her, dressing her . . . She swallowed back a grimace.

'Do you like the gown?' he asked and she raised her eyes. His expression was one of tolerant amusement without a flicker of nerves or fear. 'The cream color will provide a wonderful contrast to your blood.'

'It's too small,' Sophie said coldly, proud her voice didn't shake.

471

He shrugged. 'It was intended for someone else. I had to make some last-minute alterations.'

'You sew?'

He smiled, cruelly. 'I have a great many talents, Dr Johannsen, one of which is a proficiency with needles and other sharp implements.'

She kept her chin lifted and her jaw tight. 'What will you do to me?'

'Well, I really need to give the credit to you. I'd planned something far different until I heard you and your boss talking in the museum. You remember. Marie Antoinette.'

Sophie fought to keep her voice hard. 'Jumped a few centuries, didn't you?'

He smiled. 'You will be fun to play with, Sophie. I couldn't get a guillotine, so you're safe on that score. We'll have to go a little more medieval than that.'

She clucked her tongue in her cheek. 'No pun intended.'

He stared at her a moment, then threw back his head and laughed. It was a chilling sound, abrasive and . . . mean.

Mean. *Anna.* 'You tried to kill my grandmother, didn't you?'

'Now, Sophie. There is no try. There is only success and failure. Of course I killed your grandmother. I always do what I set out to do.'

Sophie controlled the wave of grief, just barely. 'You sonofabitch.'

'Language,' he chided. 'And you a queen.' He stepped back and she saw a crisp white bed sheet that had been draped across two poles. He tugged at the sheet, and she saw the poles were really tall microphone stands. With a dramatic flourish, Simon pulled the sheet away completely, revealing a raised platform surrounded by a low white fence. In the middle of the platform was a block, curved in on top. Stained with blood.

'So?' he said. 'What do you think?'

For a moment she could only stare, her brain denying the reality of what her eyes were seeing. It wasn't possible. It was insane. Not real. But she remembered the others – Warren and Brittany and Bill . . . and Greg. They'd suffered at Simon Vartanian's hand. He'd do this thing, this hideous terrible thing, of that she had no doubt.

She tried to remember everything she knew about Vartanian but could only hear Greg Sanders's screams. The block was bloody. He'd cut off Greg's hand. A scream rose in her throat and she bit her tongue until she'd forced it back.

Simon Vartanian was a monster. A sociopath with a hunger for power. A need to dominate. She couldn't let him. She couldn't play his game, feed his hunger. She'd play it ballsy, even though every bone in her body shook with fear.

'I'm waiting, Sophie. What do you think?'

Sophie drew on every dramatic drop of blood in her body and laughed out loud. 'You have got to be kidding me.'

Simon's eyes narrowed and his expression went dark. 'I don't kid.'

And he didn't like to be laughed at. She'd use that. Considering she was still bound hand and foot, she'd have to use anything she could think of to get away. She injected a note of amused incredulity into her voice. 'You expect me to walk up to that block, put my neck on it, and hold still while you cut off my head? You're crazier than we thought.'

Simon stared at her for a long moment, then smiled mildly. 'As long as I get my film, I don't care what you think.' He walked to a tall, wide cupboard and pulled it open.

Sophie had to really work to keep her mocking expression from changing to horror as her heart stumbled to a stop.

The cupboard was filled with daggers and axes and swords. Many of them were very old and pitted with age. And use. Some were shiny and new, obvious reproductions. All of them looked lethal. Simon tilted his head, considering his stash at length, and Sophie knew he was preening for her benefit. It was working. She remembered the dead man in the graveyard. Warren Keyes. Simon had disemboweled him. She remembered Greg Sanders's screams as Simon cut off his hand.

Fear was again rising to close her throat. Still she kept the loose smile on her face.

He took out a battle-ax, similar to the one she carried on the Viking tour. He rested the handle on his shoulder and smiled at her. 'You have one just like this.'

She made her voice cold. 'I should have followed my instincts and used it on you.'

'It's generally wise to follow your instincts,' he agreed affably, then put the ax back. Finally he chose a sword and pulled it from its sheath slowly. The blade gleamed, shiny and new. 'This is a sharp one. It should do the job nicely.'

'It's just a reproduction,' Sophie said with disdain. 'I expected better.'

He looked at her for a moment, then laughed. 'This is fun.' He brought the sword over to her and held it in front of her face, twisting it so it caught the flickering light. 'The old swords are useful to get an idea of weight and size and balance. How someone moved while wielding one. But they're ugly and rusted and really not that sharp.'

'Well, we'd want them to be sharp, wouldn't we?' she said dryly, hoping he couldn't hear the thundering of her heart.

He smiled. 'Unless you want me hacking at that pretty neck of yours.'

He was baiting her again. She made herself shrug. 'If you use the sword, you can't use the block. It's like wearing suspenders and a belt. It just isn't done.'

He considered her again, then walked to the platform, picked up the block, and placed it off to the side. 'True. You'll kneel. I'll get a better view of your face that way anyway. Thank you.' He pushed a camera on a rolling tripod into place.

'Any time. So, did you let your other victims handle the old swords?'

He looked over his shoulder. 'Yes. I wanted to capture their movements. Why?'

'I was wondering how it would feel to hold a sword nearly eight centuries old.'

'It feels like it had been sleeping all those years and woke up, just for you.'

Sophie's mouth fell open as she recognized her own words, and when she spoke her voice was barely audible. 'John?'

He smiled. 'One of my names.'

'But the . . .' The wheelchair. *Oh, Vito.*

'The wheelchair?' He expelled an exaggerated sigh. 'You know, people don't consider old people or handicapped people a threat. I was able to hide in plain sight.'

'All . . . all this time?'

'All this time,' he said, amused. 'You see, *Dr J*, I'm not crazy and I'm not stupid.'

She got control of herself, forced the tremble out of her voice. 'You're just bad.'

'You're just saying that to be nice. Besides, "bad" is one of those relative terms.'

'Perhaps in some parallel universe that's true, but in this universe, killing lots of people for no good reason is bad.' She tilted her head. 'So why did you?'

'What? Kill lots of people?' He pushed another camera into place. 'Various reasons. Some got in my way. One I hated. But mostly I just wanted to see them die.'

Sophie drew a deep breath. 'See? Now that's just bad. You won't—'

He held up a hand. 'Don't say I won't get away with it. That's trite, and I'd really hoped for better from you.' He moved a third camera into place and stepped back, dusting his hands. 'That takes care of the cameras. I have to do a sound test.'

'A sound test.'

'Yes, a sound test. I need you to scream.'

Go ahead and scream. She shook her head. 'No fucking way.'

He clucked. 'Language. You'll scream. Or I'll use an ax.'

'Either way I'm dead. And I'm not giving you the satisfaction.'

'I think Warren said that. No, it was Bill. Big bad Bill the black belt. He thought he was so tough. In the end he cried like a baby. And he screamed. A lot.'

He came over and touched her hair which was still braided in a crown from the last Joan tour the day before. 'You have lovely hair. I'm glad it's braided up. I would have hated to cut it.' He chuckled. 'Although it does seem silly to worry about cutting your hair when I'll be cutting something more important.' He ran his fingers across her throat. 'Right here, I think.'

Panic was making it hard to breathe. Taunting him was going to buy her no more time. *Vito, where are you?* She jerked her body back, away from his fingers.

'Which one was Bill? The one you disemboweled?'

He was visibly startled. 'Well, well. You know more than I thought. I didn't think your cop boyfriend would give you the details.'

'He didn't have to. I was there when they were dug up. You cut off Greg Sanders's hand.'

'And his foot. He deserved it, stealing from a church. You said so yourself.'

Horror turned her stomach inside out. He'd used her words, her lessons to murder so vilely. 'You sick sonofabitch.'

His eyes went dark. 'I've given you some latitude because you amused me. But that time is done. If you are attempting to unnerve me, it won't work. When I get angry, I become more focused.' He grabbed her arm and yanked her off the table to the floor.

Sophie winced as her hip hit hard concrete. 'Yeah, like you did with Greg Sanders.' He'd cut off that man's hand . . . *and his foot*. Because he'd stolen from a church. But it hadn't been what she'd said. That wasn't right. *He'd made a mistake*. He didn't become more focused with rage. He made mistakes. She'd have to use it.

He dragged her across the floor and she struggled out of his grasp. Then saw stars when he smashed her head against the floor, using her thick braided crown as a handhold. 'Don't try that again.'

She rolled to her back and blinked up at him, breathing hard. He was huge, especially from this angle. He stood, fists on his hips, his face like stone. But he was breathing hard, too, his nostrils flaring.

'You fucked up with Greg, you know,' she panted. 'The amputated foot didn't go with the Church. Only the hand. You got so angry that he tried to steal from you that you messed up the details.'

'I messed up *nothing*.' He reached under her neck, grabbed a handful of the gown, and twisted until the velvet cut at her throat, cutting off her air. More stars danced in front of her eyes and she bucked, trying to get away. Abruptly he released her, and she dragged air into her lungs.

'Fuck you,' she snarled, coughing. 'You can kill me, but I'm not giving you anything for your precious game.'

Simon grabbed the bodice of the gown in both hands and effortlessly lifted her to her feet, then higher, until she was eye to eye with him. 'You will give me what I want. If I have to nail you in place you will not fight me. Do you understand me?'

Sophie spat in his face and had the pleasure of seeing his face contort with rage. He drew back one fist, still holding her with one hand and she lifted her chin, ready for the blow. But it never came.

'I won't mark your face. I need it . . . pretty.' He wiped at his cheek with his sleeve and lowered her to her feet.

'What's the matter?' she taunted deliberately. 'Can't you see past a few bruises when you immortalize me in your stupid game? Or can you not function without an exact model? It must be frustrating, only being able to copy. Never creating anything on your own.' She swallowed hard and lifted her chin again. 'Simon.'

His jaw tightened as his eyes narrowed and once again he jerked her off her feet. 'What do you know?'

'Everything,' she sneered. 'I know everything. And so do the police. So go ahead and kill me, but you really won't get away with it. You'll get caught and you'll go to prison where you can paint clowns all day long and not need to hide them under your bed.'

A muscle in his jaw twitched. 'Where are they?'

Sophie smiled at him. 'Who?'

He shook her, so hard her teeth rattled. 'Daniel and Susannah. Where are they?'

'They're here, looking for you. Just like Vito Ciccotelli is looking for you. He won't rest until he finds you.' She narrowed her gaze. 'Did you think no one would know, Simon? That no one could find you? Did you really think that no one would hear?'

'No one has found me,' he said. He lifted her higher and she winced which made him smile. 'No one did hear me,' he said. 'And no one will hear you.'

Fury gave her courage. 'You're wrong. All the people you killed screamed long after you buried them. You just weren't listening. But Vito Ciccotelli was and he always will.'

He forced her to her knees. 'Then I'll kill him, too. But first I'll kill you.'

Sunday, January 21, 7:45 A.M.

Selma Crane had lived in a tidy Victorian house before Simon had buried her next to Claire Reynolds in the Winchester field. Vito crept up to the attached garage, weapon in his hand, and looked in the window. Inside was a white van. He nodded to Nick and Liz who stood behind a cruiser at the end of the driveway.

Behind Nick and Liz stood the SWAT team, ready to storm the house on Vito's signal. Vito joined them. 'It's a white van. I don't see any sign of movement inside.'

The leader of the SWAT team stepped forward. 'Do we go in?'

'I'd rather surprise him,' Vito said. 'Hold for now.'

A car approached, Jen McFain behind the wheel. Daniel Vartanian was in the front seat, his sister in the back. They approached in silence, leaving their car doors open.

'Is he in there?' Daniel asked quietly.

'I think so,' Vito said. 'There's a back door that leads into the kitchen. All of the windows on the back side of the house are boarded up and covered in black tarp.'

'Then this is his place,' Susannah murmured. 'Simon wanted to control his lighting so he blacked out the windows of his room and installed lights he could dim.'

'McFain filled us in,' Daniel said. 'She told us he has your consultant. Let me go in.'

'No.' Vito shook his head. 'Absolutely not. I'm not letting you go in there half-cocked because you feel guilty that you didn't turn him in ten years ago.'

Daniel's jaw twitched. 'What I was going to say,' he said carefully, 'is that I'm SWAT trained and a trained negotiator. I know what to do.'

Vito hesitated. 'You're still his brother.'

Daniel didn't look away. 'Now you're just being mean. I'm offering my help. Take it.'

Vito looked at Liz. 'When will our negotiator get here?'

'Another hour,' Liz told him. 'At best.'

Vito checked his watch, even though he knew exactly what time it was and exactly how much time had passed. Sophie was in there, he could feel it. He didn't want to think about what Simon could be doing to her right now. 'We can't wait another hour, Liz.'

'Daniel is a negotiator. His CO told me so when I checked up on him the other night. Do you want me to take over and make the call?'

It was tempting. But Vito shook his head and looked Daniel Vartanian square in the eye. 'You follow my orders in there. No questions, no hesitation.'

Daniel lifted his brows. 'Think of me as a consultant.'

Vito was shocked he could still smile. 'Suit up. You and I go in the front, Jen, you and Nick go in the back. SWAT stays at ready.'

'I send them in at the first shot,' Liz said and Vito nodded.

'Be prepared for anything. Let's go.'

Sunday, January 21, 7:50 A.M.

Sophie was kneeling, Simon's fingers tunneled under her braid. Fiercely he gripped her head, yanking her upright as she struggled. 'Scream, damn you,' he gritted, twisting, making her scalp burn but Sophie bit her tongue.

She wouldn't scream, wouldn't give him what he wanted. She wrenched to one side, awkward with her wrists and ankles tied, still kneeling. Simon's foot crashed down on her calf, holding her legs in place. He jerked her up again by her hair and fumbled behind him. She heard the singing of the sword as he pulled it from its sheath, then the sheath fell on the floor in front of her. His left hand was yanking at her hair, pulling up so that he had free access to the back of her neck while still pointing her face at his cameras. He raised his right arm and Sophie bit her tongue again.

Do not scream. Whatever you do. Do not scream.

'Scream, damn you.' He was furious, shaking.

'Go to hell, Vartanian,' she spat. His foot crashed down on her calf again, sending pain radiating up her spine. She bit down on her tongue even harder and tasted blood. She strained to try to spit it at him, but he dug his fingers in deeper. Her head throbbed from the pressure on her scalp as he held her head in the palm of his huge hand.

He yanked up and she was lifted almost off her knees. Then she heard a noise from upstairs. A creak. Simon's body jerked. He'd heard it, too.

Vito. Sophie spat the blood from her mouth, filled her lungs with air and screamed.

'Shut up,' Simon gritted.

Sophie wanted to sing. But she screamed again. Screamed Vito's name.

'You stupid bitch. You're going to die.' Simon raised his arm, bearing his weight on her legs with his good foot.

Good foot. Abruptly Sophie rocked right, then left with all her might sending her shoulder into Simon's artificial leg. He swayed for a split second, then toppled. The sword clattered from his hand as he tried to break his fall. She rolled to one side, barely avoiding becoming his crash pad. But his hand was still in her hair and she couldn't get away. The door at the top of the stairs opened and footsteps thundered.

'Police! Don't move!'

Vito. 'I'm down here,' Sophie screamed.

Simon came up on his good knee, then reared back, pulling her into him. Making her a human shield. 'Go back,' he called. 'Go back or I kill her.'

The footsteps continued until Sophie saw Vito's feet, then his legs. Then his face, dark with controlled fury. 'Are you hurt, Sophie?'

'No.'

'Don't come another step,' Simon warned. 'Or I swear I'll break her fucking neck.'

Vito was still on the stairs, his gun trained on Simon. 'Don't touch her, Vartanian,' Vito said, his voice low and ominous. 'I will shoot your head right off your shoulders.'

'And risk killing her? I don't think so. I think you're going to go back up those stairs and call off your dogs. Then we're going to walk away, me and your pretty girl.'

Sophie was breathing hard, one of Simon's hands twined in her hair, his other arm crossed over her throat. There was no way Simon could have planned this better, no way he could have found a deeper vulnerability, capable of stopping Vito in his tracks.

'Kill him, Vito,' she said. 'Kill him now or he'll just kill again. I couldn't live with that.'

'Your girl has a death wish, Ciccotelli. Come closer and I'll make her wish come true. Let me walk away and she lives.'

'No, Simon.' It was a soft drawl, calm and steady. 'You won't. I won't let you.'

Sophie felt the sudden tense of Simon's body at Daniel's voice and she jerked to one side, but he came with her and they crashed to the floor. He flattened her against the concrete floor, his weight knocking the breath from her lungs. He jerked back to his knees, dragging her with him. She swung her bound hands but hit only air. He twisted her hair harder and tears stung her eyes.

She swung her hands, scrabbling for any hold, any way to put enough distance between them so that Vito could get a shot. She toppled again, but this time her hands touched metal. Simon's shiny sword. Sophie kneeled over it, fisted her hands around the hilt, twisted her body so the blade skimmed her side.

And jabbed backward with all her might. The sword met flesh and kept going, plunging deep. With a startled gasp, Simon fell backward, dragging her with him. She let go of the hilt and rolled to her knees, bowed forward, twisted painfully, his hand still gripping her scalp. For a moment all she could hear was her own labored breathing, then footsteps thundered down the stairs.

Simon lay on his back, his own sword plunged into his gut, the blade leaning at an awkward angle away from his body. His white shirt was rapidly becoming red. His mouth was open and he gasped for air. Still his eyes burned with hate and rage and he lunged upward, his free hand going for her throat.

'Don't move a muscle,' Vito said. 'Because I really want to shoot you.'

Breathing hard, Sophie straightened as much as she could, her eyes still on Simon's. 'Go ahead and scream, Simon.'

'You bitch,' Simon spat. His eyes narrowed and once again he lunged, and too late Sophie saw him jerk his wrist outward, bringing the slim blade he'd hidden in his sleeve into his hand. She heard the shots at the same time she felt a searing pain in her side.

The hand in her hair sagged, dragging her so that she knelt at Simon's side, her neck twisted at an unnatural angle. She could see up, but not down. From the corner of her eye she saw Vito step back and holster his gun.

What sounded like an army thundered across the floor upstairs and down the stairs.

'Scene is secure,' Vito said loudly, but his voice shook. 'Call an ambulance.'

Sophie could smell the acrid odor of gunpowder and the iron scent of blood. A wave of nausea hurled up from her stomach. 'Get his hand out of my hair,' she gritted out. Then she sagged against Daniel as he worked Simon's big hand out from under her braid. Carefully he laid her down on her back and she clenched her eyes against the sharp pain in her side.

'*Merde*,' she muttered. 'Goddamn, this hurts.'

'Chick?' It was Nick's voice from the stairs. 'What happened?'

Vito scrambled to her side. 'Call another ambulance, Nick. Sophie's hit.' Using the blade, he cut the gown into strips and pushed them against her, stemming the flow.

'It's not deep,' he said. 'It's not deep.'

She grimaced. 'Still hurts like hell. Tell me he's dead.'

'Yeah,' Vito said. 'He's dead.'

Sophie looked over to where Simon lay, less then three feet between them, sightlessly staring at the ceiling. He had two more wounds, one in his head and the other in his chest. She was grimly satisfied to see the sword still stuck in his gut.

'I guess Katherine will figure out which one of us killed him,' she said.

'You can't feel guilty, Sophie,' Vito murmured. 'You had no choice.'

Sophie scoffed. 'Guilty? I hope it was my sword that killed the fucker. Although whoever got the headshot is probably taking home the grand prize.'

'That would have been me,' Vito said.

'Good,' Sophie said. She looked up at Daniel who had grabbed the skinny blade and was sawing through the rope that bound her hands. 'Sorry.'

'For what?' Daniel asked. 'That he's dead or that I don't get the grand prize?'

She studied him through narrowed eyes. 'Whichever answer is the right one.'

Daniel laughed softly. 'I think we did the world a service today. So, Sophie, other than the knife wound, are you hurt anywhere else?'

'Maybe my tongue.' She stuck it out and both men flinched.

Daniel gently took her chin, angling her face toward the light. 'My God, girl, you nearly bit it clear through. You might need stitches there, too.'

'But I didn't scream,' she said with satisfaction. 'Not until I heard you upstairs.'

Daniel smiled grimly. 'Good for you, Sophie.' He took one of her hands and started rubbing her wrist where the rope had chafed.

Vito took her other hand, and his were shaking now. 'My God. Sophie.'

'I'm all right, Vito.'

'She's all right,' Daniel repeated and Vito's eyes snapped up to glare at Daniel.

'What the hell kind of negotiation was that?' he ground out in fury. '"*No, you won't walk away. I won't let you.*" What the fuck kind of negotiation was that?'

'Vito,' Sophie murmured.

'You wouldn't have let him leave,' Daniel said. 'You know that. Simon hated to be told what to do, by anyone. I could only hope he'd get mad and Sophie could use it to her advantage.' He smiled down at her. 'You did good, kid.'

'Thank you.'

'I need to tell Suze.' Daniel stood up. 'I'm sorry, Vito. I didn't mean to scare you.'

He shuddered. 'It's okay. She's safe. He's dead. I'm happy.' When Daniel had walked back up the stairs, Sophie squeezed Vito's hand.

'My gran?'

'Holding on.'

Sophie drew her first good breath, despite the pain in her side. 'Thank you.'

Vito smiled down at her unsteadily. 'That was some fancy sword work.'

Her lips curved. 'My father and I used to fence. Alex was a champion, but I wasn't too bad. If Simon had seen the Joan tour, he would have known that.'

Vito remembered the way she flourished the sword to the delight of the children on the tour. He wasn't sure he'd ever be able to watch her do so again. 'Maybe we should retire Joan. Expand your repertoire,' he added, mimicking Nick's drawl.

Sophie closed her eyes. 'That's a good plan. But I don't think I'm touching Marie Antoinette with a ten-foot pole after this.'

Vito brought her hands to his lips, his laugh shaky. 'There's always that topless Celtic Warrior Queen.'

'Boudiccea,' she murmured as new footsteps thundered down the stairs. The paramedics were here. 'The after-hours X-rated tour. Ted'll have Theo's college tuition saved up in no time.'

Chapter Twenty-Six

Sunday, January 21, 7:50 A.M.

'Vito, come and check this out.' Nick motioned Vito back in the house. 'Upstairs.'

From Selma Crane's driveway, Vito watched the ambulance carrying Sophie pull away and squaring his shoulders, went inside to do his job. He got upstairs and took a slow turn, his eyes wide. 'I suspect this was not the way Selma Crane left the place.'

'Um, no. But what you really need to see is over here.'

Simon Vartanian had made himself at home. Gone were all the interior walls on the upper floor. With the exception of a king-size bed in the far corner and a state-of-the-art computer station, the entire space was a huge studio. Vito joined Nick at the far wall and moved sideways, studying the macabre series of paintings.

For a very long moment, Vito could only stare and wonder at the mind that had been able to . . . create this. For they weren't simply copies. Simon Vartanian had achieved something in his victim's eyes. A light or maybe the extinguishing of a light. 'The moment of death,' he murmured.

'He was experimenting with the stages of death by torture,' Nick said. '*Claire Dies, Zachary Dies, Jared Dies*, then series for Bill, Brittany, Warren, and Greg.'

'So our last victim is named Jared. It's a start.'

'We might never know who he is. Simon might not have known more than the boy's first name. He kept good records for all of his "models," but not Jared.' Nick motioned him to Simon's computer, where a folder sat in the middle of a spotless desk. Nick put his hand on the folder when Vito reached for it. 'Remember Sophie's okay. All right?'

Vito nodded, then ground his teeth in new anger when he saw what was inside the folder. 'Photos of Sophie's Viking tour.' She stood in front of awestruck children, her expression intent as she held the battle-ax over her head. He closed the folder. 'I'm just glad he didn't see the Joan tour. That element of surprise saved her life.'

'Look at this.' It was a diagram linking Kyle Lombard to Clint Shafer and Clint to Sophie in a vertical line. Alan Brewster's name was connected to all three.

'So Alan was involved,' Vito said.

'That would be my guess.'

Vito narrowed his eyes. 'You found Brewster?'

'I think so. I did find out what the squeaking sound was on the tape.' He walked to the wall that ran along the staircase and opened a small door. 'A dumbwaiter.'

Vito looked inside with a grimace. The man inside was nude and missing most of his head. 'It almost looks like his head . . . exploded.' He leaned in to study the man's hand. 'His signet ring says AB, so I'd bet this was Brewster.'

'The dumbwaiter goes all the way down to the basement and also has a loading area on the first floor. It's how Simon got his victims and heavy equipment downstairs. It looks like he might have even brought his dead victims up here to paint them.'

'That is so gross.'

'Well, yeah.' Nick reached into the shaft and tugged on the ropes, sending the platform and Alan Brewster halfway down to the next floor, then brought him back up. The squeaking echoed just as it had on the tape. 'His time machine.'

Jen came over from Simon's living corner where she'd been collecting samples. 'What about the church?'

'It's in the basement,' Vito said. 'He partitioned part of the basement off to be the crypt. He's got posters of stained-glass windows down there and everything.'

'So there was no church.' Jen sighed. 'That was hours down the drain.'

'Jen, thank you,' Vito said and swallowed. 'Thanks to both of you.'

'I'm glad she's okay.' She cleared her throat. 'I found what's left of Simon's lubricant. I'll test it against what we found on Warren's hands, but I'm sure it'll match.'

'So what about the paintings?' Nick asked. 'I mean, we'll take them in as evidence, but what will the Vartanians ultimately want done with them?'

'Burn them,' Susannah Vartanian said from the stairs. 'We want to destroy them.'

'We connected some dots of our own,' Daniel said, passing his sister on the stairs, then offering his hand to pull her the rest of the way up. 'Our mother suspected our father had done some covering up of Simon's sins, but she never believed he was alive. When Stacy Savard sent that picture to my father, my mother saw it and thought there had been a big mistake in identity, that Simon might not even know we'd thought he was dead. But when she and Dad got here, she started to put things together. The final straw was Dad trying to get information out of the old Russian man at the library.'

'She came to the same conclusion that Sophie did,' Susannah said. 'She hired someone to watch my father. She realized he'd found Simon and never intended to tell her. She left us word that she planned to meet Simon to see for herself what had happened all those years ago. Her letter said if she never came back, that we had been right and Simon was as evil as we'd tried to get her to believe.'

'I'm sorry,' Vito said. 'It's too little, too late, and nobody wins.'

'Simon really is dead now. Who knows how much longer he would have gone on killing people.' Daniel looked at the paintings. 'I mean, he'd been looking for that spark all his life.

He finally found it, and he never would have let it go. He would have kept killing. So today, we all win.' He shook hands with the three of them, a forced smile on his face. 'I'm going home and getting back to work. If you're ever in Atlanta, holler.'

Susannah didn't smile as she shook their hands. 'Thank you. Daniel and I have been waiting for resolution nearly all our lives.'

Jen hesitated, then shrugged. 'We found a bear trap, Daniel. We also found a drawing of you, stuck in it.'

Daniel nodded unsteadily. 'So that was to have been my end. I'm not surprised.' He took his sister's arm and started down the stairs.

'Wait,' Vito said. 'I need to ask. Where will you bury Simon?'

'We won't,' Daniel said. 'We already decided that burying him will add to his notoriety. We don't want hordes of serial killer aficionados descending on Dutton.'

Susannah nodded. 'So we're going to donate his body to the medical center in Atlanta. Maybe somebody can learn something useful.'

'Like about the brain of a sociopath?' Jen asked.

Daniel shrugged. 'Perhaps. If nothing else, some med student can use him to learn how to save lives. We're going to catch a ride back with one of the patrol cars, so don't worry about driving us, Sergeant McFain.'

The Vartanians left. Gathered at the top of the stairs, Vito, Nick, and Jen could watch through the front door as the brother and sister stopped at the gurney that held Simon's body. Susannah's shoulders sagged and Daniel put his arm around her.

'This time, he's really dead,' Vito said quietly. 'And I'm glad he is.'

'Ahh, about that.' Nick reached into his pocket and pulled out three videocassettes. 'Simon had the cameras on the whole time. You and Daniel did the right things, but . . .' He put the tapes in Vito's hand. 'You might want to keep these someplace safe.'

Vito started down the steps. 'Thanks. Now, I'm going to get a shower, go back to the precinct to do the paperwork for shooting Simon, then buy six dozen roses.'

Jen's jaw dropped. 'Six dozen? Who for?'

'Sophie, Anna, Molly, Tess. And for my mom, because no matter how bad I ever thought she was, Sophie's mother is a million times worse.'

'That's only five dozen, Vito,' Jen said.

'The last dozen are for a grave.' He'd drive out to Jersey tomorrow, a week late, but it was the thought. Andrea would have understood that he'd had a busy week.

'Vito,' Nick sighed.

'It's resolution, Nick,' Vito said. 'And closure. But after that, I'm good.'

Sunday, January 21, 1:30 P.M.

'Harry, wake up.' Sophie shook his shoulder. He'd fallen asleep sitting up on the sofa in the little family room outside the cardiac care unit.

With a snap his eyes flew open. 'Anna?'

'She's sleeping. Go home for a while, Harry. You look beat.'

He tugged her down to sit on the arm of the sofa next to him. 'So do you.'

'Just a few stitches.' It was more like fourteen stitches, and her side and tongue were sore as hell, but she was so happy to be alive that her words were barely a fib.

Harry rubbed his thumb over a bruise on Sophie's face. 'He hit you.'

'No, he didn't. I did that diving for the sword. You should have seen me, Harry,' she added lightly. 'It was the stuff of Errol Flynn. *En garde.*' She pretended to lunge.

Harry shuddered. 'I'm imagining it just fine. I don't ever want to see it.'

'Too bad. I understand there's a tape. Maybe we can watch it together next time you have insomnia.' She grinned at him and he laughed in spite of himself.

'Sophie, you're incorrigible.'

She sobered. 'Go home, Harry. Stop hiding here.'

He sighed. 'You don't understand.'

At her own insistence, Harry had told her what had transpired between him and Freya. Sophie kissed the top of his bald head. 'I understand you love me. And I understand you have a wife who you also love except for this one thing. I don't need Freya to love me, Harry. It would be nice if she did, but if I were the cause of a rift between you two, I'd just die.' She winced. 'Bad choice of words. So go home. Be with your family. Sleep in your easy chair, and if I need you, I know where to find you.'

He pressed his lips together. 'It's not right, Sophie. You didn't do anything to her.'

'No, I didn't, but I look at it this way: I have a dad and a mom – you and Katherine.'

'That's not a real family, Sophie.'

She laughed softly. 'Harry, my "real" father was my grandmother's lover and my "real" mother is a thief. I'd rather have you and Katherine as parents any day of the week. Besides, I get to pick my family. How many people can say that?'

He put his arm around her, carefully hugging her to him. 'I liked your detective.'

'I like him, too.'

'Maybe you'll have a new family soon,' he said, wily again.

'Maybe. And I promise you'll be the first to know.' She leaned close. 'If I were you I'd be dusting off that tuxedo. You may need to be walking a girl down the aisle soon.'

Harry swallowed. 'I always assumed it would be Alex. I guess now that he's—'

'Sshh.' Tears sprang to Sophie's eyes for the first time that day. 'Harry, even if Alex were still alive, I still would have asked you. He knew that. I thought you did, too.' She pulled him to his feet and pushed him out the door. 'Now go. I'll stay with Anna a little longer, then I'm going home, too.'

'With Vito?' he asked cagily.

'You bet your Bette Davis collection.'

She waved him down the hall, then smiled. As Harry's elevator closed, another opened and Vito stepped out, a dozen white roses in each arm. 'Hi.'

He gave her that smile that turned him from magazine handsome to movie-star gorgeous and Sophie's heart went pitter-pat. 'You're up,' he said.

'Treated and released,' she said and lifted her face for a kiss that made her sigh. 'I don't think they'll let Anna have those roses in the cardiac ICU. I'm sorry.'

'Then I guess they're all for you.' He put them on a table in the waiting room, then slipped his hands under her hair, searching her face. 'Truth. How are you?'

'Fine.' She closed her eyes. 'Physically anyway. I've had a few bad moments thinking about what might have happened if you hadn't shown up when you did.'

He pressed a kiss to her forehead and pulled her close. 'I know.'

She rested her cheek against his chest and listened to the soothing beat of his heart. It was exactly what she needed. 'You never did tell me how you found me.'

'Hmm. Well, there was an old woman buried next to Claire Reynolds. She used the same investment brokers as the woman who'd once owned that field. We didn't know her name, so we tracked brokerage clients who lived near quarries.'

She pulled back to stare up at him. 'Quarries?'

'The fill dirt from the graves came from near a quarry. But we still had too many names and it was almost dawn. Katherine had learned that the unidentified woman had dental work that placed her in Germany before the 1960s, but none of our names were European. We didn't want to risk calling the actual clients, because we were afraid Simon might pick up the phone. So we started calling the contact information on each person's brokerage application until we found a woman whose father had been a diplomat in West Germany in the 1950s. Her name was Selma Crane.'

'So Simon's house really belonged to Selma Crane. And Selma Crane is dead.'

'Simon found the perfect location and killed for it. He buried her next to Claire, then continued to pay Selma's bills. He even sent out her Christmas cards for two years.'

'He told me he'd killed those people to watch them die.'

'And then he'd paint them. On canvas. He wanted to be famous in his own time.' He tipped her face up, and she saw the shadows in his eyes. 'I watched the tape. You really should be an actress. The way you goaded him . . .'

She shuddered. 'I was so scared, but I didn't want him to see.'

'You said that the people he'd killed continued to scream and that I heard them.' He said it with a kind of wonder, and Sophie realized she'd paid him the highest compliment possible.

'And you always will.' She leaned up and kissed his mouth. 'My white knight.'

He grimaced. 'I don't want to be a knight. How about I just be your cop?'

'What do I get to be of yours?'

He met her eyes and Sophie's heart did a slow, delightful roll. 'Ask me in a few months and I'll say "my wife."' He lifted a brow. 'For now, my Boudiccea will do nicely.'

She smiled up at him, content. 'You're bad, Vito Ciccotelli, bad to the bone.'

He slipped his arm around her shoulders and led her toward her grandmother's room. 'You're just saying that to be nice.'

She glared up at him as they were buzzed into the CCU. 'You saw Simon say that on the tape didn't you? You rat.'

He chuckled. 'Sorry. I couldn't resist.'

Sunday, January 21, 4:30 P.M.

Daniel stopped his rental car in front of the train station. 'I wish you wouldn't go, Suze.'

Her eyes were so sad. 'I have a job, Daniel. And a home.'

Interesting, how she'd ordered the two. Job, then home. It was exactly how he ordered his priorities in his own mind. 'I feel like I just found you again.'

'We'll see each other next week.' At their parents' funeral in Dutton.

'And after that? Will you visit?'

She swallowed hard. 'Back home? No. After we bury Mom and Dad, I don't ever want to go home again.'

His heart hurt just looking at her. 'Suze, what did Simon do to you?'

She looked away. 'Another time, Daniel. After everything that's happened . . . I can't.' She climbed from the car and ran toward the station, but he didn't drive away. He waited, and when she got to the station door, she paused, turned, and watched him watching her. She looked fragile, but he knew that inside she was as strong as he was. Maybe stronger.

Finally she waved, just once, and she was gone, leaving him alone with all his memories. And all his regrets.

Then sitting there in the quiet of his car, he reached into the back seat for his laptop case. From inside he pulled a thick manila envelope. He slid the contents from the envelope and paged through the stack of pictures one at a time. He'd given Ciccotelli a copy, keeping the originals for himself. He forced himself to look at each snapshot, each woman. The pictures were real, just as he'd thought they were so long ago.

To each woman he made a silent vow to do what he should have done ten years before. One way or another, no matter how many years it took, he'd match these pictures with the victims. If Simon had perpetrated crimes against them, he could at least notify their families that justice had been done.

If someone else was responsible . . . *I'll find them. And I'll make them pay.*

And then maybe he'd finally find peace.

Epilogue

Saturday, November 8, 7:00 P.M.

'Everyone.' Sophie tapped the microphone. 'Can I have your attention, please?'

The conversation gradually stilled and everyone in the crowded room turned to face the podium where Sophie stood, looking elegant in an evening gown of shimmering green. Vito, of course, hadn't taken his eyes off her all evening.

Much of the evening, he'd been at her side, if for no other reason than to run interference against the skinny old philanthropists, who, although they'd helped make this night possible, still didn't get that they weren't allowed to pinch Sophie's butt.

Pinching Sophie's butt was Vito's job. He had the hardware on his left hand to prove it. Sophie met his eyes and gave him a wink before addressing the audience. 'Thank you. My name is Sophie Ciccotelli, and I want to welcome you tonight to the opening of the new wing of the Albright Historical Museum.'

'She's sparkling tonight,' Harry murmured and Vito nodded, knowing Harry wasn't referring to the evening gown that hugged Sophie's every curve. The sparkle was in her eyes, and the energy in her face was contagious.

'She's worked hard to make this happen,' Vito murmured back. Which was an understatement. Sophie had labored tirelessly to create a complex of interactive exhibits that had caught the eye of newspapers and several national magazines.

496

'So many have contributed to the success of this endeavor,' Sophie went on. 'Were I to read all their names, we'd be here all night. So I won't. But I would like to recognize those who've put in tireless hours to create what you're about to enjoy.

'Most of you know that the Albright Museum is a family operation. Ted Albright started the museum five years ago as a way to continue his grandfather's legacy.' She smiled fondly. 'Ted and Darla made a lot of personal sacrifices every day to keep our operating costs low so we can keep our doors open to everyone. To that end, we enlisted the help of family to build the exhibits. Ted's son, Theo, and my father-in-law, Michael Ciccotelli, have designed and built everything you'll see inside. Your guide will be Ted's daughter, Patty Ann, who many of you enjoyed as Maria in the Little Theater's production of *West Side Story*.' Patty Ann smiled, and Ted and Darla beamed. It was off-off Broadway, but Patty Ann had finally found her niche and seen her name in lights.

'We have three separate sections. In 'The Dig' you can get dirty searching for artifacts. There's 'The Twenties,' where you'll walk through science, culture, and politics of the twentieth century and hear firsthand the stories from the people who lived it. And finally, we have our 'Freedom' exhibit, which will be constantly changing, spotlighting people who have paid the price for freedom. The first of these will be *Cold War*.'

She looked to Yuri Petrovich Chertov. 'Are you ready?' She carefully placed the scissors in his hands, then handed Ted and Darla their own scissors.

'I don't know how she's keeping it together,' Harry whispered harshly.

Vito's throat had closed, knowing what was coming. But Sophie smiled as Yuri and the Albrights took their places by the big red ribbon that stretched across the door to what eleven months before had been an empty warehouse.

'Very good.' Sophie leaned toward the microphone. 'It's my

pleasure to dedicate the Anna Shubert Johannsen Memorial Wing.' She stepped back amid flashes of cameras to let the three with scissors cut the ribbon. She'd taken this job to pay for Anna's nursing home. She'd kept it to work through the grief after Anna had died quietly in her sleep a month after Simon Vartanian's attack damaged her heart beyond repair.

Katherine had declared Anna's death a homicide, bringing Simon's list of victims to nineteen.

Vito didn't think hell was hot enough for Simon Vartanian.

But it wasn't a night for sadness. Sophie had come down from the podium and was mingling once again, trying to catch Vito's eye. She looked at Harry's wet eyes and gave Vito a little nod and a smile before turning to talk to the reporter from the *Inquirer*.

'Harry, I need to get up there and make sure the butt pinchers keep their hands to themselves. Can you get Sophie a drink? I think the lights up there were hot.'

Harry nodded, pulling himself straight. 'What's she drinking? Wine? Champagne?'

'Water,' Vito said. 'Just water.'

Harry's eyes narrowed. 'Just water? Why?'

'She can't have alcohol,' Vito said and let his grin escape. 'It's bad for the baby.'

Harry turned to Michael, who was still wiping his eyes. 'Did you know?'

'Just this morning. She tried to eat lox with her bagel. It wasn't a pretty sight.'

Vito grinned. 'Dad's already planning the crib.'

'Which Theo here will build.' Michael beamed at the boy who'd done what none of Vito's siblings had been able to do – carry on their own father's art. None of them had a lick of woodworking talent. Turned out Theo Four had enough for all of them.

'No big deal,' Theo mumbled.

'No big deal,' Michael scoffed. 'He's already finished one of the cribs for Tess.'

Who, after trying for two years, was having twins, and Vito couldn't have been happier. It was a second wave of Ciccotelli grandchildren. Which just added more family.

Which, in Vito's book, made him the richest of men.

About the Author

Karen Rose is an award-winning author who fell in love with books from the time she learned to read. She started writing stories of her own when the characters in her head started talking and just wouldn't be silenced. A former chemical engineer and high school chemistry and physics teacher, Karen lives in Florida with her husband of twenty years, their two children, and the family cat, Bella. When she's not writing, Karen is practicing for her next karate belt test! Karen would be thrilled to receive your e-mail at karen@karenrosebooks.com